The Flood Girls

The Flood Girls

a novel

RICHARD FIFIELD

GALLERY BOOKS

New York   London   Toronto   Sydney   New Delhi

Gallery Books
An Imprint of Simon & Schuster, Inc.
1230 Avenue of the Americas
New York, NY 10020

First Gallery Books hardcover edition February 2016

GALLERY BOOKS and colophon are registered trademarks of Simon & Schuster, Inc.

For information about special discounts for bulk purchases, please contact Simon & Schuster Special Sales at 1-866-506-1949 or business@simonandschuster.com.

The Simon & Schuster Speakers Bureau can bring authors to your live event. For more information or to book an event, contact the Simon & Schuster Speakers Bureau at 1-866-248-3049 or visit our website at www.simonspeakers.com.

Interior design by Jaime Putorti

Manufactured in the United States of America

10 9 8 7 6 5 4 3 2

Library of Congress Cataloging-in-Publication Data

Fifield, Richard
 The flood girls : a novel / by Richard Fifield. — First Gallery Books hardcover edition.
    pages cm
1. Single women—Fiction. 2. Friendship—Fiction. 3. Small cities—Fiction. I. Title.
 PS3606.I375F56 2015
 813'.6—dc23   2014039373

ISBN 978-1-4767-9738-0
ISBN 978-1-4767-9740-3 (ebook)

For my mother, Loretta Jones. As always.

for refuge. The space belonged to him, and he furnished it with a lawn chair and a waterproof tub that held his paperbacks, a parasol, and a pile of cassette singles. He sat on the roof through most of the year, sat there for hours, even in winter, when he sat until he could no longer bear it. His perch had revealed who was having affairs with the UPS man, who was eating too much when they thought nobody was watching, who was stealing checks from mailboxes. Jake was not a private detective, but he had a private-detective outfit. He also had several piles of polyester leisure suits and a complete set of motorcycle leathers.

Jake listened only to Madonna when he was on the roof. He listened to Madonna and watched the sky instead of the dirty loop of trailer houses; it was too painful to regard his tiny universe, the town seemed so foreshortened and filthy. His Walkman had a voracious appetite, and Jake had lost many cassettes, had tried to repair the ribbon when it stretched and wound until it broke. He fixed most of them with a cunning little piece of Scotch tape, and it usually worked, only a little blip and squeal before the gospel choir kicked in during "Like a Prayer."

He had found rosary beads at the thrift store, and he wore these as he listened to Madonna, even though he was not religious. He wore three necklaces at a time: glass, baby-blue stones, and wood. He knew he was supposed to say a prayer and finger every bead, but instead he named his enemies. It seemed impossible that he had fifty-nine enemies, but the football team took up thirty-two, and there were twenty-seven other bullies and assholes in town. According to Jake's math, he disliked one-sixteenth of the town. Frank was not one of them.

The cats came around despite the freezing weather. Some nights, Frank built a tiny fire in a washtub. He played his harmonica, surrounded by piles of empty cans of cat food, and the flames shone on the tins and cast the snowy yard in waves of reflected light.

When Frank wasn't playing music, he recited facts and observations to Jake: the harmonica was the Special 20, model number 560 manufactured by Hohner, plastic comb instead of wooden. Frank told Jake that feral cats woke at four in the afternoon, that their hunting parties went out at six, and then they went back to sleep after he fed them. The cats woke

The
Flood
Girls

Harmonica, December 1990

★   ★   ★

*E*very night, Frank played harmonica for the cats.

Jake Bailey watched as the feral creatures emerged from the carcass of a 1978 Ford Granada, from the piles of fiberglass insulation beneath the skeleton of a trailer that had been immolated by fire. The cats were skittish around people, yet they came to his neighbor's yard each evening. At seven o'clock sharp, Frank would play his harmonica and put out cans of food, and the cats would gather and rub up against his legs.

The two would talk to each other, while Jake sat in a lawn chair on the roof of his trailer house. Jake's mother, Krystal, found it odd that Frank talked at all, told Jake that Frank was the shyest person in Quinn, the only permanent stranger in a town of 956. Unlike Frank, his mother was well known, and as a nurse, she was useful. His mother refused to wear any makeup, despite her thin lips. Krystal had enormous green eyes and glossy brown hair that hung past her shoulder blades, content to be a natural beauty. She wore her hospital scrubs at home, and no jewelry. Jake found it frustrating to shop for his mother.

Jake had been coming to the rooftop since he was seven years old, when Krystal stopped noticing what he was doing as long as he was in the yard. From the roof, Jake could see all of the trailer court and parts of the town. He was twelve now, and he no longer spied on his neighbors After five years, he realized that they were gross. Now he came to the roo again at three in the morning, foraged for the next three hours, slept all day. Jake thought that they were much like Bert, Krystal's boyfriend.

Bert was a human barnacle that had attached itself to Jake and Krystal's trailer house in 1989. He courted them with shopping trips to Spokane, boxes of garage sale books, a new furnace for the trailer. He promised to be a father figure. As soon as Bert moved in, he never moved again, leaving the couch only to go to the bar. He was surly and possessive, drunk and useless, and worst of all, fertile. Krystal was pregnant within a month.

Before Bert came, Frank had built a small storage shed for Jake, shoved up against the siding, between the back door and Jake's bedroom window. Frank knew that Jake's thrift store purchases were piled to the ceiling in his bedroom, each article of clothing perfectly folded but sandwiched so tightly that Jake was constantly ironing. Frank worked silently, building the shed out of cedar, so Jake's clothes would smell less like old people and more like expensive people. He added a gambrel roof, sturdy enough to support Jake's weight. Now Jake could climb out of his bedroom window and use the roof of the storage shed to push himself up to the flat metal panels on the top of the trailer house.

After Bert moved in, Frank built a privacy fence around his entire property in the summer of 1990. Bert had started trapping Frank's feral cats in the alley, collecting them in metal cages. He drove to the boating launch and threw the cages in the shallows of the river. Bert described this process in detail but was secretive about what he did with the bodies. Frank's fence was six feet high, enough to shield Frank from the sight of Bert drinking in the yard, the sight of Bert entirely.

Jake's best friend, Misty, lived with her mother on the left side of Frank's new fence. They had grown up together in the trailer court, walking endlessly around the unpaved loop of twenty-six houses and a Laundromat, throwing rocks at swallows' nests. Misty blasted heavy metal at all hours.

Bert caused just as much commotion. When he had no one to fight with, Bert fought with himself, and loudly. Bert was the kind of drunk who fell on and off the wagon so many times that he called everybody at the bar by their last names and everybody at AA meetings by their first.

Frank was surrounded by this chaos but never called the cops. He was meek, a slight man with a thick dark beard. When he wasn't feeding the cats, he watched the mountains with binoculars. He told Jake that he used to spend his summers in the fire lookouts and that these habits were hard to break. He looked for fire, even in the winter. Frank wore only bright yellow work shirts and dark green pants, and he told Jake that he had retired early from the Forest Service but never explained why.

The week before Christmas, Jake combed through the thrift shop, found several suits that looked like they would fit. Frank was silent when Jake brought them to his front porch, wrapped carefully, freshly cleaned by hand.

"I guessed your sizes," Jake said. Frank said nothing, just accepted the neatly folded pile. "I thought you would look best in earth tones," explained Jake. "Browns and greens, mostly. You'll love the ties. I even found one with pine trees. There's also a gray-and-red plaid jacket, and I figured you could wear it with blue jeans. Do you own any blue jeans?"

Frank remained silent.

The next night, Jake took his place on the roof, careful not to trip on the wires of Christmas lights Krystal had draped over the gutters. He had finally bought the entire "Like a Prayer" album, and a different rosary for every track, upping his collection to fourteen. Plastic or pearl, he had a necklace for every song and wore them on the outside of his snowsuit. He wrapped himself in blankets; the lawn chair was covered in new snow, and he sat on a plastic bag so his pants wouldn't get wet. Frank began his concert for the cats, but ended it early after only twenty minutes. He blew into his bare hands, which must have been frozen; Frank could not play harmonica with mittens. The cats ate greedily, and Jake watched a skinny pair fight over a can of pork and beans. Inside the trailer, Jake and Frank could hear Krystal and Bert fighting about getting cable television, and their new baby was crying. Frank walked over to the fence and threw the harmonica up to Jake, and then he turned away and went inside his house, without speaking a word.

The ambulance came the next day. Krystal heard the details on the police scanner and told Jake to go to his room. He watched out his window as the volunteer firemen came in their massive vehicles, followed closely by the van of the volunteer ambulance. There were no sirens. Then the cars came to the trailer court—the onlookers. It was as if every person who lived in town had heard the dispatch on the police scanner. Jake snuck out of his window and found Misty on the street. Even in the freezing cold, Bert lay drunkenly in the yard, tangled up in a lawn chair, but the crowd paid no attention. Misty and Jake hid in the alley, behind a Dumpster that was missing a wheel, and Misty smoked a cigarette as the volunteer fire department surrounded the stretcher.

Jake and Misty watched as they brought out Frank's body.

"I bet it was suicide," pronounced Misty. "That's fucking hard-core."

"He never told me he was sad," said Jake.

"I wonder if he used a gun," said Misty.

They watched until they were spotted by Krystal. "You shouldn't be seeing this!" she yelled at them as they tried to cower behind the Dumpster.

The winter grew thicker and darker, and Jake still thought of Frank. He kept the harmonica under his bed. Every morning, Jake shoved open the back door, kicked at the snow that had piled upon the cinder blocks of the back steps, and trudged in his slippers to the storage shed. He thought of Frank as he picked out his clothes for the day. Krystal would not speak of Frank's death, would not declare it a suicide. Bert claimed that the cats had eaten him.

For a few weeks, Jake bought cat food and stood in Frank's backyard. The cats came, but Jake could only hum. Jake hung his glass rosary on Frank's doorknob. The last week of January, Bert caught him and gave him a split lip for trespassing.

After that, Jake watched from the roof as the cats came around for a few more days, mewling and licking at the empty cans. Eventually, they found somewhere else to go. Jake hoped they were welcomed and sere-naded, hoped they had found a new home.

By the time Jake's lip healed, there were no more cats. Bert had trapped them all, Frank was gone, and only the harmonica remained. Frank's yard and trailer stayed untouched, the snow piling in deeper drifts around the front door.

Fireman's Ball, 1991

★   ★   ★

Rachel Flood clutched her can of diet soda, flinched at the acid in her mouth, and counted the men in the fire hall she had slept with, all before she had turned seventeen. Not for romance, not in courtship; these had been numbed things, animal rutting. At the time, she hadn't cared that some were married. There were eight in this room. Or eight and a half, because she had once given a blow job to the fireman who was currently pumping the keg for her mother.

Nine years had passed since she had left town, and these men had become beasts: Phil Faciana, fifty pounds heavier, a beard that crept up just below his eyes, a werewolf face. Doug Applehaus, still handsome, but now with a crazy look in his eyes, wearing a long black trench coat, like an assassin or a sex offender. The Hagerman brothers, separated by three years but balding at the same rate, built like sasquatches then and now. Standing beside one of the barrels were two firemen she sort of recognized, but she knew she had screwed each individually at the drive-in theater in Ellis. She remembered their cars—an AMC Pacer and a Chrysler Cordoba, the former with no backseat at all, and the latter with a backseat as big as a couch. And there was Bud Neilson, in the shadows of the flickering light. He had been her first, old back then and even older now, face gray from chain-smoking or organ failure. He stood as still as a mummy, a taxidermied version of the man with whom she had lost her virginity, although Rachel hated to think of it as something lost—she had been eager to discard it, like people born with a tail. She had been fourteen, a firehouse groupie, skidding on her cheap heels, slipping on the oil slicks from the fire engines, desperately offering up cases of beer stolen from her mother's bar.

Rachel was here to make amends, to show up and be a productive and helpful member of the community. Normally, her amends consisted of letters mailed to old lovers, police officers, women she had beat up for no good reason. But she could not write letters to the nine hundred people in her hometown, and so she had temporarily moved back to Quinn to make things right. Her sponsor had tried to get her to just accept it, to forget that her hometown had ever existed. But Rachel could not. All of the other steps were easy, even the sex inventory, but Rachel could not stop thinking of the entire town that hated her. She had decided to be a living apology, and do her time, until she could finally move on. It was necessary to be seen at this event, to let them all know she was back in town, to be of service, to right her name.

Rachel's own mother returned every amends letter she had written. The only letter not returned contained a check for one thousand dollars. Either Laverna Flood was psychic, or she read them all along, steaming and resealing the envelopes. The check was cashed. Rachel came to the fire hall to find her, figuring that although her mother would most likely be drunk, there would be witnesses, in case things took a violent turn.

Rachel was nervous as she regarded the fire hall, and it was an uncomfortable feeling. She felt no fear for more than a year, managed to replace it with her version of faith. Rachel didn't have much experience feeling things—it was only in the last few years that the suit of armor she had worn since junior high had begun to be removed, piece by piece. She hardened herself from an early age, to protect herself from an occasionally cruel mother and a constantly judgmental town. Feeling would have left her vulnerable, and she had no interest in being a victim. She needed to injure and destroy and move quickly, before she was caught and figured out. In the last year, most of her homework involved grace, and acceptance, and moving on. But she could not move on from this.

The fire hall was roasting, shimmering with heat from the two metal barrels stuffed with kindling and the cardboard detritus from cases upon cases of beer. Both garage doors were wide open—she could see the snow falling outside, the wind catching it and sending it into curlicues. The space smelled of heavy machinery and light housekeeping, of mouse-traps that were never emptied, bathrooms that only men would use. It was uncomfortably hot; she needed space, so she pushed herself through the crowd and found a place against a wall, the metal cool from the winter storm whipping around outside.

She stood there, trying to make eye contact. Few would look at her, and if they did, it was to stare and they seem startled. Hers was a face everyone in the room would always remember. She did not look like anybody else in Quinn, an alien among the rough, the common, and the interrelated. She was tall, broad through the shoulders for a woman, but her hips were narrow. She had big feet, and small breasts, and a stubborn mound of beer belly, even after a year. It was the only round part of her; she was a woman made of severe angles. She was a natural blonde and a notoriously cheap date, and at one time, she believed that these were her only redeeming qualities.

The volunteer firemen were celebrating their fortieth anniversary. Someone had decided that the Quinn Volunteer Fire Department was formed, more or less, in 1951. There had never been any reliable record keeping, but they had designated this night a special occasion. There was going to be a raffle for a gun. Rachel had been bullied into buying ten raffle tickets, at one dollar a piece, by four schoolchildren, filthy ones, who refused to leave her alone, despite her attempts to explain to them that she was a vegetarian and a firm believer in gun control.

The only other person standing alone was her new neighbor. As she had moved boxes from her truck, Bert Russell watched from a dirty living room window. Rachel had worked at her mother's bar as a teenager, and she had served Bert often. Even though Rachel sought out older lovers, the nine-year age difference was not enough for her to flirt with him, because he was short and coarse and homely. He had nothing she had wanted as a teenage girl, just a disability check. His thick nose hooked down, nearly covering his grim mouth. When he got drunk, he sat at the bar silently, marinating in his past. All these years later, Rachel could finally sympathize.

She approached him carefully, stood next to him without speaking, as he drank and stared at the cement floor.

"I guess we're neighbors now," said Rachel. He glanced at her out of the side of one eye. "I didn't know you were a fireman."

"I'm not," he said.

"How have you been?"

This was met with silence. Bert came from one of the oldest families in Quinn, and certainly the most tragic. He had earned the right to be taciturn.

"Gosh," said Rachel. "I can't believe it's been nine years."

"Stop talking," said Bert. Rachel did not want to be seen alone. She remained standing next to him, because he was a native, and that offered her some cover. Bert's father had been a hunting guide, specializing in finding black bears for drunken, fat assholes from the East Coast, and made thousands of dollars putting down the bears the tourists had grazed with bullets. They were terrible shots and too fat to chase the wounded bears. It was Bert Senior's job to track them down and finish them off, sever the head or the paw. The souvenir depended on the cost of the package the fat asshole had purchased. Bert Senior left the rest of the body in the woods to rot.

Rachel tried to make small talk again. "I'm really here to talk to my mother," she admitted. "I knew she'd be here."

"I wouldn't do that," said Bert. Rachel regretted bringing up mothers. When Bert was seventeen, his mother went out to pick mushrooms in an area recently scorched by a small forest fire, and slipped on the new growth, cracking her head open on a bombed-out stump, bleeding to death overnight. The search lasted for a day, and Bert Senior shot himself in the head two hours after the memorial service. Bert had become an orphan in the span of five days. Instead of mourning, Bert had gone shopping. He blew his inheritance on a new truck and a trailer to haul his new speedboat. He forgot to tie it down completely, and it flew through the air as he sped toward the lake, nearly killing the people in the car behind him. A month later, Bert's new truck and trailer were found upside down in the shallows of the Kootenai River, a truck-size hole blasted through the guardrails of the rickety bridge above. Bert became a cautionary tale, just like Rachel. Bert walked away from the wreck, left it there, knowing that someone else would have to clean up the mess. Rachel could identify with that as well.

Bert finally broke the silence. "I don't want to be seen with you," he said. He fled to the rear of the fire hall, and Rachel watched as the crowd parted for him. Enough time had passed that they did not whisper, but it was clear the town still worried that his speedboat of a mind was not completely tied down.

The heaviest drinkers never left the immediate vicinity of the kegs, sunk in garbage cans, slowly settling in their shawls of crushed ice. Rachel spotted groups of Clinkenbeards, Runkles, Giefers, and Dempseys. Ginger Fitchett kicked at a strand of crepe paper that had fallen from the ceiling, and lit a long and thin cigarette, the sole person in Quinn who smoked that brand. Ginger was the richest woman in town, owner of the Sinclair, the town's only gas station. She was drinking a wine cooler with Martha Man Hands, her longtime cashier. Martha was a Russell, somehow related to Bert, but her last name was unimportant. Ginger hired Martha and her truly enormous hands twenty years ago, and the nickname had stuck. Those hands and hairy knuckles were hard to ignore, as they handed back change for a twenty, or a corn dog in a greasy paper bag. Rachel's attention was captured as Tabby Pierce opened her compact, and the fires of the barrels flashed on the tiny mirror. Tabby powdered her forehead, shiny from the heat. Ten years ago, Tabby was hired to replace Rachel at the bar. She was also tangentially related to Bert, a toddler in the car that the airborne speedboat nearly destroyed. Tabby checked her teeth for lipstick and closed her compact, rejoined the noisy crowd. Rachel realized there was an order, groups were determined by genes, marriages, or restraining orders. Rachel's mother was among them.

Rachel had not seen her mother in nine years, but she had not changed one whit. Laverna Flood was on the short side, mousy-brown hair permed and cut close to her head. Laverna's mouth was a severe line, the perfect accessory for the expectant look on her face. She owned the Dirty Shame, one of two bars in Quinn, and she had the face of a bartender, impatiently waiting for customers to make up their mind about what kind of beer they wanted, even though there were only three options, and they always ended up ordering the same thing anyway.

Rachel waved and tried—unsuccessfully—to catch her mother's eye, but Laverna was at least twenty feet away, and Rachel no longer threw lit cigarettes at people to get their attention. So she stared until her mother turned and regarded her with heavy, weary eyes. Rachel raised her diet soda in salute. Laverna turned back to her cabal of friends, one of whom was pushing the keg pump up and down so ferociously that her breast threatened to fall out of her dirty tank top. Judging by the size of the breast and the lack of bra, Rachel knew it was Red Mabel. This meant that Black Mabel was lurking somewhere else, and if nothing had changed in the last nine years, she was most likely selling painkillers in the darkest corners of the room.

A young fireman materialized before her. He was probably a senior in high school, because the QVFD recruited early, indoctrinated them as soon as their delighted parents signed the waiver, rolling their eyes at the very thought of liability. People in this town were immune to danger. There was always a bear or a drunk driver or food poisoning from salads made with mayonnaise.

This fireman had a squirrely disposition, and buckteeth to match. He twitched, rocked back and forth on his boots, but remained standing silently before her. He had probably been dared to do this, possibly by Laverna.

She took a sip of her diet soda. He remained silent.

"What?" She wanted this to be over as soon as possible.

"Dance?" His voice was deeper than expected. His face was bare of any whiskers or stubble, his sloe eyes lashed heavily, and for a split second, she wondered if she was being propositioned by a lesbian.

"Absolutely not," she said, and stared at him. He looked frightened, and then he extended his hand.

"My name's Bucky," he said.

"Of course it is." She looked past him, toward her mother's cabal, to see if they were watching all this unfold. She was reminded of the piles of mousetraps, rotting in every corner of the room. If this kid was bait, they could have done better.

"I'm a Petersen. I think you went to school with my older sister."

"Jesus Christ," she said. Rachel did remember her. The Petersen girl had been a chain-smoking cheerleader who got knocked up their sophomore year. She had been unfortunate looking, a giant head and a moon-shaped face, legs like stumps, the unshakable base of every cheerleading pyramid. This bucktoothed creature did not mention his cousin Billy, and Rachel was thankful.

"My sister warned me. She said you were a real piece of work. She didn't tell me you were hot as hell." He winked. She shuddered.

"Stop," she commanded. She considered lecturing him about feminism, or sexual harassment. "Stop, or I'm going to kick you."

"Can I get you a drink?" He gestured to the kegs, bobbing like buoys in the melting ice water. "You need to loosen up, lady."

"How old are you?" Rachel didn't really want to know the answer; she just wanted to steer the conversation away from alcohol.

"Nineteen," he said proudly. He was so eager. "So can I get you a drink?"

"No," she said. "But you can bring my mother a message." She pointed at Laverna, just as her mother belched and leaned into the softer parts of Red Mabel. "Go tell her to come talk to me, or I'm leaving."

"Why don't you go tell her yourself?"

"Red Mabel wants to kill me," she said.

"Oh," he said. "She wants to kill a lot of people. She's a real angry person."

"Go," she commanded, and he did.

She watched as he skulked away, clearly terrified, and she turned her attention to a red-faced couple attempting a lazy jitterbug, moving at half time, because the song was a ballad. They were the only dancers, although there was some movement from a few drunkards leaning up against the wall, slightly swooning, heads bobbing like sloppy metronomes, eyes closed.

Rachel closed her own eyes but opened them quickly, sensing a threat.

Here was her mother, clutching her plastic cup of beer and looming dangerously, so close that Rachel could smell the Oil of Olay and the cigarettes on her fingers. Too close, especially after all these years.

"What?" Her mother's voice was still the same, imperious and scratchy. "You'd better get out of here before Red Mabel sees you. There's guns here."

"I know," said Rachel. "I bought raffle tickets."

"You'd better start saving your cash, Miss Big City. That trailer house is a goddamn money pit."

Rachel had received a slim letter. This was how she found out her father had passed away, this official notice from a lawyer naming her the sole beneficiary. She had barely known her father but still felt something inside her tear when she ripped open the thicker envelope that had arrived two days later—papers to notarize, two keys, a typewritten list of the things of value: a 1970 Fleetwood trailer house, a small lot in a trailer court measuring ninety-eight by two hundred feet, a Stihl chain saw, a 1980 Toyota Corona, and a checking account containing exactly $2,034.08. She immediately called her AA sponsor and proclaimed it a sign.

"No," her sponsor had said. "Not a sign. It's estate law. That's how it works."

"I can't help but think of it as fate," Rachel had insisted. "It means something."

"You don't have to accept every gift you've been given," her sponsor had said, somewhat coolly. "I suspect this one might have some strings attached."

And it did. The strings were in her face at this very moment, and they had hot beer breath. Her mother extended a finger and poked Rachel in the chest. Rachel took a deep breath. This encounter would be unpredictable, a teeter-totter.

"The last time I saw you at a Fireman's Ball, they had to scrape you off the floor. Could've used a giant fucking spatula."

"I don't drink anymore," said Rachel.

"That's what you keep telling me," muttered Laverna, her shadow fifteen feet long, wobbling in the heat.

"I never told you that. You returned all my letters. I haven't talked to you in over nine years."

"Word gets around," said Laverna, somewhat ominously.

"Well," said Rachel. "I'm excited about the house."

"I take it you haven't met your neighbors yet." Laverna cackled, and then she was gone.

Rachel wondered if her sponsor had been right, that this insistence on proving herself was a mistake. She glanced nervously toward Red Mabel, who fairly resembled a black bear, burly, all haunches. Her face got dark brown in the summer, but year-round her hair was massive and black. The people of Quinn called her Red Mabel because she had Kootenai blood. The people of Quinn had chosen black to distinguish the other Mabel, because of her rotted smile, teeth long dead from too many amphetamines and too little floss. Black Mabel was a drug dealer and a thief and a pool shark and a terrible drunk driver. Not terrible because she did it often, but because she did it so poorly.

Rachel had always loved Black Mabel. Both of the Mabels were barflies, but they were never seen together. There was a begrudging respect between them, a draw. Their personalities had arm wrestled and neither budged.

The Chief of the QVFD emerged from the restroom and nodded curtly at Rachel as he passed, drying his hands on the legs of his wool pants. He had several chins and was fleshy, but not fat. He was completely bald, and his eyebrows were each as thick as a thumb.

When Rachel had been a junior in high school, this man had been the grand marshal of the Fourth of July parade. He had ridden in the back of the oldest known truck in town, and Rachel had been behind him, clomping down the streets in the marching band, attached to a bass drum, the harness pinching into her shoulders with every step. He was chosen to be the grand marshal that year because he had put out the most chimney fires in one winter, more than any volunteer who had come before him.

A creature with no eyebrows approached Rachel, chomping gum, fearless. Della Dempsey. Rachel could never forget such a face, smooth brow like a burn victim.

"Rachel? Rachel Flood?"

Rachel sighed and shook her head. "I don't know who that is," she said. And it was true, in a way. She would not have to call her sponsor; she did not tell a lie. After she sobered up, Rachel had no idea who she was anymore. She didn't know what really made her happy. She was figuring it out as she went along.

The Chief yanked at an extension cord until it dislodged itself from the wall, and the music stopped, mid-song. In the corner, the lone couple continued their clumsy dance. Della waited for Rachel to say something, anything, but just like in high school, Rachel stared right past her.

He stomped to the center of the room and pulled a flashlight from his back pocket, illuminating the cement around his feet.

"Raffle," he announced.

One of the volunteer firemen leaped to his feet, coming forth from the shadows, clutching a coffee can that was filled with ripped halves of ticket stubs. A brand-new rifle was slung across his back.

The Chief barked again: "Remington Model 870 Super Mag twelve-gauge shotgun."

Rachel did not know what most of this string of words meant; it sounded like an incantation, a curse.

"Check your stubs," said the Chief, and that was it. He was so no-nonsense that Rachel was absolutely certain she had never had sex with him. She never had sex with men who knew what they were doing.

The Chief pinched a half ticket between his giant fingers, shone his flashlight and squinted.

"Six-two-seven," he proclaimed. The revelers examined their numbers.

Some people had entire handfuls of ticket stubs. Others bolted out the door to grab tickets from the jockey boxes of their automobiles. This was going to take some time.

Rachel tried to make herself as small as possible as she slunk toward the exit.

"Six-two-seven," bellowed the Chief again, obviously annoyed, as purses were emptied onto the floor, and hands were jammed deeper into pockets of blue jeans, digging desperately.

Rachel had memorized the string of salmon-colored tickets she had bought from the schoolchildren. They had been attached to each other, spun off the roll in one long chain, numbers 624 through 634.

"Six-two-seven," shouted the Chief. She could hear the exasperation in his voice as she passed him, as she made her way out into the cold, clear night. A small brown dog darted away from her, no collar, no tags. The dog ran under a fire truck as she approached. Even the strays of this town were frightened by Rachel Flood.

She walked across the frozen gravel. She'd never had luck of any kind. She supposed she was lucky that she had escaped this town. But that had not been luck—Rachel had been driven out. There probably would have been townspeople coming after her with torches, if it hadn't been fire season.

Sweet Thing

*   *   *

*L*averna woke with a hangover, and her shoulder hurt. She blamed both on her daughter. She lay in bed, kicked at an empty can of beer caught in the folds of the quilt. It flew from the bed and rolled across the floor, came to a rest as it wedged between her high heels. She planned to never wear those heels again. They were impractical, and she fell several times at the Fireman's Ball.

Today was her birthday. There was a hair in her mouth, and it tasted like home perm.

In the kitchen, Laverna made a pot of coffee, toilet paper stuffed where the filter should be. She smoked her first cigarette of the day—her first cigarette at age forty-seven—and grimaced. It wasn't that she thought forty-seven was old, just inconsiderate, a bad thing that happened to good people, like home perms.

As the coffee brewed, Laverna dressed for her shift at the bar. It was nearly three o'clock in the afternoon. She dug out a pearl-colored blouse, a black pantsuit, a gauzy black scarf. She pulled on thin nylon socks, slid a black velvet headband across the pelt of her hair, and stepped into black loafers with no heel whatsoever. Laverna always dressed in layers, even in the thick of August. Red Mabel accused her of dressing like she lived in constant fear of strip poker. Laverna cursed when she realized she had forgotten her control-top panty hose, removed her pants and started over again. This was forty-seven. Nine more hours and it wasn't her birthday anymore, not that anyone would dare mention it. In the bathroom, she penciled her eyebrows, added more arc than usual. She considered curling her eyelashes, but her hands were shaking, and besides, it seemed excessive, and she was supposed to be in mourning.

She returned to the kitchen, sipped at her coffee and smoked another cigarette. Laverna stared out the window into the front yard. It all looked the same to her in the winter, a rerun. She hated the winters here. The only thing moving outside was smoke from wood stoves. Winter in this town trapped people in their homes, in their lives. It was no wonder trains didn't stop in Quinn anymore. Only derailed.

Laverna drove to work past the softball field, covered in snow. She slowed the Cadillac, as she did every day in the winter, making sure that everything was in its right place. She was very protective of the softball field; it was the only place that made her happy, although last season had been a catastrophe. They had won only three games, and one was by default—the entire opposing team of silver miners had gone to a Heart concert in Spokane.

The Dirty Shame was converted out of a row of railroad apartments. It was sided with oily wooden shingles that Laverna's father acquired at an outrageously low price. She took after her father; Gene Flood could talk a dog out of having rabies. He grew enormously fat after they opened the kitchen and started serving food at the bar. He died of a heart attack at one of Quinn's softball games, which was embarrassing enough, but the fact that it took six volunteer firemen to haul him away from the bleachers was mortifying. A week after the funeral, Laverna's mother answered the door and made the mistake of inviting Jehovah's Witnesses into her home, confusing them with mourners. Before a month passed, she sold all the video poker machines and fled to eastern Montana with the money and her new congregation. At twenty-two, Laverna became the owner of the bar, and twenty-five years passed, changing out kegs and breaking up fights.

Tabby threw her apron at Laverna the minute she walked through the door.

"It's all yours," she said. And it was. Of the two bars in town—Laverna proudly owned the one that served food and encouraged fighting. The other bar was the Bowling Alley, an unoriginal name but frequented by most of the volunteer firemen and folks from town who had tired of fist-fighting over the conservation of the spotted owl. The Dirty Shame was always packed with loggers, men from the highway department, and the female silver miners. The miners were her most devoted customers, so Laverna tolerated the constant cloud from their boots and their pants, piles of powder in the dustpan. The silver mine seemed to only employ dwarf-size men and giantess lesbians. The lesbians were tougher than anybody else in town, so people held their tongues.

At six o'clock, Red Mabel installed herself at her usual stool as Laverna wiped down the taps and made a fresh pot of coffee. A silver miner, already quite drunk, stood at the end of the bar waving a twenty-dollar bill. The woman looked like Fred Flintstone.

Laverna sighed. "What?"

"Can I get a White Russian?"

"Too much work," said Laverna. "It's beer or nothing. I'm in mourning." Laverna sighed again. Frank's death was recent enough for her to get away with such a statement. They had been divorced for two decades, but Laverna would capitalize on any grief to get out of making a mixed drink. Frank rarely crossed Laverna's mind. He had already become a ghost, as fleeting as wood smoke, long before he died. She always knew he would derail, but there was no conductor asleep at the wheel, no negligence. Frank had crashed his own train.

She had met Frank at her first and last yard sale. This is what he bought: A toy logging truck missing a wheel. A Pat Boone album. A mountain lion carved from a piece of cottonwood tree. A boot warmer. Laverna's bowling ball, bowling shoes, and wrist guard.

Frank had held the bowling ball, palmed it like a thick-knuckled fortune-teller, and smiled shyly.

"Now that's a sweet thing," he said, and paid with cash. They were married four months later. He was a stranger in town, a precious thing. Laverna was not going to let him get away. She was surprised that her daughter had shown up to claim the inheritance. Laverna thought of

Rachel the same way she thought about the time her appendix had burst—sometimes things could come from inside your body and suddenly betray you, nearly killing you.

Once upon a time, Laverna trusted her daughter to work at the Dirty Shame, found a lucrative use for all of that lasciviousness. Rachel brought in her own crowd, and the local cops looked the other way, ignored the fact that she was only fifteen. Rachel was a terrible bartender, but fantastic at playing the ingénue cocktail maker, at flirting with her hair. Laverna's weekend numbers tripled in size. Now it remained a dead zone, and Laverna couldn't care less. Her daughter had burned her, set her life ablaze. There would be no forgiveness, only ashes.

Red Mabel turned around on her stool and launched a cue ball at a group of dusty women who were playing truth or dare. The ball smashed into the pint glasses, shards and liquid flying everywhere.

Cackling, the miners responded by hooting and grabbing at their crotches. The miners were more feral and violent lately, and if the rumors were true, emboldened by drugs. Laverna didn't care what they were buying from Black Mabel, as long as they continued to spend money at the bar. Red Mabel's fits only exacerbated their recklessness. The miners were itching to fight someone their own size. Laverna threw the bar rag at her best friend.

"Those bitches are out of control," protested Red Mabel. "You should make them clean it up."

"I really wish you'd stop breaking things," said Laverna. "I'm in mourning."

Black Mabel staggered through the front door, eyes unseeing, bombed on pills. As usual, she had embraced her nickname, wore a black T-shirt underneath a pair of inky work overalls. She wore that cursed leather duster, dark as night, and much too big for her. She wore it every day, even in the summer. It swept across the floor, filthy with old mud splatters, the hem soaking wet from the snow. Black Mabel's feet were invisible, and as usual, she seemed to be levitating. Her face was shockingly white, surrounded by the massive collar and lapels she turned up against the wind. While Black Mabel dressed to instill fear, Red Mabel would just as soon punch you in the face. Red Mabel guzzled the rest of her drink and left in disgust. As she passed Black Mabel, Red Mabel elbowed her in the arm, but she didn't seem to notice.

The bar was more rowdy than usual. One card game had dissolved into arm wrestling in bras, and Laverna saw two of the women pass a green olive to each other on their tongues. The men from the highway department cheered at this. Laverna sent Black Mabel over to admonish the women, and watched as she ducked a shower of peanuts the drunkest silver miner threw. When Black Mabel returned, Laverna gave her a piece of beef jerky.

"I always wanted to be a miner," slurred Black Mabel. "My mother was a miner, and both my cousins." Laverna took a drink of coffee, and raised an eyebrow. This was a story she had heard many times before. "I couldn't cut it," continued Black Mabel, looking over at the table of exhibitionists as they draped themselves over the jukebox.

"Mining is hard work," said Laverna.

"I'm claustrophobic," said Black Mabel. "I went down the shaft on my first day and burst into tears."

By eight o'clock, Laverna had officially lost control of the crowd. She called Tabby for backup, because Tabby was always hungry for tips and lived only a block away. The rest of her barmaids were probably unconscious somewhere.

Of all people, Rachel had been Laverna's most dependable barmaid. When Rachel was fifteen, Laverna had fired her entire weekend shift, both girls, for stealing from the cash register. Laverna was the law of the town, and a penny-pincher, so she installed her excited fifteen-year-old daughter behind the bar on weekend days, and the money flowed. Laverna didn't care if it came from pedophiles. Rachel had been a natural—imperious and saucy and a quick learner. Laverna eventually stopped shadowing her, and for two years, Rachel transformed two of the slowest shifts into moneymakers. When Rachel was exiled, bookkeeping was the only time Laverna missed her daughter.

A man pushed his way through the crowd at the front door, nodding at each and every miner. They glared at him as he passed, at his Quinn

Volunteer Fire Department polo shirt. His eyes were locked on Laverna. He sat down next to Black Mabel and inched his stool away from her, to show some respect. He smoothed out a ten-dollar bill with his index fingers and propped his elbows on the bar.

"Scotch," he said.

"We're out," Laverna said, and wiped her hands with the beer rag.

"Beer," he declared. "And keep the change."

Laverna studied him closely. He was vaguely handsome, and looked more capable than the other firemen she had known. His polo shirt was unwrinkled, tucked into his pants.

"Thanks," Laverna said, and poured him a beer and placed the pint before him. He raised his drink to her.

"Jim," he said, and stuck out his hand. "I'm new in town." He stood up, and she had no choice but to shake. "I've been wanting to make a proper introduction."

"He's the new Jim in the department," offered Black Mabel. "Jim Number Three."

Laverna rolled her eyes and went back to the crush at the bar. Laverna did not like the volunteers in town, especially the firemen. They had enormous egos and couldn't keep it in their pants.

Frank had never come to the bar, even after they were married. He left her every June to spend five months in the woods at the Forest Service lookout, came back in November, left again in January. He spent winters maintaining snowmobile trails, not looking for forest fires, yet he returned to Quinn one April to a woman enflamed. Laverna had missed two periods.

Frank took to sleeping on the sunporch, and this was where he stayed through a ferociously cold April, shielding himself with a space heater and piles and piles of sleeping bags.

Rachel was born in September 1964, and Laverna's cold, cold heart warmed when they handed her the baby. Frank was not present at the hospital—he stayed on the front porch, working his way through another Louis L'Amour. When they brought the baby home, Frank smiled for the first time since the yard sale. And for a while, anyway, he did make some effort—he bought a crib at an auction and played the harmonica for the baby, who seemed to enjoy it. He knit a tiny pink afghan on the front porch, a skill nobody knew he had.

They passed two years this way. Frank wasn't a doting father, but he tried his best. He built Rachel a mobile of airplanes from tin-snipped beer cans, which hung above her crib until Red Mabel pointed out that if it fell on the sleeping baby it would dismember her. He gave Laverna his paychecks, stayed out of her way, occasionally cleaned Red Mabel's guns. When he decided to leave, shortly after Rachel's second birthday, he gave no clear reason why, maybe because Laverna didn't ask for one. She needed the sunporch for storage anyway, had thought about learning how to make jellies and applesauce for the baby; the woods were thick with huckleberries, and she needed the space for canning.

Frank bought a trailer house on the outskirts of town. The checks came every month, and Frank kept to himself—Laverna got a child out of the deal, and as a businesswoman, she determined that all accounts were settled.

When Tabby arrived at the bar, Laverna made a big production of wiping the nonexistent sweat from her brow, poured herself a greyhound, and limped away to the only free table in the back, carrying a bar rag with her so it looked like she still intended to do some work. She put her feet up on the chair, and watched Jim Number Three push himself off his barstool. He looked embarrassed as his boots crushed the shells of peanuts. Wiping his hand on his jeans, he pulled up a chair across from her.

"Howdy," he said. "Mind if I join you?"

"You could rub my feet," said Laverna.

"I'm a volunteer," he stated. "But that doesn't mean I do charity work."

"How many fires have you been on?"

"Four," he said as he sat down.

"Jim Number Three, you are a true hero." She sipped at her greyhound and did a quick head count of the miners. She liked to keep a tally while they drank. When they disappeared, bad things tended to happen.

"They were chimney fires," he said.

"Chimney fires can blaze out of control," she offered.

"Not these ones," he said.

Laverna excused herself to pour another greyhound. The door swung open, and Bert Russell emerged from a curtain of snow suspended in the howling wind. The door eased shut behind him, and as usual, he avoided looking at Laverna. She checked the expiration date of the grapefruit juice, and interrogated Tabby about Jim Number Three.

"Who is he?" Laverna topped off her drink with a maraschino cherry, just because it seemed like a flirtatious object. She hadn't flirted in years, except for tips. But knowing that her daughter was back in town, Laverna was determined to trap him as soon as possible.

"Never seen him before," said Tabby. "He's cute, though. You'd better stake your claim." Tabby pulled the fresh pint glasses from the dishwasher. She put a hot pint glass in front of Bert and poured the remnants of a pitcher into it. The beer was so cold that it cracked, the pint glass exploding, and the beer ran down the bar and into Bert's lap. Tabby apologized profusely, and Bert said nothing, which was typical. He moved his barstool over and let the beer drip onto the floor. Bert wasn't one of Laverna's favorite customers, so instead of handing him her rag, Laverna returned to Jim Number Three.

Jim Number Three flinched when Laverna threw the bar rag past his head. One of the silver miners was on the verge of vomiting, as the rag landed on the floor near the card game. The silver miners cursed when the tallest one unleashed three kings.

"You lose," said the tallest woman. "All of you." She tapped powder out of her boots with a beer bottle, flipped over the pile of cards that were out of play.

The vomiting began, and Laverna called for the pail of sand, kept behind the bar.

"TABBY!"

Tabby struggled to carry the metal pail, and Jim Number Three ducked when she nearly hit him in the side of the face.

"I try to keep this place respectable," said Laverna. Jim Number Three nodded.

The miners were silent as Tabby grabbed a handful of sand, sprinkled it across the mess on the floor. They knew they had done wrong.

"Welcome to Quinn," Laverna said, and raised her greyhound. Jim Number Three lifted his pint glass in return, seemingly unfazed by the body fluids on the floor. Usually, it was blood. Laverna wondered if her luck had changed, if this new man might be a gift worth keeping. It was her birthday after all.

Sawdust

* * *

Jake and Misty made pies in seventh-grade home economics as the snow fell softly outside. The teacher, an impossibly old woman named Mrs. Hansen, never let them work together; Jake was always paired with the least competent student, because Jake could make a flawless pie crust. It seemed that the teacher would appreciate his talent, but instead she seethed with jealousy.

Misty was known for giving blow jobs in the back of the school bus. Jake was always her go-between when they went on field trips, a fearless pimp, proud of her bobbing head and blue mascara. He was the one who always packed the blanket, shielded Misty and the football player from the bus driver. Misty was the bossy one; she made the other kids switch seats, but everybody watched that motion, that flurry in the backseat of the school bus, the blanket moving up and down. Misty had a reputation that she swung around like a favorite purse.

The blow job that Misty had given Sixty-Four on a trip to Glacier National Park had become mythical, and now he wouldn't leave her alone, as the pies browned in the long row of ovens. He wanted a repeat performance, without an audience of mouth-breathing football players. It was a small school, but the football players were indistinguishable: all were Applehauses or Petersens or Clinkenbeards. It was much easier to pick out members of the herd by the numbers on their jerseys, which they wore to school every day.

Jake watched now as Sixty-Four begged Misty for a date, a real date. She threatened him with a rolling pin. He walked away and spit tobacco into the garbage can, and cursed loud enough for everyone to hear.

Now the other football players in the class were glaring at Misty, and Sixty-Four grabbed his crotch and pointed at her. She spit at him and was sent to the principal's office by old Mrs. Hansen, always quick to pounce on unladylike behavior.

Jake didn't see Misty again until the last period of the day. Last period was shop, and they were making toolboxes, metal bent and folded with the press that Jake could never master. He put an edge in the metal press so many times that the paint scraped from it, and it was now just shiny tin, its edges curling hopelessly. The football players had finished their toolboxes on the very first day, and the shop teacher, who was also the football coach, had asked them to supervise while he went to the teachers' lounge. After five minutes, they began to gather around him. Sixty-Four was the first to step forward.

"Fucking faggot," he said. "You can't do anything right." He slapped Jake's hand away from the metal press.

"I'm trying," said Jake. The metal piece was beyond repair. "I'm not good at this sort of thing."

Thirty-Seven mocked Jake's high-pitched voice but added a lisp that Jake was certain did not exist. He had once asked Misty for confirmation of this.

"You're gonna make him cry," said Sixty-Four.

"No," said Jake. "This isn't anything to cry about."

"Don't be a smart-ass," Sixty-Four said, and pushed him. Jake absorbed the blow, but took a step backward.

"Sissy," hissed Sixty-Four, and pushed Jake harder, this time against a wooden workbench, and he tripped over it, landing on the floor in a pile of dust from the band saw. Jake was upset, because he was wearing his favorite slacks—gray wool—and his favorite dress shirt—jet-black polyester and shiny—sure to pick up all of this mess on the floor. Before he could start brushing himself off, Sixty-Four stepped over him and pushed Jake's face down toward the bits of wood shaving.

"Eat it, faggot." He bent down to Jake's level, his face was red from crouching. "I want you to eat it."

"I won't," said Jake, just before his head was turned, and his mouth filled with sawdust, and his teeth touched the cement floor. The football players laughed, and Sixty-Four planted a foot against his neck. Jake choked as he breathed in the fine dust of two-by-fours and whole sheets of plywood.

"Stop dressing like such a fucking pansy," said Sixty-Four. "And maybe we'll leave you alone."

Jake heard a door slam, and the foot lifted from his neck.

He pushed himself up from the floor. He stared through the legs of the football players at Misty, who was walking toward them, her hands clenched by her side.

"Motherfuckers," she proclaimed. "You leave him alone."

"Fuck you," said Sixty-Four. "Mind your own business."

"Leave him alone," repeated Misty as she picked up a finished toolbox, perfect and gleaming, from the workbench.

"Hey!" protested Thirty-Seven. "I made that!"

"I don't give a shit," said Misty. Sixty-Four spit down on Jake and kicked him once in the ribs. Jake yelped and rolled over on his side. He slid across the floor and pressed up against a metal cabinet.

He watched as Misty swung the toolbox and hit Sixty-Four in the side of the head. He collapsed, took down two benches as he fell to the floor. She held the toolbox in front of her, shoved it at the circle of football players, who all backed away. She jabbed it at them, until they backed out through the door, leaving their comrade lying on the floor.

When the door closed, Misty replaced the toolbox, now dented on one end, back on the workbench.

"Fuckers," said Misty. "All of them."

"Oh my god," Jake said, and spit on the floor. He could taste the wood shavings on the roof of his mouth; his tongue was coated with sawdust.

Misty helped Jake to his feet. They stared down at Sixty-Four, a slick of blood on his forehead, shining in the fluorescent lights. He was still.

"Maybe he's dead," said Jake.

"I doubt it," Misty said, and shoved him with a push of her foot. "He's a goddamn football player. I knocked him out, that's all."

They watched Sixty-Four's chest rise and fall, and Jake was relieved.

"Jesus," said Jake. "How are we going to explain this?"

"We're not," said Misty. "We're leaving."

She grabbed his hand and pulled him out of the classroom and into the hallway. The corridors were completely empty, except for the two girls who were hanging up the pep rally poster with electrical tape. They paid no attention as Misty and Jake, still covered in sawdust, exited through a side door.

That night, Misty's mother came to deliver news. Martha Man Hands stood on the porch, shaking her giant fists, still furious over Misty's latest misadventures. Krystal immediately sent Jake to his room. He stood in the hallway and tried to listen, but the baby was screaming, and then Martha was crying.

Krystal came into his bedroom after Martha left, and told him that Misty was being sent away. Misty had always saved him, escorted Jake through the streets of Quinn in the morning. Misty flashed a pocketknife at any assembly of boys more than three in number. Misty had been his protector, and Frank had been his friend. Losing them both was too much to bear. Something folded up inside him like a lawn chair.

He was more afraid than ever. He went to sleep holding Frank's harmonica.

Waiting for the Flames

★   ★   ★

Rachel had now been in Quinn for six days, and she finally felt strong enough to venture out, lapped the town again and again, driving in circles, safe in the night. Nobody knew who the town of Quinn had been named after, although rumor had it that the original Quinn had been a railroad hobo, who in 1910 jumped a train, fell out drunkenly, and then decided to remain in the thick woods and found the town that would become his namesake. Wildfires completely decimated Quinn in 1939, and then again in 1946, just after people had finally rebuilt. As a result, the town was sloppily organized, streets named arbitrarily, or not at all, businesses only formed out of absolute necessity, no street signs or sidewalks or traffic lights. The whole town seemed to be waiting for the flames to return.

At night, the town was dark and still, no headlights from cars. The bars shut down at two o'clock, and the Sinclair had long since closed. She was thankful for the darkness when she pulled into her driveway. In the daylight, the sight of the trailer house filled her with dread.

She stepped through the gate, carefully navigating the narrow path, unlit and uneven, stepping-stones made of giant pieces of shale that were sunk at dangerous and unpredictable depths. What remained of the porch light was a jagged black hole, rimmed with papery gray clumps of hornets' nests. Rachel hadn't bothered to lock the door. Frank had left behind nothing worth stealing, and the trailer house already looked like it had been vandalized and squatted in. She turned on the living room light, and it glared off the plastic sheeting that covered the entire east corner, where the chimney had collapsed into the fireplace. The carpet was filthy, so Rachel sat on a cardboard box of unpacked clothes and reached for the cordless phone. She had been amazed to find that her father still had phone service, despite his dying. Maybe he had known she would return like a boomerang, and had paid in advance.

Seeing all those people at the Fireman's Ball had reignited her shame. She had felt the fire in her cheeks as she leaned against the firehouse wall. She always thought that the people had been frozen in time when she left, but fatter and older versions carried on like they always had, only stopping to glare. Rachel thought she had moved past her shame, after it manifested itself in her first month of sobriety as spectacular crying jags and handwritten lists of the terrible things she had done, the things she could remember. Doing this inventory with her sponsor took two solid weeks, every evening spent unveiling yet another thing she thought unforgivable, while her sponsor made endless cups of tea. The sponsor massaged Rachel's shaking hands and assured her that other drunks had done much worse things.

Rachel's sponsor was called Athena. This was not her real name. Athena had ditched the name Louise after attending a sweat lodge where she received a vision in the teepee and decided that she was a warrior woman and not a tax accountant. Sobriety did strange things to people. Athena was hugely obese, a true warrior only when they went out to eat at restaurants that served food buffet-style.

"I feel shame again," reported Rachel, when the phone was answered on the first ring.

"We got rid of that." Athena sighed. "Come back to Missoula. I warned you this would happen. Don't fuck it up. You've only got a year."

"I have three hundred and eighty-four days," responded Rachel. "That's more than a year."

She could hear Athena sigh again, and then the catch, the scratch of a lighter.

"Rachel . . ."

"What? I've done everything you have ever told me to do. You said no big changes during the first year. I didn't even get a fucking haircut."

"Did you go to that hootenanny?"

"It was a fund-raiser," said Rachel. "For the fire department. I just wanted to make sure they know I support them. Trailers burn up quick around here."

"Did you feel the urge to drink?"

Rachel thought about this question and realized that she had not. She had been too preoccupied with her mission, distracted by the sloppy citizens of her hometown, all of those faces that were vaguely familiar. She wished they had been wearing name tags.

"No," said Rachel. "I felt the urge to spray everybody with disinfectant."

"Have you found a meeting yet?"

"Yes." Rachel had found the only meeting in Quinn, but she was too frightened to go, was too afraid of who she would run into. Although it was an anonymous program, the gossip might be worth too much. There was certainly a value for the delicious secrets of a famous, thieving, murderous harlot.

"We've been through all of the steps," asserted Athena. "I don't understand why you keep coming back to steps eight and nine." Rachel made a list of all persons she had harmed, and became willing to make amends to them all. She made direct amends to such people wherever possible, except when to do so would injure them or others. Rachel no longer feared injuring herself, figured that she had it coming.

"I'm stuck," said Rachel. "I've been able to forgive myself for everything else. I have to make things right."

"That's not how it works," said Athena. "You know that. All you have to do is be willing, and if they can't accept your amends, then forget every white-trash piece of shit in that town. Stop beating yourself up."

"Okay," said Rachel.

"I don't think you need to atone for the rest of your life. Two weeks is plenty. Paint some benches, pick up some trash, buy some Girl Scout cookies, and get the fuck out of there. Go to meetings."

"You told me pain is good," said Rachel. "You told me that pain is growth."

"I also told you that it was okay to make Debbie Harry your higher power. Just go to sleep," said Athena. "Tomorrow is a whole new day."

"That's what I'm afraid of," muttered Rachel.

Athena had been astounded at how quickly Rachel moved through the steps; she had never sponsored someone so determined to get right with God, even though Rachel really only believed in Debbie Harry. There were twelve steps, and Rachel clawed desperately through each one; she wrote letters of amends to her mother and Red Mabel, to her father and several of her classmates from high school. All but one of the letters had been returned.

Rachel threw the phone against a pile of clothes, all Quinn-inappropriate, especially her vintage Halston palazzo pants. She loved those pants, but feared that magpies or marmots would be attracted to the sparkle, drop down from the sky or emerge from the forest to gnaw at her legs.

She navigated the sinkhole in the middle of the living room. The carpet was softly cratered where the floor had given in. The list of repairs was enormous, daunting: the house seemed to be surrendering to gravity, with the left end sinking faster than the right. A tube of lipstick rolled when she placed it on the kitchen counter. Rachel felt seasick when she walked from one end of the house to the other.

Rachel made do with washcloth baths, as the tiny bathroom contained a bathtub that had fallen through the subflooring. It rested three feet down from the rest of the linoleum, in the dirt and gravel underneath the trailer. Rachel had thrown the rest of her city clothes into this pit, along with the strange clothes she had found in her father's closet. Her father owned a collection of polyester-blend suit jackets and matching pants, a pile of neckties. This was strange to her—in her few encounters with her father, it seemed that he only accessorized with sap from pine trees. She lowered herself to the toilet to pee, and it was cold and drafty in the bathroom, torturous to touch her buttocks to the icy toilet seat. At least the toilet worked. Her father had not completely descended into the depths of madness. He had just fallen into squalor, and sometimes through the floor.

The bedroom was where Rachel had spent most of her time since returning home, crying and making to-do lists. Her bed was the only thing she had brought with her, the only piece of furniture she had any kinship with.

Rachel had bought the bed after being sober for two months. It was a gift she had given herself. The last two years of her drinking, Rachel had become a bed wetter. She was a beer drunk, always had been, and it was unsurprising that she wet the bed, because during the last year of her drinking, she was consuming sixteen cans of Pabst Blue Ribbon per night.

Eventually, she bought a stack of blue tarps to sleep on. She wasn't a complete degenerate—every morning, she would remove the tarp and put it in the bathtub, turn on the shower to rinse away the urine, and drape it over the couch in her living room to dry. She threw the used tarp in the Dumpster every Sunday night, before the garbagemen came, replaced it with a new one. Rachel could still recall the crackle of waking up in the morning, the sound of her naked body on the tarp, the suction and the stickiness as she pulled herself free. It was this crackle that got her sober, made her realize that this was not normal behavior, that most people didn't piss the bed every night. Her moment of clarity about the tarps came on a Monday morning, and she called the AA number, her hands shaking so badly she had to redial several times. She had not realized that her entire back and buttocks had become slightly stained, bluish, until Athena pointed it out on a day trip to the natural hot springs, two weeks into her sobriety.

Rachel deserved this bed. She had earned this bed, and now she owned fitted sheets and a duvet. She clung to this bed like she clung to her sobriety—it was a white-knuckled sort of ownership. Now, overwhelmed, Rachel turned on the bedroom light and threw herself onto the bed. There would never be enough paper for her new to-do list. The town was a creature unto itself, wild and woolly. The people who lived there were unpredictable and could never be crossed off, conquered. Rachel could not organize and proceed methodically—she had learned in sobriety that people, places, and things were impossible to control. The world never did what you wanted. She buried her face in the pillow and recited every prayer she had learned over the past year, silently and desperately. The Fourth-Step Prayer, the Seventh-Step Prayer, the Serenity Prayer. She asked for strength to continue, and for a new bathtub. Then she felt bad for asking for things, so she tried to name all the things she was grateful for, and it was a short list, so she repeated it over and over until she finally fell asleep.

———

The next morning, Rachel sat on the front porch and drank her coffee. She did not notice the rosary at first, only spotted it hanging from her doorknob when she returned indoors for a refill. She wasn't sure who had left it—probably a religious fanatic determined to ward off her bad energy. She left it hanging, because it was a beautiful thing, the only decorative object on the entire property. Rachel fingered the yellow glass beads and drank more coffee.

It was a strangely warm day for February, and it revealed the swamp of a backyard. Lacy crusts of ice collected in the corners of the fence, and Rachel's feet sunk in the muck as she examined her property. There was no lawn here. The mud was studded with blackened clumps of dandelions, frostbitten patches of clover, and skeletal stalks of tiny aspen trees, saplings taken root.

These were a new set of problems, these things she owned. In Missoula, she left behind Athena, her home group, credit card debt, the paycheck from cleaning hotel rooms, a house that smelled like urine even though it had been bleached and all the carpet pulled. She had left behind a weekly poker game on Sunday nights with a group of middle-aged women, a sober bowling league for which she had finally paid off her shoes, the keys to three different church basements—two Lutheran and one Methodist. Now she owned a trailer house, and guilt and shame. It had been her choice, and she had felt it necessary.

She looked up at the sky and was going to offer up a prayer, but she heard dim music and realized that she was not alone.

A boy was sitting on the roof of Bert's house, squeezed into a tiny lawn chair. Rachel wasn't sure what Bert's disability was, but it had not stopped him from breeding. The boy wore an unzipped silver snowsuit, bright red moon boots, and a white kerchief tied loosely around his neck. He was so close to her that she could see the book he was reading: *Lady Boss* by Jackie Collins. She approved.

He was oblivious to her, his headphones blaring out tinny beats, pop music. His hair was so blond that it seemed silver, his face so delicate and his expression so dreamy that he could have been mistaken for a girl.

She watched him. He was a ferocious reader, and turned the pages so quickly that she briefly wondered if he was faking it. He clutched at the book as if it might be ripped out of his hands at any moment.

Rachel understood how it was to cling to things so desperately. She knew that she must cling to her sobriety, even if the pain rose over the banks, even if there was a deluge. She would find a way to float, find something to hold on to.

Hearts

★ ★ ★

The last week of February, and the nights were frigid, the air tight as a closed fist. The gales punched sideways, launching last week's powder, made it sting like slivers of glass.

This was how all of Laverna's weeknight shifts ended, playing hearts with the regulars as the washer whirred. The Applehaus brothers were drunker than usual, probably because she had offered shots at one o'clock, out of dirty shot glasses, because she wanted to start the dishwasher. Their fourth was Rocky Bailey, who didn't drink but was retarded, so the playing field was level in her estimation. Rocky drank Mountain Dew out of a can and chewed great wads of grape Bubblicious at the same time. How he wanted to spend his grocery store wages was his business, but she feared he would develop diabetes.

Bert was the only other patron, silent and sullen as always. Laverna slid a pitcher and a pint glass in front of him whenever she felt like it. He sat far away from the others, in his usual spot, under the air conditioner. He never said a word, but tipped well, especially for an unemployed asshole.

Laverna had forgiven the Applehaus boys for their indiscretions with Rachel, all those years ago. The town was too small, and patrons were too important. Anything the Applehaus boys had done with her daughter would always be dwarfed by Rachel's own betrayal. However, Laverna still held a tiny grudge and would mention her revulsion from time to time, especially when an Applehaus unloaded the queen of spades.

Talk turned to the completion of the new church. Last summer, Reverend Foote and his family had relocated from Kansas, and he had built the church by himself. He contracted out the plumbing and the electricity, so the citizens of Quinn took comfort in the fact that he wasn't totally self-reliant. He had named his church New Life Evangelical—a denomination new to Quinn. Laverna loved the Catholic church in town—even though it was a small congregation, they drank heavily, and often. They already had Lutherans, Jehovah's Witnesses, and Methodists. The Methodists were a bunch of backsliders, vaguely pious. Black Mabel sold the Methodist wives diet pills, so they were also vaguely wicked.

Reverend Foote slowly but steadily poached his parishioners from each of the other churches, proving Laverna's long-held theory that nothing stuck in Quinn, except for the snow.

The new church was a perfect square, plain, slung low to the ground, much like Reverend Foote himself, whom Laverna had chanced upon at the post office. He was a short man with thick auburn hair carefully parted. He wore brown pleated slacks and a tucked-in button-down shirt that was the worst shade of yellow, faint, like a white shirt completely stained with the sweat of a chain-smoker. She hated him on sight.

Laverna shot the moon for the final time of the night, and the game was over, because she declared it so. She pointed to the Budweiser clock mounted above the door, set fifteen minutes fast.

The Applehaus boys began gulping what was left in their glasses; Laverna had eighty-sixed people in the past for not honoring closing time, or even those who dared to argue, who pointed at their watches to compare them to the Budweiser clock.

Rocky Bailey pushed back his stool and swept up peanut shells. Bert poured the inch and a half left in his pitcher into the glass and considered it carefully; Laverna knew it was warm but didn't care. Bert was a slow drinker. He was determined to get drunk, but did so at a methodical pace. This was how the unemployed drank at the Dirty Shame. On slow nights, Laverna longed for the distraction of Red Mabel, even though she was partially to blame for the very existence of the insidious Rachel. Red Mabel was her right-hand man, and Laverna always described her as such, and nobody dared argue about the genitalia.

Twenty-seven years ago, it was Red Mabel who drove a crazed Laverna into the mountains, directions to Frank's cabin gleaned from bar patrons, nebulous and contradictory. Laverna and Red Mabel prided themselves on being adventurous, and pieced together the directions, written on the back of a receipt from the grocery store, a cocktail napkin, and the back of Red Mabel's hand. They navigated the fire roads and one-lane bridges until they found his cabin. Though the roads had thawed to muddy ruts, the snow still fell lightly. Red Mabel was used to driving in the mountains—she considered herself a huntress, although the local authorities considered her a poacher. When they found the cabin, Frank was outside, stacking firewood. When he heard the truck, he looked up at the arrival, as if he had been expecting them all along, but didn't stop stacking wood. Laverna made Red Mabel wait in the truck, and she stepped out into the mud, bearing a brand-new boot warmer and a bottle of Black Velvet. She talked her way into his cabin, by pretending she was cold, which was untrue, because she and Red Mabel had drunk nearly a third of the bottle on their journey. Frank and Laverna sat across from each other; the rough pine floor seemed an impossible distance. At least he offered her the couch. He stared at her silently.

"I can't stop thinking about you," proclaimed Laverna. He made a noise in his throat and looked down at this boots. She continued, unsuccessfully, to make small talk, until they heard gunshots. They emerged from the cabin to see Red Mabel dangling a wild turkey in the air. Unfortunately, it wasn't wild—it was Frank's pet. Red Mabel warned Frank that turkeys carried all sorts of diseases, which wasn't true. Red Mabel warned Frank that Laverna would not leave without a date, which was.

Frank came into town the next month, and took Laverna out to eat at the Bowling Alley, and quietly endured her barrage. To silence her, he took her to bed. They eloped that May, to Winnemucca, Nevada. Laverna drank with elderly showgirls, while Frank gambled on battered machines. "That was a sign," Laverna would say later. "We put a quarter in a slot machine and Frank broke the handle off."

The thought of quarters reminded Laverna of closing, and she opened the ancient cash register, pulled a zippered deposit pouch from underneath the counter. She began to stack ones and fives. Only the lesbians paid with larger currency, and they had been absent tonight. Most likely they were singing folk songs in the woods, or playing demolition derby with broken heavy equipment jerry-rigged at the junkyard, something they were known to do.

Chuck Clinkenbeard's son pushed through the door, the snow blowing in with his entrance. Laverna ignored him and kept counting the cash. He was sixteen, but he had a thin black mustache, and Laverna had served him in the past, especially if it was a slow night and there were no cops in sight. The cops drank at the Bowling Alley, so Laverna often poured for any kid who looked past the point of puberty. She couldn't remember his first name, but it was too late for last call. All the Clinkenbeards had neatly trimmed mustaches, but no beards, thumbing their noses at their name. She pointed up at the clock and continued counting. Laverna would not be serving this Clinkenbeard tonight.

Still counting, she heard a sharp thwack, and stopped to glare at Rocky, who had dropped his broom. She considered yelling at him, but then the Applehaus boys had hit the floor as well, a thud and a clatter as they took their barstools with them.

She realized then that Chuck Clinkenbeard's son had a small .410 shotgun, undoubtedly filled with bird shot. The Clinkenbeards had been on a grouse genocide mission for as long as she'd known them. He slowly raised the weapon and advanced toward her, stopping in front of the jukebox as it played a Tammy Wynette song. And then the gun was pointed at Laverna. He nodded at the cash she had been stacking in neat little piles.

Black Mabel stumbled through the front door, always looking for an after-party, and seeing the raised gun, she immediately turned around, back out into the night. Laverna looked everywhere but at the gun. It was as if she didn't acknowledge that it was happening, and by doing so, it simply wouldn't. That was how things worked in the rest of her life. Black Mabel watched from outside, through the filthy window. Rocky kept chewing his gum and pointed at the gun, as if Laverna didn't notice it.

The Clinkenbeard boy said something, but Laverna heard none of it. She had turned to look at Bert, who averted his eyes and looked down at his pint glass. The jukebox whirred and now it was Juice Newton, and Laverna finally turned and looked at the gun.

"You're not robbing me," she said. "You're a fucking idiot. You're not even wearing a mask."

"I'm leaving town," he said, and raised the gun an inch and took another step forward.

"I will destroy your entire family," declared Laverna, which he apparently did not appreciate, because she heard the catch of the safety. His teenaged face closed up like a fist: his features turned into one eye and a snarl as he looked down the barrel.

Laverna glanced out the window as Black Mabel's ghostly white face looked in. Laverna sighed and began to gather the rolls of quarters. One slid from her grasp, and she could hear a whimper as it rolled off the edge of the bar and landed on an Applehaus.

"Jesus Christ," Laverna said, and reached over for a dishrag. She had planned on waving it like a white flag, but this little motherfucker had apparently never heard of the protocols of surrender.

There was a blast. She ducked in time, but her arms and the white rag were still raised. The explosion deafened her, and she felt pain like wasp stings. The glass from the mirror behind the bar rained all around her. After the gunfire, it kept falling in giant, jagged pieces, freed from the glue that had held it behind the bar for so long. She curled up on the plastic bar mat. She saw the Clinkenbeard boy's class ring, his hands, as they grabbed for the dollars. She cradled her arms, slick with blood. Laverna couldn't believe how her mind worked sometimes, but she found herself calculating how much he was taking. It had been a slow night, except for the gunfire.

From her vantage point, she could see Bert holding a shard of glass, what remained of his pint. He seemed unconcerned.

The ones and the fives were disappearing, those stubby hands stuffing them somewhere.

Suddenly there was a grunt, and a single dollar bill flew up into the air.

She heard bodies hit the floor, and then the familiar cursing of Red Mabel, *Thieving piece of shit*, *Shit for brains*, and plain old *Dipshit*. Laverna was not sure where Red Mabel had come from, but that was how it usually went. Laverna used her knees and her one good elbow to ease herself up.

She surveyed the wreckage.

Red Mabel had the kid in a headlock, and they tangled on the floor like lovers, his face surrounded by her massive breasts. Rocky now held the gun, Juice Newton still sang, and Red Mabel squeezed the Clinkenbeard boy's head even tighter, his face turning the color of plums. The Applehaus brothers remained on the floor.

Red Mabel finally noticed Laverna and the blood. "Look what you did to her!" she screamed, and adjusted her forearm until Laverna heard the snap of a jawbone. "Look what you did to her!"

Dollar bills and broken glass had been scattered everywhere. Rocky bled from his kneecap, his khakis soaking red as he clutched at the shotgun.

"And god damn you Applehaus boys! Get up!"

They popped up from the floor. Red Mabel kept yelling as they silently accepted her admonishments.

"You're both fucking firemen! You're in emergency services!"

At that, they stepped forward to help, properly chastened.

"Take this motherfucker!" Red Mabel released the boy, and the older brother began to kick him in the stomach, while the younger pinned his arms to the floor.

Red Mabel dashed behind the bar and pulled Laverna close, despite the blood. It was unclear to Laverna if Red Mabel was crying or sweating heavily as she picked up the rotary phone with one hand and called the police.

When the ambulance finally came, the Clinkenbeard boy was unconscious, Rocky tended to the wound on his leg with paper napkins, Bert continued to sit there, and Black Mabel could still be heard shrieking outside.

Rocky attempted to sweep up the broken glass behind the bar with one hand on the broom, and the other holding napkins to his knee.

"How in the hell are you going to use a dustpan with one hand?" Laverna screamed at Rocky, half determined to get up and clean the mess herself. The Applehaus boys talked to the policeman, also an Applehaus, and Bert threw down a twenty and walked past all of the commotion and out the door.

The first and last twenty of the night.

Until She Tells You to Stop

★　★　★

Rachel was awakened by a frenzied pounding on her door. It was still dark outside, but she had no idea what time it was—the alarm clock was plugged in in the cavern of her bathroom. She pushed back the duvet cover, and she was frightened.

She still did not have a light on the porch, or a chain on the door. Rachel waited for the person to go away, but when the frenzy began again, she turned on the living room light and opened the door.

There stood Black Mabel, obviously intoxicated.

"I don't drink anymore," said Rachel.

"I ain't here for that," said Black Mabel. "Your mama's been shot." She paused. "When did you stop drinking?"

"Jesus," said Rachel, shocked. This was not good news. She needed a chance to make amends. "Is she dead?"

"Hell no," said Black Mabel as she lurched into the house. She smelled like beer and the leather of her jacket. "I saw the whole thing."

"Is she okay?" Rachel suddenly felt like having a beer; it seemed like the proper reaction to such a thing. She imagined the hiss and the crack of the tab pushing through metal, imagined sinking to the floor and downing an entire can as Black Mabel watched. Numbing was what was needed here, the ritual, having a drink when things got hairy. That's what normal people did.

"Bird shot," said Black Mabel and collapsed on the tarp draped over the corner that had once contained a fireplace.

"What?"

"It was a robbery," explained Black Mabel. "Can I smoke in here?"

"No," said Rachel.

"Shit," said Black Mabel, who had already pulled the cigarettes from her jacket. "You really don't drink?"

"No," Rachel said, and fled to her bedroom, pulled on jeans, a sweater, and socks. When she returned to the living room, she found Black Mabel staring up at the ceiling and smoking.

"This place is a shithole," said Black Mabel.

"I know," said Rachel. "Mabel?"

"What?"

"My mom?"

"Shit," said Black Mabel. "She's at the hospital in Ellis. I'm sure she doesn't want you to know."

"Then why are you here?"

"I had to tell somebody," said Black Mabel. "I've never seen anything like that in my life."

"Tell me," said Rachel.

"She was closing up. In comes the Clinkenbeard kid, with a fucking shotgun."

"Is it hunting season?"

"Them Clinkenbeards hunt year-round," said Black Mabel. "They'll shoot anything, anytime."

"Apparently," said Rachel. "What was a kid doing there so late at night?"

"They always come around at last call," said Black Mabel. "The second after the shotgun blast, Ol' Red came running, and I mean running, through the door."

"Red Mabel?"

"Is there any other?" Black Mabel spit on the carpet, to emphasize her point.

"Is my mom okay?" Rachel ignored the spit, just as she ignored the carpet itself.

"Think so," said Black Mabel. "Every time I tried to help, Red Mabel just hissed at me."

"I should go to the hospital," said Rachel.

"You sure about that? I told you Red was there. There's already been enough violence in this county tonight."

"It's what daughters are supposed to do," said Rachel.

"Can I sleep here?"

"No," said Rachel. "Sleep it off in your car."

"I'll freeze to death," protested Black Mabel.

"Fine," said Rachel. "You can sleep on the floor."

Rachel grabbed her keys and watched Black Mabel nestle into the tarp, her long coat wrapped around her head. Rachel made sure to move the space heaters a safe distance away before she walked out the door.

The drive to Ellis took about twenty minutes, the entire route an old highway that paralleled the river. The road was notorious for patches of black ice, and the route was marked with white crosses; so many people had died on these eighteen miles that a hospital was a necessary thing.

At four o'clock in the morning, there was no traffic, but Rachel still drove slowly.

She had never been a cautious driver, even after she got sober. At the moment, fear flooded her body, an engine given too much gas. Rachel knew what the fuel was, knew who had caused this adrenaline to invade her blood. Rachel's hands on the steering wheel were tight fists, white from clenching. She only released one hand on straight stretches of the highway, to wipe at the sweat collecting on her upper lip.

Athena and Rachel had done a fourth step every single time Laverna returned a letter. Each inventory had been meticulous, but Rachel never received closure. She would never admit this to Athena. Rachel was willing to admit her own faults, where she had acted out of fear or selfishness. Secretly, she held on to the belief that Laverna was responsible. Laverna loved only money and power. When her mother attempted to trust men, she got bit every single time. Rachel was willing to admit to

Athena that she had pierced her mother's skin whenever the opportunity presented itself, whenever Laverna got too close. Laverna had given up before Rachel was old enough for a bra, and that was not what mothers were supposed to do.

"Your mother did the best she could with what she had," Athena said, after every fourth step. "Your mother is just a person, with flaws of her own."

Rachel would nod, and stare at the unopened envelope in her garbage can.

As she drove toward Ellis, Rachel took deep breaths and concentrated on the worst stories she had heard at meetings. Rachel had been hell-bent on destroying herself, and she had mostly avoided collateral damage. She had never killed a family of four while drunk driving, had never left a baby to freeze to death in a car while drinking at a bar in the middle of winter. She was a relatively good person, had only broken hearts and occasionally the law.

———

The nurse at the front desk waved Rachel silently through; Laverna was the only emergency at four o'clock in the morning on a weeknight.

Laverna was still in the emergency room. Rachel stood outside the curtain and listened to Red Mabel. She could see her thick black boots, the laces untied and the tongues bulged out. Red Mabel had huge, perpetually swelling feet.

She listened as Red Mabel plotted her revenge on all the Clinkenbeards, even the infants. Chain saw attacks, poisonings, arson. Rachel could not hear her mother respond.

Rachel finally gathered enough courage to step past the curtain, and saw why. Laverna was asleep. Red Mabel held a chunk of Laverna's hair and petted it softly.

When she finally noticed Rachel, Red Mabel stumbled back and almost knocked over a crash cart.

"You," said Red Mabel.

"Yes," said Rachel.

"I told you I never wanted to see you again. I warned you what would happen." Red Mabel crossed her mighty arms, green work shirt-sleeves stained with the blood of Laverna or something poached, filthy white socks exposed as she stood on the shell of her boots to seem taller.

"I'm not scared," said Rachel, hoping that Red Mabel could not sniff out this lie. "I have a right to be here."

"You have some nerve," declared Red Mabel. "I saved her life." Red Mabel grunted and stepped forward to pull the sheet down around Laverna's chest. Rachel saw her mother's arms thickly bandaged, fingers lost in enormous mittens of gauze.

"Where's the doctor?"

"Good question," said Red Mabel. "He went to go get something for her pain. That was half an hour ago."

"Thank you," said Rachel. "Thank you for being here." She sat down on a metal folding chair. Despite the sharp odor of freshly waxed floors, she could smell the sawdust that covered Red Mabel's pants.

"The only reason I'm not choking you is because the doctor gave me a sedative."

"He gave you a sedative?" Rachel was incredulous. "And he didn't give my mom any painkillers?"

"Triage," she said. "That's what he called it."

"Can we have a truce? Just for now?"

"Let me think about it," said Red Mabel.

They both stared at Laverna, who was still sleeping.

"What did they give you?"

"Valium," said Red Mabel. "Twice the usual dose," she added proudly.

"How is she?"

"They think the bird shot shattered her arms. Broken radius, or radial, or some shit. A chip in her elbow bone. She's lucky."

"Oh," said Rachel.

"All right," said Red Mabel. "I thought about it. A truce for tonight. That's fine. I need a cigarette."

Outside the hospital, Red Mabel smoked in silence and rocked back and forth on her boots. In nine years, she hadn't aged, but her face was blank in the floodlights of the parking lot. Rachel was thankful for the double dose of Valium.

"How have you been?"

"You ain't got no right to ask me that," said Red Mabel.

"Fine," stated Rachel. "How long is she going to be in the hospital?"

"Dunno," said Red Mabel. "She was conscious in the ambulance. She was talking, and she knew her arms were shot to shit." The nurse from the front desk came through the sliding doors of the lobby and sat on a curb, lit a cigarette of her own. "You're gonna need to step up. Somebody has to cover, and you're the only one with experience. Your mother made the decision."

"I'm an alcoholic," proclaimed Rachel.

"Who isn't?"

"I'm not supposed to be around booze," said Rachel.

"Tough shit. You're gonna take the opening shift and swap with Tabby. It's already been decided. You ain't supposed to be drinking on the job anyway."

"I'm not comfortable with this," said Rachel.

"Word around town is that you need a job," said Red Mabel. "And your mama needs your help. The bar opens at eight in the morning. That's too early for you to act like a whore."

"Jesus," said Rachel. "I just don't want to be tempted. That's all."

"I worked in a silver mine," said Red Mabel. "Doesn't mean I had to own every piece of jewelry."

"You stole dynamite," Rachel pointed out.

"I've got a lot of enemies," said Red Mabel. Her face snapped out of the softness, and she snarled. "And you don't have any right to talk about stealing!"

"How long?" Rachel watched as Red Mabel stepped on her cigarette, ground it into the asphalt. "How long do I have fill in for my mom?" Sometimes the chance to make amends came out of nowhere, with the speed of bird shot.

"Until she tells you to stop," said Red Mabel. She dug into her pockets and threw a set of keys at Rachel. "You'd better be on your way," she said. "The bar opens in three hours."

————

The Dirty Shame had not changed one bit, except for the mess from the gunfire. Tabby waited for Rachel, threw an apron and the opening checklist in her direction. Both landed on the floor and began to soak through with spilled liquor. Tabby didn't say a word, just glared as she stomped out, only stopping to pull the chain on the neon sign. The bar was open for business.

Splintered holes embedded in the soft pine of the bar, bird shot wedged in its unpredictable trajectory. Bottles remained erect, although some were just spiky shards. When Rachel saw the shattered pieces of the mirror, she stopped. She thought of a dark night, nine years earlier.

The countertops and the floors were still slick and sticky with spilled booze. The smells of all the different flavors of Schnapps that had exploded combined into a pungent mix of minty and fruity. Her sneaker stuck where the aftermath had soaked into the floorboards.

She tied on her apron and lost herself in cleaning, until she began to relish it. She was cleaning up one of her mother's messes for once, and not her own. She righted the barstools, attempted to pry some of the bird shot from the bar with a butter knife. She finished sweeping up the glass and filled up a mop bucket, letting the soapy water sink into the floorboards. She sprayed the bar and the shelves behind it with Lysol, and scrubbed until the surfaces were shining. She wiped down the small tables, cleaned the bathrooms, refilled the ketchups and mustards, topped off the salt and pepper shakers, and cut lemons and limes into small triangles and stocked them in the well.

Ronda, the short-order cook, came through the door at exactly eleven o'clock, silent as always. Ronda was an older Native American woman, a giantess, over six feet tall; her neck was draped with long cords and pouches. Her hair was raven colored, but striated through with bright white pieces. When Rachel was growing up, the rumor in town had been that Ronda was a witch, but Rachel doubted it. There was only one real witch at the Dirty Shame, and she had been taken out by gunfire.

Rachel emptied the mop bucket as the first customers finally arrived, the lunch drunks. They tracked snow all over her freshly cleaned floor. All were schoolteachers, eleven in total, ten beer drinkers and her former English teacher, who ordered a White Russian. Rachel filled their lunch orders, which was easy enough. Everything was served in greasy plastic baskets lined with wax paper.

When she returned home after her first shift, the smell of Black Mabel lingered, even though the woman herself was long gone. Rachel was nervous to call Athena. She turned up the space heaters and reached for the phone. She had a job, but it was in a bar, and Rachel was still relatively new to sobriety.

"I get to make amends," Rachel said. "Living amends. I just show up and do my job and keep my mouth shut."

"That doesn't sound like amends," said Athena. "That sounds like penance. Living amends means that you decide to change your ways and don't expect appreciation for it. It's a quiet thing."

After she hung up the phone, Rachel was determined to prove Athena wrong. She grabbed her journal and began to work on a gratitude list, and the effort behind finding things to be grateful for and her close proximity to the space heaters made her sweat. It had become bitterly cold again, just like that, predictable for the last days of February.

When the knock came, Rachel pushed her face against the plastic sheeting that covered her living room window. She could barely ascertain the flash of red.

A volunteer fireman occupied her porch—they all wore red mesh baseball caps outside the hall, like a flock of brutish cardinals. They always grouped together in crowds, at basketball games and at spaghetti feeds. The fraternity of the black QVFD jackets and red heads made them look like a pack of matches.

In her sweatpants and giant New Order T-shirt, with her hair still stuck to her cheek from perspiration, she answered the door.

She caught Bucky as he was about to knock again. He stopped himself before he could knock right on her face. He was distracted, staring at the mess outside the trailer house.

"What?" She was irritated. She had a suspicion that this ugly young man had come to sell more raffle tickets.

"Heard you needed a handyman."

"You?"

"Yes, ma'am. I'm not licensed or anything, but I know my way around a trailer house."

"Jesus," she said. Rachel had forgotten how fast word got out in Quinn, how it swept through without consideration, yet another fire through town.

"I have references," he continued. "I waited a week before I came over."

"Oh," she said. She was so shipwrecked lately that she'd lost track of time. She felt that she should be carving marks in the wall with a kitchen knife to keep track of every day she spent making her amends.

"Can I come in?" He pointed to her living room. She opened the door and stepped back; her living room was a junkyard. With her foot, she pushed the gratitude list under the pillow she had been sitting on—it had been a short list anyway. One: having a job. Two: continuing her sobriety. Three: being a natural blonde.

She felt sorry for both of them. At least Bucky could blame his misfortune on his teeth. Her new home was becoming a halfway house for pathetic creatures.

He entered her living room and let out a low whistle.

"I know," she said. "You don't have to make me feel like shit."

"You got some soft spots," he pronounced, and knelt down by the giant dimple in the center of her carpet.

"You have no idea," she said, and yawned.

Crouching down, his knees stuck out, sharp enough to be another tool. He needed a haircut. His hair was jet-black, and it curled around the back of his cap. He stood up, and he was at least six inches taller than she was; he seemed to be composed entirely of gangly limbs and jutting teeth.

"Can I make you some coffee?" She had only two mugs, one of which held her toothbrush.

"No, thanks," he said. He quietly regarded the kitchen. The coffee could wait.

"There aren't any problems here," she said. "This is the one room that works."

"Black mold," said Bucky, standing in a dark corner, where the linoleum of the kitchen floor disappeared under the baseboard. Rachel had just assumed those shadows were bad lighting.

"What the fuck is black mold?"

"It's the worst kind you can get," he said. He crouched down to inspect it, dug a finger into the darkness, brought his hand over to Rachel, his whole arm extended outward as if the black mold was so dangerous he didn't want it near his body. "I suspect the whole floor is rotten."

"Jesus Christ," said Rachel. "Can I spray it or something?"

"Lady, you aren't even supposed to be breathing right now. This stuff has spores, and it poisons the air."

"Fabulous," she said. "I'm going to take my chances." Bucky removed a pocketknife from his jeans and cut away at the corner. The linoleum curled neatly in his hand. The flooring underneath was the color of cardboard, but with polka dots of black growth. He examined it carefully.

"Well?"

"It's not as bad as I thought," he said. "I can cut this whole corner out, replace the joists. It hasn't spread that much."

"Wait until you see the rest of the house," she muttered as he stomped the flooring back in place with his heavy black boot.

He followed her down the sagging hallway, stopping to tap his boot around the soft spots as the carpet cratered and the wood creaked. "This ain't so bad," he said. "The good news is that I don't see any more black mold."

"The bad news?"

"I'm gonna have to replace the entire floor."

"For fuck's sake," she said.

"I ain't gonna use new lumber," he said. "I can scavenge from the dump and from behind the mill."

"So, you're thrifty?"

"Not especially," he said. "I just know you can't afford it."

"Thanks," she said. "You're going to love the bathroom."

He didn't. When Rachel turned on the light, he grimaced.

"Fuck," he said.

"I need a bathtub that works," she said. "One that's not underneath the house."

Bucky examined the tiny room. "I can put in new subflooring and lay new linoleum and make it look pretty. Or pretty enough. But you're gonna need a plumber to hook up the water line."

"Do you know a good plumber?"

"Yep," he said. "But it's gonna be expensive. All of this. Maybe you should just burn it down and start over. Torch this son of a bitch and get a new trailer house."

"I can't believe you're advocating arson," she said. "You're the worst fireman ever."

"I'm honest," he said. "Repairing this place is going to cost you. Big-time."

"It already has," she admitted. She thought that she might start crying.

Rachel followed him through the house and out the front door. He paused on the front porch, and she waited for more bad news. It was hatefully cold outside, but he removed a pack of cigarettes from his coat pocket. "Want one?"

"No," she said. Then she reconsidered when she smelled the lit cigarette. She had quit years ago, but this was all so overwhelming. "Give me one."

"Sure," he said, and handed her the pack.

"I've got black mold," she said. "A cigarette isn't going to make a difference."

They sat and smoked, her head rushing and body tingling. She instantly felt sick to her stomach, felt like she was going to shit her pants. Oh, how she missed smoking.

"I can fix the bathroom and replace all the floors for three grand," he said. "That includes putting the bathtub back into the bathroom. The plumber is gonna be extra, and I ain't touching the fireplace."

"I can give you two grand and that Toyota parked outside."

"Deal," he said. He exhaled, and shook her hand. "I knew your dad."

"Well," said Rachel. "I wish I could say the same thing." She threw her cigarette out in the yard. It didn't extinguish, just lay there smoking on top of the hardened snow.

"Does the car run?"

"Probably not," said Rachel.

"I'll be back. First thing Thursday morning. Get all those clothes out of the bathtub, all right?"

"Yes," Rachel said, and reached out to touch his arm. She was buzzed on the cigarette. "Thank you."

"It's a job," he said. "No need." He tripped his way up the path.

After Bucky left, Rachel lay down on her dirty carpet and watched the gloom through the plastic of her living room window. She would work at the bar, and not expect any thanks. This was how living amends worked. The amends would be easy. It was the living that would be the hard part.

Winter Birds

★ ★ ★

*J*ake pushed open the back door, and the snow immediately whipped his face and barreled into the tight hallway of the trailer house. He kept a towel on the floor for this very reason. Bert was always yelling about black mold. At seven thirty, it was growing light out. He crunched down the steps and placed his slippers inside yesterday's trail of footprints leading to the storage shed. The door slid easily this morning and, shivering, he stepped inside the gloom and felt around for his flashlight. The beam swept back and forth among the carefully arranged stacks, and he began to pick out his clothes. He had a lot of clothes. He was paid to keep the official scorebook for every men's and women's softball game that was played in Quinn, and he spent the money on paperbacks, movie tickets, magazines subscriptions, and the thrift store.

He chose a camel-colored cardigan, a baby-blue T-shirt, dark brown polyester slacks, and his favorite oxfords.

He often had dreamy conversations with his mother, in which they imagined where these clothes had originated—neither had seen his purchases worn on any kids in Quinn. Maybe they had come from diminutive old men, or were brought in giant trucks from Spokane, a big city where Krystal claimed people were shorter because of their drug use. Perhaps they were shipped from Hollywood, costumes for child actors. Once,

Krystal had suggested grave robbers, but the idea had struck them both as ghoulish and incredibly unhygienic.

He slid shut the shed door, replaced the padlock. The lock became necessary after Jake caught Bert, or rather Bert's lower half, protruding from the shed doors. Bert had passed out inside. When he had been roused, he had declared that he was going to start storing his tools there, until Krystal had carefully pointed out that it had been a gift from Frank.

Inside the warmth of the bathroom, Jake dressed quickly but took extra time on his hair, which he shellacked with wax until it gleamed like gold.

Satisfied, he made coffee and took it outside. The sun was rising over the mountain, and Jake could hear the rumbles of trucks warming up all around the trailer court.

He had ten minutes before he would have to walk to school. He always left time for these ten minutes.

Quinn had flocks of winter birds, strange and colorful. Jake had found a book at the thrift store and could identify them all: snow buntings, wax-wings, black-capped chickadees, red-breasted nuthatches, brown creepers. They were fast and beautiful, and like Jake, they were constantly aware of threats. As far as he knew, Frank's feral cats had never caught a winter bird. The cats caught the occasional robin or sparrow in the spring, but never these creatures.

He scattered seed and stepped back as the birds came swooping down.

Jake stood in the front yard and waited for the fashion show, the colors of the birds bright against the dirty gray sky and banks of snow.

———

When he got home from school, Bert was gone, but a weight remained in the trailer house, a heaviness in the air, as they waited for his return. Krystal cleaned silently and furiously, checked the kitchen window every fifteen minutes.

Now that Frank and Misty were gone, Krystal was Jake's only friend. Before Bert, she had attempted all sorts of things to get him involved with other kids, but he had refused Little League, Cub Scouts, church camp. His mother was his peer group. Krystal was allergic to any kind of pet, so for Jake's ninth birthday, she bought him sea monkeys, and they waited for the tiny kingdoms to materialize just like in the advertisements, all that activity in a cheap green aquarium. The sea monkeys had died together in a clump; his new friends turned out to be nothing more than suicidal brine shrimp.

Krystal was a flighty, chatty sort of woman; years of being a nurse in a small hospital had made this worse. She talked to fill up space, narrated every activity, even though Jake was right there and had no need for her bedside manner. She remained silent on the story of Jake's biological father, a man she never spoke to, even to demand child support. He probably didn't know that Jake existed. There was only one story, and he had heard it since he was three years old, so he just accepted it. His mother was not smart enough to be a liar. Jake's father had been a physician visiting from the East Coast, flown to the hospital in Ellis to consult on a special case. Somehow, in the three days he had been in town, he managed to both seduce and abandon her. At least Jake knew from where his excellent time-management skills had been inherited.

Like his mother, Jake devoured books, and when they read, the chattering stopped. For a time, they shared novels. Jake was a precocious reader. Eventually, he discovered Jackie Collins, while his mother switched to terrible Southern romances. Krystal was drawn toward stories of debutantes overwhelmed with lust, and she talked incessantly about sweet tea, fans, tiny purses, and grand cotillion balls. Her own son was the closest thing to a prissy debutante in the entire town.

Krystal found her own terrible romance, and she waited for him now. It was too early for Bert to be at the Dirty Shame, so there was no telling where he had gone. Jake lay on the couch and worked his way through *Valley of the Dolls*. In the kitchen, Krystal smashed potato chips to adorn a tuna fish casserole.

When the knock came, Jake looked up at his mother. Bert did not like visitors, did not like his wife to answer the door. Krystal's hands were covered in shards of Ruffles, and she stared at Jake helplessly. She was usually the one who told people to go away. Jake dropped his book, just as the baby started crying in her high chair, and Krystal pivoted on her feet, back and forth, unsure of what to do. Jake rolled his eyes.

Standing on the front porch was the woman from next door. He knew she was Frank's daughter, because gossip in the trailer park moved fast, and because he had spied on her from the roof.

A towel hung over her shoulder. She held a shower caddy in one hand. He hadn't been able to ascertain if she was pretty when he had spied on her, but up close, she was dazzling. Under the towel, she wore a tight black T-shirt. Her legs were shackled in the tightest acid-washed jeans he had ever seen. She smelled like fried food. He approved of all of this.

"Hello there," she said, and leaned down to shake his hand.

"Hi," said Jake.

"I saw you on the roof," she said. "You seemed like a good omen, so I came here."

Jake had never been called an omen before, but he liked it.

"Welcome," he said. Krystal emerged from the kitchen, the baby in her arms, still crying. Jake watched as his mother stared at the blonde in shock, and shoved Jake back from the door with her free arm. She had never pushed him before, but the look on her face kept him from protesting. Maybe this was his mother's true bedside manner.

"Krystal!" The woman on the porch was genuinely excited to see his mother, but Krystal responded by handing him the baby and shutting the door until it was just a crack. He could hear his mother whispering, and the woman laughed. Krystal shut the door, and Jake could hear the blonde stomping her feet as she left the porch.

Jake held the baby as Krystal anxiously checked out the kitchen window, carefully wrapped the casserole dish in tinfoil, and slid it into the oven. He watched as she took a deep breath, attempting to gather herself. This was amazing to him, this side of his mother. When Bert freaked out, Krystal did not react, because she knew better.

Krystal drew back the curtains and opened the living room window. The winter air blasted through, and Jake could see the blonde in her own yard, waiting for Krystal, peering up over the fence.

"You have some nerve," said Krystal.

"Didn't you get my letter?"

"No," said Krystal, and Jake knew she was telling the truth. Only Bert was allowed to get the mail, and he had probably thrown it away.

"I tried to apologize," explained the woman. "I owed you that much." Jake wondered if the woman had taken the rosary he had left on her doorknob and what she had thought of it. In this town, it could be considered a warning.

"Bert told me not to talk to you," said Krystal. "He warned me you were back in town."

"Jesus," said the woman. "We used to be friends."

"Rachel Flood, we were never friends. You just used me for my car."

"That's not true," said the woman, apparently named Rachel, and apparently related to Laverna. He shivered as the winter air invaded the living room. He did not want to miss any of this, and he pulled the baby closer and snuck up behind his mother.

"Listen for his truck," said Krystal. "Bert cannot see this."

"What happened to you? We used to have fun."

"You ruined everything," said Krystal. "I haven't worn lipstick in nine years. Do you have any idea what that's like?"

"I just wanted to take a shower," said Rachel. "My bathtub seems to have fallen underneath my house."

"Gross," said Jake quietly. Rachel stepped back from the fence and held up her shower caddy. Again, he studied her. Until five minutes ago, Jake had thought that his mother was the prettiest woman in town. But here was a specimen who stared back with defiance and held herself with perfect posture. Supermodel style—chin up, tits out.

Jake considered his own outfit—he changed his clothes when he came home from school, every single day. This afternoon he had dressed in black slacks, a black sweater vest over a white button-down.

"No," said Krystal. "Why are you always trying to get me into trouble?"

"Fine," said Rachel. "I'm in town to make amends. You were on the list anyway. How can I make it up to you?"

Krystal was silent. Jake watched Rachel, stomping her feet in the cold, waiting for an answer. He wondered what kind of coat she would normally wear and was lost in this reverie when his mother's answer came, short and certain: "Softball."

"What the hell?"

"I've been living in fear of your mother for nine years," said Krystal. "Lying to her makes me a nervous wreck. It's your turn."

"No way," said Rachel. "I don't play sports." Jake was delighted, and pretended to read his book. He could not imagine this woman playing softball. She did not deserve the indignities of sweat and constantly swirling dust, sharing the field with sasquatch Red Mabel.

"Right field," insisted Krystal. "It's not really a sport."

"I don't run," said Rachel. "I mean, I've run from cops and stuff, but I don't really remember it."

"Take my spot," said Krystal. "It's the least you can do. If you leave us alone, I'll buy you a new bathtub. But you can't tell Bert. I can't stand seeing you dirty. I mean, I'm not a complete bitch."

"Are you really that scared of my mom?"

"Yes," said Krystal. "Consider it a housewarming gift."

"Fine," said Rachel. Jake heard the faint rumble of Bert's truck.

"The first practice is in a few weeks," said Krystal. "Maybe you should start jogging or something." Krystal slid the window shut and drew the curtains.

———

Jake worked on the laundry basket, folding the load he had removed from the dryer. He washed all of the laundry for the household because he was the best at it, and because he insisted. When Bert finally came through the door, he ignored Jake and his piles on the living room floor. Bert sat quietly on the couch. He held no beer in his hand and did not ask Krystal to fetch him one. Jake hoped that Bert had an infection from the cut on his hand, that he had a rare blood fever.

Krystal wiped down the kitchen table and plucked the baby from her high chair, placed her carefully inside the playpen. Bert continued to stare out into space. Bert took pills for his blood pressure, so Jake ruled out a stroke.

Finally, Bert asked to speak with Krystal privately. Jake gathered the laundry and fled to his bedroom. He turned on his stereo so he would not have to listen to their conversation.

Bert did not allow Jake to shut his bedroom door completely. Krystal appeared in his doorway, fifteen minutes later. She didn't have the baby, which meant she wanted to discuss something serious.

She sat down on his bed, in the clear space among the stacks of his clothes. She examined a vest that was black and had a dark purple backing, and pretended to admire it.

"This is nice," she said, and neatly folded it.

"You hate it," said Jake.

"It's not my style, honey."

"I'll put it in the storage shed," he said.

"Have you made any new friends?"

"No," he said.

Krystal did not respond, clearly distracted. "I have good news," she said, clasping her hands together.

Jake carefully considered this. "But you just lost the baby weight."

"Jake, you have to stop reading women's magazines. Did you notice something different about Bert?"

"Are you kicking him out?" Jake's heart leaped in his chest.

"No, honey. Something happened."

"Okay," said Jake as he folded a fitted sheet. He was the only member of the household who possessed this ability.

"He almost died. He's a different man now."

"I've heard that before," said Jake. "And nobody even shot at him. It was an attempted robbery."

"Oh, Jake," Krystal said, and sighed.

"Whatever. You are always coming in here and making promises that he's changed his ways, and that things are going to be better. And that lasts a couple of hours until he gets pissed off at me."

"He's been saved," whispered Krystal.

"From what?" Jake handed her the properly folded fitted sheet.

"Saved," repeated Krystal. "Like in a spiritual way."

At this, Jake guffawed. Krystal glared but remained calm. She smoothed the sheet with the flat of her hand.

"I figured that's what you meant," he said, and stopped grinning. He knew his mother's face and could see the pain it caused her.

"He's in a better place now," she said. "He has all sorts of plans for the future. I haven't seen him like this since we started dating."

"He's been in a bad mood for two years," said Jake. "Does this mean he's going to get a job?"

"Like it or not, we have a baby now. He's the head of this family," said Krystal. "He's had a hard life." Jake turned away from her and pretended to examine his closet, because there were tears in his eyes. He was sick of all of the excuses. "Honey, I promise you. Everything is going to change around here."

"That's what you said about the baby," said Jake.

"Bert's getting baptized next week," she said. "He really wants you to be there."

"Did he say that?" He turned and addressed her directly. "Did those words really come out of his mouth?"

"No," said Krystal.

"That's what I thought," said Jake.

"You will be the best-dressed person there," said Krystal. "I just know you have a baptism outfit somewhere in here."

"Of course I do," snapped Jake.

Krystal handed him a stack of shirts, and Jake hung them, waiting for his mother to leave, for this conversation to be over.

"I'm not getting baptized," said Jake, still refusing to look at her.

"This is about Bert."

"It always is," Jake said, and continued to stare into his closet until he heard his mother leave.

The Biggest Problem

*   *   *

*L*averna was discharged from the hospital two days after she had been admitted. They let her go early, because she was a particularly cantankerous patient.

The casts were ridiculous. Laverna felt they could have done better, done something more convenient, and told the doctor so. Her arms were stuck straight out in front of her and propped up on tiny rods attached to a removable harness. Laverna had sustained extensive injuries up to her biceps, and now she had no use of her arms.

"You can wiggle your thumbs," said the doctor hopefully. "That's a good sign."

"I don't hitchhike," said Laverna.

Red Mabel refused the wheelchair, as she and Laverna had managed to absolve themselves from any official hospital policy. Red Mabel opened every single door as they made their way through the hospital lobby, and they watched as the nurses finally relaxed at the front desk. Red Mabel's truck was jacked up on giant wheels, and she had to push Laverna up into the passenger seat. Laverna rested her casts on the dashboard as they drove back to Quinn. On the ride home, plans for revenge against the Clinkenbeards were discussed, but none seemed ruthless enough.

"I think we should capture a bear and set it loose in their kitchen," suggested Red Mabel.

"No," said Laverna. "I think we should cast a spell. We need witch books. You're going to have to take me to the library." Red Mabel ignored this, as Laverna's latest round of painkillers had finally taken effect.

Red Mabel helped Laverna inside her house and led her to the couch. She offered to make her coffee, but Laverna asked for a beer instead, although she quickly discovered that drinking was just as impossible as smoking. She sent Red Mabel to the grocery store for straws, and her truck was gone for more than an hour, most likely staking out the Clinkenbeard residence.

When Red Mabel returned, they found that the phone was also a problem. Red Mabel had to dial, and stick the receiver in between Laverna's shoulder and ear. Laverna liked to talk on the phone, liked to issue proclamations to her staff and spread gossip, or start gossip, but now it was uncomfortable for her to twist her neck for so long. Red Mabel held the phone up to Laverna's ear, and she called Tabby at home and warned her that she would need paper and a pen for all of the directions she was about to unleash.

"I don't trust Rachel one bit," said Laverna. "You need to watch her. Keep her away from the men. Keep her away from the jukebox. Do not let her talk to the jukebox vendor, or she will change every single goddamn song to heavy metal. Music like that will only encourage those silver miners to create havoc and destroy things. I've had enough destruction, thank you very much."

"Okay," said Tabby.

"Now," demanded Laverna. "Write these things down."

Laverna launched into the day-to-day operations she would no longer be able to micromanage. Laverna had memorized the numbers of the beer vendors, as well as the number of the man who leased the poker machines. Laverna had not memorized the number of the food distributor. Every week, Ronda just handed the driver her order form, silent as usual.

"I also want you to keep an eye on Ronda's orders," said Laverna. "If you think she's ordering extra food to steal for whatever goddamn tribe she's from, you call me. Immediately. I don't want free fried chicken from the Dirty Shame being eaten in every teepee across the Northwest."

"Okay," said Tabby.

"Are you writing this down?"

"Of course," said Tabby.

"Your biggest problem is going to be Rachel. She's always been my biggest problem, but I have suffered life-threatening injuries, and I simply can't deal with her right now."

"I thought he just shot your arms."

"Shut up," said Laverna.

Red Mabel took the phone away from her. She could hear Tabby squawking something, but the conversation was over as far as she was concerned.

"Light me a cigarette," demanded Laverna, and Red Mabel obliged.

Ten minutes later, Laverna asked Red Mabel to put her to bed. It took half an hour rearranging pillows and bedding until Laverna was comfortable. It was going to be hard for her to sleep with her arms stuck straight out in front of her, but the whiskey was opened, and Red Mabel administered dosages until Laverna passed out.

———

The next morning, Laverna was moored at her dining room table, using her thumbs to page through magazines, but she could not concentrate on anything she was reading. It was the first day of March, and spring remained an obscure idea. She really wanted a cigarette, but Red Mabel had left to park her truck outside of the Clinkenbeard residence. Red Mabel did this every single day, just parked there, for at least an hour. This had not brought any results; no Clinkenbeard ever emerged from their house, although Red Mabel had claimed she had seen some curtains rustling.

The local police begged Red Mabel to stay out of it, to let them handle the Clinkenbeards. They knew Red Mabel's predilection toward violence, because they had been on the receiving end of it, many times. They also knew that Red Mabel had dynamite, but knew better than to bring that up.

Red Mabel was the one who lit Laverna's cigarettes, and also the one who gave Laverna a bath every morning. At first, this was embarrassing for both of them, but the whiskey helped.

There was a knock at the door. Laverna yelled for Red Mabel out of habit, but she was gone.

"Come in!" Laverna hollered as loud as she could. She needed a cigarette and was too irritable to prop herself up on her casts and maneuver out of the dining room chair.

Krystal Bailey was laden with three pies, one tin in each hand, and the other balanced carefully in the crook of her arm. Laverna said nothing as Krystal laid the pies out in front of her.

"Two banana creams, and a rhubarb for Red Mabel," said Krystal.

"Give me a cigarette," said Laverna. Krystal reached for Laverna's pack and slid a cigarette into the corner of Laverna's mouth. Krystal lit the cigarette for her and pretended to cough.

"As a nurse, I really must warn you about smoking. It slows the healing process."

"Fuck off," said Laverna. "Can you get me some more painkillers?"

"I will ask the doctor," said Krystal.

"Would you rather I go see Dr. Black Mabel?" Laverna exhaled out of her nose, and Krystal removed the cigarette, and ashed it for her, wedged it back in the corner of her mouth.

"Of course not," said Krystal.

"I knew I could count on you," said Laverna.

"Actually," said Krystal, "that's why I'm here." Krystal sat down in a dining room chair, directly across from Laverna. The table was littered with straws, magazines, pill bottles, empty bottles of whiskey, and three different ashtrays. The pies seemed out of place.

"Please tell me that you have morphine in your pockets."

"No," said Krystal. "I have to quit the Flood Girls."

At this kind of news, Laverna's blood pressure would normally rise, her face would get hot, and her fists would ball up. The painkillers, the antianxiety pills, and the whiskey prevented this from happening. Still, she attempted to make her face appear as angry as possible.

"You better have a brain tumor or something."

"I took a new shift at the hospital," said Krystal. "It pays more, and you know we have a new mouth to feed."

Laverna knew this. She was sick and tired of hearing about the baby. Two summers ago, she had to listen to Krystal talk about it in the dugout, had to deal with the morning sickness. Krystal had always vomited discreetly, usually in a plastic grocery bag that she would neatly deposit in the metal garbage can behind the dugout. Regardless, Laverna had forced Krystal to play through her fifth month. Right field never saw any action anyway.

"I see," said Laverna. "You will be missed." This wasn't really true—Krystal was a terrible softball player. Occasionally, she would get a good hit, usually a single, but by her fifth month, her stomach was sticking out, and she struck out every single time, didn't even swing.

"I found a replacement," said Krystal. "And I don't think you're going to like it."

"You are full of good news today," said Laverna. "Ash my cigarette." Krystal obliged, and Laverna regarded the terror on her face.

"Rachel."

"You mean my daughter?"

"Yes," said Krystal. "Believe me, I asked every single female I know. I almost opened the phone book and started dialing numbers at random."

"You should have," said Laverna. "She's already working at the Shame. I don't want her wrecking my fucking softball team."

"She didn't want to play," said Krystal. "If that's any consolation."

"It's not," said Laverna. "What are you going to do with that baby?"

"Bert will be home at night," said Krystal, and at that, Laverna couldn't help but roll her eyes. Bert was useless, had never held a job. He was not suitable for child care. He had proven to be terrible in emergency situations, not that Laverna thought the baby would be held up in an attempted robbery.

"Of course he will," said Laverna. "He's a fucking deadbeat. Put my cigarette out."

"I'm sorry," said Krystal.

"You should be," said Laverna. "Rachel is uncoordinated and mouthy."

"Perfect for right field," said Krystal.

"I'd like you to leave now," said Laverna.

"Okay," said Krystal. Laverna noticed that Krystal had tears in her eyes, overreacting as usual, as she pushed herself up from the dining room table. Laverna didn't give a shit. It served her right.

———

Her second visitor arrived a half an hour later, and instead of pie, he brought flowers. They were the first flowers she had received, after an entire week of convalescence. She didn't count the poinsettia from the Chamber of Commerce because Red Mabel had already thrown it into the river.

Jim Number Three presented her with a massive arrangement of lilies and tulips. He must have gone to Ellis for these, as there were no florists in Quinn. Laverna decided that he could stay for more than ten minutes. Plus, his presence might make Red Mabel jealous, and illustrate what could happen when her primary caretaker abandoned her.

"I'm so sorry," said Jim Number Three. "If I had been there, that kid would've been taken down immediately." He placed the flowers in front of Laverna, and she leaned forward, to smell them.

"Light me a cigarette," said Laverna.

"I broke both my legs once," said Jim Number Three. "Fell off a ladder and landed on a wheelbarrow."

"Jesus," said Laverna. He gave her a lit cigarette out of his own pack.

"I was in bed for weeks," he said. "The only thing that saved me from going insane was having my mother read to me."

"How old were you?"

He had to think about it. "Forty-three," he said.

"I was kind of hoping I could do the same for you," he said. "It would be a pleasure to read a book to the prettiest woman in town."

"That's kind of strange," said Laverna. But this entire month had been odd, and he was age appropriate, and vaguely handsome. If he read to her, maybe Red Mabel would try harder.

He helped Laverna to the couch, assisted her in lying down on her back, her casts stiff and pointing at the ceiling, the plaster still so white that it was painful to behold.

He had brought *Roots*, because it was the longest book he owned, and the word around town was that her recovery was going to take months.

"Never read it," said Laverna. "Didn't watch the miniseries, either. To tell you the truth, I wasn't that interested. We didn't have slaves in Montana."

Jim Number Three ignored this statement, sat back in the love seat, and turned to page one.

He finished the first chapter by the time Red Mabel finally returned. As Laverna had hoped, Red Mabel seemed suspicious. She marched straight past them without saying a word, and stomped into the kitchen.

Laverna listened, and could hear Red Mabel eating the entire rhubarb pie.

The Hostage

★　★　★

*B*ert's truck was in the driveway, and he was never home when Jake returned from school. He was usually at the bar. This was the new Bert, the one who had the revelation, saved and shaved. No bird shot had touched Bert's body, and he claimed it a miracle. Although he had avoided its flight, he did have a bruise on his shoulder from when he had encountered Red Mabel in the grocery store. She had punched him for not coming to Laverna's aid.

Inside the house, Bert sat next to a redheaded man. Instead of beer, the coffee table in front of the couch held two Bibles, side by side, held open with matching macramé bookmarks. Jake removed his snow boots, and the two men watched him silently.

Jake hoped he could make it to his bedroom in continued silence. Unfortunately, the redheaded man stood up and offered his hand. Also unfortunate, because it revealed the monstrosity of the man's suit, the color of a burnt-sienna crayon. His white shirt was brand-new, spoiled by the tie. Jake liked vintage clothing, but the tie was a disco disaster, much too wide, striped in orange and mint. Nobody had ever told this man that redheads could not wear these colors, and the man was pink in the face, sweaty.

"We've been waiting for you," said the man. Jake shook his hand, aghast at the sheer number of freckles, the bright orange hair on his arm as it emerged from the cuffs. The suit didn't even fit him. Jake did not respond, because this man affronted him on so many levels. Plus, this man wore shoes in the house. Jake wasn't even allowed to wear his house slippers in the house.

"I've been at school," said Jake, dropping the man's hand. "Where's my mom?"

"Grocery shopping," said the man. "You are a lucky young man. We've all taken a shine to Sister Krystal."

"Sister Krystal?" Jake said the name, and giggled as soon as it escaped his mouth. "That sounds like that Night Ranger song." Jake could not control himself now, and was laughing out loud. All he could think of was "Sister Christian." Bert stood up from the couch, his neck a rash of fury, but the man held up a hand. Bert sat back down.

"I am familiar with that song," said the man. "There was a time when I listened to secular music." Jake could not help but notice Bert had been broken, leashed. Jake was impressed by the weird man and his unfortunate color scheme. He accomplished the impossible, and he had not tracked snow on the carpet.

"You're gonna listen to the reverend!" Bert shouted this out, and it startled the man, but Jake was used to this. Bert was suddenly meek again, eyes on the coffee table, face scarlet with impotent rage.

"Fine," said Jake. "Whatever." He sat down on the floor and leaned back on his hands, crossing one leg over the other. He was glad he had chosen green-and-purple argyle socks, wiggled his toes to attract even more attention.

He listened for two minutes because it seemed the polite thing to do, and it rolled off him like another math class. He had been preached to before.

His mother returned from the store and shocked Jake with her amiability. It seemed that she had forgotten her promises, and Jake had no choice but to listen. Krystal and the reverend were an effective team. Jake stopped listening and began to protest. They had planned this ambush, clearly predicted Jake's reactions, prepared counterarguments, and held fast to their demands. He stopped wiggling his toes and covered his face with his hands.

He would not allow them to see the defeat. Frank had given up, too. Misty had been captured, taken away. The little faith and hope that remained inside him had been hung on his mother, and now it was gone forever. He would rather be an infidel; he would never be spineless, or submissive.

He would play along. This was just another thing to endure. Even though Jake couldn't see Bert through his hands, the intensity filled the room. Bert didn't need to utter a word. Jake could not believe he had let himself be taken hostage by his mild-mannered mother and a man in an ill-fitting suit.

It wasn't Sunday school. It was more like day care. Sundays were the only day he could spend with his mother, and now they had been taken away. Bert drove Jake and the baby to New Life Evangelical before nine o'clock in the morning, and the baby was immediately shuttled off by a group of women wearing long jean skirts and homemade blouses. The blouses were all sewn from the same pattern, high-necked and long-sleeved, only varying in the shade, all faded pastels. They frightened him. If Jake had been religious, he would have offered up an honest prayer for his sister's safety.

Reverend Foote waited for him in the kitchen. Jake poured himself a cup of coffee, and stood there, bleary-eyed, as the reverend went on about the need for Brother Bert and Sister Krystal to be alone together. They were trying to save the family. Jake knew they were just having sex. His mother was not religious, but Jake feared that Bert would try to convince her of the existence of God, in addition to the existence of his penis.

Reverend Foote took Jake's coffee away and escorted him to a little room. He was horrified by the other children, blank-faced, sitting on their knees in cheap suits and dresses. The reverend sat in a chair, and instead of graham crackers, saltines were passed around on a paper plate. These just made Jake thirsty. The reverend held up Bible verses scrawled on butcher paper, but Jake refused to memorize them, just moved his mouth silently when they were asked to repeat them on command. He excused himself and sought refuge in the kitchen, and poured himself another cup of coffee.

He sat in the corner, trying to hide, and began to read. Reverend Foote found him an hour later, clearly in no hurry. Reverend Foote did not try to hide his distaste. Bert and Krystal were not around to impress, and Jake was clearly a lost member of the flock, a pink sheep. Reverend Foote tried to talk to him anyway, but Jake could tell his heart was not in it.

"There is always time to repent," he said. "There is always time to cast away the things that make you different."

"No, thanks," said Jake. "I've read the Bible, you know. I even liked some parts. Violent and pulpy." He did not like Reverend Foote's polyester slacks, and his attempts to bring Jake to Jesus seemed just as fake. He wanted to be left alone to read.

"Jesus was different than the other boys," continued Reverend Foote as Jake hid the copy of Shirley Conran's *Savages* behind his back, and leaned up against the dishwasher. "He had long hair like a woman and it is said that his eyes were lashed heavily, and that he was a pretty, pretty man."

"He also wore a dress," said Jake. "A dirty one."

"That's blasphemous," said Reverend Foote. "Jesus had a dirty robe because he worked hard. Our Lord and Savior was different from the others, but not because of his clothing."

Jake's own outfit that day included black-and-scarlet plaid pants, a black polo shirt that was a vintage Penguin, and a black fedora with a scarlet band.

"Maybe this isn't the right place for you," said Reverend Foote.

"I kept telling you that," said Jake. "I'll make you a deal. I'll let Bert drop me off here every Sunday, and leave them alone all day. I'll go to the library, and be back in time for him to pick me up."

"That would be a falsehood," said Reverend Foote.

"It's beneficial to everyone," said Jake. "He's spreading the good word to my mother."

"I can't argue with that," said the reverend. "I wonder how she's taking it."

"On her back," muttered Jake, and grabbed his paperback. He pushed past the reverend and hurried to find his coat.

The Lineup

★　　★　　★

*L*averna arrived at the Dirty Shame early. As coach, she always tried to set a good example. She also wanted to catch Tish slacking on her weekend shift. But with her arms in these torture devices, she could not be sneaky. She could not even open the door. She kicked at it until Tish appeared, opening the door for Laverna with a flourish and a small bow. Tish and Tabby were sisters, and Tish got the looks, and Tabby the tits. Tish could never play for the Flood Girls. After surviving Bert's flying boat as a child, Tish developed a nervous condition and would not ride in a car, ruling out any away games. And somebody had to cover the bar when the Flood Girls played.

Like Tish, Laverna never played softball. At first, she didn't even understand the game. She was a born leader, an inspiration, frightening. Coaching was perfect. Laverna paid the fees to play in the league, paid the dues for every single player. When they mouthed off, she held that over their heads.

"Those casts are something else," said Della Dempsey, the other new recruit, as she took her seat. Laverna regarded Della coolly, the skin on her face tight and pink, like a burn victim. And she didn't have any eyebrows. She did have a discount at her parents' hardware store, which Laverna hoped would prove useful. "It looks like you're getting ready to choke somebody."

"Fuck up on first base and it might be you," pronounced Laverna.

It was Saturday, and the silver miners claimed their usual tables around the jukebox, the air around them blue with cigarette smoke. Laverna squinted, and it appeared they were having some sort of cribbage tournament. Shirts versus Skins. Laverna hated the dirty bras but loved the business.

Tish ferried drinks to Laverna's kingdom of tables, pushed together in a semicircle, arranged around a stool. Laverna perched on this stool like a throne; she used the height advantage to appear imperious. Tish managed two pitchers of beer and a stack of pint glasses on one single tray, returned with the single can of Diet Coke requested for Rachel. Tish looked anxiously at the tables, trying to figure out where to place it, finally deciding that Rachel would most likely sit as far away from her mother as possible.

As the team arrived, Red Mabel stood and helped Laverna sip at a double Canadian Club, even though the pink straw was shameful. Laverna looked at her watch. It was ten past three. They heard the truck slide into the gravel of the parking lot. Rachel burst through the door—she had curled her hair, and wore black slacks, a black turtleneck, a black blazer, and three-inch heels.

"This isn't an art opening," said Laverna. "Why in the hell are you dressed like that?"

Rachel didn't answer. She saw the empty chair and the can of Diet Coke, and took her seat. Laverna seethed in her sweatpants and a giant white T-shirt. Rachel's outfit filled her with rage, clearly some passive aggressive move to remind Laverna of her beloved armor, her layers.

Tish argued with a silver miner at the bar. The miner was a regular, one of Laverna's favorites, because she resembled Elvis Presley. Tish's voice raised as she accused lesbian Elvis of trying to pass a counterfeit bill.

"Go tell your sister to take her medication," said Laverna, and Tabby leaped from her seat and began to dig through Tish's purse. Red Mabel gave Tish a nickname once, but "Twitch" had not stuck. Laverna, in a rare moment of kindness, declared it too on-the-nose.

Laverna pointed to the stack of papers in front of Red Mabel, who had broken into the elementary school to use the town's only mimeograph machine. "Pass those out," she commanded.

Dutifully, Red Mabel handed out the smudged copies of the roster and contact information. Laverna believed in phone trees, demanded the infield call the outfield the morning of every game and practice. The Sinclairs did not have a phone. They lived in a strange compound behind their namesake gas station, four trailer houses arranged in a square, surrounding a garden and massive compost pile. More than three mobile homes were considered to be a trailer court in Quinn. There were many Sinclair children and many Sinclair husbands, and a goat that stood on top of a doghouse at all times, despite the weather. The sisters played left and center field, because Ginger, their employer, made them.

Tabby returned to the tables, and Tish took deep breaths behind the bar. Laverna watched her daughter study the list. Rachel's hair did look bouncy, sporty—blonde locks athletic as they moved. Laverna nearly asked Rachel what kind of conditioner she used but, thankfully, was stopped by a ruckus in the back. A cribbage board slammed into the door of the men's bathroom. The miners were competitive, and violent. It was too bad they were dismissive of organized sports.

Della and Rachel were the wild cards. Diane Savage Connor, the shortstop, was the best player on the team, and a legend in the league. Diane was a math teacher at the high school, and was renowned for her fast reflexes, as she snatched up grounders and all the bachelors in the county. Tabby was a surprisingly adept second base player, although she was short and missed most anything that flew through the air. Working at the Dirty Shame had taught her how to stop things, however, and transferred the fearlessness from breaking up bar fights into launching herself into the path of women who dared run to third base. She was so sweet that the umpires always believed the tackles were accidental. If runners made it to third base, they encountered Red Mabel, a beast on and off the field. (This was another reason Laverna had depended on Krystal—her nursing skills came in handy when there was carnage.) Ginger Fitchett pitched, always consistent and calm, attributes the rest of the Flood Girls sorely lacked. At catcher, Martha Man Hands just had to sit on her ass and be Ginger's target, both things she was born to do. Laverna's outfield was always a cluster fuck. Ronda played rover, but barely. On the rare occasions she moved, she was painfully slow, and Laverna suspected that Ronda did not like participating in yet another white person's game. The Sinclairs tripped over their cursed jean skirts, refusing to wear shorts or sweatpants, and would not dive for balls, claiming modesty. To top it all off, Martha Man Hands decided last summer that she would no longer run past first base, despite how far and deep she smashed the ball. Unfortunately, Martha had decided this in the middle of a game, and the first-base coach (Red Mabel) cursed her and pushed her off the bag. Martha declared she would walk to second base, if necessary. Of course, Laverna was apoplectic, but Ginger offered up her teenage daughter as a designated runner. Shyanne Fitchett upped their beauty quotient, could hit the shit out of the ball, and filled in whenever Red Mabel was in county jail.

Laverna's own offspring was currently examining her makeup in the mirror of a small compact.

"I think all of you know my daughter," said Laverna. "Or at least you've heard of her." There were nods all around.

"You screwed my older brothers," said Della. Her tight face and lack of eyebrows made it hard for Laverna to figure if Della was angry about it.

"Probably," said Rachel.

"Drive-in movie," said Della.

"AMC Pacer and Chrysler Cordoba," said Rachel. "I remember that."

"Engine Number Three," said Ginger.

"Excuse me?" Rachel clutched at her turtleneck.

"My husband," said Ginger. "You fucked my husband in a fire truck."

"Oh," said Rachel. "Sorry about that."

"Don't be," said Ginger. "He left town. I should buy you a drink."

Laverna was impressed by all of this teamwork.

"I'm putting Della at first," announced Laverna. "She says she can handle it." Laverna's former first-base player moved to Spokane to open a tanning salon. Laverna couldn't begrudge her for it, as she believed in the power of women in small business. "Krystal quit the team."

"Where I'm from, quitters get scalped," said Red Mabel. In response, Ronda moved her chair away from Red Mabel, silent as always.

"You were born in Pasadena," pointed out Laverna, sighing. "I'm going to be blunt," she said, although this was hardly necessary. Laverna was always blunt. "Rachel has never played a sport in her life. She's in right field for a reason."

Rachel smiled, not realizing that her mother was insulting her. Behind Rachel, lesbian Elvis put another miner in a headlock, took her down to the floor. This was common when there was cheating, at cribbage or in relationships. Laverna ignored it and continued. "And we have another problem. Ellis is fielding a new team this year," said Laverna. "High school girls."

"Athletic little bitches," said Red Mabel.

"Exactly," said Laverna. "So that makes an even eight teams in the league."

"We should send Winsome Shankley over there to fuck them until they're crippled," offered Red Mabel, met with toasts and cheers from Martha and Ginger.

"Enough," said Laverna, and the cheering stopped. "They are teenagers, and that is disgusting." She leaned forward and whispered to her team. "I made a deal with the Ellis cops. If those goddamn little princesses get caught with beer, they're out. I've already arranged a kegger in the woods."

The cheering began again. Red Mabel stood and helped their coach sip more whiskey through the pink straw.

"The tournament is in Missoula this year," said Laverna. "We just need to win half of our games. I have faith."

Rachel raised her hand. "Have we made it to the tournament before?"

"Shut up," said Laverna as Tish returned with another round of drinks, including a fresh can of Diet Coke. "We've got a good team," said Laverna. "Minus a few question marks." Red Mabel pointed at Della, who blushed, and Rachel, who ignored her. Rachel watched as the headlock in the back degenerated into some sort of crabwalk leg wrestling. The cribbage boards had been abandoned. "I'm certain that you veterans will help whip these girls into shape."

"You got it, Coach," said Diane Savage Connor, always the team cheerleader.

Laverna scowled. "First practice is in a week. Get your gloves out of the closet, girls. This year, let's try not to embarrass ourselves." Laverna's version of a pep talk elicited cheers from the usual suspects. Her entire outfield remained quiet.

The other teams in the league had uniforms. The other teams in the league had burly batters and outfielders who darted for balls like they were lottery tickets falling from the sky. The other teams practiced four times per week. The Flood Girls had Laverna, and this year, she had already been shot and hijacked by the return of her daughter. Nothing worse could happen.

Her positive thinking was interrupted by the silver miners, as usual. Elvis and her crew yanked another miner by the feet, pulled her past the Flood Girls. Laverna checked to make sure the woman was conscious. The miner sliding across the floor had a baby face, and a shaved head that struck the legs of several empty chairs. Drinks sloshed out of cups. Laverna called for napkins as the baby-faced miner was pulled out through the entrance. The open door blasted away the gloomy haze inside the Dirty Shame, and the team squinted and shielded their eyes as the sun reflected off the snowy banks piled on the street. The Flood Girls watched her feet slide through the dirty slush on the sidewalk, followed by the last of the miners, making her way outside. The door shut by itself, extinguished the light of another winter day in Quinn.

———

Laverna could not acclimate to the casts. She knocked things over with her permanently outstretched arms, coffee mugs, ashtrays, wall clocks. Red Mabel always cleaned up the mess.

The worst part was the sleeping. She was still in considerable pain, even though the doctor promised that it would get better, day by day. Like most men, he was a liar. Laverna was now sleeping on her side, one pillow under the cast on her left arm, and three extra painkillers just to make that tolerable. She found herself waking every other hour, stuck there, partially mummified, and she would peer at the bare left wall until she could sleep again. She decided to get a piece of art, a seascape or something, so at least she'd have something to stare at.

The second worst part was the itching inside of her casts. She begged Red Mabel to burrow around, stick objects inside, combs, a fireplace poker, a toothbrush, anything.

Tabby or Ginger came at lunchtime to feed her. Red Mabel was always busy at lunchtime. Laverna doubted it was anything nefarious, just that Red Mabel was exhausted from caretaking. Laverna endured the chatty Tabby saying complimentary things about Rachel, while spooning tomato soup into Laverna's mouth, and stabbing cut-up pieces of grilled cheese sandwich with a fork. Ginger was slightly better. She always brought real food from a restaurant, and while she fed Laverna she talked about business and filled her in on the gossip she pocketed at the Sinclair.

Laverna had a plan. She needed Black Mabel, and Ginger agreed to find her. Ginger had survived cancer and tried all of the experimental therapies. There were rumors in Quinn that Ginger continued to grow marijuana in her greenhouse.

That evening, Laverna heard the distinctive rumble of Black Mabel's Subaru Brat. She did her very best to come to a sitting position on the couch, and this act took so long that Black Mabel was already in the door by the time Laverna accomplished it.

"Jesus Christ," said Black Mabel. "It's roasting in here."

"I need drugs," said Laverna.

"Okay," Black Mabel said, and unzipped her long leather jacket. Many pockets were hand-sewn into the lining, and Laverna knew they contained Black Mabel's stashes. Laverna was nearly salivating.

"I need something to help me sleep, and I need something to get rid of this itching."

Black Mabel considered this. "I don't have anything to help with the itching. All my pills make people itch even more."

"I don't care," said Laverna. "Just give me something that will knock me out. And light me a cigarette."

Black Mabel stuck a lit cigarette in Laverna's mouth and began to unzip pockets. She pulled out Baggies and Baggies of pills, and laid them out across the coffee table. She began to move the Baggies around, in some strange order, like it was a shell game. Finally, she held up a Baggie that contained seven small green pills.

"This oughta do the trick," said Black Mabel. "Truckers love them when they're trying to come down off of speed."

"Fabulous," said Laverna. "There's a twenty on the kitchen table."

Black Mabel came back with the money. She ashed Laverna's cigarette. "I hope they help. You look like shit."

"I need another favor," said Laverna. "You've got to put one in my mouth, and get me some water."

"It's only seven o'clock," said Black Mabel. "Are you sure you want to go to sleep right now?"

"Goddammit," said Laverna. "What the hell kind of drug dealer are you? Give me two."

Black Mabel did not protest. Laverna swallowed the pills she placed on her outstretched tongue.

"Do you want me to come back later and check on you?"

"No," said Laverna. "I want you to leave."

An hour later, she lay in bed, incapacitated, too drugged and dreamy for sleep.

When Red Mabel showed up, she cursed Black Mabel for drugging her friend. Laverna could barely talk, just muttered about the pills.

"Do you itch anymore?"

"No," said Laverna. "I can't feel anything."

"That's good," said Red Mabel.

"I can't stop the thinking."

"That's not good," said Red Mabel. "What is it?"

"Rachel," said Laverna.

"Of course," Red Mabel said, and sat down on the bed, held Laverna's hand.

Laverna had no more words. She lay there and thought of the year her life burned down.

Snow White

Jake was on the roof again. Rachel drank coffee and spied on him through her kitchen window. He wore a pair of thickly padded snowmobile overalls, black and neon green. She knew he did not snowmobile. He wore a black fake fur coat that was much too big for him, and a black wool cap with fake fur on the brim. Even the beads in his hands were black. He stopped briefly at each bead as he pulled the chain through his fingers. His pauses were too short to be prayers, and he didn't seem the religious type. He stopped when the light caught the small silver cross at the end, and dangled from his hand. She was transfixed, and could watch this for hours. She did not need cable television. Rachel knew for certain that he had left the rosary on her doorknob.

Fourteen years ago, she had spied on the house she now owned, watching and waiting for her father, who never seemed to be at home. Rachel had come full circle, but her path had been circuitous and reckless, unlike Krystal's: she had never moved from the same trailer. Krystal lived in the trailer with her brother, Rocky, and just like everyone else, he was in love with Rachel. Unlike everyone else, he was bashful about it. They were orphans, or maybe their parents had abandoned them in Quinn like kittens in a cardboard box. The trailer was unsupervised by real adults—Krystal and Rocky were simple, like children, living on macaroni and cheese mixed with tuna fish, and Rachel slept on their couch and learned to love their casserole. Laverna was just grateful to have Rachel out of the house.

Jake opened his Walkman and flipped over the cassette. Perhaps the love of music was genetic. Rachel and Krystal had taken a road trip to Seattle in September of 1977 to see Fleetwood Mac, and they were both in love with Lindsey Buckingham. Rachel was twelve going on eighteen, and Krystal was eighteen going on twelve. Krystal proved this by getting high on cocaine and having sex with a stranger in their hotel room. To be fair, he was a glamorous stranger, an actual roadie for the band, although he was only responsible for wiping down Mick Fleetwood's cymbals.

Krystal found out she was pregnant, and that's when the fun stopped. Rocky took care of Krystal and the baby. Rachel returned intermittently, to give Rocky cash for beer, and she pretended to be interested in the baby while Rocky went to the gas station. Krystal was just another young mother in Quinn, unwashed hair, fat and poor in clothes from the thrift store. Rachel watched out the window to avoid looking at Krystal, focused on any sign of life in her father's trailer. It was a relief when Rocky would finally return with a twelve-pack.

The trailer remained the same, and the boy took to the roof to escape it.

She continued to spy, drinking cup after cup of coffee, until the boy had to flip the cassette again. Rachel looked at her watch and cursed. The coffee was an attempt to propel herself to an AA meeting, the first one she would attend in Quinn. She had chosen an outfit and fixed her hair and makeup hours ago, then forgot about her nerves while she spied on the boy. All she had to do was grab her coat and purse, and drive.

Before the truck warmed, she smoked the last cigarette in her pack. She had forgotten how small her hometown was, and out of habit, had scheduled twenty minutes of travel time. In Quinn, twenty minutes would get you to the next county. She had time to buy more cigarettes.

The gas station was empty, and the cashier was her new teammate. Rachel attempted small talk with left field, and the woman was terrified. In her truck, Rachel turned up the heat, cracked her window, and lit up. Once again, Rachel had become a smoker.

Athena had turned to food after she sobered up. Athena had stuffed herself to create a buffer for protection from any outside threats. Rachel tried to find serenity, was told to pray until it found her. In Quinn, she said her prayers out of routine, and they did not make her feel stronger, just confused and angry, overwhelmed. The claustrophobia, the actual weight of all that snow, had caused doubt to grow around her edges. Like black mold.

She needed a meeting desperately. She smoked another cigarette as she fishtailed out of the gas station parking lot, rewound a Depeche Mode song as she drove. She heard only half of it; the library was a two-minute drive.

Inside, as she passed the librarian, Rachel turned her face away. That was Peggy Davis, and she had been the sole librarian in Quinn, the only employee since it had been built in 1954.

Rachel rushed past, through the stacks and the aisles and the rows of microfiche machines. She walked so fast that the pages of *Redbook* magazines ruffled in her wake.

Once she entered the room, Rachel's plans to pretend to be someone else were dashed. She knew every single one of these old men: Mr. Tyler, her former biology teacher. Mr. Fisher, the conductor of her high school marching band. John Fitchett, Ginger's former brother-in-law, who had always driven the snowplow in Quinn, which made him more invaluable than the mayor. Pat Garrison, Black Mabel's father. PJ Garrison, Black Mabel's older brother. Larry Giefer, the owner of the grocery store. And the Chief of the Quinn Volunteer Fire Department, who did not seem to possess a real name. He identified himself as the Chief, and just like in the fire hall, he did not fuck around.

Seven old men, and her. She felt like Snow White. She stared at the seven dwarfs around her; they weren't particularly short, just wizened and gnarled from years of hard drinking. She poured herself some coffee, sat down on a metal folding chair, and checked her watch.

John arranged the books carefully, passed a small wicker basket to Pat Garrison, who put in a dollar for the Seventh Tradition. When the basket was passed to Rachel, she dropped in a five-dollar bill. That was approximately the number of meetings she had chickened out of since returning to Quinn. John cleared his throat, and began. "Hello, my name is John, and I'm an alcoholic."

"Hello, John," said all of the men.

"I guess I'm chairing the meeting tonight."

"Damn right," uttered the Chief.

Larry read "How It Works," and Pat read "The Promises."

John looked right at her when he announced the topic. "This morning, I read out of the big book, like I always do, and I couldn't get any peace out of the damn thing. I just kept thinking about the fucking snow." The men laughed at this. "The snow pays my bills, I guess. I've been really depressed since my daughter left. She was only here for two days, but she managed to bring up every single shitty thing I ever did to her. She hasn't seen me drunk for eight years. I guess she needed to poke the bear, or something. But I've been depressed ever since. So, this morning, I called my sponsor." John winked at the Chief, who nodded. "He reminded me that my past is just a reference book, like here at the library. I can put it on a shelf and leave it there. I only take it down to open for a fellow drunk when I need to share my experience. I don't have to live in that shit. Thanks."

"Thanks, John," said all the men in the room. Rachel tried to avoid small meetings, because it meant that everybody had to share, or share several times. She discovered that Mr. Tyler's first name was Jack, and Mr. Fisher's first name was Jerry. She learned that two of the men in the room had served time in prison for felonies, and one had been committed to the state institution. Rachel knew this meeting would make her feel better, and wished she hadn't been so damn scared. She listened as each man shared how they dealt with their past, and looked at her watch. There were still twenty minutes left. She would have to speak.

"Hi. My name is Rachel, and I'm an alcoholic."

"Hello, Rachel." She had feared there would be an edge to their chorus, but there was not.

"Thanks for the topic, you asshole." The men laughed, and Rachel knew that she had officially broken the ice, earned her chair in the room.

"I'm back in Quinn because of my past. I've been sober for over a year, and I've worked all the steps, but I haven't found peace. I certainly haven't found joy. So, I'm back." The men nodded their heads, and the Chief stared at her curiously. He did not seem like a man who had ever involved himself in town gossip. "You all knew me as a little girl, and then a teenager. I still get sad when I think about what I did to this town. I think about all the wives of the men I slept with, think about their children. I think about my mother, and Red Mabel." Larry Giefer grimaced as Rachel mentioned the name.

"After I left, things got even worse. I went to college, and I should have been discovering who I really was, and who I wanted to be. Instead, I discovered that I could black out if I drank enough. It was the cure to the pain, I guess. I set my sights on being the prettiest girl at every punk rock show. If not the prettiest, the wildest. I thought I was hot shit. Tried to be my own parent, and sucked at it. But I kept going." Rachel stopped, took a sip of her cold coffee, looked Larry Giefer directly in the eye. "And then I wasn't the prettiest girl at the punk rock shows anymore. People stopped writing graffiti about me. I thought I had all these friends. All I had was a bad reputation and a bunch of venereal diseases. I failed out of school, and took a bunch of shitty jobs, and kept drinking. Nobody could tolerate my bullshit, so I drank by myself. And I kept drinking. I didn't want to clean up the mess I made, so I kept drinking. I was scared. And finally, I ended up in these rooms." Rachel paused and made eye contact with the Chief. "I came back here to make things right with this town. It took me until now to realize that I need to make things right with myself. Thanks."

"Thanks, Rachel."

She used the ladies' room after the meeting and regarded her reflection in the mirror. She combed her fingers through her hair and applied lip gloss.

Outside the library, the men were smoking, as eddies of dustlike snow swirled in the street.

Mr. Tyler had a cigarette waiting for her. Even though she had a pack in her purse, she accepted it gratefully, leaned in as he cupped his hand around the flame. He did not seem surprised to see her. Rachel wondered if she had given off a future-alcoholic vibe in biology class—she had refused to dissect things but would tear herself apart later in life.

The Chief spoke first. "Them Clinkenbeards ever pay your mother?"

"No," said Rachel.

"Big mistake," said Pat Garrison.

"We're all big fans of your mother," said John.

"He's lying," said the Chief. "Your mother scares the shit out of us."

"I know the feeling," admitted Rachel.

"You did something right," said Larry Giefer. "You joined our favorite team."

"The Flood Girls?" Rachel blew her smoke toward the street. "Why are we your favorite team?"

"My brother don't support Ginger," said John. "I figured I could."

"He talked the rest of us into it," said Larry. "And we keep coming back, every year."

"Thanks," said Rachel.

"Nobody plays ball like the Flood Girls," said the Chief. "It's never boring." Rachel didn't know what to think. "Young Bucky says you need a plumber."

"Word gets out fast," said Rachel.

"Stay away from Bucky," said the Chief. "He's too tenderhearted. I need him for chimney fires."

"I'll remember that," said Rachel.

"Listen," said the Chief. "I know a few things about plumbing. Be happy to help you out."

"I just got a job," said Rachel. "I won't be able to afford it for a while."

"I know," said the Chief. "You don't need to worry about paying me. I'm happy to be of service."

"He is," said John. "He's so happy that we all hate him most of the time."

At this, all of the old men laughed. Rachel couldn't help but smile. She had found her people. She said a silent prayer of thanks, took another drag.

Hustle

★　★　★

After a long, cold winter, Laverna knew the softball field was still frozen in spots, where the bleachers provided shadows during the day. The usually muddy field was full of unyielding ruts. There would be no sliding. There wasn't supposed to be sliding anyway, league rules, but sometimes the ladies on the other teams had a little bit too much to drink and just tried to get to the bags any way they could, occasionally headfirst.

She woke up that morning in pain, something she was now accustomed to. She would have to grit her teeth until the cursed casts were finally sawed off, discarded forever. Red Mabel arrived at nine, made Laverna coffee, and gave her a bath.

Before leaving, Laverna had Red Mabel dial Bucky's phone number and put the phone between her shoulder and ear. The cord stretched across the kitchen table.

"I need you to hit some balls today," she said.

"I've got stuff planned," he protested.

"I don't give a shit," she said. "You owe me. Two hours." She let the phone fall from her shoulder, knowing that she could not hang it up, not caring that her line would remain busy until the nurse returned.

Red Mabel arranged her pills as always, lined up in piles on the counter, so she could reach down and bob for them, like apples. She swallowed one of Black Mabel's bootleg pharmaceuticals and her blood pressure medication at the same time, a combination that pleased her.

Laverna eased herself down in her recliner just as she felt the pills kick in, and she floated in this way, lost in a plot to poison the Clinkenbeard family. Laverna had a long list of people she wanted to disappear from this earth. Unfortunately, one was going to be playing right field, and was blood kin.

Rachel was not athletic, or graceful, or coordinated. Rachel was good at destroying things, and flirting with her hair. Right field was the logical place to stick her, because nothing ever happened out there, unless there was a lefty at bat.

Laverna wanted to keep Rachel close, within eyeshot. Rachel claimed she didn't drink anymore, but Laverna didn't trust her daughter's sobriety. There was nothing trustworthy about Rachel. Thinking about Rachel made her start to panic, and before she knew it, she was bobbing for the antianxiety pill. In her experience, something always went wrong when she let down her guard. Laverna kneeled, the blood rushing to her head. She attempted to nudge the phone toward the linoleum, the carpet burning her shins as she was successful in moving it inches, and then a foot. She was sweating, and concentrated so hard on the phone that she forgot the cord had grown tight, caught by her shoe. The phone suddenly rocketed around her, came to rest even farther than she had dropped it. She would not give up. She wanted a beer, decided she would have Red Mabel bring the birdbath from outside and fill it with Bud Light in case of emergencies such as this.

It took ten minutes, and Laverna had finally sandwiched the phone between her breasts and the wall, standing slowly, easing the phone up, mindful of the cord. The phone clattered on the kitchen counter as she navigated it over the Formica. She was sweating obscenely now, and rested, could barely hear the busy signal over her panting. She dipped down and opened her mouth wide, closed her teeth around the receiver. When she stood, her casts knocked a cookie jar from the counter, and it smashed on the linoleum. It was an owl, a gift from Ginger, and Laverna stared down at the shards. A piece remained perfectly intact, and of course it was an eye, and of course it was staring right at her. Laverna was really high on pills now, but determined, and faint from breathing through her nose, she replaced the slobbery receiver in the cradle. Her casts always had a mind of their own, her arms deadened and unfeeling, and the heavy plaster had knocked into the things thumbtacked around the phone. A Chippendales calendar and a recipe for Ritz mock apple pie lay at her feet, half of the phone tree of the Flood Girls remained on the wall. The other half had been ripped free and was stuck to her sweaty neck.

"Jesus fucking Christ," Laverna said, and collapsed on the sectional. She was exhausted.

The phone rang, and Laverna screamed profanities from the couch. She could do nothing but let it go to the answering machine. Rachel seemed to know that Red Mabel was not around to run interference, and began to deliver a monologue.

"I just don't think it's a good idea. I don't work well with others, especially women. I know you're in a tight spot, but you've got a couple of weeks before the first game. There has to be somebody else who can play right field. Put Bucky in a dress or something."

Laverna closed her eyes, tried to get the floating feeling back.

"I know that you're really serious about your team, and I know you've worked really hard to keep it going, and I appreciate that, I really do. Tabby said you guys won only three games last year, and one was by default."

Laverna screamed and twisted her head, tried to bury it in pillows to block out Rachel, but only succeeded in further cementing the phone tree to her neck.

"I want you to win this year. I don't think you can do that with me on the team. I'm a distraction. Every woman in the county knows about me, and I'm afraid they are going to try to hit me with the ball. I don't want any more soft tissue damage. You would not believe how easily I bruise. I'm not the type that recovers quickly from a subdural hematoma—I think I have a vitamin deficiency, or maybe I'm a hemophiliac."

Laverna screamed at the answering machine. "It's because you're a goddamn vegetarian!"

Laverna listened for Rachel to hang up, but she didn't. She could hear Rachel breathing. Laverna suspected that her daughter was pretending not to hang up in order to use up all of the tape on the answering machine. Instead, there came a beaten-down voice, one that Laverna had never heard before.

"Fuck it," said Rachel. "I'll see you at two o'clock."

The tape in the machine whirred to a stop.

———

Two more painkillers later, Laverna finally floated. She could barely feel the road beneath her as she walked to the softball field. Driving was out of the question, and she was tired of asking Red Mabel for things. She didn't care if the people of Quinn saw her zombie-walking through the streets. In fact, she kind of relished it, hoped that it might scare some children.

Bucky was the first person there. Laverna was not tolerant of players who showed up late, or showed not at all. She had seen other teams fall apart that way. She arrived at the field at a quarter to, and there was Bucky, unloading his bags. He carried them out into the field, bare of bases, and he kicked at the frozen dirt where home plate would be. He went back to the truck, and returned with two buckets of softballs.

"Laverna," he said, and nodded.

"We've got two newbies. The worst in right field. I want you to hit it to her as much as possible."

"Rachel," he said. "I heard."

"Right field. Hit it there."

"You know I don't have that kind of control," he responded. "I suck at softball."

"And you suck as an ump," she said. "At least you're consistent."

Red Mabel emerged from the woods behind the bleachers. Laverna was thankful she wasn't carrying the corpse of some animal. She did have her rifle slung across her shoulder, so it wasn't out of the question to worry about such things.

"Go get me some beer," said Laverna, collapsing on the wooden bench inside the dugout.

"Got some in my truck," said Red Mabel. "It's even cold."

Laverna closed her eyes and rested against the fence. She could hear Bucky whistling inanely. Laverna thought it was Hank Williams, and then she thought it might be Paula Abdul.

"You even suck at whistling!" she screamed this at him, her eyes still closed.

Red Mabel returned, with beer and a plan. "I don't have any straws in my truck," she said. "I got my knife. You're gonna shotgun these mother-fuckers."

Laverna didn't argue. "You are a really good nurse," she said. She had grown up in Quinn, so she was used to shotgunning beers. The men of Quinn considered it foreplay. Red Mabel nested the beer into the space between the two boards of the bench, and she stabbed the can with her knife. Laverna sat down in the dirt and put her mouth over the hole. She nodded to let Red Mabel know she was ready. Red Mabel pulled the tab, and the beer shot into Laverna's mouth. Laverna guzzled almost the entire can, foam all over her mouth and chin. She leaned back and belched, and Red Mabel slapped her back.

"Again," said Laverna. Red Mabel was happy to oblige.

"Why don't you just hold it up and let her sip at it?" Here was Bucky, trying to be helpful.

"Fuck off," said Red Mabel. "We haven't done this for years!"

"Nurse!" Laverna could tell she was slurring, but she didn't care. She weaved a bit as she called out from the dirt floor of the dugout. "Give me another!"

Red Mabel delightedly stabbed the can, and Laverna filled her mouth again. She blinked, tried to bat away the sting of beer that shot into her eyes.

Red Mabel slugged a beer down in one gulp, the old-fashioned way. She wiped her mouth with the tail of her flannel shirt and helped Laverna up from the dirt.

Laverna attempted to compose herself as the Flood Girls began to arrive in their cars. Red Mabel dusted off Laverna's jeans, wiped the beer from her chin, and kicked the empty cans underneath the bench. Satisfied, Red Mabel jogged out to third base.

Rachel showed up five minutes late, her truck rattling from the stereo. To make things worse, she brought somebody. Krystal's son.

"What is he doing here?" Laverna gestured at Jake with her casts.

"I picked him up on the road. He told me he was our scorekeeper," said Rachel. "Why is your shirt all wet?"

"He's the scorekeeper for the entire league. He doesn't belong to us. He belongs to all the teams in Quinn," said Laverna. "And I think he knows that." Jake shrugged, and Laverna belched lightly. He sat down next to her anyway, immaculate in his suit and tie, like a tiny Jehovah's Witness. He carried a small satchel, from which he removed a sketchpad and a pencil case.

"Maybe he can teach you how to play right field," said Laverna. She tried not to sound drunk as she addressed Jake. "This isn't a game, kid. Don't think you're getting paid."

"I am well aware of that," answered Jake. "You don't cut the check anyway."

The Flood Girls began to warm up on the field, while Rachel wandered around the outfield, smoking a cigarette. She dropped it into the brown grass when Diane jogged out to her, handed her a softball glove. Laverna watched as Rachel pointed to her fingernails.

"Wear the goddamn glove," shouted Laverna. "You can't catch the ball with your hands."

"Jesus Christ," Red Mabel said, and spit on the ground.

The Flood Girls took the field, and the sun was out. An icy patch remained in the outfield, conveniently located between the Sinclairs. They were like pioneer women anyway, and could no doubt navigate it. Laverna suspected that if a grizzly bear came charging on the field, between the Sinclairs and Red Mabel, it wouldn't stand a chance. And that was without Red Mabel's rifle, easily accessible in the grass near third base. Guns were not allowed at regular league games.

Ginger Fitchett warmed up on the pitcher's mound. Bucky lugged a bucket of balls and carefully arranged them before her. People in Quinn still treated Ginger like she was sick, but Laverna knew that Ginger was made of much stronger stock. Ginger had kept her hair short after the chemo, even after remission. She was a no-nonsense woman, and a hell of a pitcher. She was two years older than Laverna, and almost as mean, and she warmed up by swinging her arms around and around, wiggling her fingers. Ginger had been on the team for the last eight years. She and Red Mabel were the only original members.

"C'mon!" shouted Red Mabel. "Let's get this shit going."

Bucky flipped her off and picked up his bat and pointed it toward the outfield. Ginger snickered.

The first pitch was wild, and clattered against the chain link that caged off the bleachers. Jake startled and dropped his sketchpad.

The second pitch glanced off Bucky's bat, and it dribbled along the third-base line. Red Mabel barely moved. She scooped it up and threw it to Della at first. Della gossiped with Tabby and was not paying attention. The ball hit her on the thigh.

"Fuck!" Della shouted, and rubbed her leg. The ball rolled toward the dugout. "What was that for?"

"You need to pay attention," said Red Mabel.

"You are not the coach," Della said, and looked at Laverna for backup. Laverna said nothing, would not discourage the gossip. Della and Tabby had married the same man at different times, so they understood each other, and Laverna learned from years of coaching that communication was paramount to the success of the infield. Shortstop almost always threw to first.

The next pitch was good, and sailed into the outfield. The shorter Sinclair caught it without fuss and threw it to Della. The shorter Sinclair always smelled like freshly baked bread. Laverna assumed she was in charge of carbohydrates for their entire compound.

Ginger put the third one right over the plate, and Bucky connected, sending the ball high into the air, heading toward Rachel.

"Move!" shouted Laverna.

The taller Sinclair heeded her orders and made her way toward Rachel, who had put the glove in front of her face, cowering. The ball dropped a few feet behind Rachel, and the taller Sinclair beat Ronda by seconds and hurled it to second base.

Rachel removed the glove from her face, and began to comb out the tangles in her hair with her free hand.

"At least Krystal could make a tourniquet," shouted Red Mabel. Laverna did not like that Red Mabel was already thirsty for blood. The season hadn't even started yet.

"Nice try, Rachel," said Diane, who genuinely meant it. The entire infield laughed.

Ginger's next pitch went straight over the plate, and Bucky aimed for right field. This time, the taller Sinclair ran to assist. Rachel covered her face again, did not move an inch.

Della backed up from first and caught the ball, just barely, and threw it to Ginger, who had hustled over to cover first base.

"That's teamwork," hollered Diane encouragingly.

"Shut the fuck up," said Red Mabel.

Laverna groaned, and Jake scooted away from her. She stood up from the bench, wincing as her casts caught on the chain link. As the beer and pills rushed to her temples, and the pain sent sparks into her eyes, Laverna Flood nearly fainted. She called for her nurse.

Jake shrieked when beer sprayed in an arc from the corner of Laverna's mouth. Laverna wasn't sure if his sketchpad had been soaked, or if he was shrieking at Red Mabel and her knife. She didn't really care. When Red Mabel pulled her back up on the bench, Laverna swallowed a belch, tried to appear coach-like. The rest of the Flood Girls were staring at her.

"PLAY BALL!" Laverna cried, wiggling her thumbs, her casts pointed toward home plate.

Laverna studied her team as they shook off the winter. This year, the Flood Girls were going to be ready. Rachel would have to do for now. At least Red Mabel had not run to the outfield and punched her in the face. In that case, putting the glove over her face might have offered Rachel some actual protection.

Twenty minutes later, it was time for batting practice. Tabby warmed up, swinging the bat in circles that dizzied Laverna. Bucky replaced Tabby at second base. Laverna needed a runner.

She called out his name, and Jake looked up from his sketchpad. "I need you to run for me, kid."

"I don't run," Jake said, and pointed at his outfit. "And I'm wearing a suit."

"I'll give you twenty bucks," said Laverna.

"I don't think so," Jake said, and returned to drawing.

"Twenty-five," said Laverna. "Only because I'm hammered."

"Okay," agreed Jake.

With Jake at first base, Tabby hit a ball directly at Bucky, which he caught easily. He lobbed it to Della, once again ill prepared. Della watched it sail past her shoulder. Laverna yelled at Jake to run to second, as Della chased after the ball.

In his stiff little suit, Jake pranced to second. He had plenty of time. The ball rolled all the way to the concession stand. Laverna watched as Diane commented on Jake's pocket square and reached up to catch the ball at the same time.

Laverna looked out at the Flood Girls, at Della trying to catch her breath, at the gay kid on second base, at the princess in right field. She swore silently.

Singer

*B*uley Savage Connor owned the thrift store, and she also owned Rocky Bailey. It was unclear what a sixty-year-old, morbidly obese woman would do with Rocky, but she kept him. He lived in her house, and despite the thirty-year age difference, and the gap in mental facility, it worked. Jake did not know his uncle Rocky very well, but knew that Buley kept him busy.

"My darling boy," said Buley. "We've been waiting for you." Buley rarely rose from the giant, overstuffed chair that loomed next to the front door, her lap and shoulders covered in white cats, climbing all over her massive frame. She had one in her armpit as Jake entered the store. Buley's hair was as thin as her body was thick. What remained stood up in white curlicues around the circumference of her head, a crown of white tufts.

"As always," said Jake. He stomped his feet, dislodging the snow from his moon boots. He leaned down to kiss the back of her hand. Her arm emerged from her enormous silken gown, the meat underneath her forearm sagging, her fingers puffy but immaculately clean. This was their ritual, his tribute to her grandiosity. She behaved like a queen, a real queen, not bossy like Laverna, but innately royal and kind.

"Reverend Foote continues to poach Catholics, and you continue to reap the rewards." Buley pointed to a velvet pouch on the counter. Jake squealed with delight. "Go ahead, my boy. I left them there for you."

Jake snatched the pouch and stood before Buley, holding court. She smiled as he untied the tasseled rope, slid the rosaries out with a shaking hand. He held them up to the low light of the lamps that surrounded Buley, five lamps in all, perched on low tables and crowding the cash register. Buley did not believe in overhead lighting. Jake dangled the rosaries from one hand, and Buley raised her reading glasses and peered through them like a magnifying glass: pearly pink beads and a crucifix of careworn gold, mahogany beads and a crucifix carved from a green stone. Worn in spots from the oil from many hands, the weight of thousands of prayers spoken, and hopefully heard.

"They take my breath away," proclaimed Jake.

"Don't be so dramatic," said Buley. She reached around the cat, revealing more of her fleshy white arm as she pointed to the velveteen ottoman where she stored things for Jake. The ottoman had once been white but had yellowed over the years; the embroidered peacocks and the delicate brass hinges remained vivid. The legs were long lost, and it took on a new life as an upholstered box, Jake's favorite box in the world.

Jake sat on the edge of the thick rug underneath Buley's throne, placed the box between her puffy ankles and her silver slippers, covered in tiny bells. This was another ritual. He opened the box, and removed each item, and held it up for Buley to see. Even though Jake shopped at the thrift store weekly, Buley pretended to forget the things she directed Rocky to pull from the boxes and garbage bags of donated clothing left at the back door.

"A corduroy vest, the color of tangerines," pronounced Buley, as wide-eyed Jake held it before her. They examined the dark blue stitching, and the cerulean lining, in perfect condition. He carefully folded it, and lay it across his lap.

"That is from the seventies. Seems strange to claim it as vintage, but it has charm for days." Jake held up a T-shirt, purple, emblazoned with a slightly peeling iron-on decal, a glittering pink witch surrounded by lime-green frogs.

The final item made him gasp, which caused the cat to un-wedge itself, and leap to the top of a cedar curio cabinet. Buley chuckled, and

Jake stood up excitedly and held the pants up to his own waist. "Authentic sailor pants, black wool, cut tight through the hips. Just the way I prefer my sailors, although I've never seen the ocean." Jake traced the pants with one finger, the material blooming out into bell bottoms, the front a cunning display of giant black buttons and heavily stitched eyelets.

"Perfection!" Jake spun in a circle, the pants swinging out before him.

"I've never heard of a sailor in your size," said Buley. "Maybe they had a battleship just for midgets."

"These are breathtaking," said Jake.

"I knew you would like them," said Buley. "I probably have a sailor hat around here somewhere. Your uncle Rocky isn't here, so you'll have to look for yourself. I gave him the day off. His knee is still bothering him."

"I'll take it all," said Jake.

"Of course you will," said Buley.

"I'm going to keep shopping," said Jake.

"I encourage that," said Buley.

The store was silent today. Usually, Buley would be yelling at Rocky, who never responded, just winked at Jake and muttered the same word: *Women.* And then his uncle would sigh contentedly, return to pushing a broom, folding Levi's, wiping paperbacks down with a wet rag.

The thrift store smelled like reheated casseroles and disintegrating paperbacks. Jake hated Quinn, because nothing ever changed. But inside the thrift store, he never failed to find something new among the old and used. The things the people of this town were willing to part with were always more interesting than the people themselves.

Jake walked past the stacks of blue jeans, and the musty-smelling rack of Western-style shirts. Jake coveted the pearl buttons, but the sweat stains were disgusting.

He avoided the bottom shelf at the back of the third aisle. When he had discovered the piles of Frank's clothes, he nearly cried. He could not even look at them now. Rachel had no idea how much time he had spent picking out those suits, but Buley did. Rocky placed Frank's Forest Service uniforms on the same shelf, consolidating one man's entire wardrobe.

Jake dug through the paperbacks, even though he had passed over most of the titles before. He removed a Harlequin romance that took place entirely on a lifeboat. That was interesting. He considered buying another Agatha Christie novel, but he had made that mistake before. He shoved the Agatha Christie book back in place when he heard the front door open and the stomping of snow boots.

Diane Savage Connor, Buley's daughter, removed her coat and hung it beside the door. This was the first time Jake had seen Diane in the store. Buley held out her hand for Diane to kiss, but Diane rolled her eyes and kissed her mother on the forehead.

"Diane," Buley announced, and crossed one giant leg, the bells on her slippers ringing out through the store. "Tell me all about your latest conquest."

Diane ignored this. "Is he here?" Jake watched Diane crane her neck, peering over the enormous aisles.

"Yes," said Buley. "When are you going to settle down?" Diane absentmindedly stroked the white cat, who stretched out, luxuriating at her touch. "You are much too vivacious to end up a spinster."

"I'm only thirty-six," said Diane. "I'm exploring every opportunity."

"If that's what you want to call it," said Buley. "We had another word, in my day."

Diane ignored this as well. "Where is he?"

Buley pointed to him, and Jake stood up among the boxes of paperbacks. Diane was upon him instantly, fast as always. He could not fathom what she wanted; he barely knew her, had always worshipped her from afar. Jake couldn't help but look up from his scorebook when she burst into motion at shortstop, a blur of finely muscled limbs and glossy black hair. At school, Jake blushed when she stopped him in the hallway, even though she wasn't one of his teachers. She made a point to compliment his outfits, the only person in town who did so.

"Come with me," she said, on the move as always. "I'm sorry, but I only have fifteen minutes." Jake followed her through the store, past the woodstove, and into the back rooms where customers were not allowed. Here was where Rocky sorted the donations, and where Buley kept her hot plate. A tiny bathroom was exposed, with no walls for modesty. He watched the carefully woven braid swing across Diane's back, and she was not wearing her demure school clothes. Today she wore tight pink slacks and a black angora sweater set.

"Are you going on a date?" He was slightly out of breath. She moved so fast.

She turned around and smiled. "Of course," she said. She stopped at a small green box, latched like a suitcase. "Here we are."

"Yes," said Jake, still amazed that she had sought him out for some mysterious reason. Trigonometry and statistics were still years away.

"I didn't want to give you this at school," she said, speaking rapidly, crouching down and flicking at the latches. "I know how cruel the other kids can be, and besides, this little fucker is heavy."

"I'm not very strong," admitted Jake.

"Eat your vegetables," said Diane. The latches sprung, she lifted the cover. It was a sewing machine, an older model, the color of liver.

"Holy crap," Jake said, and covered his mouth with one hand.

"This was mine," said Diane. "Everything I wore to high school I sewed myself. It was my way of rebelling against my mother." She reached under the machine and popped out a smart little drawer. Inside, small instruments and apertures gleamed. "I even made my own prom dress," said Diane, "but I won't tell you what year it was, because a lady never reveals her age."

"I love you," said Jake.

"That's inappropriate," Diane said, and shoved away a cat, who sniffed around her legs. "I will tell you that the dress was awful. Green silk chiffon. You have no idea how hard it is to sew chiffon. I want you to have this."

"I'm freaking out right now," said Jake.

"Relax," said Diane. "I see you in the hallways, and I see your outfits, and I can tell you've got flair, kid." She checked her watch.

"Flair," repeated Jake. He let the word hang there. It seemed like a profanity in this town.

"This is a Singer from 1952. It's got a zigzagger, which probably means nothing to you." She rushed through the introductions, unlatching a green and orange box hidden inside the lid. Diane pointed at things, and Jake struggled to keep up. "Here's the foot pedal, and all your needles, and most important, instructions."

"Instructions," said Jake. Diane held up a miniature hardcover, water-stained but still legible: *Sew You Want to Learn to Sew* by Erma Thomas.

"Yes, I know it's a terrible title," said Diane. "Puns for idiot housewives." She checked her watch again. "How are your math skills?"

"Right now, my class is dividing fractions," said Jake. "I've been writing letters to Audrey Hepburn."

Diane raised an eyebrow, and replaced the lid on the machine. She crossed her arms, and addressed him impatiently. Apparently, math was no joke to Diane Savage Connor. "I believe in hard work, Jake. That applies to math and that applies to sewing. And dating, which is why I must bid you farewell. Call me if you have any questions." She was walking now, and Jake followed her to the front of the store. She continued to speak to him over her shoulder. "My mother has all sorts of fabric and I've told her to keep a look out for thread and embellishments." Jake shuddered, his body covered in goose bumps. Embellishments.

Diane kissed her mother again, and was buttoning her coat before Jake could stop her. The goose bumps were replaced by a heat in his cheeks as he realized the truth of the matter.

"I can't have a sewing machine in my house," said Jake. "Bert would kill me."

Diane paused, her hand on the doorknob. "We know your situation, Jake." She exited into the cold air, calling out to him as she left. "Make sure to thank my mother."

"I always do," said Jake sadly.

Buley reached for his sleeve. "Don't you worry, dear. I promise to keep the machine safe until you find a place for it."

"Okay," said Jake. She squeezed his hand and slowly rose, cats leaping to find another plush resting place. Buley and her bells tinkled as she made her way behind the counter, and began to ring up his purchases. As usual, she made up her own prices. Buley would never know the true worth.

Jake crossed the railroad tracks and turned toward the river. Parallel to the tracks, there was only one paved road, and it led to the newer cemetery in town. Thoughtfully, the snowplow driver had kept this road clear, and Jake passed the cedar mill on his right, built on the river. The days of transporting shingles by barge were long gone.

The cemetery spread out over acreage at the end of the road. When Jake was in grade school, the location had been a controversial topic around town. Rightfully, future mourners did not want their services interrupted by the thunder of trains passing, or the ringing of the bells at the crossing. They did not get their way. Across the tracks, Jake could see the Dirty Shame.

Frank's plot was the newest, and Jake had no trouble finding it, despite the snow.

There had been no service. Jake had asked his mother about any plans, and knew she wouldn't lie to him. Frank had been buried with no fanfare, his plot paid for by the Forest Service.

The snowbanks were still deeply furrowed from the excavators. The headstone was simple, just like the man beneath it. It was becoming dusk, and the temperature was dropping.

Jake stood there, his breath visible in the rapidly cooling air. He wanted to talk out loud, tell Frank about his daughter, about Bert converting, about the sewing machine.

Instead, he reached out and patted the headstone, and made his way back home before it grew too cold. Frank would want him to take care of Rachel, he knew that much. Just like the feral cats, Frank's daughter was a desperate creature.

Jake had heard the stories, and he hoped that some truth had been left out, over the nine years of retelling. She had once been an outcast, and Jake decided to take it upon himself to show her that she was not alone, that she was not the only one.

The Regulars

★　　★　　★

Rachel grew accustomed to her new morning routine. Every weekday began with a washcloth bath, followed by coffee and chain-smoking, and then rote praying she hoped would take root one day. She trudged out to her truck, and left it to warm, drank another cup of coffee, smoked another cigarette. By then, the windshield had defrosted, and she could see well enough to drive to work.

At the bar, she started every shift by pulling the chain on the neon signs. The Dirty Shame was open every day, at precisely 8:00 a.m. The men from her meeting appeared shortly after, drank coffee, smoked, and kept a close watch on their new recruit. She had fallen in with a gang of taciturn men older than her father, and after one meeting, they knew more about her than her father ever had.

Rachel assumed that the patrons of the bar would remember her past, would treat her with disdain. But drunks knew better than that. She had control over the thing they wanted most.

Gene Runkle showed up at eight thirty every morning. He was the dogcatcher in Quinn but was terrible at it, probably because he spent every single day drinking. The only thing he ever caught was gossip. He looked the same as he did when Rachel was a child. Rachel stopped by in the mornings to badger her mother for lunch money, and Gene Runkle was always drinking his first or second beer. Fifteen years later, he did not have the red nose and cheeks of an alcoholic. Gene Runkle was a gray man. His face and limbs were the color of shirts and sheets laundered for years, in a barely functional washing machine. His hair wasn't silver. He had a full head of it, and it was the kind of blond that had given up and faded, leached of color, yellow in some lights, the hue of old wood.

At nine o'clock in walked Mrs. Matthis, who had once been the judge's wife. Her first name was Erlene, but Rachel addressed her formally, as did everyone else in town. The judge died ten years prior, pneumonia that he just couldn't shake, a bad rasp that turned into a death rattle. After he died, Mrs. Matthis immediately took to drinking, as if she had always been waiting for the opportunity, determinedly, a little desperate, vodka and tomato juice every half an hour. She always kept her composure, and left before the lunch crowd. Mrs. Matthis sat far away from Gene Runkle—she did not engage in his rumormongering. Every day, Mrs. Matthis worked a book of crossword puzzles, sold at the Sinclair, new at the end of every month. She never asked for help with answers but was obviously not certain, for she used a pencil and brought her own pink eraser and pencil sharpener. She left the curls of shavings in neat piles around her purse. When Mrs. Matthis sharpened her pencils, it sounded like the scratchy chirp of crickets. Mrs. Matthis was the puffy kind of drunk, swollen hands and face, cheeks chapped red, pink hands clutching at the pencil so hard her joints turned white. Despite this, she erased carefully, almost daintily. The crossword puzzle books were cheap and the paper tore easily. She erased often, and Rachel suspected the boxes were filled with gibberish. Mrs. Matthis's mind was obviously pickled, and there was no way she could recall the largest of the great lakes, or the famous college football coach from Alabama.

Winsome Shankley walked into the Dirty Shame for his red beer at ten o'clock. She knew him from high school, the bad boy, the kid with money and the only new car in the parking lot. His parents moved to Quinn from California, determined to keep Winsome out of trouble. He owned the Booze and Bait, a bait shop and liquor store, and he kept dilettante hours, just afternoons, and sometimes, not at all. He was still cute enough, with the same floppy brown hair and the same sad eyes. He was handsome, because he didn't look like a local. He had originated from a completely different gene pool. Not that Winsome didn't do his best to share his DNA with the women in Quinn, and the surrounding county.

This was her morning routine. Today was Thursday, and at ten o'clock she poured Winsome's beer, and waited. Winsome was already half-lit when he walked through the door. She could tell he was drunk because he was grinding his teeth, something he unconsciously did after his fourth or fifth drink. Every drunk had a tell like a bad poker player.

"Fuck," Winsome said, and rubbed his eyes as he staggered before her. Gene Runkle kicked a stool toward him, and Mrs. Matthis bent over her crossword, her tongue poking out as she concentrated.

"Fuck is right," said Gene Runkle.

"I saw your mom outside," said Winsome to Rachel. "She's peeking through the window right now."

Rachel turned her head, and sure enough, saw the flash, the white of the casts. She expected Laverna to barge through the door, but nothing happened. Her mother was a terrible spy, had always left the espionage to Red Mabel.

"I bagged some broad from Ellis last night," said Winsome. "When I woke up, she was gone. So was my stereo."

"Lesson learned," said Rachel. "Shop local."

"She wasn't even that cute," said Winsome. "And I can't file a police report. I don't know her name, and I can't remember what she looks like."

"All those Ellis girls look the same," Rachel said, and poured Winsome a beer and a tomato juice. The girls in Ellis had mean mouths and clumpy mascara, big Swedish noses and extensive scrunchie collections. Flannel shirts tied in knots right below their breasts, tight jeans so new and stiff they resembled deep vein thrombosis. The girls in Ellis all wanted to be blond, but none had discovered toner, and as a result, they were easily distinguishable by the orange in their ravaged hair, corralled by the scrunchies manufactured by the hundreds in their home economics class.

He slid a five-dollar bill across the bar.

As if she could smell the money from outside, Laverna decided to make her entrance.

"Winsome!" Her mother stood in the doorway, the snow swirling around her feet and onto the floor. Red Mabel held the door for her. The casts made Rachel think of the zombie dance from Michael Jackson's "Thriller." Laverna's hands hung out in front of her, as if she were permanently waiting for her nails to dry.

"Fuck," said Winsome, once more.

Laverna and Red Mabel took the stools on either side of Winsome. Her mother sniffed at the air. "Jesus, Rachel. It smells like a high school girl in here."

"I put potpourri on every table," said Rachel. "Ambience." She was proud of the little dishes, filled with pine needles and cinnamon sticks and dried lavender.

"It looks like witchcraft," declared Laverna. "Give me a cigarette."

Red Mabel stuck a lit cigarette in her mother's mouth, her beefy arm knocking against Winsome's beer. It sloshed over the brim. Rachel grabbed his pint glass and wiped underneath it.

Laverna was squinting. Smoke drifted directly into her eyes.

"Where's that war whoop?"

"Ronda doesn't come in for another hour," said Rachel. "You know that. Can I get you ladies some coffee?"

"We were just stopping by," said Laverna. "I'm still on vacation."

"Sure," said Rachel.

"Your mama has never taken a vacation in all the years I've known her," said Red Mabel. "She's earned it."

"Spying isn't much of a vacation," said Rachel. Winsome hunched and cowered over his beer, as if Red Mabel was going to smack him at any minute.

"Don't worry," said Laverna. "We've got other places to be." She stood up stiffly—the cigarette still perched in place. She gave Rachel a long, hard look. "I'll be stopping by, from time to time. Nice to see you, Winsome. Hands off my daughter."

"Okay," said Winsome.

Laverna and Red Mabel slunk out the door, and Rachel exhaled. She poured herself another cup of coffee, and listened to Winsome grinding his teeth.

When she got home, it was already dark.

Bucky's truck was not in her driveway, neither was the special truck the Chief drove.

She was nervous when she stepped inside her house. The living room carpet had been pulled, and the floor was a patchwork of old and new lumber. Bucky had fixed the soft spots. Her thoughts drifted to what color of carpet she should choose, until she remembered the bathroom.

Tears came when she saw the bathtub, exactly where a bathtub should be. The fixtures gleamed, and a leftover Christmas bow was scotch-taped to the new faucet. A bottle of cheap bubble bath rested on the seat of the toilet. Krystal had somehow succeeded in hiding this expense from Bert.

Rachel said a prayer of gratitude and stripped off her clothes.

She sunk into the hot water and considered her life, shampooed her hair two times. She drained the tub and filled it again, sat in the water for another twenty minutes, until it became lukewarm.

There was still work to be done in the bathroom—molding, a new shower curtain, a vanity, new tile. But that would happen eventually. Time takes time, as Athena was fond of saying.

On the front porch, she smoked a cigarette. Her hair began to freeze in little chunks.

She could hear the engines of four-wheelers on the street outside, dads pulling their children behind them, sleds tied on lengths of rope. This was how you survived the winter in Quinn, thought Rachel. Sometimes you had to let other people pull you.

Fireman's Ball, 1980

★   ★   ★

*L*averna wore her new dress, and proudly. She felt foxy for a thirty-six year old. Love had caused her to gain fifteen pounds, in all the right places. The dress clung to her; she ordered it from the JCPenney's catalog, and it was the color of nectarines. She navigated the throngs in the fire hall, one hand clutching the hem of the rayon wrap dress. The volunteer firemen plugged in fans that year, and the room was gusty, in addition to the usual drafts from the barrels of fire. She stomped across the cement in spike-heeled sandals, swiped from her daughter's closet. She didn't know why she cared about making such an entrance. Laverna Flood had a man.

Red Mabel waved at her, and Laverna groaned when she noticed that Gene Runkle nuzzled at her best friend's neck. She was sure Red Mabel dated him out of spite, jealous that Laverna's attentions had been diverted by a younger man. At the bar, Gene Runkle had confessed that Red Mabel was a cold fish, and only allowed affection when others were watching.

Laverna pumped the keg and filled her plastic cup, as Red Mabel pushed away Gene. She grabbed Laverna with one hand, and steered her against the wall, and began describing her mink traps in excruciating detail.

"There's no mink in Quinn," said Laverna. "I asked around."

"Bullshit," said Red Mabel. "I know these woods better than anybody else." Red Mabel pointed across the room. Ginger Fitchett wore her mink, and Laverna watched as a fireman helped ease it from her shoulders. Ginger was a free woman, shedding her husband like another coat. Laverna knew her daughter was involved somehow; the divorce lawyers in the county should pay for Rachel's college. Underneath, Ginger was wearing a rayon wrap dress.

"Goddammit," said Laverna. Ginger's dress looked nothing like Laverna's—it was clearly not from JCPenney, and it was bright white. It was probably a real Diane von Furstenberg. Laverna had lived in Quinn long enough to grow bored with jealousy, competition. There was nothing she wanted. The women in this town needed something to do with their time. The men of Quinn had once been a sport, but Rachel had changed the rules, and the game wasn't fun anymore.

Laverna spent enough time worrying about her daughter. She no longer had the energy to break a sixteen year-old vegetarian anarchist with a reputation around town, a reputation that changed depending on the particular bar patron: Rachel worshipped the devil. Rachel slept with an entire punk rock band. Rachel broke up six marriages. As long as the patrons paid for their booze, Laverna would pretend to be interested. Being Rachel's mother was another full-time job, and Laverna had resigned as soon as she got a man. Laverna was in love for the very first time in her life. Frank had been something, someone, to possess. She stopped watching her figure, watching the clock on the wall of the Dirty Shame. Laverna Flood had surrendered.

Billy Petersen was new in town, a cousin to all of the Petersens of Quinn. Somehow, they had relations in Georgia, and one came looking for work. Billy was bearded, dirty, and a little desperate in the eyes. Like every logger, he was covered in sawdust and his hands were filthy with sap. She had met him at the bar, of course. Laverna flirted with him because he did not look like the other Petersens. He did not look like an Applehaus, or a Pierce, or a Russell, or a Fitchett. He was his own singular creation, twenty-four years old, and cocky. He was the only man in Quinn who wore a necklace, puka shells. He liked red beer, and Laverna served him until he had to be carried out the door by the other members of his logging company.

He came back the next night, sober, still covered in sawdust.

"Well, hello there," she said, and immediately slid a red beer in front of him. He winked, and downed it in one gulp.

"Been thinking about you," said Billy.

Laverna was currently reading the only book on astrology the public library owned, and she had been careful to keep it hidden from view of her daughter, the possible devil worshipper.

"What's your sign?"

"Virgo," he said. She studied him carefully.

"You're pretty unkempt for a Virgo."

"I'm on the Leo cusp." He had a crooked little smile.

"Do you have any plans on volunteering for the fire department?"

"No, ma'am. I'm scared of fires."

"Good," said Laverna. "I don't date them." She leaned in closer. "Tell me, Billy. Where the hell did you learn how to use a chain saw in Georgia?"

"Horror movies," he said, and winked again. He moved in a month later, much to Red Mabel's chagrin. He brought his beloved Husqvarna chain saw and an extra pair of boots. He had nine yellowed T-shirts, three pairs of jeans, suspenders printed with cartoon drawings of marijuana plants, disintegrating socks, and a copy of *Jonathan Livingston Seagull*. He wore no underwear, claimed that all men from the South did the same. She warned him constantly about getting too attached, of making promises he could not keep.

"Be careful with me," she said, so often that it finally became a joke between them. Laverna Flood was unbreakable, but in this case needed to be held with both hands.

He loved to fish, and Laverna would accompany him, pretend she did not know how to bait a hook. She was only interested in snaring Billy. Laverna's freezer grew full of his dowry. Laverna wrapped his gifts in freezer paper, found a marker and scrawled the date, his name, and a heart, because she couldn't help herself.

Tonight, Billy was in Ellis. There was no logging in the winter, and Billy had spent the entire month of February apprenticing at a butcher shop. Laverna looked around the fire hall, at the usual suspects and their boring lives. Judge Matthis held court on the running board of a fire truck, surrounded by sycophants; his snobby wife wiped the dust from the truck with a lace handkerchief before she sat down. Buley Savage Connor danced with her husband underneath a curtain of dangling crepe paper. Laverna admired her fearlessness as she moved her hands as if they held tiny cymbals, her lithe body and rolling hips captivating the crowd. Buley was exotic, had somehow mastered the fine art of belly dancing, the only mystery in another predictably oppressive winter.

Red Mabel continued talking about mink. Laverna pretended to be interested, until she noticed the red marks on her neck.

"Holy shit," said Laverna. "You have hickeys!"

"I do not," said Red Mabel.

"Nicely done," said Laverna. Red Mabel was furious, and attacked Gene Runkle, and punched him in the throat, leaving a mark of her own. Although Laverna had been at the ball for only twenty minutes, she was ready to leave. Red Mabel needed to be escorted from the premises, as there were outstanding warrants, and the judge was fewer than ten feet away.

Laverna yanked at her friend's hair and nodded at the judge. She held on to Red Mabel's flannel shirt as she bolted for the door, Laverna sliding across the cement on her daughter's spiked heels.

Laverna drove them both to her house, knowing there was a bottle of Black Velvet hidden under the seat of her truck. It was the only safe place to keep liquor—Rachel did not have keys to the car.

Billy's truck was parked outside, and Red Mabel started swearing. She hated to be the third wheel. "Go," she said. "I'll just drink in your car." Red Mabel snatched the bottle from Laverna's hands. Laverna hardly noticed, so delighted that Billy had returned.

Billy and Rachel were in her bed, the music so loud they did not even notice her.

Laverna grabbed Rachel by the hair, and pulled her backward.

She thought that Rachel had slipped out of her grasp, but then realized that she held a chunk of hair in her hand. Rachel had fallen off the bed and onto the floor, and was laughing at Laverna, clearly wasted, until Red Mabel appeared and shut her up with a slap to the face. Billy lay there, stricken; Red Mabel took advantage of his shock and jumped over Rachel to punch him square in the jaw.

Rachel sat up and fished around on the nightstand for a pack of cigarettes, and regarded her mother and Red Mabel with foggy eyes, clearly stoned on something. Red Mabel snatched the ashtray and shattered it against the wall. Rachel didn't even flinch. Billy tried to cover himself, but Laverna was suddenly upon him, punching him, yanking at the covers, screaming at the top of her lungs.

The music blared, as Billy kicked through the empty beer cans, trying to find his clothes.

Laverna was screaming in the corner of the room, launching whatever she could grab and throw at Billy. Pillows, a lamp, picture frames, and finally when the stereo was ripped from the outlet, there was silence. That was when Laverna threw the copy of *Jonathan Livingston Seagull* at him, and it clipped him right above the eyebrow, instantly drawing blood.

Billy was dressed now, and he dodged Laverna's fists as he ran out the bedroom door.

Outside, they heard him start up his truck and roar away.

Laverna stopped screaming, and then she was sobbing. She kicked her daughter in the leg as hard as she could. Rachel made no attempt to cover herself, just stared back at them, her limbs red with carpet burn.

"Get out of my house," Laverna said, and pointed to the door. "I never want to see you again."

At that, Red Mabel pulled Laverna into the bathroom. They shut the door, and she cried, and they both listened to the sounds of Rachel slamming drawers, the sounds of her leaving.

Wrinkles

★   ★   ★

*I*n the flip-top ottoman, Jake found a stack of baby-blue T-shirts.

"Don't know where they came from, dear," Buley said, and the cat on her lap was just as quizzical. White and tan, and skinny as could be, Jake thought the cat had been one of Frank's.

The T-shirts ranged in size from small to double XL, and they were in immaculate condition, fourteen of them, still carefully folded around cardboard and wrapped in cellophane.

"I think they're a sign," he said, and sat on the rug in front of Buley and examined them closely, designs taking shape in his head.

"ROCKY!" Buley was the kind of woman who yelled so much that it barely even changed her face. He appeared from one of the rows and deposited a bulging manila envelope into his nephew's hands. Jake shook the contents into his lap: iron-on numbers, thirty or so.

"Vintage," said Buley. "But I'm pretty sure the stick-'em still works."

"They look brand-new," said Jake. "Are you sure?"

"Of course, dear." The cat yawned and nuzzled into Buley's armpit. "There are some other things you are going to need, of course." Jake's head continued to swirl with ideas, and he removed his sketchpad, began to make a list. Once more, Buley called for Rocky, and he appeared silently, this time bearing the cordless phone, without being asked. Jake paid no attention to her conversation.

"Bucky will drive you," announced Buley, and Rocky was there again, to take the phone.

"Where?"

"Ellis," said Buley. "I suspect you're going to need some supplies."

———

Bucky waited outside the thrift store, honked twice. Jake thanked Buley and counted the cash in his pockets as he climbed into Bucky's truck. Thankfully, Bucky had on the heater. The March wind stung, and the small truck trembled in the gusts.

Bucky did not need instructions. As they left Quinn, he chattered away, about the upcoming softball season and his new ride-on lawn mower. Jake feigned interest, but he waited for Bucky to pause, blabbing nervously, most likely because of his passenger.

The truck rounded the curve of the river, and the highway was freshly sanded. At last, Bucky stopped the softball talk, and concentrated on the icy road.

"I saw you next door," said Jake. "Working on Frank's house."

"Yep," said Bucky.

"Isn't that weird? I mean, does your family care that you're hanging out with Rachel?"

"Don't believe everything you hear, kid."

"I don't," said Jake. "I'm pretty sure she never served time. I've read enough books to know what prison does to pretty women."

At this, Bucky smiled wryly. "Yeah. I've seen some movies."

In Ellis, Jake consulted with the owner of the fabric store before making his purchases, careful to heed her suggestions, even though he found her fashion to be deplorable. He ignored her crooked wig and sleeveless blouse made from layers of doilies. Her shirt was an arts-and-crafts disaster, but she was extremely helpful, enchanted by his twenty-dollar bill. Bucky said nothing as Jake piled the counter with spools of glittering thread, a bolt of satiny fabric. Jake suspected Bucky held his tongue, embarrassed at these purchases. In the truck, he had admitted to Jake that he needed the money, and Jake figured that Buley had paid him well.

Jake carefully knocked on Rachel's front door. He was cautious, as there was no telling what a thieving murderess would do. He clung to the rumors, because Rachel Flood was the closest thing to Lucky Santangelo; his neighbor could exist in the universe of Jackie Collins. He knew that she was not a killer but believed she was probably a thief and a slut, and he had changed his outfit three times until he was satisfied. He finally chose black slacks and a silk black shirt, a golden ascot that matched his hair. His outfit was dashing and international. It was early evening, and even though her truck was parked outside, he assumed she would be gone, on a date with a married man.

He knocked one more time. Beside him was a laundry basket and an iron with a carefully wrapped cord weighing down the contents.

She answered the door, her eyes puffy and glazed. Jake thought that she seemed kind of drunk, but the word around town was that Rachel Flood was clean and sober.

"Sorry for bothering you," he said. "I can come back at another time." He reached down for his basket.

"No way, kid." She studied him closely, and he tugged nervously at his ascot. "I was meditating. It's something I try to do every day." He smelled the incense, heard the tinkle of new age music.

"My friend Misty and I tried astral projection once," admitted Jake.

"What are you doing here?"

"The astral projection didn't work," said Jake. "Believe me, I'd rather be in Morocco."

"Your mom and Bert must be gone," said Rachel. He nodded, and was grateful that she smiled. He was used to being an imposition. "Come on in."

He lifted the basket with a little grunt and staggered into her living room. He stared around at the mess. "Have you thought about carpet colors?"

"Do they know you're over here?"

"Bert doesn't like to see me iron," he said.

"He doesn't like it when you help your mom out?" Rachel blew out the stick of incense she had been burning. Jake wondered if the witchcraft rumors were true.

"Ha," said Jake. "My mom never irons anything. This is my iron. I got it for Christmas."

"Is that what you asked for?"

"Of course," he said. "I made a list. My mom got me everything except for *The World Is Full of Married Men*. Bert put his foot down."

"Jackie Collins?"

"The only one I haven't read yet. Do you have a copy?"

"No," said Rachel. "I don't own any books."

He decided not to hold that against her. "We have school pictures on Monday," said Jake. "I would like to wear something that isn't wrinkled."

"I understand," said Rachel.

"Can I iron here?" Jake nudged the basket forward with his leg. "Do you mind?"

"Of course not. Are you sure it's okay with your mother?"

"Bert proposed to her last night, so she's kind of preoccupied with that." That was true—Jake had watched the whole thing play out over last night's Tater Tot casserole. Bert no longer wanted to live in sin, and Krystal swooned at the cheap ring, the cliché of a June wedding. "It was gross."

"Do you like Bert?"

"No," he said, examining the kitchen. Frank had never let him inside, so Jake had always wondered what it would be like, and apparently it was chaos and ugly countertops.

"Me neither," she said, and stopped herself. "I'm so sorry. I shouldn't have said that." She suddenly clapped her hands together. "I've got something to show you!"

She pulled Jake down the hallway and shoved him inside the bathroom. It reeked of fresh latex paint. She had chosen a bright yellow and a pale green, which in the poor lighting of the bathroom mirror, made his face look ashen. He kept this to himself. "It's fantastic! I'm a fan of color." Lucky Santangelo's bathrooms were usually smoked glass and stainless steel, and there was always an enormous marble bathtub with Jacuzzi jets. Lucky's bathtub would never fall through the floor of a trailer house.

"I'm so glad you approve," she said. These were not the colors of a thief or a murderess; these were colors from an outdated issue of *Good Housekeeping*. He would help her.

He eased his way past, as she followed him into the living room. "Where's your ironing board?"

"Actually," she said. "I don't have one."

He looked her up and down, at her sweatpants and Blondie T-shirt. "I guess I'm not surprised. I'll be right back."

Jake luxuriated in his empty house and gathered his new purchases from under his bed. He grabbed his beloved ironing board and tucked it under his arm. It was vintage, and he had bought it at a yard sale. It was the kind that was designed to sit on countertops. He assumed that this was so women could cook and iron at the same time. Jackie Collins would not approve.

Rachel's countertops were in terrible condition, but once again, he refrained from comment. Originally, they were a pearly white, shot through with gray veins; Jake's own trailer house had the same version of ersatz marble. But Rachel's were deeply stained with concentric circles of rust in different sizes. Frank must have left wet cast-iron pans on the countertops for months at a time. Jake eased the box of T-shirts and sewing notions from a paper bag, unfolded the board, and plugged the iron into the socket below the window. He folded his arms and stared at her as the iron hissed and began to warm.

"I lied," she said. "When I lie, I have to promptly admit it." Jake raised an eyebrow. "I forgot that I have some books. Well, it was a half truth. I don't own them, they came from the library."

"And?"

"You wouldn't like them," she said. "Laura Ingalls Wilder."

"You're right," he declared, and removed a dress shirt from the basket. He unbuttoned it, snapped it open with a quick flick of his wrist. He draped it over the ironing board.

"I loved those books when I was your age," she said.

"I'm an advanced reader," he said. "I don't like to read about people roughing it. I live in Quinn. I see it all the time. I prefer to read about people who aren't dirty. I like a clean and complex protagonist."

"Jackie Collins isn't exactly great literature, kid."

"Lucky Santangelo is a classic character," he said. "I don't remember Half Pint and Pa fighting the Mafia or flying around the world in a private jet."

"No," she admitted. "I was thinking that you might like John Steinbeck or Edgar Allan Poe."

"You thought wrong," he said, and began to iron. He smoothed down the collar and made quick work of it. It stuck out, flattened, in a wicked little point.

"*Cannery Row*," she said. "There's sex in it. And it's very political. I think you'd like it."

"I'm not allowed to read about politics," he said. "Bert's rule."

"I'll make you a deal," she said. "I'll find you the book you've been wanting, if you promise to read Steinbeck."

"That's blackmail," he said. "I learned about blackmail from Jackie Collins." He started on a pair of madras pants. "Therefore, I approve."

"I'm glad," she said. "Your high school English teacher will thank me one day."

"I'm asking to be sent to boarding school," he said. "It's on this year's Christmas list."

"That's nine months away," said Rachel.

"I don't believe in public school," he said. "Lucky Santangelo went to school in Switzerland."

"I don't think your mom can afford that," said Rachel.

Jake ignored this. "How did you make it through public school?"

"I didn't know there were any other choices," she said. "Although my mom always threatened to send me to live with the Mennonites."

He shuddered, and carefully placed the pants on the least-stained part of the countertop. He unfolded a pair of blue jeans.

"It's my only pair," he assured her.

"You iron your blue jeans?"

"Of course I do," said Jake. "Can I do your laundry?"

You Will Know the Person When You See Them

★   ★   ★

*B*ucky made three trips to his truck on the morning of Saint Patrick's Day, returning to Rachel's living room with a sewing machine and a miniature desk. She had decided upon the corner where the fireplace had been, and where the bricks remained. Upon this platform, Bucky placed a tall lamp, the fringed shade mounted on an adjustable arm. Jake insisted on doing her laundry, then proceeded to help her paint the hallway, and organize her bedroom closet until it contained everything she owned. Sorted by color, of course. She loved the help, and let his propulsion carry her.

She moved a metal folding chair behind the desk and hung a framed photograph of David Bowie just above the lamp. It once sat on her nightstand, but there was no room in this new house. Shocked that Jake knew nothing about David Bowie, she played cassettes for him the rest of the afternoon while they worked.

Rachel checked her watch, and it was quarter to eight. Bucky had left half an hour earlier, and she had lost all track of time creating the sewing corner. Jake promised to make curtains for her house, and although Rachel still feared Bert, she needed window treatments.

Jake could manage to sneak away without notice. Bert was usually gone with the reverend, and Krystal was too wrapped up in daydreams about the wedding.

Rachel left the front door unlocked, and navigated the berms of snow as she drove to work.

Saint Patrick's Day. The Dirty Shame was slammed with teachers who would probably call in sick the next day, and unemployed regulars who wouldn't need to. Rachel refused to make green beer, despite her mother's demands.

The holiday fell on a Sunday. Laverna and Red Mabel arrived at nine in the morning, scouting out what Rachel had done. They heckled her from their table in the corner. Rachel could tell they were already drunk.

Laverna was full of criticism and pain medication. She nodded off in the corner, in between heckling, dressed in an ancient, shapeless green sweater and slacks the color of split pea soup. Red Mabel plucked the cigarettes from Laverna's mouth when her eyes closed and her head slumped forward. Rachel knew that Red Mabel helped her mother dress in the morning. The thought made her uncomfortable.

The bar was lined with eight Crock-Pots, all different makes and models, that Ronda filled with corned beef and cabbage the day before. Extension cords piled in loops behind the bar, and Rachel was extra diligent not to get tangled up and spill any drinks. She refused to serve any of the food. It smelled like an outhouse. Instead, there was a tall stack of Styrofoam plates and napkins, and a new box of plastic forks and knives. The patrons would have to serve themselves for once.

Martha Man Hands and Black Mabel played Yahtzee beside the jukebox, as far away from Laverna and Red Mabel as possible.

The Chief came in and sat right near the taps, and read the newspaper.

"I didn't know Quinn had so many Irish," said Rachel as she poured him a cup of coffee.

"I know the census data," said the Chief. "Mostly Swedes and Polacks here."

She settled the coffee in front of him, and witnessed her mother kicking Red Mabel under the table. Red Mabel's mouth was full of cabbage, but she shouted Rachel's name anyway.

Rachel dried her hands on the bar rag, and walked over to them.

"I went by your house this morning," said Laverna. "I wanted to see what you've been up to."

"Did you go inside?"

"Of course not," said Laverna. "I'm not rude like that."

"Yes, you are," said Rachel.

"I wanted to get you a housewarming present," said Laverna. "And a thank-you for doing your part to help out."

Rachel stared at her mother, assuming this was a trap of some kind.

"She's really high," explained Red Mabel.

"Your yard is a swamp," said Laverna.

"Apparently," said Rachel. The clatter of the dice in the plastic cup from the Yahtzee game was unnerving.

"The guys at the county owe me a favor," said Laverna. "I don't want to get into the hows or whys."

"You should have sued those motherfuckers," declared Red Mabel.

"Anyway," said Laverna. "I got you a truckful of topsoil. They're gonna drop it off in your driveway."

"Excellent," said Rachel. She was unsure how to feel—this offer was like a kitten you pick up out of cuteness, until it hooks claws into your forearm.

"The dump truck won't fit through your gate," said Laverna. "So you'd better get some help."

"And a wheelbarrow," said Red Mabel.

"Thank you," said Rachel. "How much do I owe you?"

"Nothing," said Laverna. "Like I said, it was the least they could do." Rachel was leery of gifts from her mother, despite how hard she had been working. Laverna and Red Mabel held grudges for years, gifts for themselves, she supposed.

"Bring me a beer," said Red Mabel. "I brought my own food coloring."

And she had. She produced a tiny plastic bottle with a pointed green tip.

Just then, Black Mabel yelled "Yahtzee!" Red Mabel's hands clenched into fists.

"You're not the bouncer," said Laverna. "I don't know how many times I have to tell you that."

Rachel touched Black Mabel lightly on the shoulder as she placed fresh pints in front of them. Their table was littered with dollar bills. She did not understand why Martha and Black Mabel would gamble at Yahtzee, but people in this town would bet on just about anything.

Rachel walked back to the bar, wiped down the counter, and stopped in front of the Chief.

"You're not wearing green," she said.

"Anybody pinches me, I'll punch them in the fucking face."

Athena had told her that she would know *the person* when she saw them, and the Chief's surly words made it seem fated.

"I've been thinking," she began.

The Chief looked up from his coffee cup. "About what?"

Rachel lowered her voice. "I need a sponsor."

"Okay," he said. "But men aren't allowed to sponsor ladies."

"I don't want to sleep with you," said Rachel. "And I know you don't want to sleep with me. Are you willing?" She twisted the rag in her hands.

"I don't think I really have a choice," said the Chief. "Aren't any ladies in recovery in this town"—he looked around the bar, at the two Mabels, at Martha—"yet."

"I've already been through the steps," said Rachel. "I worked really hard. I just keep coming back to the eighth."

"Well," said the Chief. "I'm not allowed to tell you no. So I guess I'm gonna have to help you out."

"Thank you," said Rachel. "Athena said I'm the easiest sponsee she's ever had."

"That's good," said the Chief. "But you haven't worked with me. I treat my sponsees like I do the new recruits at the station."

"I'm not going to shave my head," said Rachel.

"You'll do what I tell you," said the Chief, and for the first time ever, he winked at her. She blushed. "I'm honored you chose me," he said.

Rachel leaned across the bar and shook his hand.

Across the room, Black Mabel started to cackle.

Rachel turned around to see a cop. He was a beefy creature with a dangling set of handcuffs twirling around his finger. The other hand was touching his revolver, strapped to his belt.

"Mabel Garrison," he said.

Black Mabel shook her head and stood up from the table. She rolled her eyes and shuffled willingly toward the police officer, holding out her arms.

"You're under arrest," he declared as he clicked the handcuffs into place. "Again."

The silver miners cheered, as they always did at the misfortune of others.

"I'm not even gonna ask what for," said Black Mabel as she was marched through the bar, the beefy creature close behind.

Martha Man Hands grabbed all the bills from the table, and stuffed them in her shirt.

The Scrimmage

★ ★ ★

The last week of March were days when the cloud cover lifted, and the sun was so pale and ineffectual that it did nothing to warm the gusty winds that blew sideways and rang Laverna's large collection of wind chimes. She leaned down to sip at a cup of coffee, and watched from the kitchen window as the chimes clattered against one another, producing a cacophony of sound. She could tell it was a cold wind. The river was dotted with white caps.

When the knock at the door came, Laverna didn't hear it at first, over the clanging symphony on her back deck.

"Fuck," she said, when the knocking resumed again.

"Come in," she said, and she watched the doorknob turn and the Sinclairs enter, followed by Reverend Foote. "Take off your shoes," she said.

"You," Laverna said to the taller Sinclair. "Fill up my coffee cup." The taller Sinclair did what she was told, and Laverna pointed at the couch with her bright white casts, as she settled in the recliner, the TV tray stacked with phone books, a heightened perch for her coffee cup and straw.

"What do you want?" Laverna glared at the couch, at the row of redheads.

Reverend Foote spoke, quite loudly, landing on his consonants like they fell from a great height. This was a sermon, but Laverna knew a sales pitch, even one wrapped in Jesus.

"Sister Joy and Sister Jeanette speak very highly of you and asked this morning if our church could be of service. They are two of my favorite parishioners, so of course I came over to see if there is anything you might need."

"Who the hell are Joy and Jeanette?" Laverna watched Reverend Foote blanch. "You've got nuns up there?"

"I'm Joy," said the taller, white-knuckling the droopy sleeve of her sweater.

"Jeanette," said the shorter, refusing to meet Laverna's eyes.

"Of course," said Laverna. "I'm really fucked-up on pills." She made a show of laughing, knowing these names would slip her mind the minute they left.

"The sisters tell me that they play on your softball team," said Reverend Foote. "If we had enough able-bodied women, perhaps we would field a team of our own!" He pressed his hands together, eyes lit up. "I played second base in high school, and I delighted in the camaraderie."

"If you field a team, we'll cream you," said Laverna. "These two here are pretty much useless, but they don't talk much, and I like that."

"They are quiet," admitted Reverend Foote. "I'll give you that. But they are fiercely devoted and are valuable, hardworking members of our church."

"And they have practice in two hours," she said. "A scrimmage," added Laverna, proudly. She called in her usual favors, and the Flood Girls were playing against an assortment of Little Leaguers, and maybe a few girls from T-ball.

"Wonderful," pronounced Reverend Foote. "I know you are a well-respected member of this community, Miss Flood. May I call you Laverna?"

"No," she said. "You've got to spend some money at my bar first."

"Our congregation is too frightened to bring you the usual casseroles, and for that I apologize. I try to teach them to fear no one, to walk with God, but apparently you have a reputation."

"No shit," said Laverna. "What do you want?"

"Only to reach out a helping hand, if you should ever need it." He leaned forward. "I trust you know Brother Bert Russell."

"Bert? He's in your church? He's a useless piece of shit. And he owes me money."

"And that's why I'm here," said Reverend Foote. "I understand that you employ his son."

"That's the league," said Laverna. "I've got nothing to do with it."

"Brother Bert is trying to become a better man. It would really help if he could provide for his family."

"Send him into the woods with a fucking chain saw," said Laverna. "That's what real men do around here. I'm not a goddamn job service."

Red Mabel burst through the door, stepping on the reverend's loafers and the Sinclairs' cheap white sneakers. She stood on top of the pile of shoes and stared at the couch.

"There's three redheads in this house," said Red Mabel. "That's bad luck."

"No shit," said Laverna. "They were just leaving." They stood, and Red Mabel moved from the pile of shoes. "The reverend here was asking if Bert could keep score."

"We've already got the pansy," said Red Mabel.

"Bert joined their church," said Laverna. Red Mabel laughed at this, as Reverend Foote and the Sinclairs pulled on their shoes.

"Is it a church for morons?" Red Mabel opened the door for them, and shooed them out with a flick of her hand.

"It is not," said Reverend Foote. He stood up straight, and Red Mabel puffed her chest until he had to take a step backward.

"You're letting in all the cold air," said Laverna.

"I had hoped you would be a reasonable woman," said Reverend Foote.

"Keep praying," said Red Mabel. She pointed at the Sinclairs, who had stepped out onto the porch, the wind whipping the jean skirts tight against their legs. "You two had better have your shit together today. We've got some holes in the outfield."

"Amen," shouted Laverna as Red Mabel shut the door behind them.

The Sinclairs made the mistake of arriving early. Laverna made them run laps around the chain-link fence, despite the cold wind. They would pay for bringing that terrible man to her house. Red Mabel warmed up where third base would be, jumping jacks, unencumbered by a bra.

Red Mabel's breasts became problematic when the parents began to drop off their children. The mother of one Little Leaguer covered his eyes with her hands.

"Cut it out, Red," shouted Laverna. She grasped the shoulder of the child, in full uniform, pinstriped, real baseball pants and cleats. Little League began in June, but he was ready. "Why don't you go toss the ball around?" She shoved the kid at Red Mabel, and he spit in the dirt, stomped to third base. Red Mabel looked him up and down, and began throwing grounders.

The little girls arrived in one minivan. The driver barely slowed down; the van door rolled open and the girls leaped into the gravel, landed on their feet. They moved in a pack, into the away team dugout, whispered when they saw Bucky, who had materialized beside Laverna, silent as always. This had always unnerved her.

The Sinclairs rounded home plate, red-faced.

"Keep running!" Laverna leaned against the dugout, and the little girls stared at her casts and at Bucky. Boys continued to arrive, bedecked in team uniforms, avoiding the girls at all costs.

The remaining Flood Girls arrived in groups, Della carrying a wildly struggling dog.

"Found him on the street," said Della proudly. "I aim to keep him."

"That's how you ended up married twice," said Laverna. Della and Tabby tied the small brown dog to the bench of the dugout with the removed strings from their hooded sweatshirts. The young girls took the field, still traveling in a pack, giggling at the oblivious Bucky. Laverna could not believe the amount of makeup they were wearing, and considered saying something, until her own daughter entered the dugout with Jake. Rachel's face was fully made up, the flesh around her eyebrows red from a fresh plucking. Laverna was certain that Jake had something to do with this.

"What are you staring at?" Rachel pulled on her borrowed mitt with trepidation, as if there might be spiders inside. She wore a black leather jacket over a black lingerie top, and ripped black jeans. And those cursed boots.

Jake carried a sketchpad, a case of colored pencils. He beamed at Laverna, and pointed to Rachel's face. "Your daughter has the most incredible cheekbones!" Indeed, her cheeks were emblazoned with a maroon blush, and her eyes drooped from the weight of the mascara. "I was trying to make her look just like Melanie Griffith in *Working Girl*, but we decided that she couldn't play softball in a blazer with shoulder pads. Plus, it's really cold."

"I'm glad you chose something practical," said Laverna, noting the small silver spikes dotting the lapels of the leather jacket. "And she gets those cheekbones from me."

"They all have uniforms," said Jake, pointing at the children on the field. He sat down on the bench and flipped open his sketchpad. "How come the Flood Girls don't have uniforms?"

"Shut up," said Laverna.

The last child arrived, a roly-poly little girl, braids tucked under a low-slung cap. She carried a T-ball stand over one shoulder, and acknowledged Laverna grimly. Tammi, the T-ball coach, struggled to keep up with the girl.

"This is our most ferocious player," said Tammi. "She really should be playing in an upper league." Tammi patted the girl on top of her baseball cap. "Take care of her."

Laverna called her players into the center of the field. Martha and Ronda held lit cigarettes.

"Put those out," demanded Laverna. Her catcher and rover ground the butts into the dirt.

"Hey," said Bucky. "Respect the field, ladies!"

"Yeah," said one of the little girls. "Not cool."

"This is a scrimmage," continued Laverna. "The Flood Girls need to work on their fielding." She pointed to the dugout, and the girl dragged her T-ball stand, the other children following her across the infield.

"Play ball," said Bucky, halfheartedly.

The first little boy possessed a cowlick and a mean swing, leaned in to hit Ginger's first pitch of the day. When it came back at her, Ginger jumped to avoid being drilled in the shins. Tabby tried to grab the ball, but it sped past second base, veered left, and into the land of the Sinclairs. Cowlick made it to third on what should have been an easy play. Red Mabel tried to intimidate the kid as he stood on her base, but he was not having any of her trash talk.

"Your mother is married to her second cousin," said Red Mabel.

"Small town," said the kid. "Shit happens."

A slatternly girl stepped up to the plate. Even from twenty feet away, her eye shadow visibly matched the green of her uniform. Ginger threw a strike. The T-ball girl decided this was a bad call, yelled something at Bucky about his teeth. The next pitch was solid, and the girl swung, but the ball glanced off her bat, an infield pop fly. Cowlick waited to see if Della would catch it, but it fell out of Della's mitt and tumbled to the ground, and he tagged up and ran home. Eye Shadow made it to first base.

"Hustle!" Laverna kicked at the chain link, and it rang out through the field, just as the wind picked up again. The dog snapped the string in half, and ran excitedly into the outfield, only to sit obediently at Rachel's feet.

A Native American boy was next. Laverna suspected he was related to Ronda, and studied her rover for any sign of acknowledgment. Instead, Ronda was watching the dog, and would've missed a smoke signal burning in center field. Ginger was angry, and she pitched way outside the box. The Native American kid walked to first, and Ginger turned around on the mound to compose herself.

"All right," shouted Laverna, and stalked over to the children's dugout. "My outfield needs a workout. I need a real hitter."

A boy stood up from the bench and pulled on his batting gloves. The T-ball girl pushed him down, and stomped out of the dugout, drawing a neat furrow in the dirt with her plastic stand. She nodded at Martha Man Hands, who crouched behind home plate. Martha groaned as she stood, and Laverna could hear her knees crack. They would not need a catcher. The girl arranged the stand in front of home plate and cleared her throat, glaring at Bucky, who was offering advice to Martha about deep stretches. Finally the girl snapped.

"Pay attention!" The girl pointed at the ball in Bucky's hand, and he blushed as he offered it to her. She refused to take it. She tapped the top of the T-ball stand with her bat. Bucky rolled his eyes and carefully rested the ball into the hole. The little girl was barely as tall as his waist, and she squinted into the field, as if the sun was especially bright. She pointed her bat toward Rachel and tapped three times on the plate.

"BE READY!" Laverna screamed to the outfield, just as the little girl leveled the bat and smashed the ball into the air, as threatened.

The ball sailed toward Rachel, the wind picking it up as it flew past first base, shifting it slightly away from the foul line. As usual, Rachel panicked and covered her face with her mitt. The dog remained sitting at her feet. Ronda walked to the ball, just as the little girl rounded second and barreled toward Red Mabel, who might have met her match. Instead, the girl cruised past, and Red Mabel scorched the outfield with profanities. Her invectives were drowned out by the cheering of the children in the dugout.

"You," said Laverna. The girl grabbed her stand, and spat in the dirt near Martha. Expressionless, even though her teammates screamed and rattled the cage. "What's your name?"

"Klemp," said the girl. "I ain't telling you my first name. That's my right. This is America."

"Jesus," said Laverna. "Klemp, I want you to keep hitting." Klemp propped her stand back into place. Laverna turned to Jake. "Get me a dollar out of my purse." Jake rooted around and pulled out a bill. "Go give it to Klemp." Jake opened his mouth to protest, but Laverna had had enough sass from children for one day. "I can't use my arms, for fuck's sake!"

Klemp took the dollar, but didn't have any pockets in her uniform. She tucked it into the inside of her sneaker.

"Keep hitting," said Laverna. "Just like that."

Klemp turned around and cleared her throat. This time, she pointed her bat at Bucky. She refused the ball, once again. "Do your job," she said. Bucky made a wide berth around her as he rested it on top of the T-ball stand.

Klemp pointed her bat at the taller Sinclair. The taller Sinclair flinched, lowered herself into ready position, jean skirt dragging in the grass. She pushed up the sleeves of her sweater, and Laverna's hopes rose. They came crashing back down when Klemp blasted the ball far into left field, and it grazed the mitt of the shorter Sinclair, kept on flying.

"I'm fucking with them," said Klemp. Laverna decided not to give her any more money. This continued for the next ten minutes. Klemp gave Bucky the evil eye until he arranged the ball, and Klemp bashed it into the outfield, and the Flood Girls proved to be useless. Rachel especially. Once she saw an easy target, Klemp hit it to Rachel again and again, until Rachel just held the mitt up to her face permanently.

Laverna was disgusted. She forced Jake to fetch her an antianxiety pill, and he held up the can of beer to her mouth. She could no longer watch the carnage, and she sighed. She studied Klemp, her grimly determined face and firmly planted stance. Laverna had no doubt that Klemp would grow up to be a silver miner.

"You're not even trying!" Laverna shouted to the outfield, her casts slammed against the chain link, and pain shot up her arms. The dog reached the ball before any of the outfielders, and pushed it with his nose, deeper into the grass. Ronda threw her mitt at the dog, missed by a good three feet. Finally, the taller Sinclair scooped up a ball and threw it to Diane, who had hustled out into the grass of the outfield. *At least the Sinclair had hit the cutoff*, thought Laverna. Of course, Diane had been wildly gesticulating with her hands, so she wasn't hard to miss.

The Flood Girls did not need uniforms. Laverna would rather spend the money on something useful. She wondered how much it would cost to import a ringer from Cuba, a woman who could actually play ball. She didn't give a shit about the language barrier, or the paperwork. Laverna calculated the cost of housing a foreigner, and the expense of finding plantains, or whatever Cubans ate. The hell with it, decided Laverna. She would figure out a way to draft Klemp, even though she was too young for the league.

Concealer

★   ★   ★

*J*ake found himself awake at three in the morning. This had been happening for a week. He would lie there, still as a corpse, for two hours, glancing out of the corner of his eye at the alarm clock until 5:00 a.m., when he would just give up and put on his headphones.

Jake didn't dare turn on a lamp. When Krystal worked the night shift, he made himself as unobtrusive as possible. He didn't want a lecture about Jesus, so he stayed in his room, in the dark. When he could see the glow of the kitchen light under the door, Jake knew that Bert was distracted with eating breakfast, part of the new righteous routine.

Yesterday, his English teacher had made a remark about the circles under his eyes, said that Jake looked like the mother of a newborn.

While he applied his hair wax, he studied his reflection in the mirror. This morning, he resembled someone who had barely survived being lost in the woods.

He stared in the mirror, and his teacher's remarks made him determined. He opened the cupboard below the sink and fished around for his mother's concealer.

He opened the tiny jar, and ever so carefully, began to dab a bit under his eyes. He made sure to rub it in as much as possible—he knew that he had to make it look natural.

Jake believed that he looked well rested, but just as he was applying a tiny bit more, Bert burst into the bathroom in his typically cloddish way.

Bert made a strange sound, almost a growl. He yanked Jake out of the bathroom and carried him to his bedroom.

Jake lay across his bedspread and listened as Bert yanked the drawer in the kitchen completely free. Jake could hear the clatter of cooking utensils as they spilled out on the linoleum, hear Bert cursing until he found the wooden spoon.

———

The sting of the spank had dissipated by the time he arrived at school, but his face was splotchy from scrubbing it with a washcloth. He didn't care. His homeroom was taught by a woman who despised him and rarely looked at his face.

Ms. Bray was ostensibly a science teacher, but he had decided she was a complete idiot the first month of school and had stopped paying attention when he realized she lectured directly from the textbook. In October, she had declared war on Jake when she had caught him reading a paperback behind his science book. She couldn't believe that he dared find a paperback more interesting than her lecture. She had ordered Jake to the front of the class to tell his classmates what his book was about, and why it was more important than cellular division.

Jake was flame-faced as he stood there, holding up his copy of *Lady Boss*. He showed the book to the class, careful to cover Jackie Collins's name with one hand.

"I'm currently reading a book entitled *Lady Boss*, and it is about how hard it is for women in the workplace. I think it might also be about capitalism, but I'm not sure."

He returned to his seat, and she had hated him ever since. He'd had teachers in the past who found his advanced reading skills precocious and worthy of praise. She was not one of them.

———

After school, Jake walked outside into the new snow that was slowly falling, back and forth like a feather. He knew of other places in Amer-

ica where they had things called snow days. These did not exist in
Quinn.

It was only three o'clock, but already the sky outside darkened with
the threat of another snowstorm. It took him fifteen minutes to descend
the hill and cross the streets to the library, which was irritating, considering a person could walk through the entire town in under ten minutes during the summer. He slogged his way through the snowbanks, perspiring
under his hat.

At the library, Peggy Davis pretended to roll the dates on her stamper.
Upon closer inspection, her fingers were black with ink, so maybe she
wasn't pretending. She didn't like Jake, either. He never turned in a book
past the due date, but she remained suspicious, scandalized by his sala-
cious choices in reading materials. Jake combed through the catalogs and
filled out the forms to request books from the bigger cities in Montana, but
he never got his books. He suspected that she threw away his requests, as
if she were embarrassed to obtain Erica Jong's *Fear of Flying* from Absa-
rokee, the only library with a copy in the entire state. He hated Peggy
Davis because she destroyed Quinn's best chances for a feminist revolu-
tion. Plus, she once asked him to leave during a John Birch Society meeting in the back room, even though the library was open. Jake hoped that
one day she would be replaced by a young woman with a mysterious past,
who wore only black and had an active sex life, just like the librarians in
the books he read.

Jake left the library with two Stephen King books, and skidded his
way up the snow-packed streets to the Sinclair. He knew that Martha
Man Hands was working. One of the Sinclairs mopped the beer aisle. He
wasn't sure which one it was. All he could see was a long braid and an
even longer jean skirt.

He had written Misty five letters, and bundled them with a rubber
band. He had found a half-used box of cream-colored stationery at the
thrift store—the paper was thick, and flecked with dots of lavender. Misty
would hate it, but Jake didn't care. He asked his mother for stamps and
carefully wrote his return address on the envelopes, even though he and
Misty grew up in the same trailer court. The doctors at the detention cen-

ter could be giving Misty electroshock therapy like Frances Farmer, so he didn't want to risk it. He was concerned about the weight of the paper, so he used two stamps for each envelope.

He handed the stack to Martha. As usual, she was preoccupied by the police scanner. It was chimney-fire season, and Martha, like all the other residents of Quinn, listened for her own address.

"You know where the post office is, kid." She pushed the envelopes back across the counter with her giant hands.

"I don't have an address for her," he said. "I know we got in some trouble, but I would greatly appreciate it if you could send these to her. She must be lonely."

"They've called me four times already," said Martha. "Sounds like she's already running the joint. She lit some girl on fire."

"That sounds about right," said Jake.

"I'll send them," said Martha. "But just this once."

"Thank you," said Jake. "Have you been sending her care packages?"

At this, Martha cackled, and when he left the Sinclair, she was still laughing.

The Calling

★ ★ ★

Laverna insisted that Red Mabel dress her in layers. Dressed in a pantsuit and a mock turtleneck and a scarf, she was ready to cause chaos among the patrons at the Dirty Shame. It was officially the first day of spring.

Ginger and Martha sat at poker machines, drinking wine coolers.

Laverna waited until Ginger cashed out, and Martha lost whatever she had put in, then gestured to a table with her casts.

Tabby approached the four women at the table, bearing baskets of peanuts.

"I've decided that this is a team meeting," said Laverna.

"There are only five of us," pointed out Ginger.

"We're the most important five," said Laverna. "Your drinks are on the house."

"I guess that means I'll be right back," said Tabby, and she returned with more wine coolers and another pint of beer for Red Mabel. Tabby sat backward on a chair and reached over to touch Laverna on the shoulder.

"She's useless," said Tabby.

"She's worse than Krystal," said Ginger.

"We don't have any other options," said Laverna, as Red Mabel lit a cigarette and stuck it in her mouth. She exhaled, and Red Mabel plucked it out and set it in an ashtray. "We are stuck with her."

"Are you sure?" Ginger took a deep swallow.

"Yes," said Laverna. "Patty said no, thanks; she's joined a book club. Maggie joined another team, or so she says. Maybe we have a bad reputation."

"Excellent," said Red Mabel.

"Can we make Ronda move faster?" Ginger was being serious.

"I pay the lady," said Laverna. "I can't get her to move fast at her regular job."

"Why is Rachel so afraid of the ball?" Tabby took a drink out of Ginger's bottle.

"She has a pretty face," said Martha. "She takes after her mother."

At this, they all laughed, even Laverna.

"I think she's afraid of life," said Ginger.

"When did you get so profound?" Laverna asked the question and nodded at Red Mabel for another drag.

"She used to not be afraid of anything," said Tabby. "I watched her pierce her ear in the middle of algebra class."

"I remember that," said Laverna. "She put a goddamn fishing tackle in the hole."

The door opened, and in came the silver miners, off shift, covered in the powder of vermiculite. The women had somehow captured a baby mountain lion, leashed to a length of clothesline. Laverna did not allow animals at the bar, but she was too intrigued to argue.

"When did she get so scared?" This question came from Red Mabel, of all people. The silver miners took their customary spot beside the jukebox. Tabby excused herself to pour some pitchers.

"Dunno," said Laverna. "I don't care if she doesn't catch the ball. I just don't want her covering her face like that. The other teams will die of laughter."

"Take her glove away," offered Martha.

"Against the rules," said Red Mabel. Laverna watched as the silver miners fed the mountain lion pieces of beef jerky from their pockets. She watched as the dirtiest silver miner reached into her heavy coat and removed a can of Fancy Feast.

"We need to get her drunk," said Ginger.

"She doesn't do that anymore," said Laverna. "Or so she claims." The lid was removed from the Fancy Feast, and the silver miners whistled when the cat hissed out and swiped a paw at the can, which they kept out of reach.

"Crazy bitches," said Red Mabel, as they all turned to watch the silver miners and the cub. The tiny mountain lion looked as tough as the silver miners. They were ferocious, desperate, and wild-eyed women. They drank too much, and had too little to do.

"She's sober," said Laverna. "I think it's a good thing. You all have heard what she's capable of."

"She fucked the entire volunteer fire department," said Red Mabel.

"Not all of them," said Laverna. "That's a lie." Red Mabel put the cigarette back in Laverna's mouth, as Tabby deposited the pitchers of beer in front of the silver miners, making a wide berth around the mountain lion.

Tabby returned to their table, shaking her head. "They'd better tip extra tonight," she said.

"Let's find her a man," said Martha. "Some dude who will help her take the edge off. Somebody to distract her."

"She has one," said Red Mabel. "He's a twelve-year-old little pansy."

"I don't like that word," said Ginger. "It's not appropriate. They like to be called gay now. I know these things."

"How?" Red Mabel demanded. "How do you know these things?"

"I can afford cable, you bitch." Ginger's tone had an edge to it, and Laverna couldn't help but wonder about Ginger's son, who had fled to California after graduation, never married. The silver miners were clapping now, as the cat sat up on her hind paws, balanced on her tail, coiled in a tough little spring.

"Enough," said Laverna. "Do we know any eligible bachelors?"

"Bucky," said Martha.

"Bucky," said Tabby.

"What?" said Bucky, who, unbeknownst to them, had entered the bar, in the sneaky way he always did. Bucky was underage and had an irrational fear the cops would bust him, even though volunteer firemen of any age were always absolved, and he only drank soda anyway. "Can I get a drink?"

"Have a seat," said Laverna. "Tabby, get him whatever he wants."

"Diet Coke," he said.

"Diet Coke?" asked Red Mabel. "What the fuck is happening to this town?"

Bucky sat down next to Laverna. He looked more nervous than usual, surrounded by women who were obviously scheming.

"We need your help," said Laverna.

"Look," said Bucky. "I can't help you with any more practices. The other teams are gonna think I'm partial to you, and an ump can't be partial. It's called a . . ." He paused.

"Conflict of interest," said Ginger. "You can't hit for shit anyway."

"Hey," protested Bucky. "I'm a volunteer. Respect that."

"I need to ask you something," said Laverna. "And I need you to not run your mouth."

Bucky gulped. "Okay," he said.

"How do you feel about my daughter?"

Bucky examined the faces of the other women and carefully considered his response. "She's nice enough. And smart. She's got me thinking about giving up red meat."

At this, Red Mabel spat on the ground.

"Not like that, Bucky," said Laverna. "I need to know if you find my daughter attractive."

"Shit yes," said Bucky. "I ain't blind. Just concerned about my cholesterol. I definitely am going to stop eating so many hamburgers. And do you know where hot dogs come from?"

"Shut the fuck up," said Red Mabel. "Do you wanna screw her or not?"

"Jesus," said Bucky. "She doesn't like me like that."

"How do you know that?" asked Ginger.

"Because she flat out told me so," said Bucky. "The first five minutes I ever met her."

"Sounds about right," said Martha. "She really does take after her mother."

"Quiet," said Laverna. "Are you sure she still feels that way?"

"Yep," said Bucky. "I spend a lot of time at her house. She would've jumped me by now."

"Because you're so irresistible?" said Ginger, who chortled and drained the rest of her wine cooler.

Bucky blushed. "I'm young and single and I'm a volunteer fireman. I'm a catch. Everybody says so."

"I'm thankful you have such high self-esteem," said Laverna. "You just keep thinking that way."

"Thanks," said Bucky. "I will."

Tabby brought him the Diet Coke, and he began to drink it greedily.

"Does she ever talk about any man?" Laverna leaned in close. "Is there anybody she's interested in?"

"Nope," said Bucky. "She only hangs out with Jake and the Chief."

"The Chief?" Red Mabel was incredulous. "She's already fucking a married man!"

"No," said Bucky. "They're buddies. He gives her advice about life."

"I was not aware of this," said Laverna. She felt her blood pressure begin to spike, and lifted up her arm to smash her fist on the table. This is what she usually did to accentuate her point, to let people know she had enough. Unfortunately, she still had her casts, and her arms barely budged. Angrily, she kicked at Bucky's leg, missed.

"You're not supposed to," he said, frightened.

"Oh," said Laverna, instantly calming. "This is some sort of sober-people thing."

"Not telling," Bucky said, and finished his soda.

"So she listens to him?"

"Yes, ma'am."

"Bucky, do you think you could get the Chief to teach her to not be afraid of the ball?"

"No guarantees," said Bucky. "But it won't hurt to ask."

———

Laverna wanted to keep drinking, but Red Mabel insisted that she take her home first, to change back into a sweat suit. Red Mabel was going on a mission, and as usual, it was top secret. She would not let Laverna sit at the bar by herself in clothing that could restrict her movement. There could be another assassination attempt.

When Red Mabel returned her to the Dirty Shame, Tabby helped Laverna take a few more pain pills. Laverna sipped at a shot of tequila, bending like a bird each time, using the embarrassing pink straws.

Jim Number Three came in, just as the silver miners were gathering up their coats and their wild animal. He sat down next to Laverna and watched their procession as they paraded out the door.

"Don't ask," said Laverna. "Can you light me a cigarette?"

Jim Number Three obliged. Laverna was fond of him—he continued to stop by the house most days and read to her. They were up to the chapter in *Roots* where Chicken George was gambling on chicken fights while courting Mathilda. Laverna remarked that this was everyday behavior among the men of Quinn.

Jim Number Three had been ice fishing all day, and was already drunk. He described the fish at length. He told Laverna that he was born in Alaska, and then his family relocated to Chinook, where the weather was pretty much the same. He told Laverna that he grew up hoping to become a seismologist but settled for being an electrician instead.

"Seismology is not really a science," said Jim Number Three. "Earthquakes are an art." He whispered, "Earthquakes make my heart beat fast."

"They do that," Laverna said, and leaned forward so he could remove the cigarette from her mouth.

"Chinook's main industry is sugar beets," continued Jim Number Three. "The high school football team is called the Sugarbeeters."

"That's pathetic."

"I really like you," said Jim Number Three. "I'd like to get to know you better."

"Don't say that," said Laverna.

"Why?" Jim Number Three ordered another round, ashed Laverna's cigarette.

"Because I'm a miserable person," she said.

"It's this town," said Jim Number Three, as Tabby slid another shot of tequila in front of Laverna and a pint of beer in front of him. "I think you all have vitamin deficiencies, or maybe the water is poisoned." He raised his glass to her. "Cheers!"

Laverna stared at him. Apparently, he forgot she did not have use of her arms.

The pills and the booze made her feel brazen. "Take me to your house."

Jim Number Three grabbed his keys without a word, and then he was helping her off the barstool and out the door.

He lived in Rachel's trailer court, and Laverna was thankful his house was at the end by the gravel pit, far away from her daughter.

She plopped down next to him on the couch, her casts stuck straight out in front of her. She tried to figure out a way to kiss him. He brought her a beer, and a straw, and she leaned down to the coffee table and sipped slowly. Laverna pressed her body into his side. He smiled at her, touched her face with a callused hand.

"I don't feel so miserable right now," said Laverna, and then Jim Number Three placed his own beer down on the coffee table and took her face in both hands, kissed her open mouth. He tasted like cigarettes and beer, and she loved it.

"I don't date volunteer firemen," said Laverna. "That well has been poisoned."

"I'm an electrician," he said.

"Can you build me a robot?"

"No," he said. He kissed her neck, and she shivered.

"You don't even know me," said Laverna.

"I asked around," said Jim Number Three.

"I don't like the sound of that," she said.

"I wanted to know what I was getting myself into."

"I've lived here all my life," said Laverna. "That's what you really need to know."

"Yes," he admitted. "I guess it is."

"I need to use your bathroom," she said. He helped her from the couch and escorted her to the rear of the trailer house, while opening the second button of his regulation polo shirt. He was a consummate gentleman. He flicked on the bathroom light and left the door slightly open. She did have to pee, but her arms prevented her from wiping. She could not ask for his assistance, but she didn't really care.

When she was done, she shook herself dry and used the edge of the countertop to push her sweatpants back into place. She stared into the bathroom mirror and checked her teeth, even though she hadn't eaten anything but peanuts and pills for the last six hours. She used her casts to push the door open wide enough for an exit. It was hard to flirt without hands, and she had long ago stopped wearing her hair long enough to toss. She growled at him when she returned to the living room.

He grinned at this, patted the empty cushion beside him.

"Your daughter is awfully nice," he said. "It's hard to raise kids with manners, I suppose."

"My daughter is an animal," said Laverna. "I'd prefer not to discuss her."

"Okay," said Jim Number Three. He leaned over and kissed her on the lips. "You might be the prettiest woman in this whole town. I think I've met most of them."

"Have you ever been electrocuted?"

"Not really," he said. "A couple of shocks, but that's to be expected."

"Sure," she said. "I've never really known an electrician before. I've always relied on Red Mabel when it comes to fuse boxes and shit like that."

"I went to school for it," he said. "I had a calling, I guess."

"My mother had a calling," she said. "She made the mistake of listening."

"I have a license and certification and everything." He kissed her again, and she felt her body swell with the pills, rise up to meet him. It had been a long time since this had happened to her.

"You could spend the night," he said.

"I sleep late," she said. "And I'm terrible when I wake up. Mouthy."

"Fine," he said. "I'll be gone when you get up."

An ax leaned in one corner of his bedroom. It was the regulation ax, the wooden handle inscribed with QVFD. She asked why he kept it at home, if it was a prop to impress the ladies. He nodded his head and undressed. He removed her panties, hung them from her cast.

He was careful as he lowered himself on top of her. To maneuver around her injuries, he placed his hands underneath the plaster that cut into her armpits, raised himself back up slowly. She was thankful he was in excellent shape. Jim Number Three did push-ups for the next twenty minutes.

His penis was a neat curve of flesh, slightly crooked. Her doctor would be pleased; they were being so cautious. He kissed her breasts in between every push-up. She felt top-heavy with pills, and wanted to ask him his last name. Instead, she watched his muscles bulge, and she found herself counting. At one hundred and fifty, she became his cheerleader. Excitedly, she counted out loud, delighted by his physical prowess. He was drunk but accurate, every push up truly impressive.

It felt strange to be so rigid, to have sex like this, her arms cemented in a permanent ninety-degree angle. Jim Number Three continued to do all the work. Each time he entered her, she smelled the top of his head, and she imagined she could smell the smoke in his hair, imagined that he would climb a ladder to save her.

Spin

★   ★   ★

The first Saturday of April, at 3:00 p.m., the Flood Girls were scheduled to play their first game of the season, versus the Eunice Volunteer Dispatch.

When Rachel woke up that morning, it was still snowing. She peered out her window at the billowing curtains, thick as the kinds that hung in theaters, ruffling, changing direction. She knew it was ferociously cold.

The phone call came from Ginger Fitchett at eleven o'clock.

"Game is called," said Ginger. "As you can tell, there is a blizzard outside, and as much as we hate those ladies from Eunice, we don't want them to drive here. Nor do we want to take the field. I wouldn't be able to see the batter's box."

Rachel thanked her, and thanked her higher power for sparing her from potential embarrassment. She bundled up in quilts, grateful she could spend the day with Laura Ingalls Wilder.

The next morning, the blizzard was gone. Rachel left her house shortly before noon, and it had already warmed to the midfifties. This was Quinn in April. Mercurial, stronger than you, full of surprises.

At her AA meeting, they celebrated Mr. Tyler's sobriety birthday. Even though he insisted, Rachel could not bring herself to call her former biology teacher by his first name, even though they had grown familiar. He was the only old man with enough balls to yell at Rachel for blaming her mother for everything.

When they passed around his three-year coin, Rachel held it in her palm and remembered her first AA birthday. Athena had presented the coin to her at their home group, and had made a speech about how far Rachel had come, and how she had worked for it, really worked for it, and they both had cried. Her coin was passed around the room for everyone to hold, to bless. And then there was cake and ice cream, and immediately afterward, Athena had taken her to another meeting, her version of celebration.

After the AA meeting, Rachel stood outside the library with her old men, and they discussed the prospects of the Flood Girls. She still did not understand their allegiance to her team, but they predicted a winning season.

There was a reason for the softball talk. The Chief returned from his truck and presented Rachel with a box.

She could tell it had been wrapped by his wife. He handed it over, without a word.

Inside the box was a softball glove, brand-new, a pair of black batting gloves, and an actual softball, neon green. The old men lit more cigarettes. She knew they had all chipped in on this purchase, but just like in meetings, they let the Chief provide the explanations.

"I heard you've been having some problems," he said.

"Bucky," said Rachel.

"Of course," said the Chief. "Every time you're not using this bad boy, I want you to put that ball inside the glove, and wrap the whole thing tight with rubber bands. That's how you break it in."

"Okay," said Rachel.

"Get in the truck," commanded the Chief.

———

Rachel and the Chief tossed the ball back and forth across the outfield, the air crisp and the sky completely cloudless, deeply blue.

Sometimes the Chief switched it up and lobbed it straight up into the sky to simulate a pop fly, and she lurched forward and tripped, or stumbled backward and tripped, but she could never get to the ball in time.

"You've gotta watch the batter," said the Chief. "If they are a lefty, the ball is coming to you. Before she even steps into the batter's box, you gotta move up toward the infield if you know she's a lightweight, and back the fuck up if you know she's a slugger."

"Thanks," said Rachel. She was still lying in the muddy grass as he gave this advice, exhausted after her last dodge for a pop-up. That one ended with her in the splits, sliding across the field, the ball bouncing three feet in front of her. At least it rolled toward her glove.

The Chief knelt down beside her. "You're doing all right, kid."

Rachel ripped up a clump of wet grass and threw it at him. "I don't want to be doing this at all."

"Sounds familiar," said the Chief. "Now we need to talk about putting the glove in front of your face."

"Okay," said Rachel.

"Stop with that kind of self-protection shit or I'm going to make you go to Al-Anon."

"Okay," said Rachel. Al-Anon was a threat that hung around her weekly meetings. The old men in AA did not care for Al-Anon. All of the men in Quinn went to AA, and the women went to Al-Anon. The women's meeting was double in size, and Black Mabel's father called them the Cookie-Baking Bitches.

"I need to ask you a question," said Rachel, the knees of her sweatpants soaking wet and caked with mud. This was definitely the time for humility. "I guess it's more like I'm asking for permission."

"Shoot," said the Chief.

"I'm ready to have sex," she said. She expected the Chief to stand up and walk away from her, or stammer and remind her that this sort of talk was the reason she needed a female sponsor. He did neither. He wiped the ball off on his work shirt and glared toward the third-base line. "I wanted to be honest with you."

She pushed herself up and held her palm out for the ball. The Chief moved farther away. They resumed their game of catch, shouting at each other. Her arm was getting better, and she could hit second base, and that was where the Chief stood, in the scuffs in the dirt where the bag would be secured.

The Chief fired a ball so hard at her that she caught it out of fear, as it was headed directly for her lady parts. The Chief was not a subtle man.

"I'm not going to give you permission," he shouted. "But I'll leave this one up to you. Pray on it."

"Deal." Rachel tried to throw the ball as hard as she could, but her hands were so slick that it slipped from her grasp and arced toward the first-base line. She jogged over to retrieve it.

"Hey," said the Chief. "You got a good spin on that one."

The Blizzard

★   ★   ★

The weather held, and Jake watched Rachel practice. It was after school on a Thursday, the April afternoons held light just a little longer with every day that passed. Jake brought his sketchbook, and drew Rachel in ball gowns, wedding dresses, and a black leather cat suit. She had no idea she was posing; he studied her as she practiced in the infield with her old men. Rachel called them the seven dwarfs, and Jake did not understand this, as they weren't particularly diminutive. Rachel was just really tall. Today, the eighth dwarf was Bucky—at least his name belonged with Dopey, Grumpy, et cetera.

The old men were determined to get Rachel in shape, break her of bad habits, although she had no habits to speak of, as softball was a new thing. The old men took to the field, and Rachel swung the bat again and again, sweating through her black shirt. The Chief had been pitching to her for a half hour, at least. She missed almost all the pitches, and the old men were bored, and gossiped and smoked, just waiting for action. Bucky crouched down behind the plate, and his long skinny legs poked out in severe angles, and Jake thought he looked like a grasshopper.

Outside the fence, Shyanne ran around the track, as if she ran fast enough and far enough, she could leave Quinn behind. She was a dot—the track was so far away, a dot that ran the quarter mile again and again. All he could see was hair and legs, and he approved. He looked down at his sketchbook, and Rachel's silhouette could easily be Shyanne, both blond and tall, the only two in Quinn. He began to draw clothes for Shyanne, sportswear. Rachel claimed to be Snow White among the seven dwarfs, but she and Shyanne resembled Sleeping Beauty.

He continued to sketch, waiting to hear the crack of the bat but only hearing the thud of the ball landing in Bucky's glove. Rachel swore at every missed pitch.

Then he heard thunder in the bleachers, as Shyanne ran up the wooden rows, carrying a water bottle. She collapsed next to Jake, grateful for the shade.

Even sweaty, Shyanne was stunning. She had incredible legs, and always wore athletic shorts, even in winter. She would be a senior next year, and Jake an eighth grader, but they barely knew each other. Like Ginger, Shyanne was aloof, and it was not snobbery, just resignation.

"You have supermodel legs," he said.

"Thank you," she said, and guzzled water. Jake examined her closely for flaws. Her face was pretty enough, her nose a bit wide, like most of the Swedes who had immigrated to Quinn. Full lips, eyes spaced just slightly too far apart. Her hair, however, needed some help. Despite the workout, her bangs remained crimped and sprayed, the hair spray collecting in the roots in little clumps.

"I think you should start wearing heels," he said.

"What's your name again?"

"Jake. I keep the book for the softball teams." He stared at her chest, and the absence of breasts made him deliriously happy. She needed to be sent to Milan right now, and live in a tiny, filthy apartment with fifteen other girls who looked just like her.

"Were you just looking at my chest?" She covered her breasts with a forearm, and scowled.

"I think you should be a model," he said. "And I want to help you."

"That's gross," she said. "They all have eating disorders."

"Sorry," he said. "Sometimes I just can't help myself." He closed his sketchbook, just in case she glimpsed his obsessions.

"Well, I know you're not flirting with me, so I'm okay with it. Enough with the model stuff, though."

"Can I fix your hair sometime?" Jake wanted to reach over and break up the shelf of bangs so very badly.

"Now you're freaking me out," she said. "Why are you even talking to me?"

"You sat down," pointed out Jake. "And you're the only person here."

"I used to date Number Fourteen," she said. "I know all about what happened with your psychotic friend."

"I'm not psychotic," he said. "I just think you need to know that heels would make your legs even more beautiful. You've only got a couple of years, you know. Models have a short shelf life. Like bananas."

"Stop," she said, but chewed on her lip, considering all of this. "I can't wear heels. I'm a jock."

"I hate that word," said Jake. He knew how mercurial teenage girls were, and he could not wait to travel in their pack. Up and down, vacillating between good girl and bad girl, depending on the number of wine coolers.

"Too bad," said Shyanne. "I'm a jock. I'm just a dumb jock getting harassed by a pushy gay kid. Go away."

"I was here first," pointed out Jake. "I just want to be your friend."

Shyanne burst into tears. She was definitely a teenage girl. Jake reached over to comfort her in a clumsy hug, careful not to crush her bangs.

The Chief ordered Rachel into right field, and six of the seven dwarfs lined up to bat. Bucky continued to crouch, knees near his ears. Jake watched Rachel trot out, deep into the green. She must be exhausted, he thought, but she wanted this. The Chief had taught her about ready position, and Jake watched as Rachel moved into the stance, waiting for the dwarfs to make contact. The Chief began to pitch to the owner of the grocery store, and Jake thought about bananas once more. In Quinn, the produce was shipped from far, far away. Like Rachel, most of the fruits and vegetables of his hometown were exotic, could not take root in the soil that froze solid for most of the year.

Shyanne calmed down, watching the action on the field. Rachel ran for a ball, determined as always, alone in the outfield. A cloud of dust spun around the far side of the track, a white van that did not belong there.

"Fucker," said Shyanne. "He's going to ruin the lanes."

As the van rounded the corner and got closer, Jake could see it was the dogcatcher. Gene Runkle was drunk as always, but at least the curbs around the track kept him from crashing. Jake squinted and could see a brown spot galloping in front of the white van. Jake could not help but root for the dog. Gene stopped and stumbled out, his hand holding a paper bag of dog biscuits. He called for the dog, and Jake watched Gene create a line of dog treats, a trail that led to the back of the white van. The dog was happy about this, tail wagging as he sauntered up to Gene, gobbled up the bait, too fast for capture. By the time Gene made an overture to open the back of the van, the dog had eaten all the biscuits and sped off once more. He slammed the van door and resumed the chase, the worst dogcatcher in the world.

———

It snowed a foot overnight, and the snow was still falling as Jake pretended to get ready for school. It was Friday, but there were no classes, just conferences with parents. Krystal had not met with Jake's teachers since the fourth grade. She always worked during the day. She let Jake forge her signature, and they were both grateful. His grades were just to the north of passable, but Krystal stopped caring altogether after Bert came along. She barely graduated from high school herself, and believed in practical, vocational education. He let his mother believe he would follow her path and go to nursing school, encouraged this lie by bringing home a small set of scrubs from the thrift store. He was horrified by the tiny clown heads that polka-dotted the material, but wore the uniform happily every Sunday night. Bert sought refuge at the Dirty Shame, and Jake watched *General Hospital* with his mother. Krystal videotaped the entire week, and pointed out errors in the medicine practiced in Port Charles, criticized the nursing staff for not wearing sensible shoes. Of course, this all stopped when Bert found God, and they lost cable.

In Quinn, there was no broadcast reception, no ABC, CBS, or NBC. Even with the tallest of antennas, the mountains prevented this. As Jake left his trailer house with his book bag, he stepped out into another blizzard. Quinn had six months of winter, and six months of fire season. Despite the amount of snowfall, the lightning sparked wildfires from May until November. The town of Quinn had been burned twice before, and would not be fooled again. The snow was welcomed.

He took the usual road out of the trailer court, just in case Bert was watching. He would double back in an hour, and Bert would not see him enter Rachel's back door. Jake stepped in the tracks from the snowplow, already filling again. He continued into town, past the movie theater, finally showing *Home Alone*, even though it had been released in November, five months ago. Jake continued on, past the Booze and Bait, closed as usual. Behind the counter of the hardware store, he could see terrible Della smacking her gum, and did not wave.

Buley had no clothes for him today, but that was fine. He was here for a different reason.

"AA books?" Buley was not rattled by his request, just called for Rocky. "I'm glad Bert's getting help. It's been a long time coming."

"They aren't for Bert," said Jake. "They're for me."

"Interesting," said Buley. "You are much too vain to be an alcoholic."

Jake followed Rocky to the rear of the store. For some reason, Buley kept all the self-help books with the hunting clothes. Perhaps she was trying to send a message. Jake bought a big blue book written for drunks, and several paperbacks written for the people who loved them. He didn't love Rachel, not yet anyway, but he wanted to understand her.

————

The sky was a pearly white color, and the snow kept coming. Feet of it; this was an honest-to-God blizzard, not unusual for Montana in April. Jake entered Rachel's back door, and the winds pushed the snow across her yard in great dunes that rose all the way to the top of the privacy fence. Her back door was almost frozen shut, but Jake managed to yank it open. Inside her house, he pulled the space heater into his sewing corner.

He had made progress. Five of the shirts were completely done, and hidden deep inside his bedroom closet. He worked on these shirts only when Rachel was gone. When she was home, he sewed things for her house, and clothing for himself.

Jake did not turn on the stereo, tried to remain as quiet as possible, just in case Bert was spying. When he heard footsteps on the porch, the sound of boots stomping to dislodge the snow, he dove behind the couch.

Black Mabel entered without knocking. Jake stood up from behind the couch, and she swung a snow shovel at him.

"It's just me," he protested, holding up his hands in surrender.

"Oh," she said, eyes tiny and darting. Jake could tell she was more stoned than usual, and offered no explanation as he returned to the sewing machine. It would only confuse her.

"I'm here to shovel off the roof." Black Mabel was dressed like an arctic explorer, her familiar black trench coat straining to contain the thick layers of down underneath, goggles dangling from her neck.

"Okay," Jake said, and tapped at the foot pedal as the needle began to whir.

"I don't want the roof to collapse. There's four feet of snow up there."

"You don't have to explain to me," said Jake. "I've been watching you do it for years."

"I made a promise," said Black Mabel.

"Be careful," said Jake, knowing that she was reckless. He kept sewing and lost himself in the fifth T-shirt. He listened to the shriek of the wind and the thumps and scrapes of Black Mabel. She had made a promise to Frank, and apparently it stretched through the years, extended to his daughter.

He made an extra grilled cheese sandwich, and waved out the back door until he caught her attention. He didn't want to shout her name, just in case Bert was listening. She cleared half the roof, had paused to catch her breath against the impotent chimney. She stared at him until he returned with a plate, pointed at her sandwich.

———

Above him, Jake could hear Black Mabel continue to shovel. He kept sewing, occasionally stopping to watch out the window as giant drifts came cascading down, until they piled so high that the window was blocked from snow from the roof. He had no fear that Black Mabel would slip and fall. Black Mabel was a capable woman, and if she fell, she would only land safely in the enormous banks of snow.

Mr. Sunshine

★ ★ ★

*L*averna's casts were removed in the third week of April. She was able to smoke her own cigarettes whenever she wanted to, and enjoy baths by herself. She loved Red Mabel, but she enjoyed having the house to herself. She no longer had to bite her tongue as Red Mabel bathed her; the humiliation of being naked and cradled near her best friend's armpits was exacerbated by the smell—Red Mabel needed a bath of her own.

There was one visitor who she tolerated; Jim Number Three continued to stop by in the afternoons and read to her. They were three-quarters of the way through *Roots*, and Red Mabel had taken to calling him Kunta Kinte behind his back.

Laverna bought the property on the river in 1983. She couldn't live in the house that she once shared with Rachel. Everywhere she went, she saw another reminder of her asshole daughter.

At the time, there were no neighbors. It was a half acre surrounded by aspen trees on one side, and a weeping willow on the other. Behind the house was the river—usually muddy brown, but on good days, green like an old bottle.

She took out a loan to buy a brand-new trailer house, and to place it on a permanent foundation. In Quinn, that made it a real house. Nobody could drive it away ever again.

She made the last payment four months ago, and despite the fact that it was January, she and Red Mabel had celebrated by drinking bottles of champagne and running around the yard topless.

The house was set far enough back that she had no fear of floods. The riverbank was mighty but sloped gradually. The first year she lived there, she spent a hundred dollars on crocus and paperwhite bulbs, threw them off the back deck scattershot, and now the crocuses came up in March, and then the paperwhites in May. Between those flowers and the butter-cups and forget-me-nots that grew there naturally, she considered herself a master gardener.

Red Mabel mowed Laverna's lawn, and fixed everything that needed fixing, and cleaned the gutters. She even hung the lights at Christmas.

Laverna was taken care of, and knew she would never marry again. Jim Number Three was a plaything, a diversion. Laverna wanted to live her life like a desperado, unencumbered and free to shoot back whenever necessary.

This was why it pained her to call the Chief.

His wife answered. Laverna knew her peripherally, from the grocery store or the post office or city council meetings. The Chief's wife occasionally attended the Fireman's Ball, but she always left early.

She seemed scared, however, when Laverna identified herself.

"He's not here," she said. "Do you want me to give him a message? Is there something wrong with your chimney?"

"I would call 911 if I had a chimney fire," said Laverna. "Just tell him to come see me when he has a chance."

"At the bar?"

"At my house," said Laverna. She scratched at her strange pale arms. They had grown a scraggly fur during her convalescence.

"Oh," said his wife.

"It's not what you think," explained Laverna. "This is about my daughter."

"I love Rachel to death," said his wife.

"Are you kidding me?" Laverna was suddenly angry; she hated not knowing things.

"Excuse me?"

"Never mind," said Laverna. "Just send him this way."

He arrived a few hours later, in his special red pickup truck, embla-zoned with QVFD on the door. He carried jars of something.

She met him at the door.

"Apple butter," he said, and handed her the jars. "From the missus."

"Is it like applesauce?"

"No, ma'am."

"Is it like jelly?"

"No."

"Then what the hell is it?"

"You wanted to talk to me?"

"Sorry," said Laverna. "Come in."

She ushered him out to the back deck. The river was running high, and giant pieces of bark and fallen trees rushed past, and closer to the bank, swirls of dead leaves spun in fast eddies. Today, the river was muddy, the color of the apple butter.

Instinctively, Laverna grabbed two beers from the refrigerator but then put them back and brought out Bubble Up instead. He would have to drink from the can.

She handed him the soda and sat down on a wooden deck chair. He lit a cigarette, and she pushed an ashtray toward him. They watched osprey swoop down at the water and then return to their bald perches across the water.

"I suppose you're wondering why I asked you here," she said.

"Nope." The Chief was the only man in Quinn who Laverna could not intimidate.

"How do you know?"

"There's only one thing you and I have in common, Laverna."

"How is she doing?"

"Why don't you find out for yourself?" The Chief refused to make eye contact, and continued to stare out at the river.

"I've got nothing to say to her," said Laverna. "I just need a body in the right field."

The Chief puffed on his cigarette and finally turned to look her square in the eye. "What exactly do you want from me?"

"She's scared of the ball. She covers her face with her glove and she won't swing at anything."

"Rachel isn't scared of the ball, Laverna. She's scared of you."

"I'm not following."

"If she does nothing, she can't screw it up." The Chief removed his ball cap. "She does nothing, because she doesn't want to make a mistake."

"That doesn't make any sense." Laverna looked out at the riverbank. A month ago, the crocuses had appeared, blue flowers pushed up through inches of whiteness and revealed themselves, polka-dotted the entire snowy bank.

"She doesn't want to disappoint you," he said. "I figure she's done enough of that."

"She disappoints me by not catching the goddamn ball," said Laverna.

"Then why did you put her on the team?"

"I told you," said Laverna. "I had no choice. There's only so many women in this goddamn town." They watched a giant gray log come down the river, dragging through the high grass along the shore. It was an ancient thing, riddled with holes from woodpeckers.

"You know she's no good at sports," said the Chief. "You're up to something."

"I guess I want to keep my eye on her," Laverna confessed.

"That's my job," said the Chief. "You can stop doing that."

"Can you blame me? I mean, Jesus Christ, she completely ruined my life."

"That's what kids are for," said the Chief.

"You don't have any kids," said Laverna.

"Exactly," said the Chief. "I wrecked enough things on my own. I've spent the last twenty years making it up to my wife." He stubbed out his cigarette and stood up. "I'm way ahead of you. Been playing catch with her for the last few weeks."

"Tell your wife thank you for that apple stuff."

"I will," said the Chief.

"I never thought she would come back," admitted Laverna.

"It would do you some good to forgive her," said the Chief. "It might even make you a happier person."

"You're not exactly Mr. Sunshine," she said.

"That's because I'm still trying to forgive myself," he said.

He left her there on the back porch. She heard him drive away, and she sat there and watched the river. There was no telling what could float by next.

The Flood Girls versus Quinn Lumber Mill

★　　★　　★

*J*ake predicted disaster. This was the first game of the season, and the Flood Girls were playing against another team from Quinn. The bleachers were completely full.

He arrived at the softball field at five thirty. The outfield was freshly mowed, and Jake could smell the grass from his seat on the far left of the bleachers. Bucky's white sneakers were stained green from the clippings.

Jake watched as Bucky secured the padded, puffy squares to each corner of the diamond. He laid the flat mat of home plate after using his measuring tape, and nodded to Jake in the bleachers. He and Jake were the only paid employees of the league, and they behaved like professionals.

"Nice outfit," called out Bucky. Jake wore his black sailor pants and a white shirt with epaulets. He knew that he looked like a sailor and didn't really care. If there was a flood in Quinn, Jake was ready to command the ship.

"Thanks," said Jake, ignoring the tittering among the crowd. He was used to such a reaction. "I wanted to make sure we matched." And they did—Bucky wore his umpire's uniform, also black and white, the shirt divided into vertical stripes. Bucky looked down at his outfit and shook his head.

Jake opened his scorebook, brand-new for 1991, and carefully inscribed the names into the boxes with a pencil. He had a special pencil case just for softball, and it contained eighteen pencils, two sharpeners just in case one malfunctioned. It also was loaded with cough drops, allergy medication, and a cloth handkerchief to offer others, to be polite.

Laverna had had her casts removed, and she handed him her roster on a piece of notebook paper. Her bare arms were nearly the same color as the casts had been. They looked scrawnier, too, although he doubted tending bar had ever made her muscular.

"This is going to be a shit show," she said, and waited for him to print the names into his book. Although several people in the crowd clamored for her attention, Laverna stared grimly out onto the field.

"Bucky is a professional," Jake assured, and finished copying down the last player of the Flood Girls. "He'll keep this under control."

"Might need stun guns," muttered Laverna. "I know all these people. And they're assholes." Nervously, she returned to her dugout with the roster.

Jake looked around the bleachers and wondered if the ten dollars he was paid per game would be worth it today. He was supposed to remain unbiased, but his allegiance would be with Laverna's team. His project was coming along, he supposed, the seventh shirt nearly finished. He had considered making shirts for himself and Bucky, but that would only result in cries of favoritism. The Flood Girls could use all the help they could get, but Jake would behave like a professional. He could not afford to lose this job.

The Flood Girls were playing the ladies from Quinn Lumber Mill, but the bleachers were full of firemen's wives, ex-wives, widows, or daughters. The people who surrounded him in the bleachers had sharpened their knives for Rachel, and they did not hide their hatred. They leered at her in the dugout, snickered when she let the balls roll past during warm-up. A small town never forgets, or forgives. Rachel was still a mistress and a murderess in their eyes.

The Flood Girls' fans sat in the rear corner of the bleachers. The pack of old men came to cheer on Laverna, and take delight in the chaos. They had been coming to support the Flood Girls for as long as Jake had been keeping score, and Jake supposed that Laverna's team provided the most entertainment in the league. All the old men looked the same to Jake, except for the Chief. Rachel told Jake that he was her sponsor, and Jake had read enough of the AΛ books to know how difficult the job must be. Especially today.

The ladies from Quinn Lumber Mill all wore orange T-shirts, and during their warm-up, they threw as hard as they could. Jake winced at the smack of the ball in their gloves. They were out for blood.

Before the game began, as both teams continued throwing balls back and forth on the field, Jake saw the stray dog enter the dugout. Apparently, Della was unable to tame him. The dog seemed drawn to Laverna, and sniffed at her feet. Laverna tried to shoo the dog away, but it wouldn't leave. Finally, Laverna bent down, and Jake figured she was going to pick up the dog and throw it toward the concession stand. Instead, the dog nipped at Laverna's calf. Laverna screamed, and Red Mabel was there in seconds and swatted the dog in the head with her baseball glove. The dog yelped and bolted out of the dugout.

"For fuck's sake," said a voice behind Jake. He turned around and saw one of the volunteers from the ambulance hand his beer to his wife and make his way down the steps of the bleachers. "This game hasn't even started yet!"

The volunteer took his time getting to the dugout of the Flood Girls. Laverna was cursing, and Red Mabel threw the duffel bag that contained the first-aid kit at the volunteer. Jake watched as he pushed up Laverna's slacks, and cleaned the area with antiseptic and wrapped it several times with gauze.

The warm-ups were over, and Bucky dusted off home plate and addressed the bleachers.

"Play ball!" Jake knew that Bucky loved saying those words.

Rachel's first at bat came during the bottom of the second inning, and she was wearing her usual punk rock clothes. Her T-shirt was much too big for her, and the neck was stretched out from years of wear. The gaping T-shirt revealed the strap of a lacy black bra and her small amount of cleavage. Jake was scared. If Rachel had been sixteen, Laverna would have sent her back to the house to change.

Jake wanted to close his eyes for the first pitch.

Bucky had no problem pronouncing it a strike. Rachel didn't even bother swinging at it.

"That bitch has some nerve," declared a woman, prehistoric-looking, all brow and jaw.

"Please watch your language," said Jake. Huffily, he turned back to await the next pitch.

The bleachers snickered at him. The troll toasted the man next to her, and beer slopped on Jake's elbow. He turned to glare.

"Look," said Jake. "I've got a job to do. I need to keep a clean and accurate record of this game. Especially the clean part." He made a show of wiping away the drops of beer on the corner of the scorebook.

"Shut up, freak," said the troglodyte. Jake inched away from her.

Jake observed Rachel in the batter's box. Something was wrong. She had let the ball go sailing past her with a purposeful nonchalance. She dressed more provocatively than usual. This seemed to be the old Rachel, and he wished the Chief would descend from his perch to give her a good talking-to.

The next pitch also flew directly across the plate.

Bucky called the ball as it smacked into the catcher's mitt. "Strike!"

"Slut!" The woman next to him waited for this exact moment, watching the pitch closely, shouting at almost the same time as Bucky's call.

The bleachers whooped at this, and someone slapped the troglodyte on the back. Jake wanted to curl up and put the scorebook over his head as the laughter continued, but instead stared down at Rachel, who stood in the batter's box, attempting to appear oblivious, even though the woman's voice had been loud enough to hear in the outfield.

The third pitch went wild, and someone else had yelled out "Whore!" before Bucky even had the chance to declare it a ball. The entire infield from Quinn Lumber Mill chortled.

Jake knew it wasn't the troglodyte, as she was sitting right next to him. This was a man's voice, and Jake didn't bother turning around to determine the source.

"Please," said Jake, speaking to the air in front of him. "There are rules for unsportsmanlike conduct."

"We ain't playing, princess." The voice was familiar, and Jake wondered if it was Ron, the owner of the movie theater. "Ain't nothing you can do."

Bucky finally realized something wasn't right, and swiveled his neck to stare into the bleachers. He looked as confused as always.

Jake put his face in his hands, and then reluctantly, he studied Rachel again. She was staring at the pitcher, expressionless, as if she couldn't hear any of the heckling.

The pitcher, doubled over in laughter, managed to regain her composure. She grinned as she lobbed another perfect pitch to the catcher.

Before Bucky could call Rachel out, the bleachers bombarded the field with slurs. There were many voices this time, and all around Jake they hollered out.

"Slut! Slut! Slut!"

Red Mabel leaped from the bench and ran into the bleachers, and Laverna didn't even attempt to stop her.

The Flood Girls stood up in the dugout as Red Mabel tore through the bleachers, beer flying everywhere as she took hold of some woman's hair and yanked her down the steps. Jake wished it had been the troglodyte, but Red Mabel's anger was never accurate.

The crowd was on their feet, shouting out profanities, and yet Rachel just stood there, waiting for a pitch that would never come.

Two other women jumped on Red Mabel's back, which was a mistake. They surely should have known better. One got an elbow to the mouth, and the other was thrown through the air and slid across the wooden steps.

Jake shrieked and ran just as the beer started being thrown, as four volunteer firemen took each one of Red Mabel's limbs and dragged her from the bleachers. She cursed and spat in their faces.

The volunteer firemen pulled Red Mabel into the grass, and two of them sat on her. Red Mabel managed to bite one of the firemen, and that was when Bucky finally called the game, over after two innings.

Rachel calmly walked back to the dugout. She dropped the bat in the dirt as if nothing had happened.

After the crowd dispersed, Jake walked onto the field and tried to hand over his scorebook to Bucky, who frowned and kicked at the dirt around home plate. Bucky threw his count clicker to the ground.

The Flood Girls were silent as Jake approached the dugout. The women were packing up their duffel bags. Martha and the Sinclairs were already gone. Laverna comforted Red Mabel. The gauze on Laverna's calf was perfectly white. Jake wondered if the dog had even drawn blood.

Jake stepped into the dugout and grabbed Rachel's hand.

"You should probably come with me," he said. "If anybody tries anything in the parking lot, I can give an excellent and accurate witness statement."

The parking lot was still full of vehicles, but they made it to Rachel's truck without incident. There were a few catcalls, but the riot Red Mabel caused seemed to temper them a bit. For a full minute, Rachel sat in her truck and stared out at the empty field. If she was going to drive, this would not do. Jake shook her arm, until she turned, and regarded him with heavy eyes.

"There's something you need to see," he said.

"I'm not in the mood," said Rachel.

"Please," he protested. "We need to flee this scene. As soon as possible."

"I just want to go home," she said.

"They could be waiting for you there."

Silently, she turned the key in the ignition and followed his directions.

———

At the cemetery, they stood in front of Frank's plot.

"I haven't seen this before," said Rachel. "That makes me feel like an asshole."

"I loved him," said Jake. "He was the only man who was ever nice to me."

They stared down at the plot; clumps of grass emerged, and dandelions had popped up, beginning their march to take over the bare soil.

"I don't know what to say about today," said Rachel. "I guess I was kind of expecting it this whole time, to tell you the truth."

Jake reached out for her hand. "You remind me of him," he said. "Good and bad. You've taken really good care of me, and you don't have to. But today you had that look in your eye."

"What look?"

"Frank got that look sometimes. Like he wanted to burn everything down. Like he was staring past everything already and he could see the ashes." Jake stared at Rachel until she looked at his face. "He had that look the last time I saw him."

"I don't want to burn anything down," said Rachel. "I'm done with destroying things."

"Exactly," Jake said, and continued to hold her hand, as the sounds of a riding lawn mower began, and they both ignored it.

When they drove back through town, they saw the dog. It ignored the nonexistent traffic, and galloped across Main Street, still on the run.

Fireman's Ball, 1981

★ ★ ★

As sixth period finally ended, Rachel drew a pentagram in the center of the pig, the only mark on the paper. The rest of the biology class actually dissected pigs, and the room was filled with the sounds of popping and ripping. Rachel refused. Her pig remained on Mr. Tyler's desk, Saran wrapped in a cake pan. Her customized assignment was to consult her textbook and draw the circulatory system. She also refused to do this, and put on her toughest face when the bell rang. She entered the halls of her high school, a place where she had once been beloved. She sought protection in the freshmen corridor, walking to the last period of the day, study hall. Before, being wasted and slutty had been charming, had elevated her status. But crossing Laverna was unforgivable. Parents had apparently warned their children to stay far, far away from her, had encouraged them to say awful things right to her face, to scrawl terrible things on her locker door. She thought that the girls in her class would eventually get their fill, would gobble up all the blood in the water. A year later, the knives were still out.

After class, Rachel just wanted to get the hell out of the building, go home, and get ready for the Fireman's Ball. She was going tonight, despite Black Mabel's and Krystal's warning her of the carnage.

Rachel's locker door was open.

Inside her locker, a pile of fetal pigs.

The smell rose up, and she nearly gagged. She heard the laughter, and was surrounded by the bravest girls in her biology class. Rachel's coat and purse were soaked with formaldehyde. She would not let them win. She grabbed her coat and shook the bodies onto the floor. More laughter, as Rachel slammed shut her locker door.

Della Dempsey tried to stop Rachel from leaving. She boldly stood in her path, and screamed with the others. "Murderer!" "Slut!" Rachel was a foot taller than Della and threw an elbow, caught Della right on the chin. Della cried out and fell to the floor, dramatic as always. Rachel stepped over her, kept on walking. She had a bus to catch.

As she strode down the hall, other girls waited with contraband from biology class. Rachel kept walking, even as they threw tiny hearts and stomachs in her hair.

That night, Rachel was going dancing.

———

She rode the bus to the trailer court, shivering in her seat. She had stuffed her coat into a garbage can. She had carried her purse onto the bus, and the bus driver cursed at the smell.

She sat in the back, surrounded by empty seats. The bus ride took twenty minutes, and Rachel removed the soggy SAT study guide from her studded purse. She memorized vocabulary words during every bus ride. She had to think about college. She spent the weekends on math, the math she had once cheated on. She no longer had peers to terrorize for answers. She had always known she was a smart girl but had never wanted it to define her. She used to be the fun girl, the promiscuous girl, the dangerous girl. Now she was determined to be the girl who was leaving.

Riding the bus was embarrassing, but Rachel no longer had friends with cars. Krystal had a car, but Krystal also had a baby. Her sole friend was not only dumb but boring. She was the very definition of average; her only distinguishing characteristics came from a makeup bag. Style had changed, but Rachel could not persuade her friend to put down the electric blue Maybelline eyeliner, or the Avon lipstick, Neon Orchid. Krystal's pink lipstick was her thing, just like Rachel's was surliness.

When Rachel had been kicked out of her mother's house, she lugged her two giant army duffel bags to the Sinclair, called Krystal from the payphone. Rachel's scalp burned where the air touched the wound, and her upper thigh ached from her mother's kick. Nothing hurt on the inside, because Rachel would not allow it.

Everything fit in the backseat of Krystal's Datsun. Krystal didn't even ask what had happened. She knew that Rachel had done something bad, because that was just what Rachel did. It was Frank's problem now.

Her father's door had been unlocked, and the house was dark. Rachel sat on the couch and rolled a joint, put on her headphones and listened to Blondie, got so stoned that she envisioned herself as a punk rock Goldilocks, and decided not to raid the refrigerator, just in case the bears showed up.

She rolled a second joint, and her headphones were so loud that she didn't even notice that he was suddenly standing above her.

She pulled off the headphones, untangled them from her hair. It still hurt where her mother had partially scalped her. She realized that the house was thick with pot smoke.

"I'm living with you now," she said.

He stared at her.

"I'm Rachel," she said, and he nodded. "You can stop sending child support checks."

He didn't seem to be bothered by the pot smoke, in fact, none of this seemed to surprise him at all. She reached out and extended her hand, an offering of a handshake. He surprised her by pulling her toward him in a stiff, awkward hug. She rolled her eyes.

"I'm used to sleeping on couches," she said. "You won't even notice I'm here."

"I'm in the woods most of the year," he said.

"Also, I'm a vegetarian."

"Good to know," he said. She lit the joint again and took a deep drag. She offered it to her father, but he shook his head.

"I mostly eat french fries," she said. "But I guess I won't be allowed at the Dirty Shame anymore."

"Is it really that bad?"

"Yes," admitted Rachel. "I'm going to need an allowance."

He sighed. "I figured this day would come, sooner or later," he said.

"Really?"

"Even in the woods, I hear stories," he said.

Black Mabel delivered her allowance every Friday night. Frank had some sort of arrangement with her, and Rachel could not understand it, because her father was a big square. Black Mabel mowed the lawn in the summer, shoveled in the winter, switched out the filters of the furnace, and changed the lightbulbs. This had been going on for years. In return, Black Mabel had a place to hide from the cops, or sleep off her binges. Black Mabel lived in a garage on her father's property, but he did not tolerate her drug use. He locked her out of the garage when he suspected she was high. Thus, Black Mabel was mostly homeless.

———

Rachel soaked her purse in the kitchen sink, dumped in an entire box of baking soda. She did not pay attention in chemistry class, but vaguely remembered that baking soda counteracted acid. She wasn't sure if formaldehyde was an acid, but she was determined to save the purse. While it soaked, she called Krystal.

"We're going," said Rachel. "Don't even try to argue with me."

"Why do you call me? I'm right next door."

"Rocky gives me the creeps, and your baby is always shitting."

"It's a bad idea," said Krystal. "I heard Red Mabel got a hold of a flamethrower."

"Don't wear hair spray," said Rachel. "And it's not a bad idea. It's a fun idea."

Krystal was too easy. "I guess," she said.

"I've got wine coolers," said Rachel. She waved at Krystal from the kitchen window. "Hang on a second." Rachel decided to check Black Mabel's stash. She left the phone on the kitchen counter, removed a brick from behind the impotent fireplace. She waved the glassine envelope at Krystal and picked up the phone. "And coke!"

"Come over at seven," said Krystal. Rachel watched her hang up the phone, her lips so pink they were visible across the gloomy yard.

The purse was not salvageable. Rachel dug in her closet for another purse. There was so much time to kill. She chose a pink T-shirt she had cut in half, cut again into fringes, each fringe weighed down with a giant safety pin. She had to wear clothes for a quick getaway, so she reluctantly put on jeans, black denim, splattered with bleach. Instead of heels, she wore army boots. She might need to run. Despite the threat of the flame-thrower, she sprayed her hair into giant blond curtains.

Satisfied, she sat on the couch. She still had an hour to kill, so she opened her spiral notebook and continued the work on her application essay. She was determined to go to the University of Montana and study business, get a degree, and learn how to be cutthroat, and return to Quinn for a hostile takeover of the Dirty Shame. Her essay was about her drunken mother abandoning her, for pity points. Rachel left out the parts about fucking her drunken mother's boyfriend, and the subsequent negligent homicide.

It had happened on that couch.

Rachel had lost interest in Billy within a week of seducing him. He could not understand why she turned so cold, but kept coming to Frank's trailer. She tolerated him for months, because she had no other friends. He was in the same boat, kept getting his ass kicked every time he came out of the woods. Even the other Petersens turned on him. Rachel could not understand why he didn't return to Georgia—Laverna's power did not extend past the Continental Divide. Billy was needy, and Rachel hated needy. But she was lonely, and he worshipped her. She tried to break up with him, but he kept returning, every weekend, Frank's house the only safe place outside of the woods. When winter came, and the logging crew disbanded, Billy returned to the butcher shop, which made Rachel even more disgusted. She made him shower two times before fucking.

On Christmas Eve, he showed up at Frank's trailer with a mangled face. He had been beaten up so badly he couldn't see out of his left eye. Whining, ugly, and smelling like steak, Rachel could barely tolerate him. Thankfully, Black Mabel had a new line on painkillers, and Rachel popped four Percocets, and stared out the window at Krystal's house, where it seemed like Christmas. Rocky had hung lights. There was no Christmas cheer in Frank's house, just Billy's complaints and Rachel's drug haze. At least the house hung with green smoke.

Billy drank fourteen cans of beer in two hours, lined up each empty on the coffee table. He usually drank, but not this much.

"Your mother has a vendetta," he slurred.

"Duh," said Rachel.

"I want to take you away," he said.

"I don't think so," said Rachel. "I think it would be better if we went our separate ways. It would be harder for Red Mabel to track us down."

"I can't leave without you," he said, tears seeping out of his one good eye.

"Please," said Rachel. "Go. Without me. Like, tomorrow."

"I ain't leaving you," he said, sobbing now.

Rachel rolled her eyes and pulled away from him. "My mother would report you for kidnapping her teenage daughter and transporting her across state lines. That's a federal crime and shit."

"I WON'T LEAVE YOU!"

"Jesus Christ," said Rachel. "You didn't even get me anything for Christmas." This made Billy cry even harder. Rachel opened the pill bottle, shook out five Percocet. "Take these." Billy squinted with his good eye, swallowed them with a swig of beer. When he was still talking, half an hour later, she made him take four more. He finally passed out, and Rachel lay in her bed, too high to sleep. Through her bedroom window, she watched the lights next door.

Christmas morning, and there were no presents. She lay in her bed, and remembered the holidays with Laverna, who always spoiled her, no matter how bad she had been.

In the living room, Billy was blue. He was on his back, vomit all over his chest and mouth. Rachel felt nothing, just an urge to protect herself.

Rachel pounded on Krystal's door. Even though they were opening presents, Krystal left Rocky and the baby, could see the panic on Rachel's face. Krystal was still in her first year of night classes, but knew enough to call it cyanosis.

"Holy crap," she said. "I've never seen this in real life. I mean, I've seen pictures, but he's really, really blue. What did he take?"

"He was drunk," said Rachel.

"That's it?"

"I gave him some pills," she said.

"Downers?"

"Painkillers. He was in pain! And I wanted him to shut up."

"It worked," said Krystal. "It's called aspiration. He choked on his own vomit."

"Fuck," said Rachel.

"Merry Christmas," said Krystal.

When she called the volunteer dispatch, Rachel drank a beer to steel herself. She didn't even want to think about the people at home, listening to the police scanner, even though it was Christmas morning. She drank another when the sheriff showed up and pronounced it an overdose. She was grateful that the ambulance did not disrupt the trailer park with sirens, but the people came anyway, watched as the heavy black bag was carried out through the driveway.

Rachel and Krystal parked in the Datsun and snorted lines of coke on the dashboard, even thought it was dusty, and they kept sneezing.

Inside the fire hall, Rachel and Krystal were so high that they barely noticed the stares, the glares, the admonitions. They needed to be seen by as many people as possible, needed an alibi. They were waiting to be seen by Laverna and Red Mabel. Holding hands, they did a lap around the fire trucks, at warp speed. Rachel's mother was nowhere to be found.

A kid with the biggest buckteeth Rachel had ever seen carried a coffee can, wrapped in pink construction paper. Scrawled with a sloppy Magic Marker, the can solicited donations for the Petersen family. The kid was pathetic-looking, and Rachel was angered when she realized how much money he would collect. Billy's extended Montana family did not deserve any compensation, but passing the coffee can was a tradition in Quinn.

Rachel and Krystal checked the bathroom, and no Laverna. Rachel cut more lines on the mirror of her compact, and tried to pick a fight with Krystal about her lipstick and eyeliner. After another line of coke, Krystal finally acquiesced. Rachel was applying a shimmery blue eye shadow when the women's bathroom door burst open, and the small space was invaded by a trio of large women. The women saw the cocaine, and shut the door behind them. The women had moved to town to work in the brand-new silver mine. They wanted to touch Rachel's hair, and she let them. She needed all the friends she could get. Krystal was slightly terrified, and excused herself to cower in the bathroom stall.

On the dance floor, there were nine more of these women, and they surrounded her, protected her from flying beer cups. Ginger Fitchett pushed her way through the ring of silver miners, swatting at them with her expensive purse.

"You've got some nerve," said Ginger, pointing a finger at Rachel's chest.

"Fucking snob," said Rachel, and let the tallest silver miner dip her backward. Krystal danced by herself, one shimmery eye twitching. Ginger would not allow Rachel to ignore her, and grabbed her arm.

"I'm serious," said Ginger. "Hasn't there been enough suffering?"

"Oh my god," said Rachel. "Go away!" Ginger screamed as two of the miners picked her up, lifting her off the floor and depositing her near one of the flaming barrels. Ginger kept screaming, and stomped her foot, ineffectual because the floor was cement and the disco was incredibly loud. "She's underage! Underage!"

Krystal flew across the room and waved a finger in Ginger's face. "She's not drinking! Don't be such a twat!"

Ginger was horrified by this outburst, and they watched as she commandeered the judge. Apparently, seeking legal advice.

The silver miners cheered for Krystal and hoisted her up on their shoulders. Krystal was not used to this admiration, and basked in it, and was smiling when she joined Rachel on the dance floor.

Rachel cornered the kid with the buckteeth in a smoky corner. She dug in her pocket and gave him six dimes and a penny. He gawked at her in silence while she deposited the coins through the slit on the plastic lid. He didn't say a word when she snatched the coffee can from his hands.

"Let me help you out, kid." Rachel tucked the can under her arm, made sure no one was looking. "I'm the prettiest girl here." At this, he nodded. "I bet I can get way more money than you." The kid continued to stare in shock, until she shooed him away. In the bathroom, she covered the can with paper towels, buried it at the bottom of the wastebasket. Thirty dollars and ninety-four cents, sixty-one of which came from her. She stuffed her pockets with the cash. She had earned this money.

When she returned to the dance floor, a group of volunteer firemen dared to enter the circle, and the most barrel-chested asked them to leave.

"No," said Rachel. "I paid for tickets."

"I'll give you your money back," he said. "You're causing a scene. The judge sent me over here."

Rachel tossed her hair and laughed. She pointed at a short fireman with a long beard. "I fucked him," she said. She twirled, pointed at one of the Applehaus boys. "And I fucked him. And his brother." She blew the barrel-chested fireman a kiss. "Sorry you missed out."

"My brother is a cop," said the barrel-chested fireman. "He's right over there."

"Fine." Rachel pretended to look around the fire hall. "I'd like to report the Applehaus boys for child molestation."

"You aren't a child!" The older Applehaus stepped forward. He was recently married, and furious. "You were never a child!"

Krystal wheeled into the middle of the circle. Somewhere, somehow, she had been given roller skates. "They're here," she called out, executing a perfect barrel roll. Krystal continued her impressive orbits. She crouched down on her skates and stopped herself with her hands. She beckoned Rachel over to a fire engine, out of sight from the left side of the fire hall.

"They're here," she repeated, one roller skate remained in the air, wheels continuing to spin.

Rachel peeped through the truck window, and there was her mother and Red Mabel. Ginger was sobbing to them, and Red Mabel craned her neck, ready to seek and destroy. Rachel could barely see her mother's outfit through the warp of the glass, but it seemed to be all shoulder pads and severe waistline. Laverna had lost weight.

Bolting out into the February gales, they leaped into the Datsun, Krystal taking the time to turn on the heat, because her socks were frozen.

"GO!" Rachel reached over and pulled the gearshift into reverse, but Krystal was too addled, and the car lurched backward, nearly clipping Ginger's brand-new Mazda RX-7. Screaming with joy, they tore out of the parking lot, although the velocity was unnecessary. The Dirty Shame was only two blocks away.

Krystal parked in the snowy alley, and they dashed to the back door of the bar. Rachel prayed her mother was still cheap and had not changed the locks. Krystal jumped from one foot to the other, her socks soaking with snow. Rachel kept her key from her weekend shifts, and the door opened easily. The good fortune continued, as a train barreled through town, would cover up any noise.

Krystal kept an eye on her watch, as Rachel crawled behind the bar, just in case anybody walked past and peered into the window. There was a twinge in Rachel's heart, as she opened the safe. The combination was unchanged—Rachel's birthday—09/27/64.

"Hurry up!" Krystal wiped at her nose and tapped on her watch. Rachel began removing stacks of bills, stuffed them into a zippered vinyl pouch. There was a crashing sound, and Rachel swore and dove to the floor.

They had not been caught. Krystal had smashed the mirror behind the bar, throwing shot glasses as hard as she could.

"JESUS FUCKING CHRIST, KRYSTAL!" Rachel could not stop her. There wasn't enough time, and Krystal was coked out of her mind. Rachel dug in the back of the safe for the rolls of quarters. She was determined to leave nothing behind, empty her mother completely. The envelope was too full to zip, and Rachel kicked shut the safe and leaped to her feet.

One piece of mirror remained in the frame, and Krystal had apparently decided it was the perfect size for a message. Rachel wanted to punch her but settled for grabbing Krystal by the hair. The Neon Orchid lipstick flew out of Krystal's hand, pink and gooey and smashed from scrawling on the mirror. Rachel watched helplessly as the uncapped tube rolled under the jukebox, but remembered that Laverna never cleaned under there anyway.

The piece of mirror hung right behind the cash register.

LAVERNA AND RED MABEL ARE LESBEANS.

Krystal found this hysterically funny, and Rachel yanked her through the bar as quickly as possible, careful to avoid the shards of glass. Krystal was shoeless. And a shitty speller. In the Datsun, as they spun out in the snow, Rachel hoped that this message would be a red herring. The only prize Rachel had ever won came in the fifth grade, and Laverna had been there to witness her daughter crowned the county spelling bee champion.

––––––

Rachel checked her watch, and they had been gone for only twelve minutes. The Datsun sped back to the fire hall. Rachel knew that Laverna would return to the Shame after the ball was over, hosting her usual afterparty. There was no way Laverna would connect the destruction to her daughter. Rachel had been spotted on the dance floor, and the twelve-minute disappearance would go unnoticed. Rachel waved at Ginger as she locked the bathroom door and counted the money. $1,975.08, and she struggled with her math as she divided it in half. After solemnly promising to avoid pink lipstick for the rest of her life, Krystal was given another fifty dollars. Rachel removed every trace of Neon Orchid on Krystal's lips. This had been the most lucrative night of Rachel's life.

The lesbians greeted them warmly, and the entire group invaded the dance floor. Inside the circle of miners, Krystal and Rachel danced for hours. It was easy to be conspicuous. When the toughest miner grabbed Rachel's face and kissed her directly on the lips, she surrendered. Rachel could hear the commotion, despite her heart beating in her ears, full of cocaine and the calisthenics of dancing. She had no doubt that Laverna and Red Mabel were watching; she could feel it on her skin. Rachel had no fear of flamethrowers or the judge or the future. She spun around the cement floor until her hometown was a blur. If she remained in motion, and did not look back, her hometown would disappear entirely. Rachel Flood would leave this all behind.

The Flood Girls versus New Poland At-Home Sales

★   ★   ★

*T*he second game was actually their fourth. It was the first weekend of May, and the Flood Girls had a victory, without even taking the field.

As promised, Laverna carefully organized a sting, set the Ellis High School girls up in an underage drinking bust. Winsome brought a free keg from the Dirty Shame like a Trojan horse, flirted with the curvaceous seventeen-year-old captain of the Ellis High School girls in the parking lot of the Town Pump. He offered up the keg as a gift, in exchange for an invitation to their weekend party in the woods, where he promised to make out with her around their bonfire. Laverna knew that high school girls would do anything for the attentions of an older man—Rachel taught her that much. Laverna didn't pay Winsome a dime. He loved the subterfuge, the chance to get revenge on the thieving, indistinguishable girls from Ellis. The cops were greedy, however, and Laverna slipped a fifty-dollar bill into an envelope for the Ellis chief of police. Thus, the Flood Girls won game number three by default. Laverna was comfortable going into the fourth game of the season with a one-and-one record, and one rescheduled due to a blizzard.

On the day of their fourth game, Laverna woke up smiling, and she believed that her luck was changing. The Flood Girls won a game, even if it was a forfeit. In addition, the word around town buzzed—the Clinkenbeard kid got kicked out of juvie, shipped off to a facility in Arizona, where Laverna hoped he would die from sunburn or a scorpion bite.

Today, they played the ladies from New Poland At-Home Sales. It was an away game, and the Flood Girls carpooled the forty-seven miles. The team from New Poland was a conglomeration, an affiliation of housewives who also happened to do at-home sales in their free time. Laverna especially hated them, because they believed they were real businesswomen.

This team wore nonmatching uniforms, T-shirts advertising their brands, always selling. These bitches had phone numbers on their T-shirts, as if somebody would write down a phone number in the middle of a ball game. They came to games bearing receipt booklets.

In the dugout, Laverna declared that she would murder any Flood Girl who was distracted at bat by a conversation about a new set of self-sharpening knives, which the catcher from New Poland had the market on.

In addition to the knife lady, there were several representatives from Mary Kay, an Avon saleswoman, twin sisters who sold Hoover products, and their rival from Electrolux. The entire outfield was Amway, and Laverna hated them the most. Once, in a show of league spirit, Laverna and Red Mabel let themselves be dragged to one of their parties. Of course, Red Mabel had been coarse, and completely drunk, and burned the hostess's couch with a cigarette on purpose. Laverna bought a punch bowl just to make up for it. That was five years ago. They still called Laverna every three months and sent her catalogs.

The field in New Poland drifted with fluff from cottonwood trees. Half her team was sneezing before the game even began, and the remaining Flood Girls unaffected by allergies were skittering, sliding across the piles of pollen that collected in their cleats. The fluff was everywhere, floating down in great motes, catching the wind and blowing into the faces of her starting lineup. Laverna swore she saw a great pile of it, rolling across the field like tumbleweed.

In the dugout, Diane was complaining about her new boyfriend. "He's just not very romantic," she said, and pulled her knee high socks furiously. "I like to have men court me."

Ginger rolled her eyes and addressed Laverna, who was denying the tickle in her nose and eyes were related to the cottonwood. She was tougher than allergies. "Diane is dating her doctor."

"He's not just a doctor," said Diane. "He's a specialist."

"Gynecologist," declared Ginger.

"He's already seen the goods," said Laverna. "There's no romance left."

Laverna's attention was distracted by Martha Man Hands, who had already disobeyed. She saw Martha ordering candles through the chain link from an industrious young woman. Martha also made promises to attend a Pampered Chef party, even though Laverna knew Martha had never cooked, just brought home day-old corn dogs and congealed nachos from the gas station.

"Scram!" Laverna slammed her hand against the chain link, and the saleswoman left in a hurry. Laverna knocked the beer out of Martha's hand, told her to focus on the game.

Once again, Rachel was useless in the outfield, wearing her ridiculous gothic wardrobe and refusing to move, the cottonwood fluff creating a crown around her long blond hair. After the second inning, Laverna sat her daughter down on the bench, attempted an inspiration speech.

"Every woman on this team has seen how fast you can move," said Laverna. "When you want something, I mean."

"This is sports," said Rachel. "I warned you."

"You've already got a reputation," said Laverna. "I think you've broken nearly all the Ten Commandments. Let's not add sloth to the list."

"I don't covet my neighbor's husband," said Rachel.

"You live next door to Bert," Laverna pointed out.

"That's true," said Rachel.

Thankfully, Shyanne was there. The Flood Girls were worthless, and Laverna sent Shyanne out into right field, to control the damage. Rachel never had to swing a bat.

In addition to their tenacious business acumen, the women from New Poland At-Home Sales were fierce on the field. To make matters worse, several residents of Quinn had gone to the city council, asking that Red Mabel be suspended, or fined. They claimed she had started the fight, and nearly injured several children. None of this was true, of course, but Red Mabel was determined to play the rest of the season. Chastened by the warning, Red Mabel was solicitous as she tagged out runners to third, apologizing profusely. Laverna was disgusted. In the fifth inning, she requested a time-out and called Red Mabel in from the field.

In the dugout, Laverna begged. "Shake it off," she said. "You're the beast of this team, and we're getting creamed. Fuck the city council."

"I can't pay any fines," said Red Mabel.

"I'm sure you could trade some pelts or something," said Laverna. "I don't really give a shit. If it comes down to it, we'll sue."

"I don't have very good luck in court," pointed out Red Mabel.

"Fuck 'em," said Laverna. "Go out there and kill somebody. I've got a savings account." She punched Red Mabel on the shoulder. At this, Red Mabel began to howl, despite the double takes from the New Poland At-Home Sales. She trotted out to third base and proceeded to elbow and spit at any runners who dared come near.

Despite the return of their beast, the Flood Girls could not combat the onslaught of heavy hitters.

Bucky called the game at the top of the sixth inning, as they had been completely shut out, seventeen to zero. This was known as the mercy rule.

When the game ended, the Mary Kay ladies were the worst. As both teams shook hands in a long line, a league ritual that ended every softball game, the Mary Kay ladies seemed to be laughing at them, and this was bad sportsmanship. Laverna was worried that Red Mabel would rip out their earrings.

———

Laverna rode home with Tabby Pierce and the Sinclairs.

She and Tabby talked about the Clinkenbeard kid, and how it was proving impossible to get any restitution from his derelict family. Even when Red Mabel stood on their front porch, armed with a crossbow, the Clinkenbeards offered up only jars upon jars of pickled tomatoes. They claimed that they didn't have any money, and Red Mabel threatened to kill all their chickens if they didn't pay Laverna back within the month.

"That's like two hundred chickens," said Tabby Pierce. "Red Mabel couldn't shoot them all. Chickens move fast."

"Red Mabel has a machine gun," said Laverna.

A peep, much like a baby chicken, came from the backseat of the car. The Sinclairs had been silent until then, as always. Not even a sniffle. The taller Sinclair tapped Laverna on the shoulder.

"There's something you should know," she said, and Laverna craned her neck to see her in the gloom. "We're leaving Reverend Foote's church."

"What does that have to do with me?" Laverna turned back around. She found the Sinclairs to be incredibly irritating, especially the fact that they played softball in those cursed jean skirts, but she kept them around because they didn't talk back and took direction well.

"He insists that we can't play softball anymore," said the taller Sinclair.

"Bullshit," said Laverna. "I hate Reverend Foote. He is ruining this town. He is a terrible, grotesque man."

Tabby tried to be kind for the sake of the Sinclairs. She spoke in a gentle voice. "If you can't find anything nice to say about someone, maybe you shouldn't say anything at all."

Laverna glared at Tabby. "If you can't find anything nice to say about someone, maybe you should just set them on fire."

The shorter Sinclair spoke, in full voice, and rapidly. Laverna was stunned. "It's also about Jake," she said, her pale face and red hair glowing from the backseat. "We have to leave the church because of Jake. We can't listen to the things they say about him."

"What?" Tabby turned around, and Laverna jabbed her with a finger to redirect her attention to the road.

"Who is saying these things?" Laverna tried to interrogate the shorter Sinclair as kindly as possible. "And what are they saying?"

The shorter Sinclair took a deep breath. "Reverend Foote says that we cannot be around him. Reverend Foote says that the devil is inside Jake, and if we get too close, it will jump out and come inside us."

"Jesus," said Laverna, and then quickly apologized. "Sorry."

"It's okay," said the shorter Sinclair. "I just thought you should know. We both really like Jake. He's one of our favorite customers. He's very respectful."

"The whole congregation holds hands and prays for Jake's salvation," said the taller Sinclair. "And to keep Quinn safe from the devil inside him."

"Holy shit," said Tabby. "What does Bert say?"

"Nothing," said the shorter Sinclair. "He just prays. And then everybody hugs him at the end."

"We don't hug Bert," continued the taller Sinclair. "We've never really liked him anyway."

"I think I need to tell Rachel about this," said Laverna.

"Please don't," said the taller Sinclair. "Like I said, we're leaving the church. We want the outfield to be a harmonious place. We're going to start going to church in Ellis."

"Ellis is a terrible place," said Laverna. She reconsidered her statement and looked out at the forests whizzing past. "But any church there would be lucky to have you. Thank you for bringing this to my attention."

"You're our coach," said the shorter Sinclair. "This is about the team. We know that Jake and Rachel are close, and we don't want Rachel to have any distractions."

"Amen," said Laverna, and she meant it. She continued to watch for deer, disturbed by this news but refusing to acknowledge it out loud. Nothing could be done about the reverend. He had proven to be insidious and sneaky, and normally Laverna admired such things. He had a whole church on his side, and Laverna's fan club were mostly drunk and unorganized. She would have to do this on her own. For now, she could offer Jake her support, and keep watch for any wildlife on a suicide mission.

A Name for Men like You

★   ★   ★

*B*ert planned for a trip to Idaho Falls, a revival meeting. Krystal and the baby would accompany him, for the entire weekend. Bert knew that Jake would only cause a distraction, and Krystal paid Martha Man Hands for babysitting, even though Jake protested he was almost thirteen and was capable of more housework than women three times his age. Martha gladly took the money, and two hundred dollars more from Rachel. Hush money. Martha did not want to babysit anyway.

Jake showed up fully prepared the next morning, just as Rachel was drinking her first cup of coffee. He carried his tiny suitcase, and a small tin briefcase that contained a camera from the 1960s, complete with effect lenses and an impossibly compact tripod.

"I'm ready," he announced. He wore a newsboy cap and a scarf wrapped four times around his neck.

"Travel clothes? You look like Amelia Earhart." Rachel laughed. "Are you sure you don't need goggles?"

"That's not funny," said Jake. "Take me to the city, please. I made a mixed tape for our travels."

Rachel finished her coffee, and he watched as she threw some things in a duffel bag, and refrained from commenting when he noticed that she did not fold her clothes.

The drive to Missoula took three hours, and the trees and the rivers looked just like the trees and rivers in Quinn, but there seemed to be more sunlight in the air. His ears popped as they left the lower elevation and ascended in her little red truck. The road followed rocky cliffs, carved out of the mountains.

When Rachel reached the turnoff and entered the interstate, Jake had to take a deep breath. The field trips he took at school were always just hour-long drives into more of the same wilderness, but today he was destined for a city of seventy thousand people.

Low-slung cars zipped around Rachel's truck, not the giant trucks and beaten-up Jeeps he was accustomed to. A gargantuan casino covered an acre of land, and the electronic reader boards flashed out promises of upcoming concerts and theme nights. Jake noticed every single exit ramp, all flanked by enormous advertisements for multiplex movie theaters and tourist traps— a museum devoted entirely to agates, an exhibition of dinosaur bones at the university, an amusement park that offered up a zero-gravity experience.

In the distance, he saw streets weaving through, tucking under the interstate. He observed streetlights, actual traffic signals. The billboards were everywhere, including one that advertised a shopping mall. He clapped his hands together delightedly.

"What is it?" Rachel turned the volume down on a particularly raucous song by the B-52s. "What's got you so excited, little dude?"

"The mall!" He screamed the words, and Rachel grimaced.

"That place is a nightmare," said Rachel. "I thought you had better taste than that."

"I never get to buy new things," said Jake. "Unless I get them through the mail."

"Maybe we can stop there," said Rachel. "Every stylish person deserves new things. But we are not going to Wal-Mart. That place is a fucking black hole." She turned on her blinker. "Sorry for swearing."

"I love it!" Jake clapped again as they turned onto the exit ramp.

Rachel drove into the city of Missoula, and Jake's head turned in all directions. A record store. A dog-grooming business. A real estate office with three floors. A park that was built on purpose. In Quinn, the parks were uninhabitable tracts of land the city had repossessed. Jake saw a post office that was built with actual stone columns and had a grand entrance of cement steps. A courthouse with gothic-looking architecture, built around an impossibly tall clock tower. And then, on the front curb of the courthouse, sat the first black person he had ever seen in real life. They had stopped at a red light. The black person looked normal enough, drinking something steaming from a Styrofoam cup. He did not appear to be dangerous, although Jake did not approve of the giant, baggy muscle pants, the legacy of MC Hammer. Jake took pride in the fact that he did not lock his car door.

"My first black person," declared Jake.

"You poor thing," said Rachel. "We're eating Chinese food tonight. I hope you don't have a stroke from all the multiculturalism."

"This is the best day of my life," said Jake as the light turned green, and they drove farther into the city.

They continued driving, past a parking garage, a Taco Bell and a Kentucky Fried Chicken, restaurants Jake had only ever seen commercials for.

Rachel took a sharp left and came to rest in the parking lot of a Red Lion.

"Have you ever stayed in a hotel before?"

"No, ma'am."

"Maybe this really is the best day of your life," said Rachel. She reached over and removed his hat to ruffle his hair, and he could not stop smiling.

———

Rachel changed in the bathroom and emerged wearing a man's blazer over a pink bodysuit, sleeves rolled up. A tiny and tight black miniskirt, and her legs tucked in tights of shiny pink. Purple wool socks, giant Doc Martens. Jake sat on the hotel bed and watched as she put on her makeup: lip liner, the color of plums. Lipstick, the color of pink carnations. Silver eye shadow and blue mascara. Her hair looked the same as it did in Quinn, but she added mousse to the hay-colored tangles.

Jake had packed a black suit and a pink dress shirt. It was a wedding suit, he was sure of it, especially since it had been accompanied by a tiny cummerbund. Rachel assisted him with his bow tie, took his hand, and led him out to the truck.

"Athena is a very large woman," said Rachel, as she turned out into traffic. "She's also very loud. I wanted to warn you ahead of time."

"I like large and loud," said Jake.

"She's the best teacher I ever had," Rachel said, and continued down-town, across a giant, well-kept bridge, so unlike the rickety one lanes in Quinn.

A row of women, all in black, stood like crows, holding hands. All eleven silently watched the traffic crossing over the bridge.

"Those women are famous around here," said Rachel. "They come to the bridge to protest the war. Every single week."

"Are we in a war?"

"These women have been coming here for the last twenty years."

It was true that the women seemed ancient, and Rachel honked her horn. They did not react to the honk, did not smile or acknowledge that Jake was flashing a peace sign.

Rachel turned onto a street that led to a parking lot, the lights just flickering on, as the sun had nearly set.

She parked in front of a restaurant that was built out over the river. The Mustard Seed, "Fine Asian Cuisine." Jake had an egg roll once, but it had come out of a microwavable box.

Again, Rachel took his hand and led him into the foyer. They waited on narrow wooden benches, low to the carpet. The entire entrance was walled with fish tanks, goldfish the size of his baby sister.

The hostess was dressed in black, and all Rachel had to do was say the word *Athena* and they were whisked off to a table that looked right out on the water.

"RACHEL!" Athena eased herself from the banquette and com-pletely consumed her. Rachel disappeared into this embrace, and Jake stood there, until Athena pushed Rachel away with considerable force and bowed down to shake his hand.

Athena was also wearing black, layers of it, scarves, a long glittery blouse over a black lace camisole that strained, and a flowing skirt that did not. If it wasn't for the gray crew cut, Jake would have mistaken her for Stevie Nicks. Just as he had imagined, everybody in the city wore black.

Athena did not seem that fat to him, just exotic, and full of life.

"Pleased to meet you," Athena said, and wrapped an arm around his shoulder. Her arms tinkled, and he saw that her wrists were covered in silver bracelets, each strung with tiny bells. "I have heard ever so much about you. Rachel calls you her best friend, so it is truly an honor."

Rachel smiled at him, and he blushed as Athena herded them into the banquette.

"I've already ordered," said Athena. "I made sure you got your precious goddamn tofu." Athena reached across the table and touched Jake's arm. "I apologize for my language, but you'd better get used to it."

"God, I missed you," said Rachel.

"I should hope so," said Athena.

"I've got four hundred and thirty-four days," said Rachel.

"I know," said Athena. "Your new sponsor and I have become pen pals. That motherfucker can't spell for shit."

"Really? He writes you letters?"

"I spoke to his wife. I suspect that she forces him."

"How on earth did you find him?"

"I have my ways," said Athena as the food began to arrive.

Athena announced each item, as it was lowered in front of Jake: General Tso's chicken, pot stickers stuffed with pork and cabbage, wonton soup. Thin slices of barbecued pork were arranged in a perfect ring that surrounded tiny dishes of hot mustard and sesame seeds.

Rachel and Athena talked recovery, and gossiped about mutual friends from AA. Jake surrendered to the food. He was so full after ten minutes that he forced himself to stop, and stared out at the river. It had become night, and the city lights twinkled on the water. He peered around the room at the other diners, impeccably or interestingly dressed, living a city life in the candlelight.

"So, little man." Athena's arms tinkled as she pointed a finger at him. "What do you want to do with the rest of your life?"

"This," he said.

"Rachel tells me that you like fashion and the arts. She tells me that you had very firm opinions about the decoration of her house."

"Yes, ma'am," he said, blushing again.

"In the city, we have a name for men like you."

Jake almost choked, waiting to hear that word, the word that was never to be spoken.

"Fabulous," said Athena. "Fucking fabulous."

Jake exhaled.

"Goodness," said Athena. "You're white as a sheet."

"Sorry," he said. "I think I ate too much."

"Well, my fabulous little friend. I got you a special present. A thank-you for taking such good care of my girl."

"Oh no." Rachel put down her egg roll. "Please tell me it is age appropriate."

"Of course not," said Athena. "I can tell this kid is wise beyond his years."

"Thank you!" Jake was ecstatic. "That's what I keep telling my mother."

"You absolutely cannot tell your mother about this," said Athena. "But I think it's going to blow your little mind."

"Are we going *to the mall*?"

"That's disgusting," said Athena. She reached into her mammoth black purse, and removed three tickets and fanned them out across the only clear space on the table. "If you mention that cursed place, I shall give these tickets to some homeless people."

Jake clutched the ticket with shaking hands, made out the words in the candlelight.

"*The Rocky Horror Picture Show*," he said.

"Sweet lord," said Rachel.

"Sweet transvestites," corrected Athena. "You will never, ever be the same again. The show starts in an hour."

"Thank you," said Jake.

"Honey, growing up where you do, I think you need this experience."

"I used to have cable," said Jake. "I read books. I know things."

"Oh, little man," said Athena. "You have no idea."

———

When Jake returned from Missoula, he was full of hope and ideas and left-over Chinese food gobbled in the truck. They returned on Sunday afternoon, just as the clouds gathered in a portent of storm.

Rachel had to use her headlights, and they shone on Martha's trailer house. There was a stone in his throat, and just like that, the good feelings were gone. Jake had two bags of clothes from the thrift stores in Missoula, and Rachel agreed to store them in her trailer for safekeeping.

Rachel sensed his trepidation, and waited, parked in front of her own house, her truck still running. She grabbed his wrist.

"You can live in Missoula," she said. "You can wake up every morning in that town and be yourself and do the things that you were born to do."

"I know," said Jake.

"Five years," she said. "You just have to make it five more years, and then you can go wherever you want, and be whoever you want, and nobody can stop you."

"Okay," said Jake. They continued to sit there, until Rachel reached into her jeans pocket and pulled out a business card.

"This is from Athena."

"She's a tax lawyer?" He studied the card. "I don't pay taxes."

"Her address and phone number are on the back. She wants you to stay in touch with her. She likes you."

"Okay," he whispered.

"Ready?"

"I think so," he said.

They unloaded the back of her truck, and Jake made his way across the gravel to his house.

The porch light was on, which was a new thing. It was as if they were welcoming him home, but he had never gone anywhere without them, so he was unsure. He felt like knocking for some reason, but opened the door after taking a few deep breaths.

He found Bert in his usual place, quiet and reading his Bible. He didn't acknowledge Jake's entrance, and Jake hustled to his bedroom. He could hear Krystal giving the baby a bath. He removed the duffel bag beneath his bed and examined his work. He was nearly done, still had to finish two shirts, and he had decided to stitch all the collars and sleeves. He only worked on these shirts at Rachel's house, when she was not home. He slid a chair in front of his bedroom door, just in case.

He lost himself, caressing the familiar fabric, the thick stitching, but Jake felt different. He realized that he had forgotten to take any pictures. He returned everything to the safety of the duffel bag. As he collapsed on his bed, he realized that pictures weren't necessary. Some things would stay inside you until the day you died.

The Flood Girls versus Ellis Methodist Church

★　★　★

Rachel slept in, and when she woke, she said her prayers and reminded herself that this was just softball. She had no control over the outcome, but she could control her effort, and her outfit. Outside, it was raining lightly. The game was scheduled for noon. She took a bath, and meditated in front of the brick altar. She was in a Zen state when she picked out her clothes.

Rachel pulled up to the field thirty minutes before the game, as instructed. Laverna rolled her eyes at Rachel's choice of clothing: jean shorts that had been dyed black and hung with ripped fringes of hem, over neon green spandex, and a giant black T-shirt with a bloody skull on it. She and Jake had gone shopping for cleats in Ellis, even though they both despised entering a sporting goods store. She bought the first black pair in her size, but then Jake had found neon green laces at the cash register, which at least made them unique. She had practiced with the Chief in her Doc Martens, but even with two pairs of wool socks, she still ended up with blisters.

The T-shirt was actually appropriate. Rachel wished that she wore her pentagram necklace, something she bought for a Judas Priest concert in Missoula that she was kicked out of. This game would be played against the Methodists from Ellis.

All the other girls paired for the warm-up, leaving her to toss a ball

back and forth with Ronda. She watched the opposing team, all in matching uniforms: pink T-shirts with tiny gray crosses above the right breast,
gray sweatpants, pink socks. In her previous life, Rachel would have
beaten them up on sight.

Laverna recited the batting lineup in the dugout, and even though it
was raining, she removed a clothespin from her pocket and attached the
paper to the chain-link fence. Rachel watched as the ink began to run.

She could see Jake in the bleachers, a coat draped over his head and
the scorebook. The very sight of him was reassuring. A raincoat, dark
blue with violet lining, surrounding his face like a cowl, the rest of him
bedecked in varying shades of denim. Her seven dwarfs dug into a giant
cooler, unlike the rest of the crowd, it was not filled with beer. Rachel suspected that the chief's wife had made all the sandwiches, as it was something an Al-Anon wife would do.

Rachel had grown accustomed to right field. It was a lonely place, but
she crouched down into ready position every single time, even if the batter
wasn't left-handed. Most of the action went to left field, but Rachel wanted
to appear prepared.

Bucky called out, and Rachel watched her mother come to the
pitcher's mound for the coin toss. The coach for the Methodists was wearing pink but had spent too much time in the tanning beds in Boyce Falls.

From the dugout, the Flood Girls stopped gossiping long enough to
witness the nut-brown coach stop Bucky with one hand, kneel down to
pray before he could flick the coin into the air.

"For fuck's sake," said Laverna. "That's cheating."

"You could pray if you wanted," said Bucky. The coach rose to her
feet to applause from her team. The Flood Girls had a reputation in the
league, and the Methodists feared evil was contagious.

"I don't need Jesus," said Laverna. "I've got Diane."

It was true. Diane had adopted her mother's maiden name, Savage,
and for good reason. Her vertical leap was the stuff of legend, and in the
first inning, she leaped in the air, almost as high as Tabby's breasts, and
snagged a ball destined to land in front of the statue of Ronda. A line drive
peeled off the bat and nearly knocked out Ginger's teeth, who dove to

the ground just in time, as her dental work was expensive. Diane darted behind her, scooped up the missile before it could land. Like Red Mabel, Diane was a beast, but she had been raised with good manners. She helped Ginger to her feet, brushed the dust from their pitcher's perm.

Diane was the type of woman who swung at everything, on and off the field. Fearless, she reached for an errant pitch, tapped it straight down the foul line, and Bucky had to squint and stammer until he finally called it good. By the time he had made this decision, Diane was on third base. Unfortunately, Della followed their cleanup hitter, and she was also the type of woman who swung at everything but never succeeded.

"WAIT FOR YOUR PITCH!" Laverna screamed as Della attempted to hit a ball that cruised two feet outside the batter's box. This is how it had been every game. Laverna instructed Della not to swing at anything, and to step in front of a ball if necessary. A walk is as good as a hit, Laverna reasoned, and Della might as well sacrifice her body for the team. Della refused to be a patsy, and continued to swing away, hopelessly. Rachel had no fear of throwing herself in front of a pitch. Rachel had been thrown on the hood of a Nissan Maxima, had been beat with a garden hose by a gang of drunk Russian women. A softball was nothing, and Rachel kept this contingency plan in the back of her mind, just in case.

In the third inning, the Methodists were up by twelve. Their husbands were afraid of the bleachers filled with the rough-and-tumble sinners of Quinn, and lined up against the chain-link fence behind the dugout. The husbands were also devout. Rachel ascertained this by studying their outfits. Short-sleeved button-down shirts and ties, a combination that had always made her cringe. Slacks worn without belts, their hair parted so severely, Rachel watched the white flesh redden as the sun emerged. As the air warmed up, so did the Methodists, and they batted through their entire lineup before Diane unleashed another trick from her arsenal. Diane was not a sneaky person, but she had perfected a fake out, pretending to throw the ball to first base, only to tag out the unsuspecting runner who had sprung from second.

"JESUS WEPT!" Laverna screamed from the dugout as Diane ended the slaughter and the Flood Girls returned to bat for the top of the fourth inning. Klemp had joined Laverna on the bench, as if she expected to be subbed in. The girl was as grim as always, and apparently an agnostic. Red Mabel bolted to her truck and drove over the railroad ties that framed the parking lot, parked right behind the dugout. While the Sinclairs and Tabby inched around the bases, Red Mabel formulated a plan. Klemp sat in the driver's seat, instructed to play "Hells Bells" by AC/DC over and over, rewinding gleefully, doing her part. Thankfully, Red Mabel had stolen a decent stereo system, and the bass rattled the beer bottles collecting around Martha Man Hands.

The Methodists protested to Bucky, during the fifth inning, as the song blared for the ninth time. Rachel could hear him shouting over the music, telling the coach to call the police, as he was only in charge of the actual softball field, and Klemp was a minor who had gone rogue.

The husbands gathered together in a prayer circle, and Laverna took the lord's name in vain. She also took the lord's name and combined it with all the permutations of obscure sex acts she could think of. "JESUS CLEVELAND STEAMER! JESUS FELCHING CHRIST!" Rachel was impressed that her mother knew about felching, as it was something she had only heard about from her gay friends in Missoula.

By the sixth inning, the Methodists were up by fourteen, and the praying grew more fervent, the muttering lost to the blast of AC/DC. The rain returned, and the husbands prayed even harder, as Red Mabel's white T-shirt soaked through. Red Mabel believed in Jesus as much as she believed in brassieres.

Shyanne Fitchett left to make the bus for the track meet, and in the last inning, Rachel found herself on deck. Diane transformed a base hit into a double, as the Methodist on first base was captivated by Red Mabel's breasts.

"WAIT FOR YOUR PITCH!" Laverna cupped her hands like a megaphone, but Della swung and missed each time. Laverna threw an empty beer can in frustration, nearly striking Ginger, who was used to her coach's tantrums. Ginger removed her expensive sunglasses and rolled her eyes, wiped away the drop of Bud Light with the tail of her T-shirt.

As Rachel left the dugout, Black Mabel's father and brother shouted the chorus, fists pumping in the air.

Calmly, Rachel grabbed the bat from Della and marched to the plate. She reminded herself that this was just softball. She had survived much worse. She liked the bat, the weight of it calibrated perfectly. It felt like a weapon. There was no chatter from her team, no words of encouragement. Even Diane was silent.

Rachel had yet to hit a ball, despite the hours she spent practicing with the Chief. The pitcher perspired heavily, and she wiped the mix of rain and sweat from her face with the front of her shirt.

The first pitch was a strike. Rachel watched as it flew past. The second was a ball, so far out of the strike zone that it nearly struck Bucky in the throat.

At that moment, there was a commotion in the outfield, as three white-tailed deer came bolting from the forest, chased by the brown dog. The deer ducked through a curled-up piece of the chain-link fence, galloping into center field.

The pitcher was not aware of the deer, and threw the ball before Bucky could call a time-out.

Rachel noticed that the outfield and second base were completely distracted, watching the deer in awe. Perhaps they thought the deer were some sort of miracle, sent to remedy Red Mabel's immorality.

Rachel had completed enough personal inventories to know that she thrived on chaos. She kept her eye on the ball, and swung like the Chief had instructed.

She made contact with the pitch, weak contact, and the ball rolled slowly past the pitcher and right past the abandoned second base, sending Diane running to third.

Rachel was amazed she had hit the ball, and forgot to run.

Laverna screamed at her daughter, and Red Mabel jumped up and down in the dirt, and pointed at first base. Their words were lost in the music, and Rachel only ran after Bucky broke the rules and nudged her from the plate.

The Methodists collected themselves and threw out Rachel at first. Diane wisely stayed at third.

Rachel could hear Jake cheering for her. When she walked into the dugout, Laverna and Red Mabel refused to congratulate her, even though she had finally done something softball-like.

She hit the ball.

The coach of the Methodists consulted with Bucky, and Laverna put a quick stop to their protestations that the deer were grounds for a delay of game. Not that it mattered. Ronda struck out, and the game was over.

Gold

* ★   ★   ★ *

The next night was Sunday, and it was a special occasion. Jake was allowed to sleep over at Rachel's. He planned on skipping school the next day, which only seemed to fuel the decadence of the occasion. Bert had left for five days of a men's retreat with the church. Apparently, Jake was not considered a man, not considered at all, really. He took no umbrage at the lack of invitation, thankful he would not have to attend church day care. Rachel had a free Monday, as she had switched with Tish, who needed one of her weekend shifts to go find her husband, who had left town with Black Mabel.

After a trip to the video store in Ellis, they ate popcorn, drank Shirley Temples, and clutched each other as they watched Kathy Bates in *Misery*.

He slept on the couch, happily.

Rachel made oatmeal in the morning, and they ate it slowly outside on the front porch, so Jake could put off returning home for as long as possible.

A day of rain revealed a ragged version of a rock garden. The beds followed the entire length of the fence, framed by jagged pieces of shale that Frank had hauled there and sunk into the ground. Each bed was three feet wide, and Rachel told Jake that she assumed this was just more of his bachelor landscaping, a hillbilly Stonehenge covered in snow and then the slog of dead leaves.

"He always had flowers," said Jake. "I remember that."

They spotted the squirrel, glittery and golden, almost completely covered in the green mush from plants that had been cut back and left to rot.
Jake leaped from the porch, and Rachel followed in her flip-flops. She
crouched down, brushed away the detritus until it revealed itself: a squirrel statue, ceramic and spray-painted so thickly that the paint had dried
in globs and drips. A golden squirrel, like a trophy, some special achieve-
ment in small woodland animals.

Jake went home and changed into what he felt was appropriate
gardening clothing—khaki everything, including a beret. Bert had not
returned from his retreat, Krystal was asleep with the baby in her arms, so
Jake scrawled out a note and left it on the kitchen table.

Jake and Rachel knelt down in the soggy earth and began to scoop
away all the leaves, some so mushy they disintegrated in their hands,
almost decomposed into mud.

Under the cover of leaves, dark soil was studded with tiny green
spikes. The green was so pale and new, so unaccustomed to light, that it
made Jake slightly sad. He thought of Frank planting these things, hidden
from the rest of the trailer court by the privacy fence, his secret garden.
Maybe Frank had planted them for Jake's benefit. Frank didn't have grass
in his yard, but he always had flowers. Jake didn't know what kind they
were, but he remembered the colors.

"I lived here my senior year," said Rachel.

"I didn't know that," said Jake, as he scooped a handful of sludge and
deposited it in a garbage bag.

"He didn't have a garden," she said. "This was where I used to put
my lawn chair and suntan."

"Careful," said Jake. "The sun is not friendly to blondes. I'm amazed
your skin looks as good as it does."

Grayed stalks, cut down as close to the ground as possible, were hard
as sticks. They offered more evidence of flowers here, and that Frank had
made sure they were ready for winter, and maybe his death.

Rachel pointed at the grayed stalks. "So you don't know what these
are?"

"No," said Jake. "I don't know flowers. That's a stereotype."

"Sorry," said Rachel. "I've never grown anything in my life. Just hair."

"I know somebody who can help," said Jake. "You have to trust me."

"Of course," said Rachel.

———

They drove through the nearly flooded streets of Quinn and Jake gave her directions, but Ginger Fitchett's house was easy to find. It was the nicest house in town. Like Frank, Ginger surrounded her entire property with a privacy fence.

Jake pushed through the gate first, and sitting in the middle of her own secret garden, Ginger Fitchett was entertaining Diane Savage Connor. They sat at a glass café table, under a giant pink umbrella, drinking tea. Ginger already began the work of preparing her garden for spring, and it was magnificent. Every square inch of yard had been landscaped in exact beds, framed with railroad ties. Ginger's bushes were enormous, testament to a woman who spent years and years on her yard. A tiny greenhouse nestled in the corner.

"Hello there," Ginger said, and stood to greet them. Jake was slightly shocked that Ginger wasn't asking what Rachel wanted, or even seemed perturbed that Rachel had gained entry to her yard. "Do you want some tea?"

"Sure," said Jake. Rachel nodded. They sat down next to Diane, as Ginger entered her gorgeous house, all three stories of it, a giant sunporch, the whole thing painted the color of a sunset. She returned with two more cups of tea. Jake helped himself to sugar cubes, while Rachel craned her neck to take it all in.

"Diane is seeing her gynecologist," announced Ginger. She took a sip of her tea, while Diane nibbled at a Lorna Doone.

"It's nice to know you're concerned about your health," said Rachel, to break the silence.

"Dating," said Diane, after she had swallowed her cookie. "Like really seeing him."

"Oh," said Rachel.

"That's what we were talking about before you showed up," said Ginger. "We think he might be the marrying kind."

Jake couldn't stand it any longer. "We need your help," he said. "Frank had a garden. Neither one of us know what to do with it."

"Frank?" Ginger was incredulous. Diane raised an eyebrow.

"Yes," said Rachel. "He kept it a secret, just like you. I don't think anybody in the trailer court knew what was going on behind that fence."

"I did," said Jake. "He had the flowers for as long as I can remember."

"He was a mystery to us all," Ginger said, and she reached over and patted Rachel's hand.

"I want more," said Rachel.

"I really didn't know the man," said Ginger. "I'm sorry."

"No," said Rachel. "I meant more flowers."

"Oh," said Ginger. "I understand. I always want more flowers." She gestured around her property, already crammed with garden beds and groupings of small trees and shrubs. "Is there a lot of sun in the yard?"

"Just along that side of the fence," said Rachel. "The rest is blocked by the trailer house and the trees."

"Jake," said Ginger. "I trust you have a notebook on you."

Ginger knew Jake all too well. He removed a small sketchpad from one of his khaki pockets, and a pen from another, and Ginger began to dictate a list. He made sure the sketchpad only opened to the last third of pages, the blank ones—there were secrets to be kept.

───────

On Monday mornings, the Ben Franklin in Ellis was thick with housewives. The garden supplies had been arranged out in the parking lot, in small huts made of clear plastic.

Jake and Rachel filled the cart with five bags of soil, two trowels, four pairs of gardening gloves, and three flats of flowers, neatly divided like black ice-cube trays. They picked out the healthiest looking Johnny-jump-ups, echinacea daisies, and vines of clematis. Rachel bought two trellises, per Ginger's instructions.

"Can I spray-paint them?" Jake was a big fan of spray paint.

"Of course," said Rachel.

They added six cans of gold spray paint to the cart.

They returned to Quinn, and Jake scooped out the rest of the dead leaves and dragged the trellises out into the driveway to paint.

As they dried, he returned to the garden beds, and Jake and Rachel knelt along the fence line, clearing spots for the clematis, shaking out the contents of the heavy bags of soil, stirring it in with the old dirt.

They finished planting the daisies just as the sun went down.

Jake asked for permission to have dinner at Rachel's house. Krystal noted all of the black earth that stained Jake's knees and shirt, and seemed pleased. He was dirty, like any other normal twelve-year-old boy. Jake nearly ran into his bedroom to change clothes.

Rachel made beans and rice and homemade tortillas, while Jake fussed over the gold spray paint on his hands.

After dinner, Jake insisted on doing the dishes. They could hear the thunder, and then the rain drummed on the roof of the trailer.

"I have an idea," said Jake. "But I need to go home first." He dried his hands carefully on a dish towel as the thunder boomed again.

"What if they don't let you come back?"

"I'm sneaking in. Do you have a ladder?"

Rachel and Jake stood in the pouring rain, as she propped Bucky's stepladder against the wooden fence. He climbed over and snuck in the back door. He raced back to Rachel's house through the rain, as it had turned into a deluge, the sound roaring on the metal roof.

"Get your boom box," he demanded as he stood in her living room, dripping. "And some scarves."

She followed his commands, and he plugged the stereo into the living room outlet. The scarves she offered up were gauzy and purple. He switched on the lamp he had given her, and draped the scarves over the shade.

"Turn off the rest of the lights," he demanded, and as she walked to the kitchen, Jake put a cassette tape in the boom box and hit the rewind button. The living room was cast about with their shadows, the light in the room as deep purple as the sky outside.

"Now what?"

"Close your eyes," he said. He pushed play. "Open them! Dance party!"

Rachel stared at him, until the strings kicked in.

"It's wonderful!"

"It's Madonna!"

Jake framed his face with his hands, stood perfectly still. He waited for a moment, and then twirled those hands above his head and stopped again in midpose. "Vogue" blasted throughout the house, the volume shaking the objects on Rachel's brick altar.

When the music played, Jake forgot he was a twelve-year-old boy who lived in a trailer house. This was the sound of supermodels. He always thought that he resembled Linda Evangelista anyway, although he was much, much shorter.

The light from the lamps shone on the gold paint that remained on his hands as they twirled glamorously, so fast that they seemed to be on fire.

"Pose!" He pointed at her, and she marched forward, gave a few runway stomps, and stopped, looking behind her, as if she had dropped something. This was Naomi Campbell's over-the-shoulder smolder. Rachel knew her supermodels, and that made Jake love her even more.

And they danced, as the trailer shook with the storm and their choreography.

The Flood Girls versus the Boyce Beauty Stop

★   ★   ★

*L*averna loved night games, how the bats would swoop down from the sky at the balls, and how the dark made Red Mabel even more frightening to the other team. Laverna knew this game would not be marred by fisticuffs or catcalling. Tonight they were playing the Boyce Beauty Stop, her favorite team in the league.

The Boyce Beauty Stop was a team of bitter divorcées known for the quality of their permanents, and for having the only tanning beds in the county. They hated men and all that they stood for. Only their children came to the games, until they grew up and went to college, or got married and became bitter divorcées themselves.

These women were Laverna's kindred spirits, and she did not mind the hour and a half it took to get there. Boyce Falls was surrounded by rivers, and it was a beautiful drive.

Laverna rode with the infield in Diane's Suburban. Thirty miles outside of Quinn, Tabby announced that this would be her last season.

"The thing is," she said, and then stopped herself. "I don't want to say it in front of Della."

"Go ahead," said Della. "After last week's game, nothing could shock me."

"I'm leaving Dwayne. And I don't want to hear an 'I told you so.'"

"You won't," said Della. "I could only make it work for six months. I have no idea how you made it last as long as you did."

"There's something else," said Tabby, turning to Laverna. "I'm moving."

"Fuck," said Laverna. "So you're quitting the bar?"

"You can have your shift back. You seem all healed up."

"You're no doctor," spit Laverna.

"I met another man," said Tabby.

"I think love is something worth celebrating!" announced Diane from the driver's seat.

"Shut the fuck up," said Laverna. "Where are you moving?"

"That's the funny thing," said Tabby. "Boyce Falls."

"This is a town of bitter divorcées," said Laverna. "They are going to burn your house down."

"We'll keep our happiness a secret," said Tabby.

"That's always been my personal motto," declared Martha Man Hands.

Despite Tabby's news, the girls played with precision and grace, and Red Mabel didn't assault anyone in the bleachers.

Diane masterminded the first double play in the history of the Flood Girls. She tagged out a runner at second, and still found the time to throw the runner out at first. The miracles continued when Rachel actually attempted to catch a ball, ran at it, but ran too fast, and missed it entirely. Thankfully, the taller Sinclair was there to scoop it up.

And at bat, Rachel got contact on a slow pitch and bashed the hell out of it. She hit the ball deep into right field, and remembered to run after the entire dugout began screaming at her.

"Run, run, run!" the Flood Girls yelled until Rachel made it all the way to second.

Her other two at bats were total flameouts, but she was showing some spark. Laverna's girls won their second game of the year, seven to six, and this was a game they had actually played, not won by forfeit.

It was nearly one o'clock in the morning when they got back to town, and Laverna demanded that they go to the Dirty Shame to continue the celebration. Nobody dared argue.

Gene Runkle was in rare form, still upright after hours of drinking.

He was also celebrating. He finally caught the brown dog, and carried on about his own Moby Dick.

Jim Number Three sat at the bar and stared into his pint glass. Since she had her casts removed, their sex life had become pedestrian. He still came to her house with his book, and they were nearing the end.

Laverna sat down next to him, as the rest of the Flood Girls celebrated all around her.

Jim Number Three had a grim look on his face.

"What?" Laverna ordered a drink from Tish.

"I need to tell you something that you're not going to like," he said.

"I'm sure I've heard worse," said Laverna.

"I screwed up," said Jim Number Three, and then he was crying. Laverna hated when straight men cried. It made her blood boil, and she had seen enough of it as a bartender for a quarter century.

"Just say it," said Laverna. She was short with him, which made the tears come even harder. Tish looked over, concerned. Laverna rolled her eyes. His tears were making her lose interest in him anyway.

"I slept with another woman," said Jim Number Three.

"Fucking volunteers," muttered Laverna. "Should've known."

"Some widow in Idaho needed track lighting installed. One thing led to another."

"They always do," Laverna said, and stood up from her stool. She tried to walk away from him, but he grabbed her arm.

"I don't want to break up," he said. "It was just a mistake. You're the one I really want."

"Fuck off," she said, but he wouldn't let go of her arm.

"I've been building you a robot!" Now he was sobbing.

Laverna spit in his face. "Fuck your robots! Fuck Kunta Kinte!"

Jim Number Three wiped at his cheeks, at the tears and saliva. "I still love you!"

"After your drink, you get the hell out of here. You're eighty-sixed. For good."

"Please," he said.

"It's over," Laverna said, and tore away from his grasp. She walked to the back tables, and they were all silent. They had seen Jim Number Three's tears.

"What did he do?" Red Mabel cracked her knuckles.

"The same thing every man does," said Laverna. "He's just another disappointment."

For some reason, Martha Man Hands raised her glass to this, and the Flood Girls toasted one another, and their first real victory of the season.

When Laverna woke the next morning, she was in a strange mood. She was loath to admit that she had fallen, just the tiniest bit, for Jim Number Three. She wanted to know how *Roots* ended, if Kunta Kinte's family tree finally managed to buck their bad luck. She missed Jim Number Three reading to her, attempting to pronounce all the African names. But he had turned out to be a cheater, and a volunteer, and she had officially sworn off both forever.

She needed a reminder.

She found herself driving to Ellis, to the animal control building.

The woman behind the counter tried to stop her, but Laverna just held up a hand and kept walking. She could hear the dogs barking, and it was easy to ascertain which door to open.

In the third kennel, she found him. Laverna did not know her breeds, just knew that this was the brown dog that attempted to take a chunk out of her calf. She always remembered her enemies. This was turning out to be a year of injuries. It figured, because her daughter had come back to town.

Laverna crouched down in front of the kennel, and the brown dog ignored the deafening sounds of all the other imprisoned dogs and stretched leisurely. He took his time approaching the cage door. When he got near, Laverna expected him to growl, for foam to come out of his mouth, for him to lunge at her. Laverna knew that dogs that bit people had to be put down, and wished the same thing applied to human beings. This dog was destined for execution.

The animal control officer entered the room, holding a clipboard. She cleared her throat nervously. She was a mousy woman, uncomfortable in her own body. Laverna detested women who filled the air with their discomfort, their body apologizing for their very existence. They tried so hard to take such little space that they ended up filling every room.

"What?"

"Sorry, Laverna. I can't let you be back here by yourself. Liability."

"How do you know my name?"

"Reputation," said the animal control officer. "Good things, I swear."

At this, Laverna laughed. "Bullshit," she said. The animal control officer kneeled down, joining Laverna. They both studied the dog.

"He's also got a reputation," said the animal control officer.

"I know," confirmed Laverna. "I'm one of his victims."

But the brown dog didn't even snarl. He didn't bark. His counterparts in their cages threw themselves against the chain link, howling and baying for her attention.

The brown dog peered up at her, with his giant dark eyes. She supposed he was a dachshund mix of some kind. He was a mutt, and he had a history of violence. He definitely belonged in Quinn.

He wagged his tail and sniffed at the cage. Jim Number Three had snuck up and hurt her, and she needed to be reminded how it felt. She wanted the dog to bite her.

She stuck her fingers through the chain link.

"Don't," said the animal control officer. "We can't afford the liability."

"I brought my checkbook," said Laverna. She wiggled her ring finger, and the dog loped up, and licked where the ring would be.

"I think he likes you," said the animal control officer.

"Goddammit," said Laverna. The dog rolled on his back, expecting her to rub his stomach.

Laverna stood, swinging her purse violently as she left the room. She was angry. The males of any species were fickle and mysterious creatures.

Boy on the Roof

★　★　★

The next day was Sunday, clear and blue, the yard furrowed and spiked. There was a green glow to it, as the grass had just begun poking out. She scattered the seeds out of a coffee can with a lid perforated with a knife, was proud of her work. A few seeds remained on the surface of the soil, un-sprouted. They looked like rice, and reminded Rachel of Krystal's wedding. She had never heard of a wedding on a Wednesday afternoon, figured it was some weird Evangelical thing, or maybe they were hoping Rachel could not get time off from work.

Since Bucky had nothing on his docket, Rachel decided it was the perfect day to put up the new siding. She wanted wood, but Bucky drove her to Ellis and showed her the giant pieces of vinyl, weather-resistant, half the cost, a quarter the labor.

Rachel had her mind set on a house painted the color of Tiffany boxes, that very particular shade of blue, with dark brown trim and over-flowing window boxes.

The vinyl siding came in two colors: kind of white, and kind of brown. Rachel thought that the colors were exactly the same as every trailer house in her court, and she was right.

Bucky appeased her by letting her buy eight window boxes, and flats of moss roses at the Ben Franklin. He stood patiently in the paint section, while Rachel had a confusing conversation with the salesman about

Tiffany's, and then the color of robin's eggs, and then Audrey Hepburn. Eventually, she found a blue that was close enough. Bucky apologized to the salesman.

"She's very determined," Bucky said.

"I would choose a different word," said the salesman, who thought Rachel was out of earshot. She eavesdropped and pretended to study fake flowers. There was a wedding, after all, and Krystal had become so tacky in ten years that she might welcome such an arrangement.

"I hope it's not a swear word," Bucky said, and puffed up his chest.

"No," said the salesman. "Picky. That's what I meant."

"That house is her baby," said Bucky. "She wants everything to be perfect."

"What does that have to do with Audrey Hepburn?"

"Dunno," admitted Bucky. "Sorry."

The vinyl had to be delivered. A giant flatbed truck followed them back to Quinn, and the driver was kind of cute, just like the vinyl was kind of brown.

It took an hour and a half to slide the sheets off the truck and pile them on the patio.

Putting up the siding required all four of their arms, a ladder, and a sawhorse. After Bucky drilled the first piece into place, they stood back and admired it. It was like a whole new trailer house, at least this section of it.

They were hanging the second piece when the shouting started. It came from Krystal's trailer, and it was definitely Bert.

"Jesus Christ," said Bucky, drill in hand. "I thought he stopped drinking."

"Doesn't stop him from being an asshole," said Rachel.

Bucky screwed in the final corner of the second piece, and the shouting continued, louder this time. The baby started crying, and Rachel listened for Jake but could not hear him. Krystal's car was gone, so Bert had to be yelling at Jake. Bert never yelled at the baby.

A thump and a crash, and Bucky leaped from the ladder and grabbed Rachel before she could run to the gate.

"Stop," he said. He pointed to Jake's bedroom window. Jake's legs emerged, as he perched on the sill, and pushed himself up to the roof.

Jake's head was covered by the hood of a cowl-neck sweater, three sizes too big for him. He was crying.

"Are you okay?"

"Go away," he said, in a quiet voice. He buried his face in wool. The sweater hung down to his knees.

"Get him down from there," commanded Rachel.

"Don't talk to Bert," said Bucky. "Let me do that."

"No," said Rachel. "You're taller. Get Jake off the roof. He's not in his right mind."

"Neither are you," said Bucky. "You don't know what Bert is capable of."

"That," said Rachel, pointing at Jake, curled up into a ball, sobbing.

Rachel jumped up Krystal's steps and let loose on the door.

Bert opened it and stared at her silently.

"Do you mind telling me what the hell is going on?"

"Yes," said Bert. "I do." He moved to shut the door, but Rachel put her foot in the way.

"What's wrong with Jake?"

"Everything," said Bert, not red-faced or sweating, strange for a man who had just been shouting at top volume. Behind him, the baby was crying.

"I'm not leaving until you tell me what you did," said Rachel.

"He's the one that did something. And you don't have any right to talk. I know all about . . ." He stopped himself. "You're not a good person."

"I'm calling Krystal," she said.

"I already did."

"You can't yell at him like that."

"You need to get off my porch. Right now. I've got a baby who's crying, and I don't give a fig what you think."

"Did you hit him?"

"Lady, if you don't get off my front porch, I'm gonna go get my shotgun, and maybe that will make you shut the fuck up." Now his face was red. "Sorry for swearing."

"I'm calling the cops."

"Go ahead," said Bert. "Get gone."

Rachel stepped backward as Bert slammed the door in her face.

Rachel ran around the trailer, just in time to see Jake sliding into Bucky's hands. She stopped when she saw Bucky pull the boy close, Jake still sobbing, Bucky holding him as if he weighed nothing. Jake was small for his age, but Bucky had volunteer fireman muscles.

He carried Jake into the house, and Rachel picked up the phone as Bucky deposited him onto the couch.

Rachel called the volunteer dispatcher.

"Quinn Dispatch. What's your emergency?" Rachel didn't recognize the woman's voice, but she recognized the disinterest. It was an epidemic in this town. Laverna was right about volunteers.

"I need the police. A child has been abused."

"Is this Rachel Flood?"

"Jesus," said Rachel. "Yes. Can you please send somebody? Do you need my address?"

"We all know where you live," said the woman.

"That's fucking creepy," said Rachel. "Send them now, please."

Twenty minutes later, the police had not arrived. Bucky sat down next to Jake, who leaned into him. Bucky had his eyes closed, and tapped his foot nervously.

Jake stopped crying and pulled the sweater back. One eye was swollen shut.

Bucky swore and stood. He paced, eventually standing in front of the window. He pulled back the curtain.

"The cops just got here," he reported. "And Reverend Foote."

"Why didn't we hear sirens?"

"I don't know," said Bucky. "I'll go find out."

"Please," said Rachel.

Rachel retrieved ice from the freezer, and wrapped it in a washcloth.

They sat there in silence, Jake holding the ice to his eye. Rachel listened to car doors opening and car doors closing. Another car arrived. Rachel could tell from the brakes that it was Krystal's.

Jake started talking then. Bert confronted him, had ordered his step-son not to hang around Rachel, but Jake had not listened. Bert had proof that it was not the first time. He spied the day they planted flowers, and that night, he watched them dance in her living room. Jake admitted this, and admitted he had been coming over more often than that. Jake had the nerve to quote from the Bible: "But who are you to judge your neighbor?" To make matters worse, Jake recited the chapter and verse, James 4:12.

That was when Bert smacked him.

Krystal opened the door without knocking. Her eyes were dry, but her face was white, her lips set in a tight line.

Krystal sat down on the couch, and pulled Jake to her.

"Why are you wearing my sweater?" Krystal asked him this quietly, and examined his eye, while she waited for his answer. Rachel stood in front of them, arms crossed, holding her tongue. Finally, she could take it no longer.

"Where are the cops? I want to make a report."

"I sent them away," said Krystal.

"Bert threatened to shoot me," said Rachel. "I'm going to call them back."

"Please don't," said Krystal.

"Don't you even tell me that you're worried about your fucking wedding," said Rachel.

"No," said Krystal. "Right now, I'm worried about Jake."

"We've known each other for fifteen years," said Rachel. "I can still tell when you're scared. And I can definitely still tell when you're lying."

"I'm fine," said Jake.

"This is fucking ridiculous!" Rachel grabbed the washcloth from Krystal's hand.

"Bert is sorry," Krystal said, and hugged Jake again. "He's very, very sorry, and he's going to make it up to you."

"You always say that," muttered Jake.

Krystal turned to Rachel, pleading. "I'm not a bad mother."

"I didn't say that," said Rachel. "You were the most loyal friend I ever had. Why can't you be loyal to your own son?"

"I am," said Krystal huffily.

"Then take his side for once," said Rachel. "He comes here because he doesn't feel safe."

"Our home is safe," said Krystal. "Jake likes to be dramatic."

"Bert hit him," said Rachel. "Did you leave your baby with that dirtbag?"

"Mrs. Foote has the baby, and the reverend took Bert for a drive." Krystal smoothed Jake's hair. "Bert's not going to be home when you get there," she said.

"You're afraid of him, too." Rachel wanted to hear the words come out of Krystal's mouth, wanted her to admit it.

Instead, Krystal began crying, but Rachel could tell these were selfish tears, the tears of someone overwhelmed. Krystal cried out of hopelessness, not out of concern for her son.

"Okay," said Krystal, after she regained her composure. "I will tell Bert to lay off. Jake is welcome to come over here anytime he wants. As long as it's okay with you, and as long as he lets somebody know."

"Thank you," said Jake.

"But you need to mind your own business," said Krystal, addressing Rachel. "Stay out of my marriage. Don't forget that I've known you for fifteen years, too. And I've seen you ruin plenty of relationships."

Rachel said nothing as Jake left with his mother. As usual, Krystal didn't get it. Rachel was angry all over again, and went into the yard, where she kicked at the tiny tufts of grass, and the bare spots where the new soil and seed had yet to take root, until Bucky restrained her.

"She's not pressing charges," said Rachel.

"I know," said Bucky.

Although she knew it was a private ceremony, Rachel still found herself begging Bucky to be her date. He made excuses.

"I've only got one suit," he said. "It's black. And I need to save it for funerals. I get a lot of mileage out of that thing. Especially around here."

Instead, he promised that when she got back, he and Black Mabel would have the rest of the siding installed.

The church was so new that it smelled like plastic wrap and carpet glue. It was a small space, with room for fifty: ten pews on each side, every seat taken.

Rachel did not see one familiar face. She was wearing a simple gingham sundress and uncomplicated brown sandals, but she still felt overdressed and inappropriate.

The congregation sat in their rows and whispered lowly to each other at her entrance. She took a seat, and stared back at them, boldly.

The men were in identical suits, purchased at Pamida. Every woman wore a long jean skirt, with panty hose visible at their ankles, and each had a white long-sleeved blouse that Rachel recognized as a Simplicity pattern. She shuddered.

The front of the church was bare, except for a freshly built platform, and a tall, freestanding candelabra. None of the candles were lit.

Krystal walked down the aisle without a veil, without bridesmaids, without flowers. Rachel couldn't help but think she deserved it.

At least she got to wear the wedding dress she had chosen months before, when Bert was still a heathen. Thankfully, she had the foresight to choose a dress that was long-sleeved and demure.

The ceremony was insanely boring, endlessly polite. Rachel kept her eyes on Jake, who stood up front, and off to the side. He kept the swollen eye out of sight, so he stood at a weird angle. Most of the time, he looked down at his shoes.

She was shocked at his outfit. No flair whatsoever. Brown slacks, brown jacket, white shirt. No tie, no pocket square, no hat, no shoes with platform heels. Plain loafers, the kind with no tassels.

The reception was held outside. Rachel found Jake immediately, and they sat together in the grass, watching the line of people lay out hot dishes and cold salads on folding card tables.

Bert glared when he saw them together, and Rachel met his eyes without fear. Jake's hand reached up to touch his eye.

Reverend Foote approached them, and Jake busied himself with

blowing the tiny stars from dandelions gone to seed. Rachel knew that this was how dandelions spread, multiplied, and hoped they would infest the entire church property.

"Reverend Foote," he said, and held out his hand.

"Paula Sherwood," said Rachel, and shook.

"I'm pretty sure that's not your name," said the reverend.

"It's the name my satanic cult gave me," said Rachel. "I know it sounds awfully pedestrian. We like to remain inconspicuous."

"Thank you for coming." He pulled his hand back and reached down to touch Jake's head. Rachel put an arm around Jake as he flinched, narrowed her eyes at the reverend.

"I'm here for Jake," said Rachel. "And the macaroni salad." Rachel flashed devil horns on her right hand, until the reverend left, stammering. They continued to watch the wedding party, and Rachel lost herself in counting shoes with Velcro closures.

"Why isn't Rocky here?" Rachel assumed he would have been invited.

"Bert says we've already got one freak in the family." Across the lawn, Bert was kneeling in the grass, deep in prayer, as the parishioners filed past him. Instead of wedding gifts, they dropped baskets of food as they passed. A tradition for the man of the family, perhaps, cheap plastic weaves straining to hold the cans of beets and green beans. It was up to Krystal to thank them, as Bert remained in prayer.

"We're not poor," said Jake, as he watched this parade of cheap dress clothes, offering up dusty cans from their pantries. "We don't even go to the food bank."

"This church is weird," said Rachel. Bert continued to kneel, and Reverend Foote placed his hands on Bert's shoulder blades, a blessing. Rachel could see Bert's forehead, sweating with the calisthenics of prayer. He was shaking now, and the parishioners shouted out glad tidings as they continued to pile the food around him.

"If he starts speaking in tongues, I'm kidnapping you," said Rachel. "This is some fucked-up church."

"I think I caught him speaking in tongues at home," said Jake. "Or he was choking on a piece of steak."

Rachel pulled a dandelion from the grass and held it in front of Jake's face.

"Your mom didn't get her flowers," she said. "But I think you need a corsage."

Rachel took the dandelion and slipped it through the buttonhole of Jake's jacket. They watched the wedding guests milling about, until the reverend's wife announced that it was time for pictures.

"Aren't you going to go up there?"

"No," said Jake. "I refuse. I don't want to be in any of the pictures. Because of this." He pointed at his eye, still swollen, ringed with a circle of yellow and blue bruises.

Jake's absence didn't seem to bother Krystal or Bert. They held the baby and stood with the pine trees proud and sturdy behind them.

The reverend's wife gave them directions on posing, something Jake should have been doing.

Bert held the baby while Krystal leaned over to kiss him on the cheek.

"My family!" He announced this to applause as the camera flashed.

Rachel could not bring herself to look at Jake. She sat in the grass and reached for his hand.

The Flood Girls versus Sullivan's Best Western

★ ★ ★

*L*averna drank her coffee, until her reverie was interrupted by Red Mabel, pushing her way into the house, holding a box of yellow cake mix.

"It's my birthday," said Red Mabel. "I share this day with Joan Van Ark and Geronimo." Red Mabel pulled two unbroken eggs from her coat pocket, and gifted these as well.

"I'm not going to make you a cake," said Laverna. "I've got shit to do." She handed the eggs back to Red Mabel, who pitched them into the sink. Red Mabel left, and Laverna stared at the eggs, cracked and dripping all over the dirty dishes.

———

Krystal's car was gone, as usual. Laverna craned her neck, but could not see Rachel's yard, because of the fence. Ginger had told her that Rachel was gardening, of all things. Laverna could see the new siding, and for a split second, she was proud. She put on her mean face when she stepped up on Krystal's porch.

Laverna resented women who took care of deadbeats, and she carried this resentment with her when the deadbeat answered the door. Word had traveled fast, and Laverna had no tolerance for child abusers.

"Bert," she said.

"Laverna."

"You owe me close to a hundred dollars," she said.

"What?"

"Your tab," she said. "Just because you got right with God, doesn't mean you got right with my bookkeeper."

"You keep the books," pointed out Bert.

"Fact is, you never settled up. But seeing you now, I'm reminded how nice it's been not having you around." Laverna adjusted her scarf and gave him dead eyes.

"I'll make things right," said Bert. "I've been trying."

"You let me take Jake for the day, and we'll call it even. I need help reorganizing my closets. Due to my extensive collection of layers, it will be quite a job."

"He's qualified," said Bert. "Jake!" He yelled down the long hallway of the trailer house.

She looked him in the eye and lowered her voice. The cigarette smoking added a scratchy tone, and she hoped she sounded like a mafioso. "You lay a finger on that boy again, I'll rip your fucking nuts off."

"I'm not that man anymore," he said.

"Bullshit. Get a job, you goddamn lowlife." She muttered this before Jake could hear.

She grabbed Jake, who appeared from the hallway already dressed, in gabardine slacks and a dress shirt the color of mustard. He didn't protest as he was yanked out to Laverna's car.

"Road trip," she announced as she backed her Cadillac out in a hurry. Laverna turned out of the trailer court and headed toward the highway.

"You have a game today," he said.

"I'm well aware of that," she said. "You're coming with. Watch for deer." The town of Sullivan had their own scorekeeper, but Laverna was feeling magnanimous. Truthfully, she was sick and tired of riding with the other Flood Girls, listening to them bitch about boyfriends, split ends, Democrats.

Jake sat next to her in the Cadillac. Ten miles out of town, Laverna and Jake gossiped like old women. In addition to having the only hotel in the county, Sullivan was best known for being the birthplace of an actual serial killer, who murdered three homeless prostitutes in Spokane.

Of course, they both had read the book, called *The Murderer Who Came Down from the Mountains*. Laverna was delighted that Jake shared her opinion that the serial killer could have tried harder. Three murders was a spree, not a serial killing.

At a McDonald's drive-through, Laverna ordered an iced tea, nothing else. She could not understand why McDonald's was considered such a treasure. The Dirty Shame was just as cheap and convenient, and had the added bonus of entertainment from the silver miners.

She handed Jake his cheeseburger. "My daughter hasn't turned you into a vegetarian yet?"

"No," said Jake. "I am the captain of my own ship."

"It's one weird ship," said Laverna, and returned to the highway. She watched out of the corner of her eye, as he unfolded paper napkins across his lap and delicately peeled away the wrapper from the burger. "Can I ask you a question?"

"You may," he said, and paused before taking the first bite. His manners were exquisite.

"How are things going with Bert?"

"I'd rather not talk about him," Jake said, and chewed silently.

"Does he mind you spending so much time with my daughter?"

Jake swallowed. "He says she has a bad reputation."

"He should talk," said Laverna. "What does your mother see in him? She's so pretty, I mean."

"I'm just thankful the baby is my half sister," said Jake. "If she grows up to look like Bert, I can get away with being half-concerned."

"Your mother deserves better," said Laverna.

"I agree," said Jake. "But she got knocked up, and I think she wanted to see if she could get it right this time."

"You are a nice young man," Laverna reassured him. "You are the only male in this town who I approve of. As you probably know, my daughter picks inappropriate men. She makes dumb choices."

"No," said Jake. "That's the old Rachel." He accentuated this by pointing a french fry. "I'll tell you something. Rachel is one of the smartest women I've ever met. You're lucky. It was an awful day when I finally realized my mother was not intelligent. My mom might be a nurse, but she's an idiot."

"No comment," said Laverna. She wanted to ruffle his hair, or touch the back of his neck. She shook off her motherly instincts, resumed her usual laser focus. "I need some help with something."

"Okay," said Jake.

"It's about the Fourth of July parade," she continued. "I want to win the float competition this year."

"You've never had a float," said Jake. "The Flood Girls usually ride in the back of Red Mabel's truck and throw candy at people."

"Exactly," said Laverna. "Not this year. I want a float, a real float. Like the firemen and the Shriners and the pep club and the rotary club."

"And the John Birch Society," added Jake. "Even though they are a bunch of white supremacists," said Jake. "They shouldn't be allowed to decorate anything."

"Correct," said Laverna. "I want to win. And only you can help."

He considered her carefully. "You're right. I've just been counting down the days until I'm old enough to decorate a prom."

"Well?"

"I'll make you a deal," said Jake. "I will create a float for the Flood Girls, but you have to do me a favor."

Laverna shuddered. "Fine," she said.

"Black Mabel takes care of your daughter," he said.

"If that's what you want to call it," said Laverna. "I believe the authorities would call it drug dealing."

Jake ignored this. "Now I want you to take care of Black Mabel."

"Is she in the clink again?"

"No," said Jake. "I want you to pay to have her teeth fixed."

"Jesus," said Laverna.

"Anonymously," he said. "I know how much you like to take credit for things."

"Fine," said Laverna. "I'm not a complete glory hound, you know. I'm leaving the float completely up to you. It's your baby, and I want nothing to do with it. Except to win, of course."

"Why are you picking me? I mean, really?"

"You've had a rough couple of months," said Laverna. "You deserve a little glory of your own."

"Is this a secret?"

"Just the Flood Girls know," said Laverna. "And Bucky. Don't tell anybody else. I want this to be a shocker."

"You came to the right kid," said Jake. "I promise it will be unlike anything this town has ever seen."

———

In Sullivan, Laverna discovered that Rachel had also made the trip with a surprise guest: Bucky. Laverna promptly gave him an assignment, to protect Jake in the bleachers. Laverna warned him about pickpockets, made sure he had brought his knife.

As her team warmed up, Laverna watched the ladies from Sullivan's Best Western. As if the serial killer wasn't enough, Sullivan also had uniforms. The women wore actual polo shirts, provided by the hotel. Laverna was suspicious of the shortstop and rover, as they were Mexicans. Laverna assumed they were illegal immigrant housekeepers, smuggled across the border to play softball.

The white women on the team were heavy drinkers. Laverna usually made sure her own girls waited until the second inning to crack a beer, but the ladies of Sullivan always showed up half-lit, and traditionally fell apart by the bottom of the fourth inning.

It was easy for Ginger to strike out the drunkest ladies—they were either seeing double, or kept one eye shut to maintain perspective.

In the middle of the fourth inning, Rachel caught her first ball. Laverna was amazed, and watched as Rachel stood still and the ball fell right into her glove.

Of course, she forgot that she was supposed to do something next, so she stood there, surprised like everybody else, as one of the Mexicans tagged up and continued her run from second to third. Laverna felt a scream rise in her throat, an invective aimed at her daughter, but swallowed it. Thankfully, Red Mabel's heart had not softened. Or her voice.

"Throw that fucker!" Red Mabel was ready at third, and Rachel, snapping out of her reverie, launched it in her general direction. It wasn't anywhere near third base, but the Mexican runner stopped, probably because Red Mabel looked like a female *chupacabra*.

The Flood Girls won, fourteen to six.

———

She dropped Jake at home, and found Jim Number Three sitting on her front porch. It was the longest day of the year, and still light out. Laverna swore when she saw the roses.

"No," she said, and slammed the car door.

He stood, left the roses behind. He offered up a bulging envelope, a better gift.

It took Laverna a few minutes to count two thousand dollars, all singles and fives.

"From the Clinkenbeards," said Jim Number Three proudly. "An electrical fire in the middle of the night. Strangest thing. Told them I was pretty sure it was pack rats. I was happy to help rewire their shack. Expensive as shit."

He waited for acknowledgment, but Laverna brushed past him, kicked the vase of roses. The water drained between the boards of the porch.

She tucked the envelope into her purse and gave him the finger. She had no more words for Jim Number Three. She locked the front door and watched out the window until he drove away. Laverna counted to one hundred, brought the roses inside. Laverna Flood was a practical woman. It was Red Mabel's birthday, after all. Tonight, she would receive flowers, probably for the first time in her life.

At nine o'clock, the sun had not set, and it made Laverna restless. She removed bags of apples from the freezer. Red Mabel picked them last year in the fall, and they spent an afternoon peeling and coring, stuffing them into freezer bags. Laverna filled her kitchen sink with hot water, and left them there to thaw.

While she waited, she took a cup of coffee onto the back deck, and sat and smoked and watched the enormous suckerfish on the edges of the bank. The river was running high, and the suckers wended their way around the tall grass and the buttercups that were now submerged.

Laverna spent the next few hours making applesauce, boiling down the apples in a giant pot, smashed them into pulp before she added Red Hots, the cinnamon candy that was her secret ingredient. She filled the mason jars, and sunk them in a cauldron of boiling water.

Laverna went into the house and returned with a rifle. She flicked at the safety with her thumbnail.

She fired at the suckerfish. They seemed unaffected by the splash, by the sound. They continued to scuttle along the bank. Laverna fired again, and her hair was the only thing that moved.

"I am through with this bad luck," said Laverna, to no one in particular.

Through the screen door, she could hear the pops and snaps of mason jars rattling in their cages.

"No more volunteers," said Laverna, and fired again. The gunshot echoed across the river, and then there was silence, save for the sound of applesauce righting itself, lids sealing themselves shut, the sound of settling.

Feathers

★ ★ ★

*J*ake dressed with purpose that morning, had to root through the storage shed to find certain pieces. He decided upon boot-cut black slacks, a crisp white shirt, a black vest with a barely perceptible white pinstripe, black boots, and a black beret. Finally, he was satisfied. This is what a designer would wear.

Misty's bike still leaned against Martha's trailer, and Jake borrowed it for his mission today. He was going to need speed as he went looking for Bucky. It was a Friday morning, and he had almost finished Rachel's house, so Bucky could be anywhere.

Jake cruised around the streets of Quinn, past the sprinklers, a Kool-Aid stand, trucks still parked at the bars from the night before.

He found Bucky drinking coffee outside of the hardware store with Della Dempsey. She rolled her eyes at his outfit, stomped out her cigarette.

"I need to talk to you," he said to Bucky.

"You're freaking me out," said Della. "Are you supposed to be dressed like a French person?"

"This involves both of you, actually," said Jake. He got off his bike and stood in front of Bucky, digging in his pocket for the envelope.

He passed it to Bucky, who whistled when he removed the five hundred dollars.

"We're building a float," said Jake. "Or rather, you're building the float, and I'm decorating it."

"Sounds about right," said Della.

"You get to keep whatever we don't spend on materials." He pointed at the hardware store. "That's where you come in," he said to Della. "Laverna expects a discount."

"She always does," said Della.

In the hardware store, Jake started pointing at things: rolls of chicken wire, two-by-fours, wire coat hangers, ten white bedsheets.

"Does Laverna want us to dress like the Klan?" asked Della.

"No," said Jake. "This is my vision. And we already have a white supremacist float."

Jake conferred with Bucky about nails and screws. He filled his basket with cans of baby-blue and gold spray paint.

Della was at the cash register, chewing her gum, which seemed to be a job on its own.

The total was under one hundred dollars, and Bucky loaded the purchases. Jake demanded they drive to Ellis. He threw Misty's bike in the back of Bucky's truck.

On the drive, Bucky wanted to talk about Rachel. "Is she done making her amends yet?"

"You're not supposed to know about that," said Jake.

"I'm just trying to be supportive," said Bucky. "Is she leaving soon?"

"Do you know any harpists?"

"No," said Bucky. "What does that have to do with Rachel?"

"Nothing," said Jake.

"She's really something," continued Bucky. "Does she ever talk about me?"

"Out of your league," said Jake, not caring if he sounded cruel. "Don't even think about it."

At the Ben Franklin, Jake filled shopping carts with rolls of fiberglass and eighty packages of white napkins; even though it was picnic season, the manager had to bring more from the storehouse.

At the fabric store, Jake bought feathers, fifteen yards of gauzy netting, five yards of white chiffon, a case of silver glitter, and cotton batting for pillows. Bucky seemed slightly embarrassed when Jake emerged from the aisle with armfuls of white feathers.

After Jake paid, there was still two hundred and fifty dollars left.

"That's for you," said Jake.

"Sweet," said Bucky.

"But you have to do exactly what I tell you."

"You're enjoying this too much, kid."

Laverna had cashed in yet another debt, and an old flatbed truck from the lumber mill was parked in Diane's garage. It was a huge space, large enough to park three cars, and Bucky could not stop wondering aloud why a single woman needed such a large industrial space.

"Sex dungeon," said Red Mabel, who was waiting for them, along with Ginger, Shyanne, Rachel, Della, and Martha Man Hands. Ronda was cooking lunch at the Dirty Shame, and Diane was teaching summer school. The Sinclairs were tending to the gas station. Ginger told Rachel that she had to pay the Sinclairs each twenty dollars to ride on the float. Apparently, their new congregation did not celebrate Independence Day.

Jake unveiled his sketches and his design plan. The Flood Girls agreed unanimously that this was a secret worth keeping.

Bucky framed out the flatbed with two-by-fours. As each section went up, Red Mabel and Rachel wrestled the chicken wire flat, and Ginger attached the pieces to the two-by-fours with the staple gun.

Jake and Shyanne followed behind, stuffing the chicken wire, each hole threaded through with a paper napkin. When the framing was done, and all the chicken wire hung, they sat down on Diane's cold cement floor. They stuffed themselves when Laverna arrived with greasy boxes of fried chicken and french fries.

Jake approached Red Mabel and took her off to the side. She licked the grease from her fingers, as he asked her to begin a special project of her own.

"You're the best with a knife," he said, which she could not deny. "This is like whittling, but not pointless." Jake found wire on one of Diane's shelves, and Red Mabel began her assignment.

Eight hours later, the entire frame was stuffed with white napkins. Bucky had built a wall behind the cab of the trailer, had given it the illusion of a curve, with some crafty work with the remaining two by fours and a handsaw.

Diane arrived later with cases and cases of beer, and pop for those underage or sober. Work was stopped for the day; once again, the Flood Girls had something to celebrate.

Before he left, Red Mabel grabbed Jake with her strong arms, and kissed him on the forehead.

————

Three months, and Jake had become intimate with the Singer. He grew to love the hum as he stitched. He studied the book and consulted the machine's instruction manual when he was perplexed. He talked to the machine, and Rachel didn't think it was strange; she left him alone in the sewing corner. Jake and the Singer produced slowly, but he was determined to master the detail work. So far, he had made four potholders, a skirt for Rachel, and two shirts for himself.

Jake found all his material at the thrift store. In the ottoman, Buley hoarded thread for him, half spools in every color. She set aside a seam ripper, and a pincushion. The pincushion was a turtle, and shone with pins that stuck in the felt shell. Jake and Buley could not believe people were willing to part with such things.

Jake discovered a bolt of cotton fabric, sturdy but sheer, the color of the night sky, a dark blue that was almost black. Perfect for curtains, an easy project, which he was thankful for.

Last week, Jake had to admit defeat and call Diane for help with the shirts. Diane spent an hour at Rachel's house, helping him stitch the button-holes, lining them up exactly, showing him what he had been doing incorrectly and passing on a few tricks of her own. Diane also attempted to set Rachel up with one of her exes, but she declined as gracefully as possible.

"I'm not ready to date yet," said Rachel. "But I appreciate the offer."

"He's a catch," said Diane. "He's been married twice, but one ran away and one died in a freak accident. Crock-Pot explosion. Can you even imagine?"

"I can," said Rachel. "But no, thanks."

Jake was curious. "If he's such a catch, why aren't you still with him?"

Diane pointed at the stitching on the hem of Jake's seafoam-green shirt. "Sloppy," she said. "I'm not ready to settle down, I guess. I'm not the type of woman who makes things in Crock-Pots."

"How did . . ." Jake began to ask for the sordid details.

Diane stopped him with one hand. "She was making a stew. That's all I know."

Jake diligently worked on the hem of the second panel of curtains. His family was on a church trip, some sort of pilgrimage, or maybe a picnic, in Boyce Falls. Rachel watched, as she sat on the couch and drank tea.

Jake sewed determinedly, humming to himself, occasionally sweet-talking the machine. Rachel eased herself from the couch and dug through a toolbox beneath the stereo.

"Ha," she said. Jake did not look up, could hear the squeal of the cassette as it rewound.

Rachel pushed play, and stood in front of the Singer. "Fleetwood Mac," she announced. "I want to know what you think."

He did not know why she was staring at him, why his opinion was so important. The music was enjoyable enough, but she was looking at him like she expected him to come unglued.

"Pleasant," Jake said, and resumed pumping the foot pedal, zipping along the hem.

"Your mother used to love this album," said Rachel. She returned to the couch, arranged pillows under her legs. Jake could tell she was stiff and sore.

He watched her grimace, as she elevated her right leg on the arm of the couch. This kind of pain was undoubtedly new to her. He removed his foot from the pedal. "Did you ever hurt yourself when you drank? Bert broke his nose once. It was kind of awesome. He fell down our steps and landed on a sprinkler."

"I broke a rib once," she said. "But you should have seen the other girl."

"Did you make amends to her?" Jake had been working his way through the Al-Anon and AA literature. At first, he wanted to help Rachel stay sober, but selfishly, he now wanted her to stay in Quinn.

"I did," she said. "I found her last year at a strip club. She didn't even remember me."

"Who could ever forget you?" Jake slid the material through the darting needle.

"Most of the people I made amends to already forgot about me, or didn't remember it at all."

"But you did the work," said Jake. "That's the important thing."

"I think the worst was having to go in front of the entire tribal council in Pablo. I had to make amends to the twenty most important Indians. Apparently, I ruined one of their powwows. I thought I was a jingle dancer."

"Jesus," said Jake.

"Athena made sure that I never said sorry. That wasn't enough. I had to promise that I was doing the work to change, and that it wouldn't ever happen again."

"And now you're a different person," said Jake. "You're better for it."

"I'll always be an alcoholic," said Rachel.

"And I'll always be a hillbilly," said Jake. "We all have our crosses to bear." He finished the hem with a flourish.

"I don't know any hillbillies who can stitch together a miniskirt out of carpet samples."

"Good point," said Jake. The miniskirt turned out perfectly, and fit Rachel even better than he had hoped. She claimed that her tips doubled when she wore it to work.

Bucky installed a doorbell without being asked, and when it rang, Jake and Rachel were both startled.

"Come in," hollered Rachel.

The door opened, and it was the last person Jake had expected to see.

Bert stepped into the living room, carrying a package from UPS.

"This is yours," he said to Rachel, but his eyes laser focused on Jake. "I signed for it."

Rachel jumped up and crossed in front of Bert, tried to block his view. She took the package from Bert's hands. "I ordered some workout videos!" Bert continued to stare, as Rachel yammered. "Still trying to get rid of this beer belly!"

Bert pushed past her and marched to the corner.

Jake took his hands off the sewing machine, and leaned back in the chair. The album continued to play, and all Jake could hear was the refrain. *Never going back again.*

"Is that yours?" Bert pointed at the machine, at Jake's vintage Singer.

For the first time, Jake did not want to lie, or make any excuses. He stood up from the chair, and in front of the machine.

"Yes, Bert. It's mine."

Bert yanked the power cord from the wall, picked up the machine, and rushed toward the door. The foot pedals and cords drug behind him, as well as the curtain panel that was still stuck in the machine.

Jake and Rachel ran after him. They watched as he threw the sewing machine over the fence, heaved it with all his strength. Jake could hear it land, crack, and he knew it had broken into pieces.

Bert stomped up the shale path. They stood in the newly installed light of Rachel's front porch and heard him swearing as he crossed the driveway. Inside the house, the music continued, as if nothing had happened.

The curtain had been made from several yards of fabric, and the material snagged on the top of Rachel's fence, as it launched through the air.

They both watched the fabric, as it danced, moving slightly in the breeze.

The Flood Girls versus Eunice Volunteer Dispatch

★　　★　　★

*A*t the Dirty Shame, Winsome insisted on taking Rachel out to dinner. When she pointed out the lack of restaurants, and the gossip dining in Quinn would create, Winsome was undeterred.

"No chance," she said. The unspoken rule in AA was to wait a year before having sex, or making any major changes. She had received permission from the Chief. She could not think of anyone in Quinn who was mildly attractive, and it wasn't worth the gas money to travel for a one-night stand in Missoula.

"I won't drink around you," he said. "And I've got a hot tub." Rachel ignored this, continued to busy herself with slicing lemons, but her mind was caught in a familiar place. It was bargaining mode. She remembered the last two years of drinking, sitting in front of the gas station in Missoula, leaving it up to the radio station to decide if she would buy beer. If it was a song she liked, she would drink that night. Unfortunately for Rachel, at that point, she could rationalize almost anything. She would hear Michael Bolton, and decide that she had liked him all along.

"One night," said Rachel. She had earned sex, had worked hard for it, and Winsome was the only single man around these parts with a human head.

Rachel drove to Winsome's house when her shift was over. He had only one swimsuit in his house for a woman, despite the many he had entertained over the years, and it was much too large, would have fit Buley. As promised, he behaved like a gentleman, and he stayed sober. She was not breaking the rules, or sidestepping them. This was biology.

She stayed for hours. The hot tub was contained in the backyard, beneath an octagonal gazebo and shielded by aspen trees. She stayed until she could see the stars.

They both got what they wanted. This was her first sober sex, and her feet were rough and her legs stubbly, but none of that mattered. She deserved the release, and he deserved a woman who would not steal his stereo.

———

The next game was in Quinn, and Laverna scheduled extra practices. Rachel was determined. Sometimes only four of the Flood Girls would show, but Rachel was always there. This was their rescheduled matchup with Eunice Volunteer Dispatch, and this time, in the last week of June, there was no snow. Rachel sweated in her black T-shirt, emblazoned with a giant smoking pistol, and ripped-up jean shorts. She was going to have to buy a sports bra. Even with the underwire, the lacy black bra from Victoria's Secret was completely impractical, and her sweat combining with the lace made her itchy.

The Eunice Volunteer Dispatch wore black shirts, the backs a white outline of a police scanner. Rachel knew from her own experience that black was impractical, hoped they were sweating just as much as she.

Rachel warmed up in the infield, played catch with Martha, attempted to throw the ball as hard as she could, as Martha crouched down in her gear. Rachel knew that Ginger's pitches were lobs, really, but she wanted to show the people in the bleachers that her arm was getting stronger.

Martha was impressed. She stood up and approached Rachel, the ball in her hand.

"You're getting some heat on those," said Martha.

"Thank you," said Rachel. "I've been practicing extra with the Chief."

"I can tell," said Martha. "Look, there's something that I need to say. It's kind of a secret, and I feel really bad about it."

"Okay," Rachel said, and stepped closer to Martha. Rachel was certain it had something to do with lesbianism.

"It's about your friend." Martha used her thumb to discreetly point at Jake, who was sitting in the bleachers, scorebook carefully prepared as always. Winsome sat next to him, eating popcorn, sober.

"What is it?"

"He gave me some letters awhile back," said Martha. "For my daughter, Misty."

"And?"

"Well, he and Misty got into a lot of trouble together."

"I've heard," said Rachel.

"I never sent them," admitted Martha. "I guess I was angry. I suppose Jake has been wondering why she hasn't written back."

"He hasn't said anything," said Rachel.

"I threw them away," said Martha. "I just wanted somebody to know. Please don't tell him."

"That's really fucked-up," said Rachel. "You need to tell him." Martha had an ashamed look on her face as she walked back and crouched down, ready for more catches.

Several of the girls from Eunice Volunteer Dispatch were related to Della. The pitcher and first base were Della's sisters. The entire Dempsey clan was in the bleachers, and none of them had eyebrows. Jake sat in the front row, surrounded by the seven dwarfs. They had attended every home game, and offered up advice after every AA meeting. Keep your eye on the ball, wait for your pitch, running forward to catch a pop fly was much easier than running backward. Rachel couldn't help but think these suggestions were also metaphors for sobriety.

The rest of the bleachers were filled with faces that had become familiar, the people of the town. Rachel was thankful Shyanne was here to keep her out of the batter's box.

However, Shyanne twisted her ankle in the fourth inning, running like a colt, after nailing a ball clean to the fences.

She limped into the dugout. Rachel looked on nervously as Ginger immediately started fussing. Laverna pretended that she knew what she was talking about, and diagnosed it as nothing.

"Walk it off," Laverna commanded. "It's not even swollen."

That was a lie. As they all watched, it grew larger.

The Flood Girls went back to the field, and Tabby surprised everyone by catching a ball that shot three inches off the ground, diving into the dirt before it could make contact. She brushed off her chest, and waved at her sister, Tish, who was emitting bloodcurdling screams from the bleachers, off her medication once again.

"Calm down!" Laverna screamed into the bleachers. These screams were a distraction, and off-putting. "Take your fucking medication!"

Tish was chastened by this. Rachel knew that Laverna had let Tish close down the bar for a rare hour, so that she could finally see her sister's softball game. This was a mistake, as Tish was extremely excitable. Her face crumpled as she grabbed her keys and left at the top of the fifth inning. Rachel understood this—Tish would rather be serving drinks than let herself be a target for Laverna.

Ronda showed off her guns by catching a pop fly and then throwing the ball all the way from the outfield to Red Mabel at third base. This was the second double play in Flood Girl history. Rachel ran in from the field and hoped that their luck would continue, that Shyanne would be standing in the dugout, ready to bat.

She wasn't. Shyanne continued to sprawl across the bench, her ankle elevated on a pile of purses.

Rachel nervously adjusted the lineup, attached to the chain link with a clothespin, and a lump rose in her throat when she saw she was on deck.

It was the top of the sixth inning. The Flood Girls were behind by one, eight to nine, but Rachel wasn't worried about a loss. She was worried about the crowd.

As Rachel stepped up to the batter's box, the bleachers became completely silent.

Bucky turned around and strained to look through the chain link. He seemed determined to avoid a melee, because if the game was called short, he wouldn't get paid. She watched as he dusted off home plate with extra care. He winked at Rachel, and she swallowed down the fear in her throat.

Rachel swung the bat around to warm up her arm, and the crowd was still. She wondered if Red Mabel was aiming a sniper's rifle at them.

It was a ball. Bucky called it. From the bleachers came a few snickers, some tittering. Rachel could hear Jake cough nervously.

The next pitch was a thing of beauty, a high, impossibly perfect arc, and Rachel swung and missed.

"Strike," called Bucky.

There was laughter now, but no one had screamed out any slurs.

Rachel figured they were past that now. It was enough for the people of Quinn to watch her fail.

But she didn't. Rachel kept her eye on the ball and swung at the next pitch. The ball flew over the third-base line and stayed in play. Rachel remembered what to do. She ran to first. She blew her mother a kiss.

The citizens of Quinn gasped, and the seven dwarfs stood up to applaud. Rachel's single brought in Della, and the contingent without eyebrows delighted. Ronda continued her streak and hammered a slow pitch, sent it rocketing over the head of the woman in right field. Even though Ronda was right-handed, she was always full of surprises. Her triple brought in Rachel, and just like that, Bucky called the game.

The Flood Girls were victorious, eleven to nine.

————

Monday morning, Gene Runkle sat at the end of the bar. Rachel didn't mind him or Mrs. Matthis—she saved her anxiety for the appearance of Winsome, and had planned a speech where she reiterated that it had been only a one-night stand. Gene was celebrating, but he wouldn't say why, just kept raising a gray finger for another shot of Crown Royal.

For once, Rachel had to pry the gossip out of him, on his fifth shot.

"Caught that fucking dog last week," he said. "It was like Moby Dick or some shit. An endless hunt."

"Bullshit," said the silver miner who looked like Elvis. She leaned across the bar on an elbow and ordered her first beer of the day. "It was the Klemp girl who caught him."

"Whatever," said Gene. "It's done!" He raised his glass and saluted himself.

———

After her shift, Rachel sped to Ellis. Animal control was in a giant garage, built on the outskirts of Ellis, so the constant, deafening barking wouldn't bother anyone.

Rachel passed the wing full of cats, but continued down the corridor and entered the cement room that housed the kennels. She was immediately overwhelmed by the chaos of dogs hurling themselves at kennel doors, scrabbling up to greet her, barking madly.

She saw the brown dog immediately. He stared back at her, eyed her like he knew he was on death row.

Rachel went to the front desk and brought the attendant back. The attendant was young and nice, and appeared competent. She was the antithesis of Gene Runkle.

"What is that?"

"We think it's a dachshund mix of some kind." The dog was brown, transitioned into a dark red along the back, grew darker still until the hindquarters were completely black. Fangs stuck out from beneath his upper lip, vaguely vampire-like, but the springing tail and white paws suggested anything but evil.

"It looks like a gremlin."

"He's a sweetheart," said the attendant.

"He bit my mother."

"Oh," said the attendant, absorbing this information.

"Can I take him on a walk?"

"Of course," the attendant said, and returned with a leash.

"How long have you had him?"

"A week or so," she said, and unlocked the kennel. The dog stepped out calmly and stretched out on his front legs, yawned. "We call him Frank."

"You're kidding me."

"No, ma'am. The dogcatcher in Quinn insisted on it. Thought it was hilarious."

Frank bent obediently as Rachel attached the collar and leash. She walked Frank out behind the animal control building. He didn't pull on the leash, just moseyed along, stopping to smell things, lifting a leg on others.

Rachel followed him back into the office, and announced to the attendant her intent to take him home. This pleased the woman, and she slid the paperwork on a clipboard across the counter. Rachel filled out the necessary information, Frank sitting right beside her, as if he knew. He scratched his ear with one hind leg.

"Rachel Flood?" The attendant looked down at the clipboard.

"Yes."

"I've heard about you." *Oh, fuck*, thought Rachel. Her past was everywhere. Frank would never be allowed to go home with a slut or a murderess.

"Oh," said Rachel.

"My friend Diane Connor? She thinks the world of you."

"Pleasure," Rachel said, and shook her hand.

Frank and Rachel left together, and the attendant waved at them until they pulled away.

Frank sat calmly on the front seat as she drove to the pet store. Again, he bent down and accepted the leash without a peep. A half hour later, they returned to her truck with dog food, a leash, a dog bed, a bowl for food and a bowl for water. She also bought a chew toy shaped like a softball, and Frank immediately began gnawing on it.

He watched out the window as they drove back to Quinn, tail wagging when she reached over to pet him. She looked over once, and she could have sworn that he was smiling at her.

She parked in front of her mother's house, and went around to the passenger side, and clipped Frank on his leash.

They walked up to the front porch, and Rachel rang the bell.

This was the first time Rachel had ever been to her mother's house. To most daughters, this would be a strange thing. To Rachel, it just felt like another thing to brave. She steeled herself and waited for her mother to appear.

Laverna answered the door, and regarded them both. For once, she didn't seem suspicious.

"Hi," said Rachel.

Laverna crouched down and rubbed the dog's head. "I recognize him."

"His name is Frank," said Rachel.

"Seriously?"

"Yes," said Rachel. "I got him for you."

Rachel handed Laverna the leash and returned to the truck, expecting her mother to yell after her. Nothing came. Rachel collected the food, the bed, and the bowls, and brought them to the front door.

She stood there, her arms full. Laverna was already stroking Frank's head.

"Come in," Laverna said, and Rachel entered without a word, Frank sniffing Laverna's pants. Laverna unleashed him, and he began nosing around the living room. Rachel examined her mother's home, at her taste in decorations. Laverna walls were nearly full of woodprints of sunsets, carefully carved heads of Native Americans and the cowboys who hunted them, ancient snowshoes and spurs mounted on a grayed chunk of cedar. Jake would be horrified. Rachel knew these had all been gifts from Laverna's customers.

Laverna led them out to the back deck. Frank lay down in front of Laverna and snuggled into her feet. She scratched his back, and he stood and stretched, and then began to sniff around. He seemed wary of the river.

"I've never had a dog," said Laverna.

"I know," said Rachel.

They sat in silence and watched Frank, as he shambled closer to the railing, still careful of the water. Rachel wanted to tell her mother so much. Rachel wanted to give her mother something to love that wouldn't ever disappoint her, betray her, or break her heart.

Rachel considered her words, but then decided to say nothing. Maybe this time her mother already knew. It had taken ten years, but Rachel had finally accepted her mother as a person, who had done the best with what she had.

"He doesn't bark," said Rachel.

"Just like your father," said Laverna.

Honeymoon

$\star$ $\quad$ $\star$ $\quad$ $\star$

*B*ert and Krystal did not go on a honeymoon. Bert claimed there was no money for it, and Krystal claimed that what they really needed was family time. Jake had dreams of Glacier National Park, and of Bert falling into a fumarole. No such luck. He even considered giving them the rest of his softball money.

When Krystal went to work, Bert and the baby left with Mrs. Foote, to knock on doors and spread the word. Jake knew they used the baby as bait—who would turn away an infant on such a hot summer day?

Jake loaded his Walkman with Roxette, and his pockets with the sketchbook and pens to make a list. He walked through town, and the sugary Swedes in his earphones erased all fears of bullies hiding around street corners, lurking in abandoned trailer houses.

Without the Singer, he sought an audience with the queen.

For the past week, Buley had been teaching him how to embroider. He sat at her feet, and his fingers swelled, poked by a craft as ancient as prostitution, dating back to the fifth century BC. He didn't mind Buley's history lessons. She sent Rocky out for sandwiches, and only acknowledged the broken Singer once, as if she knew the depth and weight of his loss.

He arranged the materials as instructed—a wooden embroidery hoop, tiny scissors, embroidery floss, embroidery needles. Again and again, he practiced with small squares cut from bedsheets, separating the hoops, pulling the fabric tight until Buley was satisfied. For the first three lessons, Jake wrote his name in cursive on each square; cursive a skill he had not utilized in years. Buley watched him as he carefully pulled the needles through, each thread a dot until his name was outlined in thread. He cursed the loop of the J and the tiny circles in the K, and the long tail of the Y of his last name. There was beauty in this, and at last, Buley declared that he was ready to begin work on the T-shirts.

They never made small talk—Buley watched him silently, only shifting slightly in her seat to point out dropped stitches. She saved her words for Rocky, hollering across the store about feeding the cats and refilling the ink of the price gun, even though the numbers were arbitrary.

Jake knew that the lessons were over. He had not wanted to ruin this time in her court, but he could feel the coronation was complete.

"I need to ask you a question," he said. He could not look Buley in the eye, and tugged at a long piece of embroidery floss a Siamese had appropriated under her throne.

"There are no more questions," declared Buley. "You've got a knack for this. It's all about practice, at this point."

"My mom," said Jake. "I wanted to ask you about my mom."

"No," said Buley. "I have nothing to say. Nothing you would want to hear."

"I respect that," said Jake.

"ROCKY!" Buley full-throatedly called for her boyfriend, who emerged from the stacks of concentric lampshades. Rocky held the price gun, stickers stuck in the beds of his fingernails.

"Yes," he said. He attempted to flick the price stickers away, but they remained stuck, no matter how much he shook his hand.

"I need you to have a conversation with your nephew." Jake watched the ball in his uncle's throat as he swallowed nervously. Buley pointed at the rug next to Jake, and Rocky sat without a word. "Jake has some questions. And if you want meat loaf for dinner, you're going to give him some answers."

"Yes," said Rocky once more.

"Um," said Jake, looking at Buley for permission. She nodded, pulled a twinned pair of silver kittens onto her lap, as if she was the one who was seeking comfort.

"He wants to know about his mother."

"Krystal," said Rocky.

"That's the one," said Buley. She reached for a pack of grape Bubblicious on the counter and threw it at Rocky. He unwrapped two pieces and offered one to Jake, who refused. Rocky filled his mouth—Buley was trying to comfort her boyfriend, as well.

"I just want to know what happened," said Jake. "I just want to know when she became ashamed of me."

"Yes," said Rocky. He chewed his gum, attempted to fold one of the wrappers into a painfully tiny paper airplane.

"Rocky," commanded Buley. "Talk to him."

"She did the same to me," admitted Rocky. He handed the paper airplane to Jake, and the wings were no wider than a match, and the folds shook with his pulse. "My sister is real good at moving on."

"She never left," said Buley. "She's still there. You're not."

"Why did you leave us?" Jake took a deep breath, closed his eyes, waiting for the crush of the answer. A question he had never dared ask.

"Trouble," said Rocky. "She couldn't stay away from it."

"I was just a baby," said Jake. "I don't remember anything."

"That's why I left," said Rocky. He remained silent, and began to fold the second gum wrapper. Buley nudged him with her ankle, the silver bells on her skirt tinkling, causing the twinned kittens to peer around nervously.

"Rocky," said Buley. "He's the only flesh and blood you've got."

"Didn't want you to remember," said Rocky. "Couldn't stay there and let her screw you up. Like I said. She did the same to me."

———

In his bedroom, Jake unzipped the duffel bag. Four shirts left, and without the Singer, the sewing was tedious, secreted away from the eyes of Rachel or his stepfather. Counting stitches, just as he used to count rosary beads. He bit his tongue in concentration, lost in darting through the embroidery hoop, again and again. Couching. Buley called it couching, this gold work, the thread was silk and expensive, and he could not afford a mistake.

These T-shirts were jersey knit, not meant for such detail, and he tried to remain as calm as possible. One false move, and the cotton would stretch. Jake admired Rachel's rituals of sobriety, and alone in his room, he cultivated his own spirituality. When he embroidered, he lit one candle on his thrift store candelabra, the cheap brass paint flaking off in great chunks, littering his dresser in glittering piles. He lined up the books and magazines on his bedside table, pleased at the culture: the AA books, two curling issues of *Vogue* from 1978, the copy of *Cannery Row*, and last year's *TV Guide* cover of Susan Lucci, ripped and glued in a frame of construction paper. He dressed in satin pajamas, lime in color, and forced himself to ignore the missing buttons. That was a sewing project for another day. He sprayed his quilt with a bottle of Lady Stetson perfume, another thrift store find, the contents stretched with tap water. And he listened to the same song, sometimes for hours, if it was a good night, and he was left alone.

Shyanne had given him the cassette single, and that was another portent of good luck. He had gone to the Sinclair for his mother, as milk was cheaper at the gas station. Shyanne washed all the windows every spring and fall, because Martha Man Hands was sloppy and the Sinclair sisters insisted on using vinegar. Shyanne used Windex, legs so long that a ladder was not necessary. She removed her headphones when she saw Jake.

"Here," she said, and gave him the cassette straight from her Walkman. "I already have the whole album." It was true—Ginger could afford ten thousand copies of *The Immaculate Collection*. Krystal flat out refused, thwarting Jake's Christmas list once again.

"Are you sure?" Jake tried to give her the milk money in exchange, but she refused.

"I'm sick of it anyway," she said, and removed another cassette from her coat pocket. "Garth Brooks," she announced.

"I'm sorry," said Jake, and returned home with his new prize.

The cassette single was part of the ritual. "Justify My Love" was exactly four minutes and fifty eight seconds long. The B-side was the Shep Pettibone remix of "Express Yourself," and clocked in at just over four minutes. He counted stitches, and listened to Madonna, forced himself to rise each time to flip the tape. The breaks were necessary; if he got too caught up, he got sloppy with the needle, and veered outside of the ribbing on the crew neck and sleeves. Embroidery was the work of perfectionists, and Jake the type of boy who had always colored inside the lines. He saved artistic expression for his wardrobe.

Thirty-five minutes passed, time disappeared as magically as the baby blue. Glacially, the embroidery spread, millimeter after millimeter stitched with tiny darts of gold thread.

Jake heard Bert's truck, and leaped to stuff the T-shirt and embroidery hoop under his bed. He plucked the inch-long bits of gold thread that snaked, snagged in his carpet, at least a dollar's worth that he snipped with every new row. He wished he could tie them back together, return them to the spool.

He managed to remove the evidence by the time Bert knocked. He was allowed to close his door now, Bert's wedding present to his new stepson. He still entered without being asked inside. Jake stopped the cassette as Bert crossed the threshold. Jake sat down on the bed, surrounded himself with the quilt.

His stepfather looked around the room, suspicious as always. The candelabra was still lit, the only sign of possible homosexual activity. Maybe not.

"Smells like a rodeo whore," said Bert. "Excuse my language."

"Stetson," said Jake. "Aftershave." Jake was nowhere near shaving, but Bert said nothing. At least it wasn't concealer. For the first time ever, Bert sat down on Jake's bed.

"I want to make things right," said Bert. He made eye contact with Jake, and his gaze wasn't glazed by booze, framed with bloodshot. He cleared his throat and continued. "I want to say sorry for hitting you and for ruining your sewing machine."

"So you want to make amends?" Jake looked away. He still did not

Level

★   ★   ★

*W*hen Bucky and Black Mabel arrived to do the last of the work on the trailer, Jake came out to help. Rachel was nervous—it seemed improbable that this trailer house could survive being lifted without splintering into pieces.

Bucky drove a giant flatbed, loaded with cinder blocks. Rachel and Jake carried one at a time through the gate, Bucky and Black Mabel carried two each. When the truck was unloaded, Bucky went to the dump for yet another load, and when he returned, they resumed in earnest. Rachel couldn't help but watch Bucky's back, straining with the load, surprisingly muscular.

She watched as he placed the jacks under the listing north end of Rachel's house, saw Black Mabel disappear underneath to begin stacking the cinder blocks. Eventually, Rachel gathered enough bravery to bring Black Mabel more, despite the spiders and centipedes that skittered around the pieces of skirting that had been unscrewed, propped up in the yard. Jake refused to go under the trailer house, because of his outfit, and because of his fear of the pale insects.

Despite the heat, Black Mabel kept her long leather jacket on, and Rachel was amazed that she didn't sweat. Bucky was drenched. They kept at it until all of the cinder blocks were in place, Bucky working from the edges, until he finally reached Black Mabel, pinned beneath the pipes underneath the bathroom.

trust Bert, and probably never would. This seemed like his mother's doing.

"Yes, I do."

Jake took a deep breath. The power dynamic had shifted, and he was going to take full advantage. He resumed eye contact with his stepfather. "Lately, I've become sort of an expert on these things." Jake pointed at the AA book on his nightstand. "I've learned that just saying sorry isn't enough."

"What the heck do you want me to do, kid?" Bert stood up and crossed his arms, frustrated. "All I can do is say sorry."

"Amends means trying harder, and living better." Jake's voice quivered at first, and then grew more certain, as he continued. "Amends is something you demonstrate."

"What do you want?" Bert sighed and uncrossed his arms.

"I want you to build me a shoe rack," said Jake.

Finally, one-third of the house rested on cinder blocks, and Bucky removed the jacks.

Rachel and Jake helped them screw the skirting back into place, but Bucky and Black Mabel refused the twenty dollars that Rachel pulled from her pocket.

———

There was work to be done, finishing touches. They had grown to love this house.

They painted the kitchen cabinets. She had allowed Jake to pick out the colors, and he had chosen a butterscotch yellow. The linoleum on the counters had been replaced with a dark brown tile, and he was adamant that the colors worked perfectly together.

Rachel removed all the cabinet doors and placed them on sheets of newspaper on the kitchen floor. Jake unscrewed all of the knobs carefully, and he painted the doors while Rachel painted the faceless cupboards.

"I hope you're going to line those shelves," he said.

"Of course," said Rachel. "I suppose you want to pick out the shelf paper."

"I trust you," said Jake.

"You never told me what you thought about *Cannery Row*," said Rachel as she stood on her tiptoes and dabbed at a corner of the cabinetry.

"It was hard to read," said Jake. "But it wasn't bad. Not enough sex, though. And everybody was so grimy and filthy."

"That's Steinbeck, kid."

"I didn't hate it," Jake said, and began painting the first door. "If you have any other recommendations, I will accept them without question. You have good taste."

"I know," said Rachel. "Except all I've been reading lately is Nancy Drew."

"Jesus," said Jake.

"They're comforting," said Rachel. "I can't believe I never read them when I was a kid."

"You were too busy causing chaos," said Jake. "But that's all over now."

"I don't know," admitted Rachel. "I still feel like a grenade."

"Don't make me lecture you again," said Jake. It was true—Jake had read enough Al-Anon literature that he counseled her like an expert. He demanded that Rachel forgive herself but admitted it was out of his control. He finished the first door and stood up to admire his work. The butterscotch was dazzling. The wet paint shone in the kitchen lights, and Rachel could tell, without having turned around, that he had paused his work, words unsaid. She held a paintbrush, and waited.

"You didn't kill Billy," he said. "Stop living like you did. You need to forgive yourself."

At this, Rachel began to cry, until Jake grabbed for her hand. "I have something for you."

Jake removed the harmonica from his pocket.

"This belonged to your father," he said. "He always told me that it was the Special 20, model number 560 manufactured by Hohner, plastic comb instead of wooden. I remember all of that."

He placed the harmonica in Rachel's hand, and she closed her fingers around it.

They stood there for a moment, until Rachel pulled Jake close.

"Thank you," said Rachel. "I know exactly where it should go."

Rachel placed the harmonica on the tallest stack of bricks around the fireplace, the corner that had become her altar.

The house was completely level now, and they could both feel it.

———

The next morning, Rachel prepared to pay the man responsible for all of this.

The grass grew where the seeds were scattered, the furrows she kicked up in anger long since raked over, patted down, put back in place.

Black Mabel had poured cement and created a patio. Rachel bought new patio furniture from the parking lot of the Ben Franklin, and the golden squirrel was placed in the center of a small glass table.

Rachel stared out at the fence line, at the beds bursting with flowers. Orange and white lilies stood proud, unfurling with the morning sun. Clumps of purple and yellow irises, like odd fists, all things her father planted.

The Johnny-jump-ups spread, just like Ginger promised, a carpet wending itself around the roots of the taller plants, tiny striped tiger faces, pale lavender, white, and yellow. The echinacea were in full bloom. The clematis climbed two-thirds of the trellises; the giant purple blooms and snaky green arms glowed against the golden spray paint. Bucky left his ladder behind, and it remained propped against the fence, just for Jake.

Rachel called Bucky early in the morning, when it was still crisp outside. By afternoon, the last days of June were too hot to bear.

"I've got a leaky pipe," she said.

"Bullshit," he said. "Everything is brand-new, up to code."

"It's under the kitchen sink," she said. "I'm afraid it's going to warp the wood. And I know how you feel about soft spots and mold."

"My enemy," he said. "I'll be there in ten minutes."

She sat outside and contemplated the corner of the yard that had once been a giant pile of cans. She thought about planting a lilac bush, or maybe an apple tree. She thought she should honor her father somehow.

She imagined the blooms of an apple tree, and it cheered her. She stood when she heard Bucky's truck.

She waved as he opened the gate and came down the path, no longer jagged and dangerous. The walkway filled in with gravel and the pieces of shale resunk and flattened. He carried his bucket of tools, smiling as always.

"Good morning," she said.

"Not if you've got a leaky pipe," he said, and set the tools down. He flexed a muscle for her benefit. "I shall destroy any leaky pipes."

"I know," she said, and followed him into the house.

He rested his bucket of tools on the counter.

"Do you want some coffee?"

"Yes, ma'am."

She didn't make a move to pour any, knew he would attend to the sink immediately, because that was how he worked.

He crouched down and opened the cabinets. He craned his neck and swept a hand across the new subflooring, and looked up at her.

"There's no leak," he said.

"Look harder," she said.

He stuck his head in farther, until she could see only his neck. He popped back out with an envelope.

"What's this?"

"It's got your name on it, dude."

He stood up and opened the envelope. It was stuffed with bills.

His eyes widened.

"Four thousand dollars?"

"I wish I could pay you more."

"Sweet Jesus," he said.

"Make sure you pay Black Mabel her share," she said. "She's always been good to me."

"I honestly didn't think you were gonna pay me a dime," he said.

"Really?"

"Shit," he said. "Ladies make promises to pay me all the time. You're the first one who ever came through. I didn't mind the work, honestly. Would've done your house for free."

"You need to stop letting the ladies walk all over you," said Rachel.

"Can't help it," said Bucky. "And you paid for all the materials."

"But you did all the work," said Rachel. "I sat down with the Chief, and we figured out what I would've paid a contractor. You did months of work. I'm getting off easy."

"Thank you," he said, and then his face grew sullen.

"What's the matter?"

"I'm done here," he said. "I guess that means I won't be seeing much of you anymore."

"Bucky," she said. "I promise that you won't be able to get rid of me."

"Really?"

"I don't treat friends like that." Rachel reached out for his hand, even though he remained crestfallen. She wasn't sure if he was sad because the construction was over, or sad because she just wanted to be friends. "Besides," she said. "Next summer, I want you to build me a back porch."

He smiled at this, and Rachel continued to hold his hand.

Into Bloom

★   ★   ★

*J*ake, Krystal, and the baby were sitting in their usual place, in the parking lot of the IGA supermarket. Krystal brought lawn chairs and a sunhat for the baby. Bert stayed behind at their trailer house. He was doing the work, hanging eight rows of shelves on a wall in Jake's bedroom. Jake really needed ten rows for his shoes but decided to say nothing. He remained wary of Bert looking through his drawers, but at least he was trying.

The townspeople gathered at eleven o'clock in the morning, in anticipation of the parade. They sat on curbs, leaned against the bent poles of stop signs. Their usual number was thinned by half—their sons and daughters and husbands and wives would be riding on the floats.

Buley and Rocky joined them, and Krystal made painful small talk with her brother, until eventually, she handed him the baby. It was not enough of a distraction.

"She looks like you," he said.

"Thank God," said Buley.

Krystal ignored this. Mrs. Matthis stumbled across the road, clutching her crossword puzzle book. Jake could tell she was wasted—the Dirty Shame had closed for the parade, and the morning regulars were forced out into the sunlight. Mrs. Matthis plopped down in the parking lot of the IGA, sought refuge in a row of cars. She leaned against a Pontiac Firebird, her lips moving as she faked solutions.

Buley fanned herself extravagantly, a red-and-yellow accordion, Chinese dragons. Jake coveted it, could not help himself, even though his mother shifted in her lawn chair uncomfortably. Buley took notice, and silenced him with a rosary from her purse, beads the color of the cloudless July sky. Jake took it gladly, even though the crucifix was cheap white plastic.

Krystal eyed Rocky and the baby nervously, reached over to adjust the sunhat. "So, Rocky? When are the two of you going to get hitched? Marriage is the best thing that ever happened to me."

"I refuse to be known as Buley Bailey," Buley said, and folded her fan with one crisp movement. She looked at Krystal with disdain. "Sounds like a disease you catch in the Amazon."

"Indeed," said Jake. Across the street, Gene Runkle, another refugee from the Dirty Shame, waved an unlit sparkler in one hand, and a miniature American flag in the other. The people around him could tell this was not patriotism, just alcoholism. They moved away as fast as they could.

The parade began with a long line of logging trucks, strung with Christmas lights. This was how the parade always began, and it was stultifying.

"I've never understood that," said Jake, shouting to be heard over the engines. "Why do they always get to go first?" Jake was a sucker for pageantry, and believed every parade should begin with a marching band and cheerleaders. In Quinn, the cheerleaders did not twirl batons, or do much of anything. They didn't even hold pom-poms correctly—dropping their elbows and let them hang limply. Cruel-mouthed, slouchy, and disinterested, Jake could not wait to befriend them in high school. Alas, the bad-postured cheerleaders and the marching band in street clothes would come in the middle of the pack. Thirty logging trucks, creeping in their lowest gear, and Jake was already exhausted. To make matters worse, the logging trucks were completely loaded, reeking of pine sap and diesel fuel.

The people of Quinn loved their logging trucks, stuck fingers in their mouths to unleash whistles, drowned out by the big rigs.

Buley smiled at Jake wryly. "The people of Quinn do love a parade," she said.

"The people of Quinn love ranch dressing," added Jake. "That doesn't make it right."

The first float finally approached. It was Reverend Foote and New Life Evangelical, stuffed full of identically dressed parishioners Jake recognized from the wedding. The float wasn't that special—a butcher-paper banner, children dressed like lambs. They sang, and Mrs. Reverend Foote banged on a tambourine. Krystal snatched the baby away from Rocky, and forced her tiny hand into a wave.

Buley was not aware of the new church in town; she was the type of woman who isolated herself out of disgust, another reason why Jake loved her. She stared at the float quizzically.

"Moonies," she pronounced. "I bet they had a mass wedding in the football field."

"Christians," Krystal corrected her. "That's our church." She forced her baby to wave with more gusto, and the baby responded by erupting into tears.

"Does your church have a dress code?" Buley pointed at the cheap black slacks and jean skirts. The children on the float wore the same clothes but did not have the blank piousness on their faces. Instead, their identities were disguised by photocopied lamb heads, sagging with cotton balls, held aloft on Popsicle sticks.

"We're nondenominational," said Krystal proudly. "We accept everyone just as they are." Buley peered down at Krystal's jean skirt and arched an eyebrow.

Behind Reverend Foote came the ladies from Quinn Lumber Mill, shaking silent chain saws at the crowd. They wore flannel shirts, despite the heat, and Jake appreciated that they stuck to a theme. Unfortunately, instead of candy, they threw sawdust.

Next were the fire trucks, both engines, the volunteer firemen stood on the running boards and clung to ladders. They wore the red baseball caps and regulation polo shirts, and satisfied smirks. They knew they were considered the most fearless citizens of Quinn, Red Mabel notwithstanding. There was no room for Jim Number Three. Since he was the newest, he walked behind the trucks, and Jake could tell he was ashamed. But

Jim Number Three was the only fireman who had tucked in his shirt, and Jake hoped that Laverna would give him another chance, points for good grooming. The volunteer firemen threw candy, and occasionally, a smoke alarm. The crowd always loved the firemen the most, because they hosted the only social event of the season, and tonight, they were responsible for the fireworks show. Bucky was not riding with them, and the Chief drove behind the fire engines in his special truck, his wife waving proudly from the passenger seat.

The Shriners followed on their stupid little motorcycles and atrocious little hats. Years ago, Jake had asked his mother what the Shriners did, and Krystal claimed that they worked on finding a cure for cancer. They did not look like scientists to Jake; he'd seen trained bears at the circus in Ellis, and they had exhibited more intelligence and skill than these fat men, wobbling on their tiny bikes. Jake would have given anything for trained bears in this parade. Perhaps the lazy cheerleaders could ride the bears without saddles, and they would be forced to take interest, or risk being clawed.

The Rotary Club was next. The float was intended to resemble a covered wagon. Jake grimaced at the bedsheets draped over a splintery frame of two-by-fours, and the cardboard horse heads duct-taped to the grille of a brand-new truck. If Jake could have the bears, he would also insist on Ronda, shooting real arrows at these ersatz cowpokes. Underneath the bedsheets, the grand marshal sat on a bale of hay, surrounded by mustachioed businessmen in ill-fitting cowboy attire. The grand marshal was Peggy the librarian, and she didn't even bother waving.

"Why is she the grand marshal?" Rocky didn't know her; he got all of his Louis L'Amour books at the thrift store.

"I heard she's retiring," offered Krystal.

"Overdue," said Jake, but only Buley got the joke.

Here came the high school pep club's float, students dressed as knights, in homemade tinfoil costumes, engaging in mock swordfights. Jake groaned aloud.

Behind them, the high school band marched, playing the school fight song. A clarinet squeaked as they passed, and the band sweated profusely in their street clothes, hardly in a tight formation. At least the music drowned out the church singers, still audible, two blocks ahead.

Mrs. Matthis suddenly materialized beside Jake, clutching at her puzzle book and one arm of his lawn chair. She crouched down, weaving side to side. Jake was afraid she would topple them both. He uncrossed his leg and planted both of his feet firmly on the pavement.

She whispered, top lip sweaty, and he fought back the nausea as he leaned closer. She never asked for anything, always too proud, no matter if her breath smelled like vomit. He would help, because the horses arrived, marching behind the Rotary Club. Again, he didn't understand why they got a spot in the parade—people in Quinn rode horses all the time. The only thing interesting about them was the giant shits they took, and the way the floats behind had to maneuver around the steaming piles.

"Five letters," whispered Mrs. Matthis. "Princess of Monaco."

"Get out of here," commanded Buley. She snapped her fan open and waved away the smell of vomit.

"First letter is 'K,'" she whispered. A horse reared up and snorted, and Mrs. Matthis was so frightened that she toppled over, crushing her crossword puzzle book. She seemed surprised to be lying in the hot parking lot, and looked around sheepishly, as she struggled to stand.

"No," said Jake. "You must have another word wrong."

Mrs. Matthis would not admit the mistake. She lurched away, nearly falling again, but clung to the mirror of a farm truck. She backed up against the truck and slid along the door and over the wheel well. She sidestepped cautiously, her back filthy with dust, until she reached the bumper. She collapsed to sitting, her weight causing the farm truck to creak.

"Grace!" He shouted this at Mrs. Matthis. She looked back at him, and like all really drunk people, was determined to demonstrate that she was okay, she was just fine. She stood up from the bumper and tripped down another row of cars.

"The answer is Grace!" Jake was standing now. Of course he knew the late princess of Monaco.

Mrs. Matthis stumbled onto the hood of Black Mabel's Subaru Brat. She lay on her back for a moment, slowly sat up, and shook her fist at Jake.

"Grace!" Jake was screaming now. "GRACE, GRACE, GRACE!"

"I'M DOING THE BEST I CAN, YOU LITTLE FUCKER!" The townspeople were shocked by her outburst, and Mrs. Matthis pretended to regain her composure, as she slunk out of sight behind Black Mabel's car.

Jake thought it was appropriate that the John Birch Society float came next, squishing the horseshit with their wheels. Their float was also Western themed, fat men with rifles slung across their backs, the straps too tight and straining down the middle of their shirts. It seemed like they possessed enormous breasts. They threw pamphlets that warned about Communist threats.

Behind them, four trucks of Little Leaguers, all in uniform. And Klemp. Finally, she had been promoted from T-ball, and Jake could swear she tucked a wad of chewing tobacco in her lower lip. She spit something reddish, but she was such a terrifying little girl that it might have been the blood of her enemies.

Up next, a flatbed truck rumbled down the street. The football players and the girls of the basketball team waved, surrounded by actual, store-bought crepe paper. There was no shortage of money when it came to high school sports. The school mascot sat on the tailgate, in a matted costume topped off with a ridiculously large knight's head. Although he couldn't see, the mascot remained steady and waved a large piece of butcher paper inscribed with fighting words. Sixty-Four glared at Jake, side-armed a Jolly Rancher. It bounced from Jake's knee, and Buley caught it without pause, threw it back with incredible velocity. It struck Sixty-Four on the cheek, a welt forming instantly. Apparently, Diane had inherited her softball skills.

Next came the zombie march of disenchanted cheerleaders, to the hoots and hollers from the crowd. Pleated skirts swung as they trudged, the only sign of life. At least the girls revealed some leg.

But there was a din: a low, rumbling noise, traveling from up ahead. For there was a float following behind the cheerleaders, a float he still couldn't quite see, it was obviously making quite an impression on those who could.

He knew for certain it was his float.

Apparently, the townspeople grasped the irony. The crowd shouted, laughed, and applauded. They approved.

Krystal gasped when she saw it.

"Did you do that?"

"Yep," he said, and his chest grew tight as the float pulled near.

The flatbed glimmered in the sun. Diane's boom box played "Devil Inside" by INXS, the song recorded again and again on a blank cassette. Yards of chiffon caught in the light breeze and trembled in giant waves. Bucky winked at Jake as they pulled past, but the Flood Girls remained perfectly still, arranged just as he had instructed, palms together, eyes upward at the sky.

The napkins were painted sky blue, and attached to the backdrop, the cotton batting had been shredded, resembling perfect clouds. The framework was hung with the chiffon, floating out in great sparkly sheets.

The Flood Girls were dressed as angels. Coat hanger halos wrapped with gold garland, bedsheets making long white dresses, wings made out of white feathers stretched out across their back.

Red Mabel sat above them all, pretended to play the harp, reclined on a raised platform, the ugliest angel in heaven.

Jake's throat closed up as he witnessed the glory of it all. Buley hugged him tightly.

The baby cooed and reached out toward the sparkle, as the citizens of Quinn continued to roar.

———

After dinner, Jake and Rachel walked to the football field, passed the gutters riddled with the red waxed paper of a week's worth of firecrackers, paper cones that had once been fountains, burned at one end, spent. Jake knew that the storm drains would soon be choked with the thin wires of sparklers, blackened and bent. The streets were littered with the carcasses of family packs of Bumble Bees, pyrotechnic insects that lit up and flew in circles toward the sky. The Bumble Bees left burn marks on the asphalt.

People were already gathered at the football field, even though the firemen's show wouldn't start for hours. Jake and Rachel paced around the track, and it sounded like Beirut. Jake's mouth tasted like metal, the acrid smoke of sparklers.

They found Laverna in the beer garden. She sat with Red Mabel, and they were surrounded by empty plastic cups. Laverna frowned as they approached.

"Bastards," Laverna said, and Jake knew immediately.

"Pig fuckers," added Red Mabel.

"Second place," said Jake. "I kind of figured that would happen."

"The Rotary Club won again," said Laverna. "We should've kidnapped that goddamned Peggy and put her on our float."

"It's okay," said Jake. "It was totally worth it."

"Yes," said Laverna. "You did me proud, kid. It was worth every penny."

"Thank you," said Jake. "It all seems like a dream."

Rachel and Jake navigated the cacophony of the north end of the track, where ten-year-olds shot bottle rockets at one another, launched out of empty pop bottles. The parents just sat in lawn chairs and watched their children form small armies and use garbage cans as bunkers, engaging in ground warfare.

Soon it was ten o'clock, but the sky wasn't black, not with the constant explosions. The volunteer firemen had not mounted their own expensive display; these were airborne flowers from the fireworks-obsessed denizens of Quinn, who weren't celebrating America's independence as much as celebrating other countries—their close proximity to legal firework stands in Canada, and cheap explosives manufactured in China.

Jake and Rachel rounded the bleachers and cut behind the dugouts.

Winsome Shankley clutched the chain link, barely hung on, vomited, and swung from the fencing with one hand. It was an impressive trick, doing this at the same time. Winsome was so vain and so well practiced that he did not vomit on himself, the regurgitated alcohol spewed through the fence and onto the away team's bench.

"I can't believe I had sex with him," said Rachel as they walked away.

"He had a hot tub," said Jake. "I've heard that chlorine kills sperm and diseases."

"That's comforting," said Rachel.

The firemen began their show, and housewives clapped at each explosion in the sky, screamed as the booms flowered into tails of color, fire powder transformed into bloom. The wives called out the names of their husbands, the brave volunteer firemen who tended to the tar barrels and shot paper cartridges shaped like pigeons into the sky. The volunteer firemen carefully monitored the makeshift cannons, set up the firing line in the long jump pit. Through all the smoke, they were barely visible as they scrambled around the sandy graveyard and sought protection behind the piles of hurdles, stacked and put away for the year.

Rachel and Jake watched all this from the far end of the football field, sitting on a picnic table and looking up at the sky. Rachel lit a cigarette and smoked it silently. Jake knew she was thinking about Winsome.

Rachel threw her cigarette toward the goal post, not caring that children leaped out of the way.

Above them, the sky over the football field glowed with the colors of a summer storm, trembled with the reverberations of the fireworks.

The Flood Girls versus the Ellis Talc Miners

★   ★   ★

*T*he final game of their regular season play was against their stiffest competition, the best team in the county league.

The Ellis Talc Miners were rough and raucous on and off the field. Like the Flood Girls, they had a reputation. On top of all that, Shyanne was done for the year. Her ankle was still severely injured, and Ginger would not let up about it.

In the dugout, she harangued Laverna: "Do you know how much college costs?"

"Of course not," said Laverna.

"Do you realize how much her scholarships will be worth?"

"Right now is not the time to run your menopausal mouth," said Laverna. "I'm sick of hearing about it."

Laverna walked away and brought her roster to Jake, who sat in the bleachers, Frank leashed and lying beside him. She didn't say a word to Jake, because she was nervous. This game meant more to Laverna than she was willing to let on.

Laverna returned to the dugout and clipped the lineup to the chain link. She watched Rachel, warming up with Della for the first time. This also made Laverna nervous so she eavesdropped as they threw the ball back and forth in front of the dugout, and Della chewed on her giant wad.

"I heard you fucked Winsome," said Della.

"It's none of your business," Rachel said, and threw the ball at Della as hard as she could.

"He gets around," Della said, and caught the ball with ease. Laverna was proud that they had both improved.

"You don't have any eyebrows," said Rachel. "Doesn't that bother you?"

"Not really," Della shrugged, and threw Rachel a grounder.

The Winsome thing was new information to Laverna, but she had bigger things to worry about.

Bucky called for the coaches. After the coin toss, the game began.

Not surprisingly, the Ellis Talc Miners were sluggers, and smashed each pitch thrown their way. This made up for their clumsy fielding. They moved like burly teenaged boys, sloppy and muscle-bound. They also behaved like teenaged boys, leering at Rachel's exposed bra straps and tan legs. Laverna was thankful that Shyanne wasn't there. Rachel could handle this sexual harassment, as she was a bartender.

The Flood Girls held their own. Tabby somehow managed a triple and made her way around the bases with surprising speed, despite the two packs of cigarettes she smoked each and every day. She caught her breath and fanned herself on third. This was Tabby's first triple, and she was so preoccupied that she almost forgot to run to home after a soaring hit from the taller Sinclair, deep into left field.

The run tied the game up. Laverna knew the importance of this game, as it was her job to keep track of such things, but didn't say anything to her team. She didn't want to jinx it. She looked up at the bleachers, and Jake was grinning. He had done the math.

The miners then inched ahead by one, a line drive that passed right through Ronda's legs, and Rachel surprised them all by running, galloping, to scoop it up and throw it. She actually threw it to Tabby at the cutoff, but not before the miners scored.

At the bottom of the sixth inning, Laverna was distracted. Krystal stood outside the dugout, waiting quietly for Laverna to notice her. Laverna supposed that Krystal had come to the softball game for the first time this year to show her support for her son. Laverna was wrong. When she finally turned around to acknowledge Krystal, a folded-up piece of paper was shoved through the chain link. Krystal said nothing. Laverna plucked the paper, as Krystal had left it to dangle there. It was a check for one thousand dollars.

"I'm trying to make things right," said Krystal. "It's been eating at me for years."

Laverna shoved the check into her pocket and turned back to the game, refusing to acknowledge Krystal's explanation. Laverna knew; she had always known.

Instead, Laverna listened to Krystal walk away. Secretly satisfied, she shouted for the benefit of the fans in the bleachers. "WHY DOES EVERYBODY KEEP FUCKING WITH ME?"

She glanced over her shoulder, and Krystal had reentered the bleachers, her head hung down as she took a seat beside her son.

The Flood Girls had the last at bat. Diane made it to second base, thanks to the slothful infield, and Martha Man Hands struck out.

Laverna placed an arm on Ronda's giant shoulder, as her cook warmed up by swinging two bats at the same time, always a bruiser.

"You've got this," said Laverna. Ronda, expressionless as usual, just handed Laverna the extra bat and marched grimly to home plate. Laverna was on the verge of needing an antianxiety pill, but Ronda entered the batter's box stoically, no fear registering on her face. Laverna watched the outfield back up toward the fence—when Ronda beat her bat on home plate, they backed up even farther.

Ronda stepped into the batter's box and swung with all her considerable might, the ball sailed over the fence, and the game was over.

The Flood Girls won, nine to eight.

Jake came running into the dugout, and as expected, he had done the math. He jumped up and down as the Flood Girls gathered around Laverna. Math had never been their strong suit, but they knew something was different.

"We've made it!" Laverna put an arm around Ginger, kissed Tabby on the cheek. "The Flood Girls are headed for the tournament!"

The old men in the bleachers continued to applaud, even as the crowd dispersed. Bucky threw his cap into the air. The Flood Girls were shocked, but hoisted their coach up in the air, Red Mabel doing all of the heavy lifting.

Lucky

*   *   *

*J*ake's thirteenth birthday was on the second day of August. School was still out, and he was thrilled to finally, officially, be a teenager, although he wasn't expecting much.

It took him almost an hour to dress and prepare himself for this auspicious day. He knew there was no party planned. Unlike his classmates, there would be no roller rink rented for an afternoon, or a trip to the water slides in Spokane.

Jake decided on white linen. He had the pants, and a short-sleeved button-down. It was not muddy, and this was one of the five months of the year that didn't seem like winter. White linen would be safe, because the sun had finally come out to stay in Quinn.

After rummaging around, he discovered that he did not own any white shoes, and this came as a surprise to him. He chose a pair of light brown loafers, soft leather, and a straw fedora with a dark brown leather band.

Krystal made his favorite breakfast—cold spaghetti. It was an odd choice for a favorite breakfast, but Jake grew up with a single mom, and he always loved leftover spaghetti in the morning. Krystal obliged, prepared it the night before, mixed the sauce and the noodles together, put the entire pot into the refrigerator.

They sat together at the kitchen table, and Krystal watched him eat.

"Do you feel any different?" Krystal handed him the salt and pepper shakers, which had actually been a birthday gift to her, found at Buley's when he was nine years old. The shakers were pewter candles, in matching pewter holders, with orange glass flames perforated by tiny holes.

"Laverna always says that age is just a number," Jake said, and carefully wiped the corners of his mouth with a cloth napkin.

"Do you have any big plans?" Krystal waited for Jake to respond, but he kept eating spaghetti. "I'm going to make you a cake this afternoon," she said. "Do you want to invite Rachel over?"

"Sure," said Jake. He knew that Krystal had to work at seven, so there would be no party, just the cake and the presents, and then she would put on her scrubs and drive to Ellis for yet another night shift.

After breakfast, Jake walked around the trailer court and then ventured farther into town. He had on his headphones, the cassette playing as loud as it could possibly go, despite the repeated warnings from his mother. The headphones were old, at the point in their life that he had to repeatedly wiggle the connection in order to get both sides of them blaring. Once he found the sweet spot, he held his thumb there.

He wanted to see if Quinn looked different as a thirteen-year-old. He walked past the Dirty Shame, and he wanted to have coffee with Rachel, but Tabby's car was parked in front.

He cut across the softball field, the grass still wet from the sprinklers. His loafers stained from the water, and it pained Jake that he would have to ask to borrow Bert's boot spray. He continued up Main Street, listening to Sinead O'Connor, and passed the post office. The movie theater had no poster outside, and the marquee announced that it was closed for repairs. This happened a few times per year, when Ron, the owner, went fishing in Idaho, or when the roof collapsed. The roof was constantly leaking, and more than once, Jake had been caught in a sudden deluge during a movie. Ron offered no refunds for this. Sometimes, little pieces of the ceiling would fall during a screening, coating the audience with tiny clouds of plaster. Jake was amazed that nobody had been injured—even going to see a movie in Quinn was a dangerous proposition.

He finally decided that thirteen didn't feel any different. His shoes were wet, and he had not worn socks, so he squished his way up the front steps and entered his house.

Rachel was waiting for him, sitting in the kitchen with his mother. On the kitchen table, there were two things: a gift-wrapped box and a pale blue envelope.

"Happy birthday, kid!" Rachel leaped up to hug him. "The box is from Athena."

Inside were a *Rocky Horror Picture Show* T-shirt, the sound track on cassette, and the movie itself, the VHS still wrapped in cellophane.

"You'd better hide those from Bert," warned Krystal, as she began to clean up the baby, who still had some red sauce on her cheeks.

The envelope contained a fifty-dollar gift certificate to JCPenney.

"From the Flood Girls," explained Rachel. "Ginger has this idea that your underwear and socks come from the thrift store, and they won't stand for it. I didn't want to correct them. I know that Krystal buys you those things."

"I do," said Krystal as she picked up the baby. Jake could tell that she was trying to prove she was a good mother.

"The nearest JCPenney is in Boyce Falls," pointed out Jake. "This is great. I can use it to order stuff from the catalog, right?"

"Wrong," said Rachel. "I'm driving you there. Today. And we're hitting every thrift store on the way. You can buy whatever you want. My present to you."

———

Jake bought two complete suits in the town of New Poland, one seersucker, the other houndstooth, and a half-used can of leather spray. In Boyce Falls, Jake purchased two pairs of slacks, one pair bright red, and the other gray with tiny pink squares. He also picked out a stack of paperbacks and a winter coat, green wool with a giant black fake-fur collar. Rachel paid for everything.

At JCPenney, he used the gift certificate and spent twenty-nine dollars on new white T-shirts, packages of socks, and a collection of boxer shorts in every color. He spent the remaining twenty-one dollars on a pair of white sneakers, a purchase that Rachel balked at. Jake insisted that she trust him, and he promised that he would never, ever use them for sports.

They drove back to Quinn, Rachel slightly speeding. The trip to Boyce Falls and back had taken the whole day, and it was six o'clock when they arrived in Rachel's driveway. They carried his bags of purchases into his house, and he was thankful that Bert was still gone, on yet another long drive with Reverend Foote. He would be home within an hour, because somebody had to watch the baby. Jake would not. It was his birthday.

They ate yellow cake with chocolate frosting, and Krystal gave Jake presents: Bert gave Jake a bag of deeply discounted birdseed. Krystal gave Jake a new Walkman and new headphones. As they ate the cake, Krystal began telling tales from her nursing career about teenagers with tinnitus. She was interrupted by a knock on the door.

Krystal came into the kitchen with Laverna, who was holding a black bandana. Knowing Laverna, Jake did not think this was particularly strange.

"We've got a date," announced Laverna. She approached Jake with the bandana and tied it around his eyes.

"Okay," Jake said, and he trusted all of them, so he said nothing as he was led out of the house. Rachel held his hands, and he could hear a car door opening, and then he was sinking down, and he knew they were in Laverna's car. Jake remained silent as the motor roared to life, and listened as Laverna gunned it once they hit smoother streets, revved it to make a spectacular noise.

"We just passed Bert," explained Rachel. "Don't worry. We made sure to wave."

They slowed, the car making angry sounds as Laverna slid to a stop. Rachel helped Jake out of the bucket seat. She led him into a building that smelled familiar, and then she was assisting him down a slight slope. Rachel maneuvered him into a cushioned chair.

He was confused when the blindfold was removed, because he was in a dark place. He could sense Rachel on his left and Laverna on his right.

Then he smelled the popcorn.

Just then, the movie screen flickered to life, and in the bluish light, Jake turned around in his seat in the front row and realized the entire theater was empty. It was just the three of them.

Rachel presented Jake with popcorn and a soda.

"Laverna arranged all of this," she said.

"Ron owes me a favor," said Laverna.

"Thank you," said Jake. "It must have cost you a fortune."

"Just wait, kid. It's gonna be worth it." Laverna popped a handful of Junior Mints into her mouth, and she squeezed Jake's shoulder with the other hand.

The movie began, and Jake shivered.

Somehow, Laverna had performed a miracle.

It was the new Madonna documentary, *Truth or Dare*. It had been out in the big city theaters for only a few weeks, but Jake knew that it would never, ever come to Quinn.

Tonight, it had. Jake was certain it was a one-night engagement.

———

The movie was amazing. It seemed that Ron even turned up the volume. The concert footage was thunderous.

After the credits rolled, and the screen flickered out, Jake could talk again.

As they entered the lobby, there was Ron, who sighed as he stood beside the popcorn machine.

Laverna stopped Jake with one hand. "Ron has something for you."

Ron grumbled and reached below the counter, and handed Jake a rolled-up poster. Jake pulled off the rubber bands, revealing the movie poster for *Truth or Dare*. Madonna was lying in the foreground, one hand disappearing into her crotch, wearing a black dress and surrounded by silky bedsheets. She looked out at them expectantly. Above the title, the tagline read: THE ULTIMATE DARE IS TO TELL THE TRUTH.

Jake swooned and hugged Laverna fiercely. He hugged Rachel, too, as Ron crossed his arms and stared at the three of them.

"Not really my cup of tea," said Ron.

Jake knew exactly where the poster would go—behind the clothes hanging in his closet. Bert would never see it, but Jake would know it was there, always there, and that was enough.

He knew it was an unlucky number, but thirteen might just be his best year yet.

The Tournament

★   ★   ★

*B*efore Laverna booked all their rooms, she called Rachel.

They went to Jake's house together, waited for a time they knew Krystal would be home. They hoped both Floods together would be enough of a persuasion.

"He's part of the team," Laverna explained.

"He's really the heart of our team," Rachel said. "He's like our good-luck charm."

Bert, like a wall, shielded their view of the living room, rising up, his face scarlet, upper lip slick with perspiration.

"No," he said. "Absolutely not." He reached his arms up and supported himself on the doorframe. "Our debts have been paid in full."

"Krystal paid her debts," pointed out Laverna. "You still have a bar tab."

"I'm not afraid of you, Laverna Flood." Bert stepped out onto the porch, and Laverna found herself stumbling backward. The heat from Bert was palpable.

"You're done," he said. "You're done filling my kid's head up with nonsense. We're trying to teach him some humility."

Rachel peeked around Bert. Laverna was impressed that her daughter was so fearless, but she knew her attachment to Jake was a deep, unexplainable thing. Laverna could see Krystal on the couch, the baby on her lap.

"Krystal," said Rachel. "You know this is ridiculous." Laverna pulled Rachel back as she pled, as Bert began to clear his throat, a sound that could have been mistaken for a growl.

Bert took another step forward, and Laverna stood in front of her daughter. Bert would not dare strike Laverna Flood. She waited for Krystal to respond, barely visible in the darkened living room and the shadow of her husband.

Krystal refused to look at them. Meekly, she pulled the baby tighter and spoke through the blanket, her voice muffled, but the words rang out clear enough. "I don't think so," she said. "And I would prefer it if he didn't know it was an option. I don't want to feel guilty."

"See?" Laverna protested. "You know how much this would mean to him."

"The answer is no." Bert's face was a flame, and fittingly, he grabbed a piece of kindling from the pile beside the door. He pointed the splintered piece of wood at Laverna's chest. "We're trying to spend more time together as a family."

"Jesus," Laverna had said.

"Watch it." Bert snapped the piece of kindling in half. Laverna flinched at the crack. "We're circling the wagons."

"I know an Indian," said Laverna, and before she could lie and insist that Ronda was handy with a bow and arrow, Bert shut the door.

———

The Flood Girls took four vehicles to Missoula, mostly because Diane and Rachel had overpacked. Laverna reserved a block of rooms at the Thunderbird Motel, including one for Bucky, even though he did not umpire at this level. He tried to pay Laverna for his room, but she wouldn't hear of it. Laverna trusted Bucky with Frank, and hoped he would help keep the girls in line.

At seven, Athena knocked on Laverna's hotel room door. Laverna couldn't fathom how this woman could have possibly saved her daughter's life. Athena wore a black dress, and between the enormous breasts hung ropes upon ropes of necklaces. The dress was empire-waisted, the skirt full and dangling with ribbons. She looked like a fat wife of a medieval king.

"Aren't you hot?"

"You must be Laverna," Athena said, and pulled her into a hug.

Laverna glared at her daughter over Athena's shoulder. "Don't believe everything you've heard," she said. Doors opened down the hall-way, and the Flood Girls emerged, all of them dressed for a night on the town. Except for the Sinclairs, whom Athena was especially taken with. Although the Flood Girls were ready for dinner, they waited while Athena somehow sweet-talked the Sinclairs into lip gloss and chignons. They refused to abandon the jean skirts.

At a Mexican restaurant, Laverna grew entranced with Athena, and the margaritas. She never blended drinks at the Dirty Shame, because it was too much work, but this was something to reconsider.

Halfway through her third margarita, Laverna told Athena the entire story of Jim Number Three, and grew a little weepy. A waiter made the mistake of approaching her.

"I'm really sorry, but dogs aren't allowed in here." The waiter, a pudgy brown-faced man, pointed at Frank, curled up between Laverna's heels.

"Fuck you," said Laverna. "Your people eat dogs."

"That's Koreans, ma'am."

Laverna slammed her fist on the table. The waiter took a step back-ward; Athena jumped from the table and reasoned with him, gesturing around the room at the lack of customers, at the banquettes filled with paired members of the softball team. Frank was allowed to stay.

Rachel sat with Bucky at another table, and Laverna caught her roll-ing her eyes. She threw a balled-up napkin across the restaurant, and it landed in Rachel's enchiladas.

Laverna was hopped up on tequila. She hollered across the room. "Athena says that my break up with Jim Number Three is symptomatic of my low self-esteem!"

"You don't have low self-esteem," said Rachel. "I'm pretty sure about that."

"She said that I push people away before they can hurt me," shouted Laverna. Red Mabel raised a margarita in the air.

"That I agree with," said Rachel. "Too bad you didn't push away that Clinkenbeard kid."

"Your mother was victimized," said Athena. "There's a lot of trauma there."

"My mother has traumatized an entire town," pointed out Rachel. "Even the children."

"Your mother is an alpha female," declared Athena. "I've never met any woman quite like her. She's ferocious."

"She bites," warned Rachel. Laverna responded by baring her teeth.

After dinner, the majority of Flood Girls wanted to find single men and dance. The minority (the Sinclairs) did not, as they had cable television in their room. Laverna sent them away with Frank, and instructions on how to find the porn channels.

With Athena and Rachel as designated drivers, the Flood Girls invaded Missoula. At the Forest Lounge, Laverna once again commandeered Athena, because she was a really good listener, and she had no desire to flirt with the dirty hippies and the rowdy fraternity brothers.

Laverna brought Bucky to help out, but he was useless after his third margarita. She had never seen him drunk before; apparently drunk Bucky had issues with gravity and depth perception. Terrified, he took refuge on the top of a Def Leppard pinball machine, and Ginger and Rachel took turns babysitting.

All night long, Laverna tried to be a good coach. She had finally found an excellent assistant coach, and her name was Margarita. When Laverna caught Diane and a hippie smoking marijuana in the women's bathroom, she snatched a handful of the hippie's long beard and flushed the joint down the toilet.

She bought Ronda six beers in total, and although Ronda did not speak, she smiled each time Laverna appeared with another bottle. The tequila filled Laverna with emotions, and she delivered a speech, thanked Ronda for her years of service and apologized for white people. Ronda stopped smiling, and escaped onto the dance floor. Laverna was shocked, but apparently Ronda had a thing for George Michael.

Ronda was the only person dancing to the beat. Tabby, Della, and Martha slow danced to "I Want Your Sex," despite the tempo. They had been slow dancing to every song, clinging to a trio of pimply and overweight frat boys who couldn't believe their luck. Laverna stumbled onto the dance floor every twenty minutes, making sure the boys did not get too handsy.

At some point, Laverna lost Diane. She and Athena checked every Suburban in the parking lot, but Diane had just disappeared into the night.

"I don't care if she's high on dope and howling at the moon," said Laverna. "As long as she doesn't get arrested. She's the best shortstop I've ever seen." Laverna began weeping, and Athena patted her hand, pulled her back inside the bar.

Red Mabel drank at the bar with the better-looking frat boys, all transplants from the Eastern Seaboard. Adoringly, they bought Red Mabel drinks all night long, and she regaled them with hunting stories. When a handsome boy from Pennsylvania dared question the veracity of Red Mabel riding on the back of a mountain lion, she got into the first and last fistfight of the night. Laverna knew she was justified, and was delighted when his fellow frat boys booed him and drenched him with beer. Of course, Red Mabel was victorious, and nearly broke the nose of the boy from Pennsylvania, careful not to injure her hand. There was a big game tomorrow.

When she wasn't policing her softball team, Laverna continued her therapy session with Athena. When her obsession with layering was diagnosed as issues with intimacy, Laverna did not punch Athena. She held her tongue when Athena called her out for being a control freak, and a martyr. Instead, she wept openly, buried her face in Athena's massive breasts. She apologized for being drunk, but Athena encouraged her to let it all out. So she did, and the rest of the Flood Girls were just as carefree and feckless.

An hour before closing time, Laverna had lost count. She was a bad umpire, as far as tequila was concerned. Ten? Twelve? She was loaded, just as she hoped the bases would be in the morning.

She could hear Athena counseling her, or maybe talking makeup secrets, as she was apt to do. It was just noise at this point. Laverna's ears and eyes were full of tequila, and her senses narrowed to one corner of the bar. Rachel tossed her hair and massaged Bucky's shoulders. Laverna leaped from her seat, could not feel the table slam across her thighs, hear the crash of shot glasses and the screech of Athena's chair skidding backward.

Laverna had a handful of Rachel's hair, and she screamed as she yanked her daughter away from Bucky.

"What the FUCK?" Startled, Rachel grabbed her mother's forearm, and Laverna could barely register the pain as Rachel pinched until her mother let go. Now Rachel was standing, and Laverna was ready for this. This was why she did not drink tequila. Laverna alternated between quaking with sobs and blind rage.

"DON'T TOUCH HIM!" Laverna pointed to Bucky, who stared up from the floor, frightened.

"It's okay," he said, in a small voice.

"NO!" Laverna shoved Rachel against the wall, and Athena was there, stepping between them. Red Mabel attempted to shove a pool stick into Laverna's hand, and encouraged her to beat her daughter with it. Athena knocked it out of Red Mabel's hand, and it clattered to the floor. The noise was not enough to free Laverna from her tequila tunnel. She shoved Rachel again, and her hands wrapped around her neck.

"YOU RUIN EVERYTHING!" Laverna realized that Rachel was not fighting back. Her daughter closed her eyes, as her face grew red. Rachel had resigned to die at her mother's hands, and that made Laverna even angrier.

The bartender pulled Laverna away, and she kicked him in the knee. Red Mabel provided interference with her massive body, and Athena backed her up, and the bartender was shoved away from the corner. He threatened to call the police.

"Please don't," said Athena. "This has needed to happen for a long time."

"I don't give a shit," said the bartender. "You bitches are out of here."

"This is nothing," said Red Mabel. "Come drink at the Dirty Shame sometime, kid." She reached into her heavy wool logging pants, and forced a fifty-dollar bill into his hand. He accepted the money begrudgingly, and was descended upon by the horny Flood Girls on the dance floor.

"WHY? WHY DID YOU TAKE BILLY? WHY DID YOU RUIN MY LIFE?" Laverna's hands returned to her daughter's throat. Rachel's eyes remained closed, tears streaming down her mottled cheeks. Bucky crab-walked backward, barely missing the shards of broken shot glasses.

"You are choking her," pointed out Athena. "She can't answer your questions right now." Athena did nothing to pull Laverna away; instead, she put a hand on Laverna's shoulder.

Laverna dropped her hands. She breathed heavily, gasped as if she had been choked herself.

Rachel opened her eyes and remained against the wall. Laverna could not believe that Rachel was making direct eye contact, no challenge there, no fury. Laverna wanted Rachel to fight back.

. "ANSWER MY QUESTIONS!" Laverna stomped on the floor, nearly lost her footing in the pool that spread from the overturned table.

"I don't know," said Rachel. "I don't know why I did the things I did." She continued to make eye contact with her mother. Laverna's hands closed into fists. "I've been trying to make things right."

"She was a teenage girl," said Athena. "She did what teenage girls do."

"Fuck that," Red Mabel said, and spit on the ground. "She was the devil! THE DEVIL!"

Laverna reached back, and punched her daughter in the eye. The bartender was upon them again, but Laverna did not need to be restrained. Rachel's head hit the wall, but she didn't flinch. She stood there, and Laverna felt the arms of the bartender wrap around her, take her down to the wet floor.

Rachel's face was bright red, her eye already swelling and seeping. She said nothing as she stepped past her mother. She paused only to squeeze Athena's hand, as she walked across the dance floor and out the front door.

Laverna sputtered as she was yanked to her feet. The bartender pointed to the exit.

The Flood Girls gathered their purses. None seemed shocked at the violence; Laverna's team had been waiting for this.

Only Athena spoke. "She's your only child," she said, as the Flood Girls began their exit, accompanied by the groans of frat boys. "She's your daughter."

"She's our designated driver," Laverna said, and pushed past Athena. The tequila roared through her, and all Laverna Flood could think about was how they were going to get back to the hotel.

Of course, they woke with hangovers. The Sinclairs were used to this behavior from their teammates, but not before such an important game. Laverna sent them to the lobby to find aspirin, ordered the sisters to begin praying in earnest.

Laverna had never seen such a sorry lot. She felt fear in her throat as they caravanned, and the other Flood Girls were visibly nervous as they parked in the complex of the softball fields. These greens were actually green, not polka-dotted with knapweed and spotted with gopher holes. Today, there would be no invasion of white-tailed deer, tumbleweeds of pollen, gales of blizzard, or riots over Rachel. Three separate fields, flanked by grandstands, and an enormous tiered structure of restrooms, concessions, and a perch for the announcers. She saw the microphones and the PA system, and said nothing. The fields, divided by tall white clapboard, glittered as the automatic sprinklers ratcheted and stopped, sinking back into the earth. The Flood Girls trudged and dragged duffel bags, sought similar refuge in the cool of their cement dugout. The infield collapsed on the freshly painted bench. Martha vomited, and the noise of the splatter sent Della into dry heaves, revealing yet another weakness. Laverna's outfield was in better shape, but white-faced with nerves.

Although she was not hungover, Rachel appeared the most battered. She had bruises on her throat, and her eye almost completely
swelled shut. A long and thin cut, crusted with blood, just below her
eyebrow. Laverna looked down at her ring, Black Hills Gold, set with a
tiny sapphire, the prongs of which had done the most damage. Laverna
double-checked to make sure the stone was still there. She couldn't care
less about Rachel's face.

Diane appeared as she had disappeared ten hours before, mysteri-
ously, stoned out of her mind.

"I'm really high," she apologized, avoiding eye contact with Laverna.

"No shit," said Laverna. Diane whimpered, skittish and cotton-
mouthed, whispered to Della for gum and fled to the farthest corner.

The bleachers began to fill, even though the game would not begin
for an hour. Laverna saw the cluster from Quinn—Bucky cooed to Frank,
Rachel's old men studied the tournament programs, and the Chief crossed
his arms, stoic as always. Rocky held a bursting picnic hamper on his lap,
sandwiched between Buley and Athena, oversized and overdressed. All
of their costume jewelry sparkled and dazzled, alit in the summer morning. Laverna, amazed that her daughter had somehow grown a fan club,
blinked back tears. Her hands shrunk into tight fists, fingernails dug into
palms; she refused to acknowledge these new emotions, feared they were
a harbinger of menopause.

Angered at the thought, pissed that they still had an hour to kill,
Laverna erupted, screamed at her girls. She needed to feel normal again.
"This is the big dance! Get your shit together right now! For Quinn! For
the love of the game!" She realized that these were all sports clichés, and
that made her even angrier. The infield sat upright but then cowered
against the cement wall, as Laverna began kicking dirt at them.

She was restrained by Athena, and could not free herself from the lock
of meaty arms and massive breasts. She continued to kick dirt until the
great wall of Buley rose up to shield Diane.

An umpire poked his head into the dugout, clearly concerned. "Is
everything okay in here?" He stared closely at Rachel's battered face.

"That's just her way," said Rocky, carrying a sagging cardboard box. Undoubtedly, the umpire had seen worse, but never from a woman.

"Warm up in ten, coin toss in twenty." He left with a smirk, a tip of his hat.

"Fuck him. Go warm up now," said Laverna, never one to follow directions. "Shake it off, ladies." The Flood Girls took to the field, making sure to give their coach a wide berth.

Athena counseled Laverna, massaged her back, as the Flood Girls tossed the ball back and forth. Across the field, Laverna watched the Ellis Talc Miners roll on the grass, stretch luxuriously, like lionesses that had just devoured an antelope.

After ten minutes, Laverna called in her team, and tried to ignore their various states of undoing. Martha's color was high, her temples sweating and beet red. If Martha had a stroke, Laverna would rip off her man hands and beat her to death.

Without a word, Rocky ripped open the box and consulted a list in Jake's perfect handwriting. One at a time, he delivered each T-shirt like a precious bundle.

Thankfully, Laverna was too dazzled to cry. The uniform of the Flood Girls, a baby-blue T-shirt, the collar and sleeves embroidered in gold. Across the chest, gold thread outlined by dark blue: TFG, and above the three letters, a foreshortened halo, also gold and dark blue. She turned the T-shirt to find a glittering gold iron-on number, the 1 seemed to be flying on hand-sewn angel wings, crisp white and carefully detailed with dark blue stitches, intricate feathers.

"Save your tears, ladies," said Laverna. "We've got a game to play."

The Flood Girls were utterly shameless, and changed into the new shirts in the open air of the dugout. Most of the girls wore sports bras, but the Sinclairs wore strange brown camisoles, and Laverna was proud of their new lack of modesty. Red Mabel was completely topless. Bucky let out a wolf whistle from the bleachers, and Red Mabel bowed toward him, breasts sagging. At this, Rachel's old men applauded.

"He asked for a team photo," said Rocky.

"He insisted on it," said Buley, and removed a boxy Pentax from her purse. Athena arranged the Flood Girls in different permutations—by height, by age, by bra size, and by batting average. Buley clicked away, until Athena was satisfied.

"Our first team picture," declared Laverna, pinching at her thigh to ward off the weepiness. First uniforms, first picture, first tournament. Laverna, the back of her uniform displaying the number one, couldn't help but beam as she posed for every single shot.

Laverna walked to the pitcher's mound for the coin toss, joining the umpire and the coach from the Talc Miners. She could hear the Flood Girls arguing about the significance of the numbers. Some claimed the digit corresponded with the batting lineup, some declared they were chosen at random. Della was happy to point out that she had one more number than everybody else. But Laverna knew. The boy had ranked the women in order of their importance.

Laverna lost the coin toss, and the Talc Miners chose to bat last. Laverna returned to her team, just as the PA system startled them with a squeal of feedback, the volume sending Della into dry heaves once more. The bleachers had filled to capacity. Laverna, as usual, had not paid attention to the umpire's instructions, and the national anthem burst forth from the speakers. She pushed her confused girls onto the field. The recording had reached the second verse before the Flood Girls finally stumbled into place, and presented themselves to the crowd, hands over hearts.

After the anthem, the girls started to walk back to the dugout, but the announcer's voice blared out again, and in the echo Laverna barely distinguished the name of her team. She rushed out onto the field, but her commands weren't needed. Thankfully, Rachel still adored the limelight, and when her name was called, she stepped forward and waved at the crowd, despite her mangled face. She tossed her blond hair, and her old men stomped and whistled, and she blew a kiss in their direction. Laverna rolled her eyes but knew Jake would be proud. Rachel had earned the number two on her back.

Number three was Diane, who was obviously still stoned. When her name was called, she tripped on her cleats but still managed to stumble forward. Number three because of the sewing machine, surmised Laverna, as Ginger was announced as number four. Jake respected Ginger's age and her status, probably assumed he would get free corn dogs at the Sinclair. Five was Martha, waving her giant hand, chosen fifth just because she had birthed a bad girl. Red Mabel had grown into a bad woman, number six, and she spit on the ground as she stepped forward. Seven and eight were Ronda and Tabby. The taller Sinclair was bashful when number nine was called, and then called again, for the shorter Sinclair. The announcer seemed confused by the two number nines, but Jake had never been one to care about regulations. Della was number ten. Jake shared Laverna's distrust of redheads.

The Ellis Talc Miners absolutely annihilated them, seven to four. The girls played terribly, bobbling the ball, missing throws, swinging at pitches they had no business swinging at. At the top of the fifth inning, Martha threw up in her catcher's mask. After the game, the Ellis Talc Miners shook their heads, disappointed at their former competition.

———

Next in the tournament bracket were the Mother Truckers, a team from the Tri-Cities. The early-afternoon sun broiled the fields. Bucky scouted their competition in the morning, and was terrified. He forced the Chief to drive him to a gas station. Bucky returned to the field with a case of Gatorade, three bags of ice, two copies of the same *Cosmopolitan* magazine, a bottle of aspirin, and for some reason, an air freshener shaped like a pine tree. Laverna removed it from the package and tied it above Red Mabel.

She was bone-tired, and maudlin. "This is it," Laverna said, her hand on Della's shoulder. "No matter what, I'm proud of you."

"Bullshit," said Ronda. Jaws dropped, not because Ronda had back-talked the coach, but because Ronda had talked at all.

"Fine," said Laverna. "We lose this, and we're done. First team out of the tournament."

"Awesome," muttered Martha, still not recovered.

"Jesus Christ," said Red Mabel. She side-armed a beer at Martha, who nearly broke her fingers catching it. "Hair of the dog." Red Mabel crossed her arms and stood in front of Martha, forced her to down the whole can. Now Martha belched in between dry heaves, but at least she was smiling as she opened her second beer.

The Flood Girls stretched on the grass, rubbing sore muscles in the roasting sun. Ginger did not leave the dugout, and looked up at Laverna helplessly.

"I'm on fire," she said. Laverna fanned Ginger with one of the magazines, but it provided no relief. Her pitcher could barely catch a breath. Laverna shouted over the country music that thundered from the PA system, until Athena heard her.

"Hormonal supplements," Ginger admitted weakly, as Athena took her pulse.

"I turned into a werewolf," said Athena, and dug in her enormous purse. "Menopause hit me and I thought I had been cursed by gypsies." She removed a battered cellophane bag, the bottom sagging with an inch of green powder.

Laverna snatched it away from her. "No more marijuana!"

"Herbs," said Athena. "Maybe you should take some, too."

"I'm still too young for that shit," said Laverna, and hoped it was true. Athena dumped the powder into a bottle of Gatorade, and when she shook it, the flecks swirled around ominously. Despite this, Ginger drank it eagerly, and Laverna sat with her until the umpire called her away for the coin toss.

Laverna lost, and the Flood Girls would bat first. As she headed back to the dugout, she spotted her daughter, sitting quietly on the bench. Laverna was not the only Flood Girl to ignore her today. She marched past her team, and pulled her daughter to her feet. Tabby gasped, expecting another assault. Instead, Laverna reached her arms around Rachel, pulled her close, rubbed the embroidery on the back of her new uniform. This time, she let the tears come.

They embraced for seconds, wordlessly.

"Play ball!" The umpire's call came, and Laverna stretched on her toes, to kiss Rachel on the cheek.

"I'm sorry," said Laverna.

"I deserved it," said Rachel, and now she was crying, too.

"Damn straight," said Red Mabel.

"Shut your fucking mouth," said Laverna. "Get out there and cream those bitches." Red Mabel was first at bat, and took to the field.

Red Mabel pounded home plate with her bat and spat at the catcher's feet. The umpire yelled at her, but Red Mabel pretended it was an accident. She swung at the first pitch, and it flew in an arc above the infield. She launched it so far up into the air, the center fielder could not distinguish it in the blinding sunlight. The Flood Girls whistled as Red Mabel tore around first base. She got caught between second and third, the two Mother Truckers throwing the ball back and forth over her head. Finally, Red Mabel charged, bloodthirsty and frightening, hell-bent on taking third base. The woman whimpered and leaped back from the bag, and missed the toss. Red Mabel was safe. She beat her chest and growled at the coach of the Mother Truckers, and Laverna knew the momentum was now firmly in their favor.

When her team took the field, Martha caught a pop-up at home plate, for the first time ever. The ball winged off the bat and shot straight up into the air, and Martha stood on creaky knees and caught it easily. In the bleachers, the fans from Quinn attempted to do the wave, but the Chief refused to stand every time. Diane hit homers in the second and fifth innings, both times the bases stacked. The herbs calmed Ginger significantly, and she threw with precision, despite the sweat running down her face. She struck out two batters in a row. Rachel ran past the foul line and dove for a pop fly, caught a ball even the umpire had written off. The Sinclairs were so eager to win, they crashed into each other, leaving the taller Sinclair with a bloody lip. Continuing to surprise everyone, Martha actually ran to second base.

"Shit yes!" Martha stood on the bag, and shook her fist in the air. She was drunk again.

During the top of the sixth inning, the Flood Girls batted through their entire line up. The pitcher was exhausted and she lobbed meatballs, right in the sweet spot of the batter's box. Everyone but Della made contact. After Ronda nailed the white clapboard in center field, Laverna studied the roster. With two outs, Rachel was on deck. Her daughter removed a rosary from the pocket of her sweatpants and kissed the cross before she pulled on her batting gloves. Rachel's higher power blessed her with a blistering grounder that tore past the shortstop.

Laverna did not know who Rachel had prayed to, but the divine intervention went on to help the Flood Girls beat the Mother Truckers ten to eight. They would be back to play in the morning.

Exhausted and sunburned, the Flood Girls returned to the Thunderbird. Laverna would not take any chances, and put the girls on lockdown. Laverna listened for doors opening or closing, sniffed for any pot smoke, and patrolled the stairwells, keeping watch for an invasion of hippies and frat boys. In the hallway, she played gin rummy with Athena and Rachel, as Frank guarded the doors.

The sprinklers were still spinning as the Flood Girls arrived for the first game of the day. Laverna, ignoring her own orders, drank a beer as she watched her girls warm up. The opposing team filled her with dread. Bucky could sense her nerves all the way across the carefully manicured infield, and brought Frank. He knew that she needed someone to hold on to.

The Spokane Quilting Society wore real baseball pants, metal cleats instead of plastic nubs. They dove into the dirt and practiced sliding, allowed only in tournament play. Laverna whispered to Frank that she hoped nobody got hurt.

Laverna stood for the majority of the game. She only looked away once, at the bottom of the third inning. The Flood Girls were overwhelmed by the onslaught of heavy hitters, and the Spokane Quilting Society scored nine runs in the span of fifteen minutes. Laverna couldn't bear it and turned her back as the bases filled once more. She hugged Frank tightly, and kissed him on the head. Laverna steeled herself by studying the long wooden bench, and her throat caught at the sight of the line of purses. Her girls: a designer handbag that only Ginger could afford, grommets and spikes on Rachel's punk rock wallet, a Day-Glo fanny pack for Tabby, Della's half-moon snaking with fake gold chains, cheap canvas totes for the Sinclair sisters, Diane's prim pocketbook, a drawstring bag that once held Crown Royal for Martha, Ronda's fringed leather coin purse, and a red-and-white beer cooler for Red Mabel, who would never carry something womanly. Even though they had been abandoned by their owners, the purses remained, left in the exact same order as the Flood Girls batted. This game was bittersweet.

Rachel was responsible for their only two runs, hitting the bruiser on first base in the face with a line drive. She ignored the bleeding nose and darted to second base, ran her fingers through her long blond hair when the old men screamed out her name. Her violence inspired Red Mabel to swing the bat like an ax, and her home run brought them both in. By the fifth inning, the umpire called the game. Twenty-four to two. The mercy rule.

The Flood Girls gathered around Laverna in the dugout, not dejected, not disappointed. In the bleachers, the fans from Quinn rose, stood, and clapped for the Flood Girls, despite the loss. Laverna saw the Chief embrace Bucky, and that was when she knew this season was truly something to be proud of.

Red Mabel passed around cans of beer, and the Flood Girls shook them in the air, their version of pom-poms. Diane counted to three, and when the tabs were pulled, a geyser of cheap beer showered their coach. Frank dove for safety under the bench. Drenched, Laverna was too emotional to protest, as the beer dripped down her face and her arms, pooled in the dirt at her feet.

More cans were opened, as the Flood Girls toasted Laverna, and toasted one another. The baby-blue T-shirts darkened, soaked in alcohol, and dripped as the girls pulled one another into embraces. For once, Ronda hugged back.

Klemp barged into the dugout, baseball cap pushed down to her eyes, her face as surly as always. She marched straight to Laverna and stuck out her hand.

"This is a nice surprise," said Laverna. She shook Klemp's hand, and the girl's grip was just as assured as her batting.

"Been here the whole time. Thought you were going to win the whole thing," said Klemp. She did not let go of Laverna's wet hand. "Shit happens."

"Yes," said Laverna. She leaned down to Klemp's height, her knees popping at the effort. "In ten years, you're going to be a Flood Girl, and we will be unstoppable."

"Whatever," said Klemp. "In ten years, you'll be dead."

"Jesus," Laverna said, and stood back up. She let go of Klemp's hand and pushed her out of the dugout. "I'm not that old."

Laverna knew they would return to these fields. The roster might not be the same in ten years, but they would battle their way through many seasons to come.

Quinn would always make new Flood Girls. Laverna had no doubts about her hometown, knew that it created devils and angels, queens and boy princesses, gritty souls that could survive anything.

———

In the parking lot, Laverna was silent as they loaded into the Suburban. Tabby hoisted herself up into the driver's seat, Laverna riding shotgun as always. Red Mabel and her enormous duffel bag took up the entire second row, Bucky and Rachel in the back. Hundreds of softball fans weaved through the lines of vehicles, sweating as they made their way to the fields for the final rounds of play. All these people arriving, just as the Flood Girls limped their way back to Quinn.

"Seat belts," called out Tabby cheerfully. She turned in the seat to make sure Red Mabel had heeded her orders.

"Shit," said Laverna. "We're going to have to go to that damn mall. I forgot to get something for Jake."

"We got first place," said Red Mabel, as she unzipped her duffel bag, removed dirty laundry and warm cans of beer. She smirked as she pulled the bag open wider. Inside, Laverna saw glimmers of gold. The first-place trophy was revealed. Red Mabel lifted it in the air, one corner of her smirk tugging into a crooked smile. Jake would adore the fake marble columns and the cross of sparkling softball bats, just as much as Laverna adored Red Mabel and her nefarious ways.

"Drive!" Laverna commanded, and threw a pair of filthy sweatpants over the trophy, just in case anybody was watching.

Erica Kane

★　★　★

September came, and so did an unprecedented amount of black bears. Jake's mother warned him to be especially careful at night, and early in the morning. This was normally the month for hyperphagia, in which black bears consumed sixty thousand calories per day, getting ready for hibernation. They always made appearances in town—the people in Quinn grew used to the occasional nuisance of garbage cans overturned, gardens ravaged, and crashing sounds in the middle of the night as their unpicked crab apple trees were destroyed.

But this year, there was an armada. There really was no other word. Jake wasn't scared of black bears—he knew enough that they were not a threat unless they were starving or protecting their cubs. Usually, all a person had to do was make a lot of noise, and the bear would run away. He learned this from a 1985 episode of *All My Children*, when he rushed home to see what became of Erica Kane, played by the immortal Susan Lucci, as she found herself trapped in the wilderness for some soap opera reason. A black bear charged her, and like any good soap opera, the drama was disarmed by the delivery of a passionate speech. In this case, Susan Lucci backed up against a tree and proclaimed: "You may not do this! . . . I am Erica Kane, and you are a filthy beast!" The bear, of course, knew that Erica Kane was nobody to mess with, and wandered away. The particular speech stuck with Jake, and he prepared to unleash it upon any bears that came near.

The bears invaded the town. The oldest citizens of Quinn claimed it was unprecedented. The bears traveled in packs down Main Street at night. The braver bears sunned on the bleachers of the football field, and one got stuck in the automatic doors of the post office. The Forest Service and Fish and Game stapled warnings on every pole and tree standing. Fish and Game came door-to-door at the trailer court, because apparently, black bears liked trailer courts. Cats and dogs went missing. Laverna announced to her regulars at the Dirty Shame that the number of bears surpassed the number of citizens. Special city council meetings were called, and the citizens of Quinn were told the same thing, every single time: Shoot on sight, and don't let your toddlers play unattended. Fish and Game knew Red Mabel, and prepared for a massacre.

Jake started eighth grade in September, and this year promised to be better. Peggy Davis retired, and the new librarian was barely middle-aged. The new librarian wore cashmere turtlenecks and owned at least three different pairs of eyeglasses. Her beauty made him nervous, and he had yet to ask her name. He had a new friend in Shyanne, a beautiful ally and protector. She wasn't mouthy like Misty, and Jake followed her around during lunch and waited by her locker in between classes.

First period was still Ms. Bray, At least this year he had a window seat. He wore his black sailor pants, and black boots that made him look taller. His shirt was a seafoam-green color, sewed on the old Singer.

Ms. Bray attempted to teach about continental drift, but most of the students watched out the windows, at the duo of black bears that had surrounded the flagpole. They milled about, sniffing at the lawn, curled up on top of the picnic tables that still smelled of sack lunches. All of this reminded Jake of the beginning of *Red Dawn*, one of his favorite movies, but without the Russians. He would have preferred Russians, because they probably would have shot Ms. Bray first.

Ms. Bray had enough and pulled the curtains shut. The students groaned, and Jake looked up at the blackboard to see Ms. Bray's crudely drawn version of the continental drift. It resembled a basketball with patches of eczema.

Jake surreptitiously pulled his copy of *Flowers in the Attic* from his desk and slid it behind his earth science textbook. It was his second time through the entire series, but it was delicious, and far preferable to hearing Ms. Bray opine about Pangaea.

Ms. Bray caught him, even though he was trying to keep his page turning as quiet as possible. She pointed to the front of the class, and Jake knew the routine, knew that she would give the speech about how if he found cheap paperbacks more interesting than a junior high school education, he should just go live under a bridge. It was always the same. Sometimes she switched it up, and suggested that he go live on the streets of San Francisco, which always made the class snicker.

"What is it this time?" Ms. Bray took a seat in an empty desk at the front of the class, one leg crossed over a knee, her foot bobbing expectantly. "I cannot wait to hear about hobbits or Nancy Reagan's astrologist or Jonathan Livingston Seabird."

"Seagull," said Jake.

"Don't let me stop you," said Ms. Bray. "Tell the class what is more interesting than the formation of every continent on this globe!" she shouted, which was a first.

Jake cleared his throat. "I am currently reading *Flowers in the Attic*, by V. C. Andrews, and it is a novel. This book is about a normal family, except they are all blondes. The father is killed in a car accident, and the mother takes all four of her children to live with their grandmother in a grand old mansion. The grandmother is evil, because she is not blonde, and she forces the children to live in the attic, which is okay, because it's a mansion, and it's a really big attic. But then the kids get really bored, and the oldest brother and sister start fucking each other."

The class erupted, and Ms. Bray was on her feet. Jake paused to take a deep, dramatic bow. He was not afraid anymore, and he soaked in the cheers of his classmates. Ms. Bray slapped the book from his hand, and shoved him toward the door.

"This is not funny!" she screamed at the class, who continued to howl, as she pushed him into the hallway.

"Go to the principal's office right now," she said, and shut the door behind her.

Jake could no longer hear the students laughing, as he walked down the long hall toward the administrative offices. He looked over his shoulder, and turned left instead of right, and marched out the front doors of the school. He didn't care about the black bears. He walked to the Sinclair, where Martha Man Hands mostly ignored him, caught up in all of the bear sightings squawking on the police scanner. He ate a corn dog, and returned in time for second period.

———

As promised, Shyanne waited at her locker. She still had a walking cast on her foot, but the orthopedist said she was healing well and should recover to full capacity. She told him this as they walked the empty hallways; school had ended ten minutes earlier, and the students were eager to get back out into the unseasonable air and the chaos of the black bear invasion. Shyanne was wearing her usual athletic shorts—for a while, she had worn sweatpants, depressed because she thought she had blown her chances at a scholarship over a stupid women's softball game. But here were the shorts, and those legs that still came up to his neck, and he followed her into the auditorium, where her entrance caused every boy to punch each other and stare at her legs.

At exactly four o'clock, the student council president called the meeting to order. Twenty students were present, all elected representatives from their respective classes, plus Jake. Nobody seemed to notice or care that he was there, even though he was sitting next to Shyanne, and they made an odd couple.

This was a new year, and a new student council. There were no minutes to read from the previous meeting, as they had disappeared with last year's secretary. Nobody cared about what had been discussed three months ago anyway. The student council president was the type of girl who did every extracurricular activity, in an attempt to make up for her atrocious personality. She began the meeting by introducing herself and her long list of accomplishments, and then introduced the vice president, the secretary, and the treasurer. They also were known for their atrocious personalities. Normally, Jake believed that women should have a more active voice in politics, but not in this case.

There were four representatives from every class, and Shyanne volunteered for the seniors, but the other fifteen representatives were burnouts or total nerds. Shyanne broke it down for him—the freshman class would meet and elect the most awful candidates they could pull together, in an attempt to sabotage the system. The sophomore class would nominate the mentally handicapped and the obstructionists, because they figured out how the game was played. The juniors were always hungover, or high, and they elected their two foreign exchange students and two kids who were devoutly religious. The seniors were a little more unpredictable—some volunteered, like Shyanne, because it looked good on a college transcript. Others volunteered just because they hated the new student council president.

Sarah was imperious. She sat on the stage with the vice president, the treasurer, and the secretary, who had yet to take a note on her yellow legal pad. They did all of the talking, while the representatives took a nap or did homework or threw spitballs at one another. This went on for twenty minutes—the student council president discussed the black bear crisis, the new uniforms for the girls' basketball team, the new faculty members, and the renovations to the chemistry lab.

Finally, it was time to talk about the main event. Homecoming. Sarah discussed the wood gathering for the bonfire, the pep rally, and the fundraiser, which this year was something called Donkey Basketball. Finally, she began to discuss the dance.

The treasurer raised her hand, and Sarah called on her.

"We have three hundred and ten dollars to spend this year, but we need to keep two hundred dollars in prudent reserve."

"Okay," said Sarah. "So we've got a hundred bucks to spend. I was thinking we should make it a Sadie Hawkins theme this year!" Her fake enthusiasm was grating; everybody knew she just wanted an excuse to force boys to slow dance.

"No," said Shyanne, from her seat in the auditorium.

"You need to be called on," declared Sarah.

"Shut it, Sarah." Shyanne stood up, and pointed at Jake. He immediately began to blush.

"Who is that? Is that an elementary school student?" Sarah laughed, and the vice president rolled her eyes and began to apply cuticle cream.

And then Shyanne was dragging him onto the stage, while Sarah looked confused and slightly frightened.

Nobody else paid any attention until Shyanne wheeled the chalkboard out onto the stage, and Jake unrolled his sketches and scotch-taped them in place.

———

Triumphant, Jake walked home from school, his feet barely touching the ground. His head was filled with shopping lists, with the schematics of decorating a gymnasium, with his ten minutes of glory.

He entered his yard. Thankfully, he looked up from his reverie. A black bear sprawled on his porch, and it gnawed on one of Bert's filthy boots. The bear was bald in patches, his snout disfigured by scratches that had become scar tissue. This bear was a survivor.

Jake raised his hands. The bear raised his head and looked up at him, curiously.

"I AM ERICA KANE! AND YOU ARE A FILTHY BEAST!"

The bear resumed eating Bert's boot, until Jake threw his earth science textbook at it, and then the bear yawned and stretched and lazily walked into the backyard.

Keeping Score

★   ★   ★

Rachel was thankful that Jake hated math, and was terrible at it. He just didn't care about solving for X, because he believed there was more important detective work to be done. He came in with his algebra homework for the last hour of Rachel's shift, and they gossiped and speculated about Laverna, who had been spotted with Jim Number Three. There was also the mystery of Red Mabel, and why she had shaved her head. Jake assumed that it was head lice, but Rachel had it on good authority (and the rare sober authority, as it was not bar gossip, but discussed at AA) that the two Mabels had teamed up for some sort of project. Rachel was just grateful for Jake's presence, serving him Shirley Temples until he was vibrating from sugar, and she often called Diane Savage Connor from the bar phone for assistance with the algebra problems that stumped them both. Rachel found herself missing softball, the sunburns, the furrowed scrapes on the knees, waking up in the morning so sore she could barely walk. She missed riding back from games with exhausted women, spent and silent, an easy quiet that could only exist among sisters, or veterans of the same war.

Lately, the distraction of Jake had become the only sane part of her day. The silver mine had closed down for a month, after a section had caved in, and safety inspectors were flown in. They still had not given the all clear, and the lesbian silver miners had become day drinkers. They tipped terribly, and there had been some sort of fissure among them, perhaps a blame game over the cave in, or perhaps a love triangle gone wrong. The miners had divided into two camps. Usually, ten or so would sit in the back by the jukebox, playing the same Anne Murray songs over and over. The other camp was a small one, really just one lesbian who Rachel had always thought was the alpha of the pack, now relegated to sit by herself at the bar, heckled mercilessly, watching in the mirror nervously for the projectiles that were often hurled at the back of her head. The split had been a vicious one. If the outcast tried to use the bathroom, she would be blocked by a flank of surly women. They had matching crew cuts now, to further distinguish their solidarity. The outcast kept her waterfall of crunchy black hair, shaved on the sides, a frizzy tail that fanned out across her shoulders. Rachel stopped herself from forbidding the public urination, and stopped Jake from offering to deep condition her hair. The banishment had caused the outcast to have some sort of breakdown, which was surprising, because every lesbian Rachel had ever known had been a reticent creature. The fistfights were never fair, and always ended up with the outcast on the floor, her former coworkers pouring beer on her. The outcast returned to her barstool, guzzling drinks, only leaving to urinate on the sidewalk.

It was a Friday afternoon, and it had been an odd week. Mrs. Matthis was still drinking, even though lunch had come and gone. She finished two entire crossword puzzles, and the floor beneath her was covered in pencil shavings. In addition to the lesbian psychodrama, Rachel had felt a tangible buzz throughout Quinn, noticed a bloodthirsty look on the faces at the grocery store and at the Sinclair. Tomorrow was the first day of deer-hunting season. Jake was the only normal person in town, and his outfit especially pleased Rachel, even though it was a rare repeat. She adored the smart gray suit, as it hung on him perfectly, and this time he had paired it with a black button-down, the butterfly collar fanning out across his shoulders. She would check his shoes later.

"I'm going hunting tomorrow," he said, and stabbed at a maraschino cherry with a plastic cocktail sword. For the first time ever, he avoided making eye contact.

"I hope you are talking about the thrift store," said Rachel. "Please tell me you are stalking the elusive Yves Saint Laurent sweater vest."

"In this town?" Jake had finally secured the cherry, and popped it in his mouth. He laid the stem delicately across the edge of the napkin. "And that's not very funny. I really want one of those."

"Sorry." Rachel was confused, and the outcast had brought taxidermy with her today, adding to the insanity. The outcast had propped up a badger on the stool beside her, mounted on a circle cut from the stump of a pine tree. It was a cheap job, the eyes replaced with pure black marbles, much too large, bulging from the sockets. She had staple-gunned plastic Easter basket grass along the edges. The whole thing was unnerving to look at, made worse because something had gnawed off a front paw. Rachel was aghast when the outcast stroked the badger during the lunch rush, but now she almost called her mother, because the alpha had begun to whisper to it.

Jake whispered also. "That is really, really weird."

Rachel wiped the bottom of the glass before she returned it to the napkin. Jake would say something about a ring of condensation. "I guess you aren't going to clarify," said Rachel. She slid the math book down the bar, and leaned on her elbows. "Why on earth would you go hunting?"

"Jesus Christ," said a gravelly voice. "This is America, sweetheart." Rachel looked up at the miner, waiting at the bar with an empty glass. She was Laverna's favorite, and despite her crew cut, she still resembled young Elvis. "Are you some sort of communist?"

"Vegetarian," Rachel said, and tilted her pint glass, pulled the tap. While it filled, Elvis extinguished her cigarette on the head of the badger, and the outcast said nothing. Elvis squinted at Jake's drink.

"Is that a fucking Shirley Temple?" Elvis was drunk, and obviously looking for a fight. Unfortunately, she had picked the two most fearful people in Quinn.

"Yes," said Rachel, reaching for the bar phone.

"They are delightful," Jake announced, and picked up the plastic cocktail sword, as if he planned on using it as a weapon.

"You should be drinking a Roy Rogers, kid." The miner snatched the sword out of Jake's hand and flung it at the outcast, and it stuck, trapped in the static of her hair. "Little boys drink Roy Rogers. Little girls drink Shirley Temples."

"Thanks for the tip," said Jake. Rachel winced at the defiance in his voice. "I certainly don't think you, of all people, should be giving me advice on gender conformity."

"Speak English," said Elvis. "This is America!" Mrs. Matthis tried to ignore Elvis, even though she was uncomfortably close. She valiantly sharpened another pencil, and turned another page.

"You've already said that," Jake said, and stood up from his stool. Rachel began to dial her mother's number, her other hand scrambling in the soapy water of the bar sink, as she tried to find something more vicious than a teaspoon. Elvis stared down at Jake, two feet shorter.

But all at once, the showdown was over. Mrs. Matthis stabbed her in the hand with a freshly sharpened pencil. Elvis screamed; the pencil had been brought down so hard that it continued to stick in her hand, even though she shook it wildly, in pain.

Mrs. Matthis did not react, picked up another pencil and sharpened it nonchalantly. The bar filled with the sound of crickets, as she continued to twist another pencil back and forth, creating an armory.

Elvis screamed as she was rushed out the door by her brethren, on their way to the hospital in Ellis. There would be no retribution—even the silver miners knew Mrs. Matthis still had friends in the court, even though she was now armed and dangerous.

The outcast was delighted by this turn of events, but did nothing to stop the fire that smoldered in her taxidermy.

"You need to be more careful," said Rachel. "Those women are lunatics. You can't challenge them to a fight, Jake. Especially not in that suit."

"Whatever," said Jake. He faked a yawn. "Overdressed and unimpressed."

The smell of burning fur had reached Rachel, and she wrinkled her nose. "Let's talk about this hunting thing."

"Not my idea," Jake said, and accepted his drink. "Obviously."

"Are you even old enough to hunt?"

"I don't really know," he said. "This morning, there was a brand-new camouflage shirt and matching pants on the kitchen table. In my size. And one of those horrendous orange safety vests."

"How awful," said Rachel. "Do you even have shoes for that sort of thing?"

"Loafers," he said. "I'm kind of worried about the traction. I'm pretty sure hunting was my mother's idea. Or maybe Bert's. Whatever. They're trying."

"Maybe things are better."

Jake lifted his glass and saluted her, just as Tabby came through the front door. The sudden burst of daylight lit the Shirley Temple, and it glowed as he held it in the air. "I owe that to you."

He took a drink, as Tabby halted, grimaced at the badger. The drape of smoke made the scene even more surreal.

"The miners," explained Rachel. "Don't worry. I'll clean it up."

Tabby said nothing as she walked behind the bar, tied an apron around her waist. This was the Dirty Shame, and Tabby had apparently seen stranger things. She poured a beer for the outcast, and began to busy herself opening the cash register and counting the till. It was the beginning of another shift.

The outcast, silhouetted by the thick, acrid smoke, whispered something. A prayer, as she poured out the contents of her pint glass. The outcast asked for another beer. She sipped until the embers stopped glowing, until she was certain her friend was no longer on fire.

————

Four days before Halloween, and all of the flowers in the garden had been cut down to their nubs. Somehow the clematis continued its march. The vines had overgrown the trellises and wrapped around the planks of the fence. The plant was still blooming, and Rachel let it go. The squirrel kept watch for the first frost of the year.

She had to wear slippers now, and a coat. She could no longer sit outside in her pajamas. For the hundredth time, she thought about quitting smoking. She exhaled, and decided that there were bigger things to think about.

She heard the latch of the gate, and the creak as it swung open.

She turned around to see Jake, bearing a brown envelope and two carefully gift-wrapped packages, dressed in his most ridiculous outfit yet. As threatened, he wore the camouflage pants, a camouflage long-sleeved thermal shirt, and a mesh vest the bright orange of hunters.

"Don't even start," he said, gesturing to his clothes. "Just remember that Bert built me a shoe rack. He's trying."

"He's got a long way to go," said Rachel.

"I'm done with fighting," said Jake. "Bert isn't going anywhere." He pulled up a pant leg, and he was wearing the pinkest socks she had ever seen.

"Thank God," said Rachel. "You were starting to scare me."

"Here," he said, and thrust the envelope at her. "I've been meaning to give it to Laverna, but you'll do."

Rachel opened the envelope. Jake had compiled the stats for the season, and typed them in his usual, fastidious way. She found her name, and when she saw the numbers, she wished that she hadn't.

"I'm done with keeping score," said Jake. "Acceptance," he said. "I learned that from one of your books."

He pushed the gift-wrapped packages at her, and she tucked the envelope under her arm.

"Presents?" Rachel was mystified. He had given her enough.

"Not for you," he said. "I finally finished the uniforms for Bucky and Shyanne. I know it's late. I made Bucky number thirteen, and Shyanne number zero. Zero is the runway sample size. We're going to have to work on her diet."

"Of course," said Rachel.

Jake flashed his pink socks at her one more time. He tipped his hat to Rachel Flood, and walked up the path, let himself out of the gate.

———

An hour later, the Chief came to her house for their weekly meeting. They no longer met on the field, no longer threw a ball back and forth. Softball was over. Now they sat across the couch from each other, and they actually used the literature.

"I wanted to tell you something." He reached into the pocket of his jacket.

"It better not be bad news," Rachel said.

"No," said the Chief. He removed a blue ribbon from his pocket. FIRST PLACE, SCIENCE FAIR, 1961. "Sorry. It's the only first place I ever got." He placed it in her hand, wrapped her fingers around it. "As your sponsor, I think you are officially done making your amends."

"What?" The ribbon seemed to weigh ten pounds.

"You're done here," said the Chief. "You can leave this place."

"Where am I supposed to go?" Rachel felt frantic. She assumed she would know when she was done, that there would be an obvious conclusion.

"I think you've made peace. You can go wherever you want to go," he said.

Rachel began crying, and the Chief was quick to hold her.

"It's all so overwhelming," she said.

"I know," he said.

She never thought she would feel reluctance at leaving Quinn. Just months ago, she had barely endured each day. Once upon a time, envelopes returned to her, unopened. The people of her hometown marked them RETURN TO SENDER, and now Rachel Flood wrote her amends so wholeheartedly no envelope could contain them. No words were necessary; she would let grace and humility end this story.

If she wanted, she could go create a whole new tale, leave this chapter far behind, put the book on the shelf. If she wanted, she could go back to Missoula.

She could wait there. In four years, Jake would be old enough to join her.

Meadow

★　　★　　★

*J*ake's stomach was growling. He hadn't had a chance to eat breakfast, and it took Bert nearly an hour to pack his truck. Jake felt obligated to stand and watch, because it seemed respectful. All Bert needed was a gun and their lunches, but it was all for safety's sake.

Mrs. Foote arrived in her station wagon, said something encouraging to Bert, but Jake paid no attention to her. Waiting for Bert was painful enough. Mrs. Foote left with the baby, and Bert cleaned his rifle, even though Jake was certain it had been taken apart the night before. Krystal placed their lunches behind the driver's seat and kissed her husband good-bye. Saturdays, she worked the day shift. Jake peeked inside the paper bags as Bert finally turned the key in the ignition. Bologna sandwiches, potato chips, and a pudding cup.

Lunch was all Jake could think about as Bert drove toward the mountains.

It began to rain, softly at first, and then picked up until Bert had to put his wipers on. The wipers were the only sound in the truck. They did not make conversation. The silence became a tangible thing after Jake crossed his leg, and Bert caught a glimpse of Jake's pink sock.

Jake could tell Bert was angry by the way his stepfather clenched the steering wheel. Bert flicked off the heat in the truck so hard that Jake thought the switch would break in his hand. Jake wished they could turn on the radio, but Bert did not believe in popular music anymore.

The rain kept up, and the truck got colder as they wound their way up the mountain and turned off onto a logging road. They had been driving for an hour. Jake had no idea where they were. The geography of the mountains that enclosed Quinn never interested him. All Jake could think about was the lunch his mother packed and getting home as quickly as possible.

Bert was a deer hunter. The freezer in Krystal's trailer was a testament to this. Jake pretended to look for deer in the brush, but he was secretly rooting for them, and would not have let on, even if he did spot one.

Twenty minutes up the logging road, Bert pulled the truck into a gravel turnaround and parked.

"This will do," he said. These were the first words he had spoken all morning.

It was still raining, and Jake cursed Bert silently for making him get out in all of this wetness. At least Jake didn't care about these clothes.

Bert grabbed his rifle from the rack above the seat, and Jake reached for the cooler sitting next to him, hoping they were bringing the lunches with them, but Bert shook his head.

It was drizzling as they began to descend into the thickness of white pines. They slid their way down a shale embankment. He tried to follow Bert's path, because he was a man who knew what he was doing in the woods, and Jake did not want to be left behind.

Jake's mind was preoccupied with his plans for the homecoming dance. He was trying to figure out how to create a giant papier-mâché castle facade. He had no doubt that it would work out exactly as planned, but it would require some assistance from the teacher of the shop class.

The rain became less of an issue when they reached the deeper woods. The giant pines provided shelter and as Jake inhaled, the glorious smell made him feel better about all of this. They rose up so tall that they became the sky. The gray sky was barely visible through the canopy.

They kept going, deeper into the forest, Bert stopping occasionally, and holding up one hand. Jake knew to stop moving when Bert did this, just as he knew not to talk, not that there was a chance of conversation. The rain changed to sleet, and Jake shoved his hands deep inside the pockets of his jacket. He did not have gloves.

He moved his fingers along the rosary in his right pocket. He no longer wasted his time thinking about his fifty-nine enemies. He had finally stopped keeping score.

Madonna had a new album, and he had enough money to buy it. He knew Rachel would take him to Ellis, make a special trip. They were both tired of *Like a Prayer*. He continued to move his fingers along the chain of beads. He kept the rosary hidden from view, because it felt good to have a secret. There was Catholicism going on inside Jake's pocket, and Bert would never know.

They passed through a brief opening in the trees, a tiny meadow, the tall grasses brown after summer. Full of rain, the vegetation soaked the legs of Jake's pants.

Bert held up a hand and Jake stopped obediently in the middle of the meadow. He was starting to shiver. He saw other hunters during their descent, saw the flashes of orange. This was the first day of hunting season, so that was to be expected. But they hadn't seen any hunters for a while, and Bert looked around and cocked his head, listening for sounds in the brush.

Jake stood still, patiently, thinking about a movie that Laverna might actually enjoy, something that had men with mustaches. Definitely not a musical.

There was a rustle in the brush, and then the flight of birds, their bright colors as they took to the sky. His winter birds. A flock of black-capped chickadees. A burst of yellow as a trio of cedar waxwings hopped from limb to limb, wearing their robber masks.

Jake watched the birds, until a doe stepped into the meadow. The deer did not notice them. Jake remained so still that he could hear the doe chewing, the sound of grass ripped from the soil.

Bert turned suddenly, his face just as expressionless as always.

He looked to the right, and raised his rifle.

Thank God, thought Jake. Maybe they could be done with this.

And Bert turned, just as the sleet began to fall in heavy sheets, and Jake could hear the patter on his shoulders as Bert aimed the gun at him.

Jake didn't have time to realize what was happening.

A flash, and then nothing.

No Lights Flashing

★　★　★

Rachel finished reading the forty-ninth book of the Nancy Drew series, *The Secret of Mirror Bay*. She could finish these books in a few hours, figure out the villain within the first fifty pages, and unravel the mystery within the first seventy-five. This brought her comfort—despite the mystery of her own future, at least she was always a step ahead of the girl detective. Perhaps that was where her future lay; Rachel was still young enough to be a police officer.

She listened to the rain for an hour and thought about her future.

Eventually, she got up from the couch and called her mother.

"Jake and I are coming over," she said. "I just wanted to warn you."

"I appreciate that," said Laverna. "I'll make dinner. I've got some steaks in the freezer."

"That's not funny," said Rachel.

"Sure it is," said Laverna. "It's not my fault you have a crappy sense of humor."

"It might be," said Rachel. "There's a good chance it might be genetic."

"I refuse to tangle with you," sighed Laverna. "Athena told me not to engage when you bait me." She hung up the phone, and Rachel laughed. Her mother was full of surprises. Apparently, Laverna was also full of Al-Anon.

Rachel filled the sink, and stacked dirty dishes under the running water. She turned on the stereo, and the cassette whirred to life. Madonna blasted through the kitchen, rattling the speakers. She did not hear the knocking.

The music stopped. Rachel spun around, and the Chief was standing in front of the stereo. She waited for him to speak, and kept her hands in the soapy water. She heard Bucky's truck pull up in the driveway.

"Rachel," said the Chief. "There's been an accident."

Rachel's mind went many places, all of them dark. "What do you mean?"

"It's Jake," he said. "There was a hunting accident."

"Jake?"

"He's gone, Rachel."

She saw Bucky was running through the door and he was in the kitchen in time to help the Chief ease Rachel to the floor.

She didn't cry. That's what she would remember, days later. She just went into a gray place. She could recollect sitting on the couch, Bucky and the Chief on each side of her, the phone ringing and ringing. None of them made a move to answer it. Rachel only rose to the corner of the living room, and she wiggled the loose brick where the fireplace had once been. She slid it from the mooring, reddish dust piling at her feet, from passing years and new construction. She wanted to get high. The Chief and Bucky said nothing. Inside the hole, more dust, a neatly cut line of mortar and creosote.

Rachel eventually spoke, and it was to insist that she be the one to tell Laverna. Rachel felt that her mother needed to hear that their good-luck charm had been undone by bad luck of his own. For the first time in her life, she needed to be near Laverna. The Chief and Bucky thought this was a bad idea, but they did not want to fight her. They found her a coat, and the Chief insisted that he would drive.

Rachel was in shock as she regarded the scene in Krystal's driveway. It seemed like a dream. Krystal's car was gone. The Chief said she was at the hospital with the body.

A city cop car was parked outside, and the long sedan of the sheriff. Bert sat in the dirt, a cooler open beside him, and he ate a sandwich.

Rachel rushed him. He didn't flinch as she tore across the gravel. He was expressionless as she lunged, as if he had been expecting it all along. She was yanked backward by Bucky, pulling at her T-shirt until it began to tear. She heard screaming, a wail that could be heard throughout Quinn, another siren. It took a moment until she realized the uncontrollable keening sound was coming from deep within her.

The Chief pushed Rachel into his truck, and they both waited for Bucky, who was talking to the cops. Bert kept eating his sandwich, even though it had started to rain again. They watched as Reverend Foote appeared, gingerly holding the rifle.

They watched as Reverend Foote handed the sheriff the gun, as the reverend walked up to Bucky and put his hand on his shoulder. They watched as the reverend said something, his brow furrowed as he attempted an expression of concern.

Bucky reached back and punched the reverend so hard in the face that he stumbled backward and tripped over Bert. Reverend Foote landed on his back, arms cast out in a perfect cross, as if it would break his fall.

Both cops did nothing, just stood there. Bucky crossed the driveway and got into the truck with them. He was shaking. He asked the Chief to turn on the heat as they backed out, and Rachel looked over as they drove away. Bert continued to eat his sandwich, and the reverend remained prone in the gravel.

Rachel watched the sheriff slide the rifle into the backseat of his car, no lights flashing.

The Mercy Rule

*   *   *

*L*averna already knew, just as the Chief had suspected. It was Ginger Fitchett who called, Ginger Fitchett who had the police scanner going all day and all night next to the cash register at the Sinclair.

After Ginger called, Laverna went out to the back deck and drank a beer and watched the river. The sleet warmed back into rain in the afternoon, made the water a sheet of ripples, turned the surface gray with motion, gray with reflection of the storm clouds above. Laverna removed her corduroy blazer, despite the damp air. She slid the red velvet headband from her hair, threw it at the wind chimes, missed by feet. Kicked off her low-heeled pumps, the same gray as the river. She tugged the gauzy scarf from her neck, dangled it beside her chair in hopes Frank would snatch it away and bury it in the yard. There was no more need for armor.

She drank her beer and waited. She knew Red Mabel would show, and that they would get drunk, and she would cry, and Red Mabel would sit beside her and smoke, because that's what always happened when somebody died. This was how they mourned.

Frank crawled on her lap, and they watched the river together. He tucked his head into her armpit. She had come to learn that it was his favorite place on earth.

She heard the truck pull up, and she could tell it was not Red Mabel.

She lifted Frank from her lap, set the beer down, and went to the front door.

The Chief and Bucky helped Rachel inside. Frank came galloping from the back, and sniffed at their legs, as Rachel lowered herself to the couch. Bucky tucked an afghan over her, and they stood there, all of them, waiting for Laverna to do something.

She sat down next to her daughter, and asked Bucky to fetch a beer and an ashtray. Rachel handed her the piece of paper Jake had given her that morning. Finally, the tears came as Laverna read the statistics, the careful columns of runs batted in, errors, runs scored, and batting averages. Jake paid close attention to each one of the Flood Girls, and there would be nobody who could possibly take his place.

She drank while Rachel smoked, cigarette after cigarette, and not a word was spoken.

The Chief and Bucky took turns rolling a ball across the carpet for Frank, until the dog had enough, and he nosed the ball under the couch. He crossed the room and lay across Laverna's feet.

Bucky built a fire, because it was the only thing he could do.

When Red Mabel sped down the driveway, and lurched to a stop, the Chief stood up and kissed Rachel on the forehead. He and Bucky left as Red Mabel rushed in.

Perhaps they thought that grief was women's work, or perhaps they were afraid of Red Mabel's anger.

Later, Rachel finally spoke. "I can't go to his funeral."

"I know," said Laverna.

"I imagine it will be at Reverend Foote's church," said Red Mabel, attempting to be helpful.

That was when Rachel broke, and Laverna reached over and pulled her close.

"None of us will go," said Laverna. "We'll do whatever you want."

"I hate him," said Rachel, still sobbing, and Laverna didn't know if she was talking about Reverend Foote or Bert, but figured that it didn't really matter. All Laverna could think about was the mercy rule. She wished for an umpire to call the game.

There had been enough loss.

––––––

Laverna stopped by Rachel's house every single night. She sat with Rachel while she worked her day shift, tried to give her some time off. Rachel refused. Laverna understood, had also lost herself in work when her heart had been broken, nine years earlier.

The funeral would be Saturday morning. There was no announcement in the newspaper, just a small article on yet another hunting accident. The report did not even mention the names of those involved, those absolved. At the Dirty Shame, Laverna learned that the funeral was private, and only for the congregation.

Laverna knew her daughter well enough, knew that Rachel could not stay away. The other Flood Girls would not have gone to the service. The other Flood Girls were ready to burn the church to the ground.

Benediction

★   ★   ★

Rachel slept fitfully, and between every nightmare, she smoked a cigarette on the front porch. The last hours of night bore a dampness, a threat of snow, the temperature the coldest in months. Summer and softball seemed like impossible things.

She lay there, and said her prayers, and forced herself to pray for Krystal, even though she didn't want to.

Today was the funeral, and all Rachel could think about, all that preoccupied her mind, were the clothes he was going to be buried in.

She knew she had no say, knew that he would not have left directions. As organized as Jake was, he would not have thought it necessary to create a will.

Bucky was going, because the Chief demanded it, even though the funeral was private. Closed to the public, and closed casket, because the injuries were so devastating. There would not be a chance for Bucky to see what he was wearing and report back to her.

Jake had so many suits. A storage shed full of them. Krystal probably bought a cheap black suit from Pamida, brainwashed. Reverend Foote would approve. No ascots or funny hats or pocket squares.

Rachel settled into the fact that she would never have any way of knowing. Instead of plastic flowers, she would bring something with flair to where he was buried, every year, until she herself was gone.

She found herself thinking of the women in black, the women in Missoula, standing solemnly on the bridge.

She was lost in this distraction when she realized Bucky was calling her name from the hallway.

"Rachel?"

"What?"

"Are you decent?"

"Yes," she said. He stood in the doorway of her bedroom, impossibly tall and slim in his dark suit. They had spent enough time together that she had grown accustomed to his teeth. He was handsome.

"I knocked and knocked. You really gotta start locking your front door."

She rolled over, away from him, and pretended to look out the window.

"Leave me alone, Bucky."

"It's not right, Rachel. It's not right for you to stay here. You have to come with me."

"I'm not going," said Rachel. "None of us are."

"That's why you have to go," said Bucky. "Somebody from the Flood Girls ought to be there. He was one of you."

"You're going."

"Chief's orders," said Bucky.

"Well, he's not the chief of me."

"I thought he kind of was."

"Not about things like this," said Rachel. "I don't want to see Bert, okay?"

"I get that."

Bert was a free man, absolved, clean. He continued to insist on the sudden appearance of a deer, that Jake stepped in the way. The coroner and the sheriff declared it a hunting accident. They were so common around Quinn, that it was probably not even investigated. Rachel wished that Nancy Drew was real, but this was a mystery that would never be solved. How Krystal could stay with Bert was perhaps the biggest mystery of all.

"I don't want to see Krystal, either."

"It's not always all about you, Rachel."

"Fuck you, Bucky. I hear that enough at AA meetings."

"It's not," he said, and sat down on the bed. "You are gonna hate yourself later if you don't go."

"I don't want to go to the church. I don't want to see that stupid fucking reverend. I don't want to see Krystal. I don't want to see Bert. That's it. I'm done arguing."

Bucky got up from the bed, and started sliding hangers on the rod he himself had hung, looking for clothes.

"Do you want a dress?" He held up the first black thing he found, which was actually a sundress. "Just tell me, and I'll find whatever you want."

She sat up in anger, and was ready to yell at him, but did not. She wasn't angry with him. Her chest got tight, and she pushed herself out of bed, and the tears started coming.

"Is it snowing?"

"A little," said Bucky.

"I guess I'm going to need a coat."

She shoved him out of the way and began to choose things from her closet.

As she stepped out onto the front porch, she saw Bucky's ladder, still propped up against the fence. The snow had collected on every rung.

———

The snow fell harder as they drove to the church. There were not many cars in the parking lot. The church looked the same, but the roof was white from the snow. She recognized the Chief's truck, and the same station wagons and vans from the wedding.

It broke her heart a little bit, to see that the parking lot was barely a quarter full.

When they entered the church, it was worse than she expected. The front row was empty, except for Krystal, Bert, and the baby. Nobody sat in the pew across from them. The rows behind were occupied, contained all of the people she remembered from the day Bert and Krystal were married. Those plain people in their plain clothing. They were dressed identically, and it infuriated Rachel to see them in their cheap dark jackets and black pleated dresses.

Only Krystal was distinguishable. Rachel could see her from behind, in the seat closest to the aisle. She wore lipstick. Bert sat next to her, in a dark gray sweater. He was holding the baby, and Krystal rested her head on his shoulder.

The Chief and his wife sat in the back by themselves. Bucky steered Rachel over to them, and she sat down next to the Chief, who was holding on to his wife's hand tightly.

There were no flowers. Rachel hated this place, the plainness, the cheapness; apparently there would be some sort of wake afterward—one wall was lined with those same card tables, covered in things wrapped in tinfoil and wax paper.

The door of the church opened, and a girl with dyed-black hair stomped past in heavy boots. She wore a black leather jacket and torn blue jeans. The congregation turned to stare. Rachel could smell her leather jacket as she sat down in front of them, the leather wet from the falling snow. The Chief tapped her on the shoulder, and she turned around and glared at him.

"Misty?" The Chief seemed flabbergasted. "How did you get here?"

"Hitchhiked," she said, and turned back around.

"There are no flowers," said Rachel, and nobody responded.

She wanted to stand up and scream at the top of her lungs. This place was so empty and quiet and everything was too new, and Jake was a kid who appreciated things that were loud, things that had a previous life of their own. Jake's funeral should have been held at Buley's, not a place that still had pieces of masking tape around the doorjambs, a place that still smelled of fresh paint.

As if she had been conjured, Buley and Rocky entered the church. Rachel knew that nothing would keep Rocky away from his nephew's funeral, even if his presence was unwanted. He helped Buley sit in the empty pew across from Krystal and Bert, a pew meant for family.

Bucky put his arm around Rachel, and the Chief's wife offered her a handkerchief, the real kind, cloth, and the fact that Jake would have appreciated that made her cry even harder.

Reverend Foote came out onto the raised stage, entering from a little door off to the left.

Rachel gritted her teeth as he walked to the pulpit.

He led them in prayer. Rachel glanced over at Bucky, who was watching her closely.

She could not focus on his words, just kept staring at the row of card tables, thinking about how none of these people who belonged to this church belonged to Jake; they were here out of duty, and then to eat.

The parishioners began to sing "We Shall All Be Reunited." The Chief opened up the songbook and placed it on her lap, but she refused to acknowledge it, and it fell to the floor and made a thump as it landed. It slid beneath Misty's bench, and Misty kicked at it, and it came to rest between the third and fourth row.

Reverend Foote smiled when the song was over, and began to talk about lives cut short, about how God had a plan for each and every one of them. She could see Bert nodding his head.

Rachel found herself staring at the coffin. In truth, she had suspected that the size of it would gut her, but it wasn't terribly small. Jake had been a little over five feet tall. He had just seemed so waifish and slight in real life. The coffin was plain, and brown, and didn't look like expensive wood. It didn't even seem polished. It didn't gleam in the lights that shone on the reverend.

Reverend Foote was speaking about the survivors, Krystal and the baby, and Bert, and those in the church who had gotten to know and cherish Jake. At that point, Rachel was ready to start throwing casseroles, but she just pulled her jacket tighter around her.

Reverend Foote talked about lambs in heaven.

Rachel heard the door as it opened behind her. She didn't turn around.

Then Rachel smelled something familiar. She immediately twisted in her seat.

She would know Athena's perfume anywhere.

In came Athena, lightly dusted in snow, wearing her usual giant black shift dress, but a scarf in all the colors of the rainbow, tied around her neck.

The parishioners turned in their seats to stare, and the reverend stopped his sermon, as the long line of women marched behind Athena, up the aisle, and Rachel didn't recognize them until they were upon her.

Each squeezed her shoulder before taking a seat in the pews.

Here was Ginger Fitchett, in an exquisite vintage Chanel suit, black wool, the skirt hitting just at the knees, pillbox hat pinned to her dark hair, and a thin polka-dotted veil.

Shyanne was right behind her, wearing a long silk sheath, the décolletage and the hem framed by fans of delicate black lace. The sheath was split up the side, and one of her long, beautiful legs was revealed with every step. She was wearing opera-length evening gloves and a giant black hat. A small stuffed bird perched along the brim in a nest of feathers. She was wearing turquoise heels.

The Sinclairs came next, in matching dresses, long, ebony silk, flapper style, the hems heavily beaded, fringes hanging and clattering, the strands of beads making a racket as the Sinclairs eased into the pew. Their hair was up in complicated buns and twists. They had enormous amounts of hair, and it had been secured all over with black lacquered combs, sparkling with tiny rhinestones.

Della Dempsey marched behind them, in a cunning little cocktail dress, dark as night, the top formfitting, satiny and scalloped at the bustline. Her skirt was covered in peacock feathers, and she floated past them, and took her seat.

Martha Man Hands followed, and the girl named Misty turned away, in an attempt to hide herself. Martha wore a top that was jet-black and corseted tightly. Her arms and shoulders were bare, and her voluminous skirts were made of piles and piles of dyed dark taffeta. She wore a single ostrich feather in her short hair, clipped in place by several black barrettes.

The procession continued with Diane Savage Connor in a little black dress, the kind Audrey Hepburn made famous, white gloves, long strands of pearls, a black hat with a white satin bow pinned in her long black hair.

Next came Ronda, in a ball gown, black and enormous, skirts turning into a train behind her, wet from the snow. The train was two yards in length. A rhinestoned jacket covered her shoulders. The dress was surrounded by a cloud of black chiffon that began at her waist and followed down to the train. In her dark hair was a giant headband, bejeweled with tiny green amethysts. This was a giant dress for a giant woman, and she had trouble sliding into the aisle.

Tabby had been attempting to hold Ronda's train, and her breasts threatened to spill out of her dress. She wore a tiny black bustier, made entirely of rosettes, and a full skirt embroidered with a dazzling bird of paradise.

Red Mabel followed closely behind, and there was an audible gasp from the church as she stepped forward. Red Mabel wore a black tuxedo with tails, a black shirt and a white bow tie, a cummerbund the same material as Athena's scarf. She wore a shiny top hat, which she removed and tipped at Rachel and Bucky. Red Mabel stopped, waiting for the woman she was escorting.

Laverna revealed herself, making a late and grand entrance as always.

Rachel burst into tears again, but for all the right reasons.

Her mother had been saved for last.

Laverna's gown glittered and sparkled, and it threw off light all around the bare walls of the church. The bodice was tight, and Rachel was surprised at her mother's curves. It clung to her, cap-sleeved, every inch covered in silver rhinestones and black bugle beads. Her skirt was Western style, complete with a black crinoline that grazed the floor. It swelled out and around her, the skirts layers of black ruffles, each peaked with a dusting of rhinestones, every layer roped with black pearls. Her hair was a wig, a giant blond beehive that was Victorian in style, ropes of the same black pearls orbiting it, a giant black butterfly with jeweled wings perched at the very top. Following behind was Frank, unleashed, wearing a little black sweater, rhinestones glued to his collar.

At this point, Laverna could not fit in the pew with the rest of the Flood Girls, so she sat down next to Rachel, lowered herself with her hands, her legs stuck out in the aisle, the crinolines and hoops too large to fit. Frank jumped up on her lap, and made a nest in all of the bustles.

After Laverna had wedged herself in, Reverend Foote cleared his throat.

The parishioners ignored him, still turned around in their seats, mouths open. Rachel could see Bert's face, scarlet with rage.

The walls of the church were cast with flickering lights, the reflection from all the rhinestones.

Rachel knew that Athena and Buley had organized all this. The dresses had come from the thrift store, had been rented in Missoula, or stolen outright. Buley might have sewn some herself. Rachel nodded at her former sponsor. Athena clutched at her scarf made of rainbow colors and smiled sadly in return.

The reverend clapped his hands together, to regain the attention of his congregation, and resumed the service. Rachel didn't mind, because she was surrounded by her team, surrounded by the Flood Girls.

She held Bucky's hand, and she held her mother's hand, and things seemed the way Jake would have wanted, and she was content.

The reverend began speaking again, and then Frank let out a sharp bark and jumped down from Laverna's lap. They had never heard him bark before, and watched as he marched up the aisle. The front rows murmured as he made his way to the front of the church. He turned around when he reached the platform, and sat in front of the coffin, staring defiantly at the entire congregation.

Frank guarded the boy who was going to be buried. The reverend called for the owner, but Laverna ignored him.

This time, Frank wasn't going anywhere.

Fireman's Ball, 1992

★　　★　　★

*T*he Fireman's Ball, 1992, and the fire hall was stifling hot, as usual, but Rachel stood by the barrels of fire, reluctant to leave the side of Red Mabel, who was telling some story about a grizzly bear. Red Mabel did not like it when people abandoned her in the middle of a story.

Rachel was in the corner with Laverna, Red Mabel, and Martha. They were drinking beers, while Rachel sipped on her soda. Conversation turned to Rocky Bailey, who had been made an honorary volunteer fireman.

The jitterbuggers made asses of themselves in the back, tripping on hoses, but dancing on, carelessly, recklessly, happily. Rachel admired them for this.

Martha's daughter, Misty, was hiding in the corner, sucking face with one of the volunteer firemen. Martha was too drunk to notice her, and Rachel didn't feel like warning Misty about what her future held.

Across the hall, the Chief was in deep conversation with Bucky. Bucky held the coffee can with the ticket stubs. He had apparently been promoted.

During the last four months, Red Mabel had been preoccupied, plans spinning behind her eyes. She was a huntress, and Rachel hoped the assassination would be messy, but remain covert. Bert had it coming.

Jake was buried behind New Life Evangelical, and there wasn't anything the Flood Girls could do about it. He was the first to be buried there, which would have pleased him. Ginger and Rachel planted a dogwood bush behind the headstone, despite the reverend's protestations. To silence him, Ginger promised to return with one of Red Mabel's guns. In the winter, the bare branches of the dogwood were a bright red, the only bright thing in all that snow. Laverna and Rachel hung a rosary from the branches, and the parishioners kept removing it. There was no shortage of rosaries at the thrift store, and Buley was happy to provide replacements.

Rachel watched as Laverna nearly fell into a barrel, but Red Mabel reached out and caught her in time. Diane was deep in conversation with her latest beau, the hippie from Missoula. Rumor at the Dirty Shame was that the two were building an A-frame out in the wilderness. They danced together by the utility sink, so close they seemed to be melting into each other. A flash from the dark corner, Black Mabel and her new white teeth, selling something illicit to an impressionable young fireman. The Sinclairs were nowhere to be found. They did not, and never would, attend such things. Ginger Fitchett and Della argued about something that had to do with the decorations. Ginger kept pointing upward and shaking her head. She appointed herself the decorator of the entire town of Quinn, her version of continuing Jake's good works.

Ronda attempted to sell raffle tickets, but she just stood silently in front of people until they grew uncomfortable and emptied their pockets. Jim Number Three gave her a twenty-dollar bill. He was the only volunteer who took care of his uniform—his polo shirt was neatly ironed. Rachel respected that, and she also admired his tenaciousness. He approached Laverna, but stopped short, pretended to inspect a fire extinguisher latched to the wall. Rachel did not understand the necessity of a fire extinguisher amid all those hoses, but understood being nervous here. Once upon a time, she had stood by herself, trying to appear inconspicuous.

Rachel touched his arm as she passed him, and Jim Number Three smiled gratefully. Her mother lectured Red Mabel about machine guns.

"Everyone will know it was you," Laverna said, and accepted a kiss on the cheek from her daughter.

"I can't help it," said Red Mabel.

Rachel wrapped an arm around Laverna's neck, and agreed with Red Mabel. "You have flair," said Rachel. "You should never be ashamed of it."

"Thank you," said Red Mabel. A year ago, the bullets were meant for someone else. Rachel laughed at the memory, leaned close to her mother, whispered in her ear.

Laverna sighed and threw her cigarette into the barrel. Jim Number Three beamed when she approached. Rachel and Red Mabel made plans for Laverna's birthday, to be celebrated for the first time in years.

Rachel checked on the rest of the Flood Girls, made sure they all had rides home. She stopped to gossip with Tabby about the newest volunteer in town. Thankfully, his name was not Jim. Rachel crossed the cement floor to join the Chief, who stood next to her favorite volunteer fireman.

She stood on her tiptoes to kiss Bucky on the lips. After all these months, he still blushed.

She grabbed the can from Bucky's hands and searched all over until she found a young fireman with bad skin and a crooked nose. Rachel handed him the tickets, and told him that he was in charge, and warned him not to screw it up.

She walked back over to Bucky and yanked at his arm until he followed her outside into the cold and clean air of another February night.

He did not want to miss the raffle, but she promised she had a better prize, waiting for him at home.

Acknowledgments

This book would not have been possible without the love and support of my family—my sisters, Lisa Cooper, Launa Baas, and Dana Wallace; my awesome stepfather, Gary Jones; my nieces, Mykah and Britt Cooper; and my superstar of a nephew, Brian O'Neill. I thank all the rest of my relatives for putting up with me.

My friends are everything to me. Amber Boyce, Laura Kamura, and John Runkle kindly offered me the space and time to write. My recovery family in Missoula have offered me hope and faith—I am honored to travel the road of sobriety with you. A special shout-out to my kids at Young Guns— keep on trudging, and never wear socks with sandals! I must thank my readers and editors, for helping to make this book sing: Kris Frieswick, John Myers, Haili Jones Graff, Mari Passananti, Jenn Grunigen, Lorna Doone Brewer, Kori Erickson, Mike Paulus, Charles Garabedian, Sharma Shields, Queen Jackie Collins, Laura Moriarty, and most of all, the miracle that is Deirdre McNamer. I would also like to thank Erinn Ackley, Sara Trotter, Sandra Maggi, Sydney Lytle, Diane More, Stacey Walker Old-ham, Rhian Ellis, Robert Gerber, Jeff Ferderer, Greg Shanks, Dana Fiengo Pruner, Lar K. Autio, Gregory Gourdet, Erin Giefer, Lisa Hunt, Janelle Jones, Lucy Hansen, Lesley Lotto, Patrick Ryan, Kelly Faciana, Julie Her-genrather, Jennifer Hendrickson, Robin O'Day, Kenzie Kovick, all of my former coworkers at 2675 Palmer, the Creative Writing Department at the University of Montana, and the Zootown Arts Community Center. This book took root in a workshop with the truly incomparable Jenna Blum.

My team is flawless and ferocious: Lucy Stille, Jenny Bent at the Bent Agency, and Alison Callahan Kilkelly at Simon & Schuster. Thanks for taking a chance on me!

Finally, this book was inspired by the good people of my hometown, Troy, Montana, and especially all the beautiful women who played softball. They taught me about grace, strength, and self-acceptance. I thank you all!

XOXO, Richard